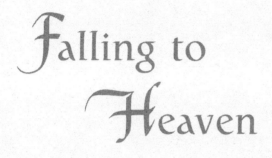

JEANNE M. PETERSON

Falling to Heaven

THOMAS DUNNE BOOKS

ST. MARTIN'S PRESS 🐾 NEW YORK

This is a work of fiction. All of the characters, organizations, and events portrayed in this novel are either products of the author's imagination or are used fictitiously.

THOMAS DUNNE BOOKS.
An imprint of St. Martin's Press.

FALLING TO HEAVEN. Copyright © 2010 by Jeanne M. Peterson. All rights reserved. Printed in the United States of America. For information, address St. Martin's Press, 175 Fifth Avenue, New York, N.Y. 10010.

www.thomasdunnebooks.com
www.stmartins.com

Design by Jessica Shatan Heslin/Studio Shatan, Inc.

Library of Congress Cataloging-in-Publication Data

Peterson, Jeanne.
  Falling to heaven / Jeanne Peterson. — 1st ed.
    p. cm.
  ISBN 978-0-312-53392-2 (alk. paper)
  1. Quakers—Fiction.   2. Tibet (China)—Fiction.   I. Title.
  PS3616. E84284F36 2010
  813'.6—dc22

                                                        2009041643

First Edition: April 2010

10   9   8   7   6   5   4   3   2   1

To Julian and Hayden

ACKNOWLEDGMENTS

It has been nearly a decade since I began the journey that brought *Falling to Heaven* into being. I say this as a caveat: the passage of time and raising children have taken their toll on my brain cells, so if I've forgotten anyone in this list of acknowledgments, my profound apologies.

First, thanks to all the generous fellow writers in the San Diego community who have helped me in a wide variety of ways, especially Judy Reeves, Roger Aplon, Suzanna Neal, Patrick McMahon, Sarah Zale, Jill Hall, Peggy Lang, and Chet Cunningham.

For their invaluable help in my research into Tibetan Buddhism, I am grateful to the community of Drikung Kyobpa Choling, and especially Drupon Samten Rinpoche, Michael Essex (Wangdu), Tsering, and Peter. Any misunderstanding of Tibetan culture or religion in this book can be laid at my doorstep, not theirs.

To all of my fellow Quakers at La Jolla Quaker Meeting, thanks for opening your hearts to me and taking me in as one of your own. Thanks especially to Jim Summers, Jane Peers, and Kerstin Waschewsky.

My warmest gratitude to the following individuals for making travel to Tibet a joy: Hira Dhamala of Karnali Excursions, Nga-wang, and Tashi, as well as my friend DeeDee, who'd never trav-eled in the developing world before stepping foot into Tibet to accompany me.

I am deeply indebted to my tireless agents, Ros Edwards and Helenka Fuglewicz, who toiled with such patience and faith, al-ways believing in the book's potential. And great thanks to my editor, Katie Gilligan, at St. Martin's, whose insight and sugges-tions have taught me so much as a writer.

Last but certainly not least are my loved ones who read through countless versions of the manuscript and provided unstinting sup-port: my mom, Kathleen Smith; my sister, Nancy Holt; along with Marcie Goldman and Paula West. Love to my two children, Hayden and Julian, for being their lovely selves and providing me with so much material from real life.

Prologue

Imagine God with feet. With ten toes, toenails, perhaps even a divine bunion or two. And if perchance God decided to touch those feet down on the earth's soil, picture one of those feet planted on a cloud, and the other foot dangling, reaching down to find purchase on the wildly spinning blue ball beneath it. What might the divine foot touch first on the earth as it stretched from the lower reaches of the heavens? Why, the roof, of course. The roof of the world. The highest country on the earth, encased on all sides by the Himalaya, Karakoram, and Kunlun mountain ranges, like a sapphire nestled in its protective setting of gold. So the Divine One might land on the serrated edges of the Himalayas and perch upon those chiseled peaks, inhaling the thin air that is winged by vultures.

From this vantage, the divine eye could gaze upon the antlike human figures bustling about the small hamlets and larger cities of that country that rests on the roof of the world, the land of snows, what is known in human circles as Tibet.

Were this visitation to take place anytime during the tenth through the nineteenth centuries, as Western humans reckon time, the sights beheld would show little change. The peasant with black hair braided into a long queue down his back, wielding his scythe in golden fields of barley. A bronze-skinned woman bent over a flowing creek, singing as she rinses laundry in the cleansing waters. A young girl tossing dried chips of yak dung into the oven in her kitchen. A man in red robes, incense in his nostrils, sitting erect with a mind as empty and still as a frozen pond. The mountains sheltering the land of snows make it so difficult to reach that its inhabitants lived relatively undisturbed and unchanged for hundreds of years.

Were the Divine One to have touched down during the year of our Lord 1954, however, the all-seeing eye would have witnessed scenes sharply at odds with those of earlier centuries.

Groups of men in uniform the color of Tibet's soil. They move from the east, from the Land of the Dragon, across the jagged landscape of Tibet, each battalion moving in concert as the legs of a great spider might move the whole across a vast desert. Each carries a rifle in his arms with the devotion of a mother for her infant. In a monastery to the south, monks hold their breath. They sit in a circle around the sacred mandala they have prayerfully fashioned with many-colored grains of sand; their normally placid faces contort as the uniformed man with the shiny black boots sweeps his foot across their oeuvre. In Tibet's eastern lands, soot rises in black curls from a city in flames as one of the legs of the spider leaves it.

Hard words float up from the cities into the thin mountain air, words never heard before in this region, out of the mouths of the uninvited guests from the Land of the Dragon. *We will liberate you. Eliminate foreign imperialists. Long live Chairman Mao.* From the houses of natives, wails are heard and words like *taken to prison camp* and *disappeared*.

In Lhasa, the capital, an old man called Tenzin in russet monk robes sits on the damp floor of a Chinese prison, his face so lined it resembles a topographical map. Although his gaze rests on a spot of urine on the stone floor before him, his shining eyes see beyond the walls that cage him and his cellmates. He has been beaten until his back is an open sore. His wounds ache, but he sits, undisturbed.

In the city of Shigatse, smoke floats up through the hole in each flat roof. Should that divine eye peek down through one of those holes into a kitchen, it might glimpse the woman called Rinchen, who stands on aching feet, shredding goat meat. Beside her on the stove bubbles a savory broth with bits of garlic, grains of black pepper, and chopped onions dancing within it. Peering into this steaming pot is her young boy, Champa, standing on a wooden stool, his seven-year-old eyes pricked and smarting from the steam and the onions. She says affectionately, "Such a naughty boy. If you touch that soup pot again, you'll be sleeping out with the goats tonight!"

Outside her kitchen window she can see her husband, Dorje, tending to the animals sheltered within the walls of their square courtyard. He holds grains of barley up to the warm, snuffling mouth of his favorite mare, who nuzzles at his hand contentedly. He strokes the velvety neck of the horse as he whispers sweetness into her cocked ear. On the opposite end of this corral, two enormous, hairy yaks stand tolerantly, searching the ground for treats. Leaning against one wall are twenty bales of wool to be loaded onto the backs of these last patient beasts. Tomorrow Dorje will prod them and others of their kind onto the dusty paths of his trade route.

To the west, on a high pass of the Himalayas, a man and a woman can be seen trudging upward. They wear clothing that, to a distant observer, disguises their origin and their white skin. But there is more to this picture, a remainder that only the superior senses of the deity could perceive. The blood that has been oozing into the heels of the woman's leather boots for some days now, mixed with skin worn off the delicate flesh of her heels. The throbbing that pulses in the man's head, signaling another altitude headache, blinding the traveler and ending his rumination over whether they will be caught and deported from the country they are entering unlawfully. The packs these two carry on their backs grow dangerously light as their food supplies dwindle. Only the all-knowing mind could discern what mysterious purpose propels these two dogged travelers forward with their Sherpa guide—a purpose that none, not their family members, not their friends, and especially not their unwilling hosts, can fathom.

Part
One

Dorje

My mother taught me how to do prostrations as soon as I could walk. *Bring hands together over your head, then to your chest, then go down like Abu on all four legs, touch your forehead to the earth. Hold your love for His Holiness in your heart every moment.* Abu was our little puppy, and my mother taught me prostrations in this way, with me pretending to be Abu. She brought me to the temple with her every day, teaching me how to say prayers for all sentient beings. She said to me, "Even though your father is Chinese, you will learn to be a good Tibetan."

When I became a little older, my mother noticed I could put myself in the place of others and understand them. She said, "Perhaps it is because you have two kinds of blood. It is your destiny to be the friend of the tiger and the rabbit, although these two are enemies."

I suppose this is a good thing, being a friend to the tiger and the rabbit. When my mother told me this, I was too young to imagine the ways in which it would prove to be true. But now, in my country, we are feeling the jaws of the tiger. And the teeth can be sharp, like the prick of many blades.

I am speaking of the Chinese. We Tibetans talk about the

Chinese all the time. When we sit and drink our tea, I hear how Palden had his yaks taken by the Chinese. Or when we thresh barley on the roof, I hear about my neighbor Tashi, who had his barley taken by the People's Liberation Army.

Whenever we talk about the Chinese, I remember my two kinds of blood, but I do not feel Chinese. At least not the way my Tibetan friends think of them. My father was from Amdo, where more Chinese people were close by than here in Shigatse. So he and my mother were married because their families knew one another, just living side by side without any problem.

In these last few years, things with the Chinese are very different. There is no more living side by side without any problem, because the Chinese say they have come to *liberate* us. When I first heard this, it made me laugh. Other Tibetans also laughed at such a silly idea. We wanted to ask, *Liberate us from what?*

But now we have a bad feeling, a hardness in the stomach, a feeling of anger. And we are afraid.

Over the years, the Chinese have come and gone and come again. When they would go, we would drink *chang* to celebrate and tell ourselves the trouble was over. But each time they would come back, they would stay a little longer, and we would pray harder for them to leave.

It seems now that they are staying.

We don't like it when we are reciting our prayers and we see a Chinese person laughing at us openly. Without respect.

Because here in Tibet, nothing is more important to us than our religion.

So I feel the anger of my people, but I can also put myself in the place of the Chinese.

It is not hard for me to look into the face of one of these young Chinese soldiers and see into his heart. He has pride. He believes he is bringing the superior wisdom of Chairman Mao to us. He looks at us and sees superstitious peasants with dirt on our faces. He looks at the soil under our feet and sees Chinese soil.

I speak Chinese and Tibetan, and so my people often come to me asking for help when they have a problem with the Chinese. That is when I stand between the tiger and the rabbit, and I think of my mother's warm hand touching my cheek when she said this, so long ago.

This is hard for my wife. She says, "When you help all these people, you put your family in danger."

I tell her, "It is my destiny to help people in this way," and she says, "Oh, the tiger and the rabbit and your destiny! What about our family?"

In these moments I am reminded that people here say my wife does not have good manners. She came from the province of Kham with her family when she was just a girl, so she has the rough Khampa ways. It does not bother me that she is like this because I know it is only on the outside. Inside, her heart is tender and sweet.

Lama Norbu told us Rinchen was a panda in her previous life, and I know it is true. Rinchen was a she-bear, with a soft black coat and big black eyes, and also long, sharp claws. I saw the bear incarnation one day in Rinchen. A communist soldier came on the street when we were walking to the temple with thermoses of *dri* butter to refill the butter lamps. He went over to touch our son, Champa. The soldier was smiling, and I think Champa had charmed him. Everybody likes Champa because he is a clown. But with the soldier, Rinchen stepped in front of our son, with her hands in fists, standing strong. I think she scared the soldier because, even though he had a gun, he walked away quite fast! Maybe he saw the long claws of Rinchen's soul ready to tear him apart.

I noticed Rinchen right away when she came here from Kham. All of us in Shigatse talked about her as the girl who could tame the wild dogs. Maybe it was because she was a bear in her previous existence and the packs of dogs in the streets could smell the bear in her, so they were afraid. The first time I saw her, she was only as tall as a sheep, and she was carrying a large bag from the marketplace for her mother. In my mind, I called her "small as a sheep, strong as a bear." When she walked by the dogs in our neighborhood, they became quiet. Everyone else had to throw stones at them to keep them away, but Rinchen needed no stones. I saw her from my window on the second story of our house as she came, and I watched her go by until I couldn't see her anymore, and the whole way she went straight and peaceful with no dogs to bother her.

When I was twelve years old, I found out my parents had arranged a marriage for me with the girl who tames the wild dogs. I was happy because she was a strong, brave girl, and I thought, "We will have a good life together."

We have made a good life, but Rinchen does not like my curious nature. In the end, I have often seen that my wife is wise. I hear her warnings in my mind, telling me that my curiosity could bring us hardships, but sometimes I'm still like a little mouse nosing around.

Such as yesterday, when I greeted our new neighbor. The woman from America. Who, along with her husband, is probably being watched by the suspicious Chinese. Westerners are the enemy, the Chinese say.

The Americans arrived a week ago and have been staying next door in a house owned by the Tibetan regent. For centuries, to protect our traditions and religion from outside influences, the Tibetan authorities have almost never permitted foreigners to stay in Tibet. So it is astonishing that they are in Shigatse, and since they are staying in the regent's house, they clearly have permission to be here. I simply cannot understand the presence of these neighbors, so the mystery lives in my mind like an itch I have to scratch.

Our homes are close to each other. Each of our houses has a square courtyard with the house settled into one corner, and our two houses lie in the corners of the squares that are closest to one another. Because of this, I have caught glimpses of them through the windows. Each time I have seen them, many questions have burned within me. Was it true that they both had hair that disobeyed, curving up into waves like an ocean on their heads, instead of lying flat? Was it true their eyes were light-colored and clear so I might see all the way through if I looked right at them? Why were they here? Could I be helpful to them? I speak English, taught to me by an Englishman when the British had a mission here.

Perhaps it was destined for us to meet, because yesterday I looked up from behind the low wall of my courtyard and there she was. The woman with unruly red hair out in front of her door with a broom, sweeping up dust. Her hair was pulled back, but shorter strands of it were indeed curled up around her face, which was pale, with speckles across her nose, and pink in her cheeks. She was tall, and she wore a red silk *chuba,* I was surprised to see. She held one of her hands over her mouth shyly, but behind it I saw a smile. I was ready to say, "Greetings, madam," but instead she burst out with *"Tashi delek!"* in a perfect Lhasa accent. I was unable to speak from the shock and stood like a statue, staring into the green eyes. Next she bowed to me, and I bowed back to her. Finally I stammered in English, "Good day to you." I only wanted to wish her a pleasant day, but then I remembered this was the way to say good-bye. So of course I thought I must leave. I bowed again, and she followed with her own bow. I felt so silly, I simply walked away. She must have thought I was rude to leave so quickly.

To make up for my rudeness, I have decided to give them the "welcome *chang,*" a kettle of butter tea and a kettle of *chang.* I plan to go while Rinchen is away at the river getting water for cooking. She would yell and tug at her braids if she knew, saying, "Why are you talking with those foreigners? Do you want the Chinese to start watching us too?"

When I think of this, there is a tightness in my chest, and I wonder if I will bring trouble to us all.

Emma

May 29, 1954

Dear Genevieve,

Greetings from Tibet! We are settling in after a week and a half of being here in the town of Shigatse. We got permission to be here from the local nobleman, called the regent, and he's even letting us rent a house from him. I can't tell you how surprised we are that we're being allowed to stay. I thought he'd boot our heinies out of here as soon as he saw us. Gerald says either I charmed the regent with my fluent Tibetan, or God's hand is already at work. Personally, I figure he just needed the rent money.

It took us four weeks to walk over the mountains on foot from the Nepali border to Shigatse. We were relieved to make it here before June, when the monsoon season starts and travel gets a lot more challenging. We had a Sherpa named Tsultrim, and he promised to guide us until we got deported—he was that certain we'd be turned back! What an odd look he gave us. It reminded me of the general reaction we got from officials as we made our travel preparations: They thought we must be nuts. Or we must be missionaries, who are generally assumed to be nuts anyway. I assured him we were not missionaries, just tourists (and nuts too).

Luckily for us, Tsultrim was clever and took us on all sorts of detours to avoid running into any Tibetan authorities. The journey itself was so challenging I can hardly describe it. Gerald thought his head would burst as we climbed up as high as seventeen thousand feet. At the top of one of the highest mountain passes, I lost all feeling in my face. Tsultrim made me lie down and rest. Gerald told me I got really loopy, asking him over and over, "Did we just have a conversation?" He got worried and went into physician mode, asking me questions I dimly recognized from quizzing him for his neurology exams. When I sat up and told him to shut up already, he assured Tsultrim, "She's back to normal." Tsultrim said, "She will feel better when she comes down." As we descended the pass, the blood rushed back into my cheeks. They felt as hot as if I'd been sunburned.

The house where we're staying is filled with lovely Tibetan furnishings of carved wood, brightly painted with flowers and birds. We have two rooms, including a kitchen with a cast-iron stove fueled by, amazingly enough, the dried dung of yaks. They don't waste anything here! It hasn't been appetizing to store yak poop in the same room with all the food. Fortunately, the regent found us a helper by the name of Phuntsog. He leaves "yak chips" and food items just inside the courtyard gate for a small fee each week. The fact that I don't have to go harvest "yak patties" makes me think there must be a God, and he knows my limits!

We're working at living as Tibetans do, so we've been using a large churner to make butter tea. Tibetans drink this tea all day long, as many as sixty cups a day. It takes Phuntsog forty-five minutes to make it, but when I do it, it takes an hour and a half! First I gather the stream water, throw dung chips into the oven fire, and scrape some yak butter into the cylinder-shaped churner along with some salt. I boil the water, break off some tea, and churn it all together. I'm beginning to understand why some of the women here look as burly as the livestock.

The other thing we have in the way of food is tsampa, a flour ground from roasted barley. It tastes sort of like puffed wheat. Oddly enough, you don't use it to make anything, you just eat it. By using a few drops of tea you're supposed to form the flour into a little dollop that you pop neatly into your mouth. As we've found out, it's a lot harder than it looks. We usually end up with flour dusted in an undignified trail down our chests. When we get tired of tsampa, we move on to other Tibetan staples: yak meat, yogurt, and cheese, mainly. Acquired tastes. Enough said.

We sleep in the kitchen, and the one other room in the house has an altar in it. It seemed like an odd arrangement to us at first, but Phuntsog said, "When winter comes, you will understand why you sleep in the kitchen next to the stove." I imagine we will. As far as the altar room goes, every house here has one.

On the outside, our house looks like a typical Tibetan house: a whitewashed adobe affair situated in the corner of a square courtyard formed by four adobe whitewashed walls that are about five feet high. Everything is functional here—that is, if we chose to, we could corral our livestock within the courtyard (you know, yaks, sheep, a horse or two). At every corner of the courtyard is a set of prayer flags tied to a willow stick that juts out vertically from where the two walls meet. People here sometimes store their firewood on top of the walls, and they even use them as a drying surface for yak dung! They mix the yak dung with water and form it into disks, which they then slap onto the vertical surfaces of the walls for drying, leaving an orderly polka-dot look.

I've spent a good deal of time being fascinated by the windows on the houses. They're quite dramatic. Think of a large black square stuck into the side of a white house, then pull the two bottom corners of the black square outward to make the base of the square wider than the rest of it. Then stick a four-paned window into the middle of the figure and top the window with a white frill that looks like a bed skirt. To add to the theatrical black-on-white theme, all doors here are painted red, and it's really a beautiful effect.

Being here has forced Gerald to confront his filth phobia. When we were back in Kathmandu studying the Tibetan language, the Nepalis told us, "Those Tibetans, they don't care about being clean. All they care about is their religion." We had no idea how literally they meant that! The toilets in the cities are just pits that stink to high heaven and back down again into hell. At first Gerald wouldn't admit they bothered him. So while I was calling them "celestial cesspools" and "skunk-pots," he would lift his chin as if he could hear his father saying, "Chin up, old boy." He was trying so hard to be respectful of the culture here. He finally came off his high horse though, after numerous trips caused by a bout of diarrhea. Then he joined in, calling them "pestilential palaces." Aside from the toilets, though, the other places are relatively clean and quite lovely.

The latest big event is that we met our neighbor! His name is Dorje (sounds like dor-jay). I can't tell you how excited we were, because no one else here has spoken to us. I greeted him from our porch, and then he came and knocked on our door the next day. When I opened it, he was standing there grinning, holding two kettles. He was a little shorter than me, and he had his black hair braided in a long tail in the back. His dark hair shone, and his chest spread broadly beneath his collarbones, even as he bowed. Such dignity and such humility, all at once. He had a gold earring, in the fashion of men of means here, and he wore a nice black chuba (it looks like a bathrobe with a belt around the waist). He said, in melodious English, "I brought welcome chang." (Chang is the beer they make out of barley.) I was so touched by his thoughtfulness and his kind face that tears came to my eyes. He chuckled when I told him how we've struggled to eat tsampa. His laugh seemed to bubble up from a deep place within. He gave us a lesson on proper tsampa-eating technique. I took advantage of the chance to ask him about something that has really chilled us: nearly every door here has a swastika on it, including ours! He said that this symbol simply means "all is well," and that it is thousands of years old. It is supposed to bring well-being, in his words. I wonder what he thought of our disturbed expressions as he explained it to us. It has taken some getting used to seeing it in a country full of Buddhists who are so against killing they won't even swat a fly!

We got into a discussion about religion with our neighbor, and we explained to him that we're Quakers. Gerald told him, "We believe that God speaks to us if we wait in silence," to which he responded, "This is like meditation, is it not?" I didn't bother to mention that I'm not exactly devout, but I did chime in with the Quaker saying "There is that of God in everyone." He looked a little confused at that point, but hopefully we'll get the chance to clarify that it means we respect his religion as also being from God.

It was the first time we'd ever talked to someone who knew absolutely nothing about Quakers. So we didn't get the usual reactions of "Oh, those women with the bonnets" or "the horse-and-buggy people" or something or other about oats.

I know that some in our Quaker meeting worried about our trip here because the Reds are supposedly taking over and all that. Please let them know that although we do feel the Chinese presence, we don't feel any danger. The Tibetans seem to be carrying on their lives normally, so there's no cause for worry.

Gerald has been praying for you. I have been too, in my own way. I hope the warmer spring weather eases your arthritis pains. Please pass along our love and greetings to all the Friends, and thank them for holding us in the Light.

Peace,
Emma

I sat at the kitchen table, knowing I hadn't told Genevieve all that had really happened when we talked with Dorje. His bowl still sat to my right. I touched the bowl's wooden lip, still warm, as if it could tell me what it was about him that had made my chest ache.

He'd asked why we came here. I told him, "Gerald wants to find a guru here to learn about Tibetan religion."

Dorje asked him, "You are looking for a teacher?"

Gerald looked down and ran his hand through his blond curls, a gesture that told me he was embarrassed. He answered, "Oh,

I'm sure we won't be here long enough to find one. We'll only stay as long as the regent allows."

Dorje looked so earnest as he said, "Lama Norbu says that if your heart is pure, a teacher will come to you." His eyes opened like flowers as he said it, and he clasped his hands together in a prayer mudra at his chest.

Next to Dorje's bowl lay a photo of my dad. An old black-and-white with scalloped edges and a crease on the left corner. Dad in an alpine trekking outfit of leather boots, a fur-lined jacket, and thick woolen trousers. He stood arm in arm with a Sherpa. The other arm he held out as if to show off a flexed bicep. He grinned radiantly, with the Himalayas standing behind him like hulking shadows.

When Dorje asked my reasons for coming here, I didn't know what to say. I *had* to come. Something, some invisible cord, pulled me over those unforgiving mountains. It wasn't Gerald; it wasn't the guide. I took every step on my own, my face wrapped in a scarf to stave off the choking dust. While gasping my way up with quivering legs, I felt like a fish on a dock, gills flapping open, desperate to be back where the air is thick and nourishing. But I didn't let my legs turn around, even then.

I've explained my reasons for this trip to so many people. But when I sat across from Dorje's kind face, eyebrows arching together as he listened, I handed him the picture and couldn't say a word.

He held the picture gently and studied it.

Finally I said, "That's my dad."

"These are the Himalayas?"

I nodded. His eyes became so sad as he gazed at me, as if he already knew what had happened. I felt awkward, naked. Turning my face away, I said, "He . . . died. They never found his body . . ." My voice trailed off. Sadness stung my eyes.

"And your mother?"

Gerald took my hand and answered for me. "She died when Emma was quite young."

"And now *you* are here," Dorje said. His smile against his copper skin was bright. It held joy, a joy that came from having known—and accepted—sorrow.

Seeing it made me look down into my bowl of tea and swallow.

I loved Dorje from that moment. And I didn't sense any danger at all.

> Conscientious objection is not a total repudiation
> of force; it is a refusal to surrender moral responsibility
> for one's actions.
> —KENNETH BARNES

Gerald

The brown eyes stared up at me, glassy and unseeing. I stepped back, unable to breathe, and their gaze seemed to follow me. I wanted to turn and flee, but instead I rooted myself to the spot, even as I heard the thud of the butcher's knife against bone and the choked sound of my own breathing.

I pulled in deep breaths as I'd learned to do over the years. In a moment I'd be okay, I knew. The smell in my nostrils was the metallic scent of blood, although I'd never smelled *yak* blood before.

Old images pushed up to the surface, and I sat with them and let the picture show roll. Breathing in the blood smell, looking up at the sky, and thinking of Rufus. After my heart slowed and I was calm, I walked home with Rufus still piggybacking my brain.

Upon reaching home, I told Emma about it while we sat on the regent's magnificent couch with the colorful curlicues painted on it. "Quite the adventure today, Em. I started following this old man because he was sporting those boots with the upturned toes."

She smiled at me. "You and those boots." She had her russet

waves loose, still drying from a morning bath, and her skin glowed beneath the tiny sprinkle of freckles over her nose and cheeks.

I grinned back. "It seemed he was heading for the monastery up on the hill, and I wanted to get a closer look at the golden roof, so I followed him. But then we came to . . . the butcher's grounds."

"Oh, God!" she exclaimed, disgusted.

"I heard sheep bleating and yaks lowing or mooing or whatever they do, and there was blood *everywhere*. I saw a yak head fall to the ground after the butcher cut it off." I shuddered.

"Oh!" She grimaced. "That is *so* grisly." She paused. "You okay?"

"I'm fine. I took some deep breaths and gathered my wits and here I am."

"So it didn't make you . . . remember?"

"Rufus?" I said deliberately.

She nodded vigorously.

"I'll admit that it did remind me, but I've faced my demons and I'm perfectly all right."

Rufus had entered my life when I was eight years old. I'd been fresh from England, and he'd taunted me daily at school. "Listen to the snooty way he talks!"

I didn't want to be different. When I'd told Father about it, he'd said, "Don't let those Yanks ruffle you. Pay him no mind, and presently he'll forget all about it."

I thought Father didn't understand how hard it was to be eight and alone with a bully in a schoolyard. So I resolved to deal with it the way I saw other boys handle things.

On a rainy day in October, with Rufus jeering at me and a gaggle of children around us, I made a fateful choice. I stepped toward him and pushed him as hard as I could.

He fell backward against some stairs. His eyes opened wide as his head struck the edge of a step. His eyes looked at me and never closed again, staring.

His body went completely still. Blood ran from the back of his head—so much of it—how could a little boy have so much blood? And I heard around me first a deadly quiet, then the other children began crying, and someone screamed at me, "You killed him!"

I shook my head, backing away. "No. No, I didn't. I just pushed him."

But Rufus was dead. An ambulance came and they covered his face with a sheet and my parents were called and Rufus's parents came and I saw his mum crying.

I stopped speaking then. For the rest of that year and most of the next as well. If I didn't open my mouth, nothing bad would happen. I prayed every night. Not from the Book of Common Prayer as I'd learned at church, but my own desperate words. "God, I promise I won't hurt anyone else. Please help me to keep that promise. Please, God. Please forgive me for . . . Rufus. And bless his family." No matter what they said in the schoolyard, I didn't answer. I didn't speak in the classroom and not even at home.

After what happened with Rufus, Father wouldn't speak to me. We'd only just arrived in the States, in the small community of Middletown, Connecticut, so that Father could take a teaching post at Wesleyan College. Though he'd counseled me not to be ruffled by Yanks, I saw how it pained him when the townspeople looked at us with stony faces. He held his head high and clenched his jaw when he went out the door in the mornings.

When I would enter a room, Father's face would change. He would look down, eyebrows lifted as though he'd bitten into a sour apple, then he'd deliberately refocus on the daily paper in front of him. Mum was hardly better, with her uncertain, rabbity face that followed the scent of Father's opinions and then hopped along behind.

So, being silent was my slow atonement. I prayed, "God, please help Father to see that I'm sorry and forgive me." But he spoke only to Mum and my older brother, Tyler.

Then one night Father invited a friend to our home for supper, a colleague from Wesleyan. A Dr. Spence, father said before the visitor arrived, someone with a lot of clout in the institution. By this we knew Father wanted us to be on our best behavior, and I was dreading the thought of having to impress some buttoned-down academic.

When Dr. Spence appeared in the doorway in a rumpled shirt and khaki pants, his face bare but for one patch of hair on his chin, Tyler and I looked at each other in astonishment. This was not the sort of fellow Father would have consorted with in the past, clout or no. Had Father sunk to depths we'd not imagined?

After the evening was over, Father commented, "Seems a decent fellow, despite being a pacifist."

"What's that?" I asked. My first words in *so* long, because I had to know.

"Hmmm? A pacifist?"

I nodded.

"Let's see," my father mused. "Someone who abhors all violence and thinks we should simply shake hands and be friends. Never fight wars, that sort of thing."

Father didn't notice that I'd just started speaking again. I heard the sneer in his voice about our visitor, but from that moment I couldn't stop thinking about Dr. Spence. It had never occurred to me that one could be opposed to wars and stand against them. I could scarcely believe it. It echoed in my heart in a way that made me wonder whether I too might be one of those . . . pacifists.

He visited a few more times, and I found I so liked him. He was warm and funny and smoked strange-smelling French cigarettes. The day after one of his visits Mum told us that his eight-year-old daughter would be staying with us from time to time whenever he went abroad to conduct his research.

That was how I met my Emma. She wore trousers. I'd never seen a girl who wore trousers before, or who could belch on command, or who could climb trees better than me. Emma would not let me hide in my quiet world. She tugged me out of it by playing marbles and pitching baseballs at me and putting her hand to my ear to whisper secrets. Her eyebrows reminded me of red velvet cake, the maroonish red brows painted lushly on the silk white frosting of her skin. I adored red velvet cake. Her auburn hair lay on her shoulders like a warning flag, untamed, heated, out for adventure. When she got angry, she would flush from her chest all the way to the top of her head. I found myself wanting to wrestle with her, though I'd never had that urge before in my life.

I couldn't believe she sought my company. Nobody else did. One day I asked her, "Didn't you hear what I—what happened last year?"

"Yeah, I know. You mean that kid Rufus who died?"

"Uh-huh." I would admit my guilt. "I—"

"Yeah, I heard about it. Was it really gory? I mean, did you throw up or anything?"

I was so startled I could hardly respond. "Uh, no. I guess I didn't."

"Yeah, the Housers told my dad about it, like we should stay away from you, but he just rolled his eyes and said, 'That poor English kid—his life must be hell living in a town with people like you.'" She stood with her hands on her hips and tossed her head while she spoke.

"He *said* that?" I was nearly giddy with relief and gratitude.

"Oh, yeah, he loves telling people exactly what he thinks, and they can go to hell if they don't like it." She smiled simply.

I blinked hearing her speak so freely, and a laugh escaped me, the first time I'd laughed in a long time. She laughed too, which was even better, to laugh *with* someone. When Emma's father died, I couldn't have been more delighted that my parents took her in as one of our family.

Although Emma pulled me back into life, I still prayed for forgiveness for Rufus's death. But Emma and I talked about it sometimes, and one time she said something so simple, it helped me begin to put it to rest.

She made me show her the stairway where it happened. She made me point out the very step, while I turned green from the horror of it. She said, "I can see it. I could push you, and you could fall and crack your head open by chance too."

"But *you* wouldn't push someone like that."

She laughed. "I *have* pushed someone like that. They just didn't hit a stair." She shrugged.

Then we went and sat on the step, the lethal step, for a long time and said nothing.

Something lifted that day and I was able to put the worst of it behind me. But by the time I was fourteen, the world itself was preoccupied with death. My parents heard from relatives about the terror Hitler was spreading across Europe. They would sit in the parlor listening to reports from London on the wireless.

One night we sat eating our supper after just such a harrowing account from the battlefield. Father cleared his throat. Without taking his eyes off his food, he said, "There is nothing more important than duty. And if your country calls upon you to defend her, you must not be deaf to her call."

The next morning Tyler left for the enlistment office with Father while Mum stood in the hallway holding her doubts between pursed lips. How proud Father was that day. Brave Tyler, doing his part, not letting the side down.

I knew what Father expected of me. But every time I thought of what that meant, I knew I would never be able to kill a man, and that I didn't even want to participate from behind the front lines in helping someone else do it. As the years passed, a sense of doom grew like a plague inside me. Soon I would be eighteen and Father would expect me to enlist. Then one day I saw a man on a street corner handing out pamphlets. A woman in front of me took one. She looked at it, then threw it at his feet and yelled at the man, "Traitor!" as she walked away. When I reached him, I saw his eyes were kind, despite her harsh words to him. He said, "Son, there is another way," and handed me a pamphlet.

That was how I became a conscientious objector. I registered to do "equivalent public service" under Roosevelt's provision. I spent three years working with the mentally ill in an asylum that was purgatory itself: patients naked, covered in their own waste, the male patients forcing themselves on the poor women patients, patients chewing off their own skin.

Father was livid, and it made no difference to him that I was following Christ's example as we'd been taught at church: clothe the naked, feed the hungry, comfort the sick. It didn't even make a difference when Tyler eventually returned from the war bearing indelible scars: the thousand-yard stare and the tendency to rock uncontrollably whenever he heard fireworks go off.

In meeting other conscientious objectors, I found that many of them were Quakers who had vowed never to take the life of another human being. The silence of Quaker meetings became my refuge. I felt that God had led me to a place where I could forgive myself.

As a conscientious objector, I endured the rancor of many. One such man was Deacon Pratt at Holy Trinity. Mr. Pratt was an old American Legion fellow whose left leg still carried shrapnel from World War One. I was nineteen, and I'd decided to make Mum happy by going to church with her and Father. Even Em had assented to come along. As we all stood eating doughnuts in the fellowship hall, Mr. Pratt came over and pumped my arm in a handshake and said, "You in the service, young man?"

I dreaded what was coming, but I looked him in the eye and said, "No, I'm a conscientious objector, sir."

"What?" He eyed me with a suspicious rooster look.

Emma smiled ruefully and wound one of her locks round and round her finger, which she only did when she was bored with someone else's stupidity, as she put it. Pratt's eyes squinted, got small and hateful. He looked at my father first. Father stared down at his shiny wing tips. Around his collar, I saw Father's neck coloring. Poor Mum kept a pleasant expression while clutching her purse strap tightly as if to say, nothing bad is happening, nothing bad is happening.

Mr. Pratt spat out, "Hitler's over there murdering women and children, and you're afraid of getting killed."

Emma colored, then piped up, "He's not afraid to die. He doesn't want to *kill* anyone, got it?"

"Oh, and what do the *two of you* know about that?" Mr. Pratt barked.

My heart was pounding. This was getting out of hand. "With all due respect, sir, I—"

Emma cut in, "With all due respect, he's not the only pacifist in the world. I think possibly even Jesus was a pacifist. Love your enemies? Does that sound familiar?"

Father's eyes bulged. "That is *quite enough* from both of you," he said through clenched teeth. "I *do* apologize, Mr. Pratt. Now please excuse us."

Father took my hand and Emma's and dragged us toward the door.

I came out of this reverie when Em, still seated next to me on the curlicue couch, ran her fingers through my hair. "Sure you're all right, Geebs?"

I draped my arm around her shoulder as she snuggled into my side. "I am now," I said.

~

A day after the butcher incident I was out walking in Shigatse. I smiled, thinking, "I won't be going near that place again." I watched a young woman doing a *kora:* a circumambulation following a sacred route. She was muttering prayers and spinning a prayer wheel, a gizmo with prayers on scrolls inside.

Seeing the *ragyapa* cutting up animal carcasses had brought me face-to-face with Tibet's contradictions. Tibetans were so devout and peace-loving. They had no standing army and even tried not to disturb worms when tilling the soil. Yet they certainly ate meat, so the lowly caste of *ragyapas* was given the karma-destroying act of butchering animals for everyone else to eat, free of karma.

We all have our foibles, but I still remembered the day long ago when I'd read about Tibetans in one of the books given to Emma by her father: *Tibetans wear boots with upturned toes so they won't kill insects when they walk.* I asked Emma about it and she said, "Yeah, my dad said they don't believe in killing. Something about reincarnation, so if you kill, you could spend your next life as a yak or a donkey as a punishment."

I was electrified. "Perhaps we should go there someday."

"That seems like a long way to go to get away from Mr. Pratt, Geebs."

I laughed. "But living in a place where life is that highly valued? Can you imagine? I wouldn't have to explain myself to anyone."

"I hate to break it to you, Geebs, but we'd probably croak somewhere in the Himalayas along the way."

But we *had* made it, and now I was sitting in the regent's house, looking at Emma's small, sensitive mouth as she pursed her lips and placed them on the rim of her wooden tea bowl. The Himalayas were not the only mountains we'd had to conquer to land in this glorious moment, when the last rays of the Tibetan sun painted a golden fresco on the walls.

Dorje

It was shortly after I became friends with the Americans that our family's misfortunes began. My youngest son, Champa, began losing all the water in his body. A few days ago Rinchen noticed him holding his belly, bending over with pain, and many times a day he would go outside to make *kaka*. Soon he could not even stand up he was so weak. Rinchen cried in silent fear, holding my son, and when he would make *kaka,* which looked like a thin stream, she would clean him up. Lama Norbu came to cleanse our house of evil spirits, but my son did not get better. I sent for the Tibetan doctor, but we heard he was away in Kham province. As we have tried to decide what to do, Champa has quickly gotten worse. My wife's remedies are not helping him. Our house is dark, thick with smells of sickness and *kaka,* and Rinchen's worry fills every room.

My mother, Ama-la, has taken over the cooking. On the first day, she clucked around the kitchen, glad to take it over again since Rinchen had abandoned it to take care of Champa. But now Ama-la senses the fear we do not speak of, that Champa will not get better.

Sometimes it is good to have Ama-la cooking, but other times it is frightening. When I was young, Ama-la was beautiful with tightly braided hair and perfect silk brocades on her body. She ran our family strictly, with kindness at times and with the stick at other times. Now she has no teeth and her milky eyes see nothing. Her braids are tight from Rinchen's fingers, not her own. She laughs at things the rest of us do not see. Some people think she has lost her mind, but I know that Ama-la's mind is like a river with things passing through that do not stay as they do in other people's minds. She no longer remembers my father very well, and that is good. It is as if she has forgotten that her heart was broken when he died. Is she not lucky to be able to forget her misfortunes?

I have to watch Ama-la because sometimes she forgets what she is cooking on the stove and smoke fills the room, and we all worry that the house will burn down. When the smoke begins to gather, I sneak behind her, refilling the pot that has gone dry or taking the *thukpa* off the stove because it is burning. I say nothing because she gets cranky being told what to do in her kitchen, especially by a man. She is not often cranky, only when she does not feel well. Then she and Rinchen peck at each other like hens, because when Ama-la has her aches, she likes to tell Rinchen what to do.

So Rinchen is on the mattress holding Champa, whose watery eyes stare at the ceiling. Behind the stove is Ama-la, boiling water for tea as I stand guard in the corner with the empty hands of a man when there is sickness in the house. I pinch myself to keep from crying over Champa and watch as Samten, Rinchen's brother, holds back his tears by biting his lips. When Champa soils himself, Samten helps my wife clean him up. Samten hums songs to calm his sister and wipes Champa's face with a wet cloth.

We are a small family living in this house, only five of us to comfort and help each other when an illness like this comes. The deep crease between Samten's brows tells me he and I have the same awful thought in our minds: what will Rinchen do if something happens to Champa? We have only one other son, Dawa, but he is grown and away at the monastery. We think of Rinchen's heart and see sharp rocks that pierce and rub like gravel in her shoes.

Samten is the only other person in Rinchen's family here in Tibet. They have always been fond of each other. Long ago, when they were children, they were once left with their grandmother while the rest of the family—their parents and three older brothers—went on a pilgrimage. As they were climbing a pass, they heard a great rumbling, a sound every Tibetan fears in his heart. The snows of many winters came falling off a steep hillside, burying all the members of the party. This happened after the family had already moved to Shigatse, so the entire town heard about Rinchen and Samten's misfortune. Everyone brought tsampa and yogurt and cheese to Rinchen's grandmother, and the lamas said special prayers for them. Samten never married or made a family of his own so he could stay close to his sister. He helps me with my trading routes, and he is a good man. During our journeys, he entertains me with stories and songs, and even the yaks and the sheep keep walking without any trouble when he sings to them.

Ama-la has filled a wooden bowl with salted tea to give to Champa. As Rinchen carries the bowl to him, I see that she has a warrior face today, hard like the bowl in her hands. With this face she tries to frighten away any demons that might harm our son. She can be quite fierce in protecting our family, and I think it is because she has lost so much. On top of the misfortune of losing her family, we have also lost two children shortly after they were born. Each time we have lost a child, my wife has lain flat on her mattress for weeks at a time, looking sad enough to hate her existence.

When Rinchen is sad, it is as if the world stops. She lies in bed like a cold mountain, and it seems the rivers stop flowing, the sun stops shining, the sheep stop eating. The second time we lost a child, she stayed on her mattress for a long time. We all tended to her because her chest swelled with a broken heart.

But even when she has not lost a child, at times sadness descends on Rinchen like the seasons fall on the earth. Samten and Champa are always the best at leading her out of her sadness. Champa sings to her all the songs he has learned in his seven years of life. Samten forces her out of bed with teasing only a brother could do. One time when she was low, he said, "Oh, I have grown to be a very old man during the years of you lying in this bed. See the gray hairs on my head?" He pointed to his hair. "All the sheep have died. The cockroaches have built a kingdom in the kitchen. And Champa has run off to marry an ugly girl with no ears. Really—and she has no hair on her head either. So sad, no mother to guide him, so he made this terrible mistake."

She covered her head with the blanket and said, "Let me be. My heart is so heavy I cannot move."

"Oh, look at you, lying in bed with fleas crawling through your hair!" He dug under the covers and pinched his fingers against her head. "Oh, I got one! And cockroaches climbing into your bed to be warm, and they are thinking they will reign in the kitchen forever. And my empty, empty belly, crying out, 'Feed me!' What a sad story. I think I'm going to cry." He made weeping sounds until Rinchen sat up and could not keep the smile from her face.

Then he said, "What is this? Is something wrong with your face? It moved!"

She sat up and answered, "Oh, be quiet! You're an impossible child!" Rinchen was born before Samten, and she never let him forget that she was older.

"Who is this sitting up?" he exclaimed. "It could not be my lazy older sister—let me call Lama Norbu to cast out this spirit!"

"Enough, Samten! I will fix you some food if you shut your mouth already."

"Maybe some cockroaches, eh?"

She swatted him on the arm and got up off the mattress. We had Rinchen's delicious noodles that evening.

It is a warm memory to think of how Samten teased his sister. But that was years ago. In this moment, we are tense and frightened.

There is a knock at the door. I go to it and open it slowly. Standing before me are my two American friends. Emma bows and looks at me with a question on her face, wondering if they are welcome. She says, "*Tashi delek,* Dorje. We don't want to bother you—it's just we heard . . . crying and I saw your wife holding your son. Is he all right?"

My insides are jumping with hope. I look over at my wife excitedly, only to remember that I haven't told her anything about my new friends. But her face is a stone with eyes that are sad and far away.

"Champa is very ill," I tell the Americans.

Emma smiles kindly. "Did you know Gerald is a doctor?"

My mouth falls open, but the blond man is already walking over to Champa. My wife opens her arms to let the man examine our son. Sitting on the mattress with her, Gerald takes his tools out of a little bag and touches them to Champa. Gerald asks her questions in his simple Tibetan. Even Ama-la comes over to listen and settles herself on the floor. Samten stands back and looks at me as if to say, *Who are these people?*

Gerald's hands are large with long fingers, and they touch Champa slowly and gently. Emma joins our gathering around the mattress. Gerald turns to her and says, "Dysentery, I'd bet." Emma gets down onto her knees next to Ama-la. She takes Ama-la's hand, and Ama-la smiles wide.

Gerald speaks in Tibetan, saying, "Champa has a . . . like a bug, a bad bug in the part of his body that takes the food he eats and gets rid of the waste."

My wife nodded and said, "Yes, we know he has this. But do you have any medicine?"

"Yes, I have medicine that can help him."

A sigh pushes through my wife's lips. She hesitates, and her eyes ask the important question: *Will he live?*

Emma understands this language of the eyes, saying, "He'll be fine."

Gerald takes a bottle from his bag. He removes several small pills, but these are white, not like the brown pills we would get from a Tibetan doctor. Gerald puts them in my wife's hand and says, "Give Champa one pill each day." My wife nods, and her other hand grabs the man's wrist. Her eyes fill with tears, and she has no words. He nods back to her, then he and Emma stand up. They bow and walk to the door.

I stop them, saying, "You must stay to have tea with us, and some dinner."

But Emma shakes her head. "When Champa is feeling better. You all need to get some rest."

I bow to both of them and say with my throat swelling, "Thanks, thanks, I will pray for many blessings for you, for long life and good health, and may you have many children."

A strange look passes across Emma's face, like winter. Her skin is more pale than I have seen before. As I watch them leave, I notice my chest feels empty, and I don't know why.

Champa is well! He plays outside again with the other children, and he is exactly as before, our precious little *bö*. We gave special offerings at the monastery to express our thanks. Rinchen wants to give everything we have to our new friends, so grateful is she that they shared their medicine and their kindness with us! She had me bring some fresh yak butter to them yesterday, and we have invited them for a party this afternoon. The air that was thick with tears is now filled with ginger and garlic and steam from the dumplings Rinchen is cooking. She is also preparing a *thukpa* soup with greens and yak meat and lamb.

This morning I talked to my wife about American ways, trying to teach her so she will not offend our guests when they come. I told her, "Remember, it is not polite to ask them their age. Especially the women. For some reason, they do not like this question."

She answered, "I only want to know so I can show her the respect appropriate to her age! How could she be offended by this?"

"I don't know exactly what is the reason for this, but you must trust me. My English friend told me that the English and the Americans get very nervous with this question."

My wife looked at me sideways with her eyes pulled into small holes, as if she thought I were making this up. "I don't know, Dorje. If I don't ask, then I will not know how to act towards her."

"She is very friendly. Ask her questions about other things, about her life in America, *just not her age.*"

Rinchen pulled her stubborn head up, saying, "We'll see. I will think about it. But tell me this, Dorje: Why are these two so skinny? They are tall, with big bones, and the man has a large nose on his face. So they have big bones, but no meat on them? Is America a poor country where they don't have enough to eat?"

I thought about this. "No, I don't think so. But don't ask them about this either."

My wife's jaw was hard. She wanted to give me an answer.

But now there is a tap on the door. Rinchen goes right to the door and opens it. Emma stands with Gerald behind her. She holds two white silk *khata* scarves folded in her hands, and her grin could not be wider. Gerald is already winking at Champa, who runs through the door and latches on to Gerald's legs as if the tall man were just another uncle known to him forever. A delighted "Ohoho!" escapes the American man's mouth, and he ruffles Champa's hair. My son was so sick when he last saw Gerald, how does he even remember him?

Meanwhile, Rinchen and Emma have a much more formal greeting: my wife receives the two *khata* scarves from Emma's hands and places one around Emma's neck while she bows. As

Gerald has already got down on the ground with Champa before even crossing the threshold, Rinchen quickly puts the *khata* around his neck and we all laugh at the impossibility of a formal greeting with him on the ground.

Rinchen puts her hand on Gerald's elbow, offering to help him get up, and we laugh again. After our shared silliness, our guests come to the table and Ama-la pours them bowls of chang.

My wife says with a broad smile, "Now we have the real welcome chang for you. Not the one given to you before by my naughty husband without my knowing! Please drink!"

A few moments later Rinchen takes Emma by the hand into the kitchen and asks her in a quiet voice, "How old are you?"

Oh! She thinks I cannot hear what she is saying? Emma's eyebrows jump up on her forehead the way a sheep jumps when startled, but she says, "I'm twenty-eight." She hesitates, smiling, but then says graciously, "Are you making dumplings? Will you teach me?"

Rinchen looks proudly over her shoulder at me, as if to say, *See, I know how to make friends with another woman, even one from America.* My wife says, "To make *momos* is really simple. It is a very important Tibetan food for celebrations and parties."

Rinchen has the meat filling for the *momos* in a bowl and the dough cut into pieces on her worktable next to it. Emma bends over the bowl to smell the filling and says, "What do you have in here?" They put their heads together as Rinchen explains, then Ama-la walks into the kitchen and stands behind the two women kneeling at the table. She listens closely as Rinchen explains how to seal up the dumpling after stuffing it. Ama-la says, "No, Daughter, you must pinch together the dough this way, to shape it," bringing her fingers together to demonstrate. My wife frowns and looks at Emma, who smiles back knowingly. These two women understand one thing: living with the mother-in-law. A light smile spreads on Rinchen's face. She takes a breath and says, "Ama-la will now teach us how to make *momos*."

Emma's eyes are shining.

Later we settle down to a feast of roast lamb, *momos*, *thukpa*, yogurt, and then dried fruits as a treat. We all eat so much we are about to split open.

After the meal, Samten sings songs for us with Champa sitting at his feet. Samten's wearing his fur-lined hat as a costume and has it inside out, with the fur on the outside, because he is singing about a fox, so he has to have fur. Champa giggles at his uncle's fox movements like scratching at the ground, or hiding behind the stove and then jumping out.

Ama-la sits next to Emma at the dinner table. She has her arms around our guest, who sits looking pleased. First Ama-la says to Emma, "You saved our Champa!" A few minutes later she adds with a grin, "My grandson, he is well now." Whenever we laugh at Samten's movements, Ama-la laughs too, probably because she has had too much chang; her milky eyes cannot see what Samten is doing.

She leans over to Emma and says, "Mmm. You smell good!"

Emma grins and puts her head on Ama-la's shoulder.

I have only known my new friends for a few weeks, but as I look at all of us together, I feel a strange largeness about us, as if our bonds with each other will soon be too big to fit in one room.

Emma

"When we visit the monastery with Dorje today, I'll bow, but I'm not prostrating myself to any lamas." We sat hunched over the table, drinking sweetened tea to chase off the morning cold that crept around our ankles.

My husband pressed together his generously full lips. Despite my agitation, I felt a twinge of longing to touch them and feel their warmth.

He only pressed them tight when he was about to be diplomatic. "Emma, you tramp hundreds of miles over hellish terrain to get here, you drink disgusting tea with yak fat in it, but now you've gotten stuck on this one little point." A smile was in his smooth voice.

"Geebs, I can't help it. I don't like the way Tibetans only have male lamas—oh, sure, women can be nuns, but they can't be in charge of anything."

"You're right, Em. I'm simply concerned about giving offense." He shrugged.

We'd been here in Shigatse about six weeks, but I already felt I'd learned enough to have been here a year. Long enough to have a catalog of hates and loves and to get cranky about a few things. As we walked the dusty road to the monastery with Rinchen and Dorje and Champa, I got lost in my thoughts and tripped on a pothole as I mentally fussed over bowing. I nearly ran into Champa as I listened to Dorje talking to Rinchen because I was musing over the loveliness of spoken Tibetan, the soft consonants like velvet to my ears and the harder ones pushed through with a puff of air. And its gentle, polite way of saying things. Smooth and yielding, never pushy. I loved bowing to Rinchen or Dorje, feeling my forehead touch one of theirs, with our eyes casting warm rays between us. I was deeply impressed that Dorje kept a string of *mani* beads around his wrist and actually used them to recite prayers throughout the day. Even as we walked, his lips moved quickly, his fingers ticking off beads.

While we trudged along, I watched Gerald and laughed to myself. He was tiptoeing around to avoid stepping on insects in his Tibetan boots. I teased him, saying, "Bug! Don't step on it!"

He stopped on the spot. "Where?"

I gave him a naughty smile, and we resumed walking.

"Em, you are wicked, and you're going to be reborn as a beetle," he smirked.

"Whoa, look out, there's another one!"

"All right, young lady." He grabbed my arm and pulled me along so we wouldn't lose Dorje's family. The crease between his brows deepened. "Em, I have to tell you, as much fun as this is for you, it hurts me."

"You cannot be serious."

"Do you honestly think I'd enjoy being mocked for not wanting to kill something?"

My heart sank. "Oh, Geebs, I'm sorry. I just didn't think."

"It's all right."

After a walk of many miles, we finally made a dusty arrival at the monastery. We entered the temple and stood in a long line of pilgrims. In the dim light I saw low benches where monks sat chanting, and Buddha statues draped in *khata* scarves of every color. The pilgrims had all come to pray, and many held thermoses of yak butter to give as offerings. The scent of sandalwood filled my nostrils. I heard a man reciting prayers quietly, and when I turned to look at him, I saw he was also spinning a prayer wheel. On my back I felt the press of the woman behind me, and I noticed that everyone in the line was pushing forward. It was not a rude sensation. Just a sense of intense desire on my back, a yearning to express a feeling from the heart. They touched the feet of Buddha statues, prostrated themselves, even rubbed yak butter on the columns of the temple as offerings. I'd never been around such a hunger. So, when we came to the monuments where the ashes of revered lamas were kept, I bowed, in the exact same way as those before me and behind me. I simply could not offend that yearning all around me by being my irreverent self. It felt like a longing for God, although I wasn't sure these people even believed in God.

I got choked up and felt stupid enough to wonder, why did I hate it so much, showing respect for others' rules? When I'd joined the Kittredge family, Tyler was fourteen and Gerald was ten, and their pinched faces and school uniforms told me there would be rules in this household. Their mother, Abigail, had pushed my tomboy legs into tights. My poor legs resembled blue sausages, the top ends tied off with a plaid, pleated skirt and the bottoms with shiny hard shoes. A private-school uniform. Yech. I found out there was a proper way to do *everything:* how to put a napkin in your lap, how to answer the telephone, how to breathe deeply while "taking one's exercise." These were not relaxed English folk with bawdy jokes here and there. These were the stick-in-the-mud kind. Ugh. Even here in Tibet, Gerald held his tea quite properly, with an arc in the last finger of his right hand. He did that even though he was drinking tea out of a *bowl,* for God's sake!

The school principal once told me that because I was a poor

orphan, I should have been grateful Abby and Eddy took me in. I wanted to spit at him, but then a helpless feeling came over me. I could never make him understand how lost I felt. How angry to be forced to be someone I wasn't, to tear out every shred of the willful girl my father had made me.

I especially hated that they made me go to church because Daddy had always said, "The whole universe is God's church, Emma." Every Sunday, Queen Abby scrubbed us within an inch of our lives, then we all walked down the hill to Holy Trinity Episcopal Church on Main Street. The first time I went I wondered if I'd feel God, or at least something, because there had to be some compelling reason why people sat in a building yakking with some guy they couldn't even see. Although the pew had a padded rail for kneeling, by the end of that first service all I could feel were my sore knees. Stand up, sit down, kneel, say this and that, sing, stand up, sit down again, amen. I whispered to Geebs, "I think the reverend has gas," and he snickered, still keeping his eyes to the front.

Gerald confessed he didn't like Holy Trinity either. One day after he'd turned eighteen he came into my room and sat down on my bed. I was studying. Without a word, we did the sneaky thing we'd done many times before: we lay on my bed on our sides, looking into each other's eyes with my books like an island between us. If our parents knocked on the door, we could easily rearrange ourselves as though he were helping me with my homework.

This was not unusual, given the heavy breathing and petting we'd been doing for the past year. I'm sure if they'd known, the king and the queen would've called me a harlot and blamed me for the whole thing, but Geebs was no angel. We were expert at hiding in plain sight, showing no trace of giggliness around each other, or any mooning glances at the breakfast table that would hint that I'd had my naked legs wrapped around Geebs' naked waist the night before, or that Geebs had any idea that a French letter was anything other than a letter from France.

"I've had an epiphany, Em." He ran his hand slowly along my side.

"Really?" I shivered.

"I think I found God."

"Where *was* he?"

"Em! I'm serious." The brow crease appeared.

"You're distracting me with your hand, so it's your fault."

He grinned, then took his hand away. "I went to a Quaker meeting this morning with a CO friend."

"What's that?"

"It's a religious sect. Their worship is utterly profound—they sit in silence for hours."

"Uh-huh." I tried to look sufficiently swept away by this description.

"There's none of that dreadful claptrap at Holy Trinity, no prayer book, no sermon."

"Well, *that's* a plus. So what was God like?"

"I simply felt loved by Him," Gerald whispered. "He was a deeply loving presence, like a glowing light shining down on my head. It was incredible. I want you to come with me sometime."

I wrinkled my nose. "Ah, Geebs, you know I'm not cut out for that stuff. I have the attention span of a grape."

"You'd like it. In Quaker meetings there are mystics and rebels, and some people are both. They put their consciences above any laws. This fellow George Fox started it three hundred years ago in England, and ever since, Quakers have been getting thrown in jail for being rebels. You won't believe it, Em. They're all oddballs. And they think like your father did—they say God is in everyone."

He knew how to lure me. If these people were like my dad, maybe it was worth considering.

At my first Quaker meeting, Gerald and I entered the meetinghouse, a room with stark white walls and folding chairs. We sat down. Everyone sat with eyes closed. I felt restless, so I sat on my hands, hoping to behave myself. I told my mind to try to experience God as Gerald had. But I couldn't stop being distracted. I stole glances at old, austere Friends and young Friends with a bohemian look. A woman directly across from me was shrouded in gray from her sensible shoes to the wavy silver hairs on her head. She sat with an expectant look, her face shining like a beacon in a sea of gray. She seemed to hold some secret between smiling lips. After nearly two hours, I heard rustling and low voices around me and opened my eyes to see everyone shaking hands.

It is hard to fathom how I ever became a Quaker. I'm pretty mediocre at it. I never did experience the infinite in a meeting, and sometimes I fell asleep during meetings. But I was drawn to the quiet, and something magical seemed to happen when all of us were gathered together.

And I found a mother. After the announcements, I noticed the old woman in gray gravitating in my direction. I watched each step of her boxy shoes across the hardwood floor. I felt panicky. *What if she saw me peeking at her, and now she has targeted me for some churchy message?* Before I could flee, she caught my elbow with her soft, wrinkled hand.

"Hello, my dear." Her voice quivered in a regular, uncontrollable vibrato.

I felt bad for wanting to squash such a fragile fly. "Hello."

"I'm so impressed with your erect posture. You must have a strong back and shoulders. Couldn't help but admire that." She slid her hand gently up my back.

I found myself melting as I smiled down into her bright eyes, and they smiled back. A warm lamp lit inside me. "Well, thank you," I heard myself say. "What's your name?"

"Genevieve," she answered through a wide smile that creased her face. With vigor she shook my hand in her warm palm. "I could really use your help. Why don't you join me here Monday afternoon around three o'clock?"

"Uh . . . well, what exactly do you need me for?"

Her expression grew serious. "When I was hungry, you fed me," she murmured. "When I was in prison, you visited me."

All right, she's a little loony. But I couldn't say no to her. "Umm, okay."

"Wonderful." She took my hand and pressed it between hers, saying, "We're going to have a ball!" With that, she turned and shuffled back across the room.

Monday was a thoroughly wet and sloshy day. I didn't want to go meet her, but when I thought of not showing up, I imagined her waiting patiently in the downpour, bent and saddened by disappointment. At three o'clock I approached her as she hunkered beneath a tattered black umbrella.

"Oh, ye-es!" Her quavery voice had a cadence to it. Up on the *oh,* midway down on the *y* and the *e,* and ending with an insistent second syllable on the *yes.* "We'll just load the cakes and we'll be set to go." She attached her fingers to my sleeve and towed me along. "I made them in Jessie's kitchen because it's right here next to the meetinghouse."

She had an ashy line of flour on her left temple. I wondered how a will like hers dwelled so peacefully in such a little body. I let that will flatten me like a rolling pin on a lump of dough as she herded me toward Jessie's back door. Her eyes had streaks of blue that seemed to fizz like a sparkler. As we approached her car with the fifth layer of fist-size cakes, I said, "Can I ask what we're doing?"

"We're loading up the prune cakes for the inmates," she answered as though it were perfectly obvious.

"Prune cakes?" I asked, disbelief evident in my voice.

"Oh, yes. Keeps everybody regular, guards and inmates alike."

My brain jolted awake. "Inmates? What kind of inmates?"

"Prison inmates," she said cheerfully.

I envisioned her handing out prune cakes to a bunch of degenerates as they hurled bawdy catcalls at me. "Umm . . . Genevieve? Do the . . . criminals treat you all right?"

"Oh, of course, my dear. They're just young girls who've lost their way." Her eyes twinkled.

"Girls? These are female inmates?" I tried to keep the shake out of my voice.

"Oh, yes. Don't worry, dear, the love of God is all over that place. You'll see," she said amiably, shuffling toward the driver's door as I padded sheepishly to the passenger door. I was already in the car, its interior ripe with the sweet nuttiness of prunes, when she opened her car door. She placed her beige vinyl handbag on the seat, then she sat on it. "I take my little booster with me everywhere I go," she said, pointing to her handbag and lifting her right buttock to give me a better view of it. "Otherwise, I can't see over the handlebars."

I chuckled to myself until we pulled up in front of the imposing silhouette of the prison. MIDDLESEX COUNTY DETENTION CENTER was printed across its stern face in iron letters, blackened with ages of grime. I felt chilled. We gathered the trays from the car and approached a hulking set of wooden doors. She powered one of them open with her right hand, balancing her two tiers of cakes expertly in her left. I folded myself behind her as she led with a smile as big as a barn door.

So many impressions of that first visit moored themselves in my mind: the dank scent of concrete, the bone-chilling scrape of iron on iron as each gate slammed behind us, the tinkling of keys, the sounds of her scuff-scuff footsteps, and the air growing stale. We passed through seven portals in our descent into this hell, each one marked by Amazonian women guards and an institutional-green gate. Genevieve strode forward, unaware that I tiptoed like a shadow behind her. The solid voices of the guards softened in her presence, and that's how I knew she'd melted them too. One of the guards gently dusted the flour from Genevieve's face.

After we'd given away two full trays of cakes to guards alone, we finally arrived at our destination: cellblock D. The cells were arranged along the sides of a long, gray corridor. The smell was an animal of many limbs: cigarettes, urine, sweat, and disinfectant. The stench of boredom, suffering, and wasted lives. The women wore coveralls of bright orange with the penal-institution name stenciled on the back. They had skins of every hue, from the bluest black to the palest ivory, and they were everything from fat to raven-haired to platinum blond.

What I remembered most about that day was the image of Genevieve wrapping her tiny hands, one on top, one on the bottom, around the hand of each woman as she spoke to her. The gesture was almost unbearably tender. She didn't preach; she listened. Each prisoner drew near to those sparky eyes like a cat drawn into sleep before a hearth fire. Genevieve was right when she'd told me, "The love of God is in that place." She gave it, and she got it.

After we'd made our way back out of the prison and she'd settled herself into the car and onto her purse, I touched her veined arm. "Why did you choose *me* to do this?"

"Just following the Light," the quavery voice said. She pointed her index finger toward the roof of the car and added, "He told me to."

"He told you, 'Go invite that girl over there'?"

"Oh, no. It wasn't as clear as all that. I felt the Spirit drawing me across the room to you. I had no idea what I'd say when I actually got there. But it all worked out, didn't it?"

This time I wrapped her hand in *my* two hands. "Thank you. I will never forget this."

"So you'll come back visiting with me next month?" Her smile grew bigger.

"Oh, yes," I said, grinning.

Genevieve always said, "It's more important to *do* than to sit around talking about it." I still wasn't sure what I believed about God. If he did exist, then he had some explaining to do about taking away both of my parents. The only thing I could always say was that I believed God lived in two people: Gerald and Genevieve.

Gerald

I sat in the temple, staring round me, thanking God for letting me see this. For it was His hand I saw. Everywhere. It was too beautiful not to see and feel Him there in the gentle light of butter lamps and the sizzling they made when they sputtered. I saw His Light in the eyes of the lamas. If you sat and prayed for all sentient beings for hours each day as they did, wouldn't that change you? It must. I felt enveloped by hundreds of years of those prayers, thinking that they traveled into my lungs with each breath. What would it do to me, I wondered, to breathe them in? Chants vibrated out of the monks' throats, chants so guttural they seemed frightening, otherworldly.

I saw Emma surveying the colors shouting all around us—fiery reds, majestic golds, forest greens, and magentas, all blazing out of paintings of Buddhas on delicate, hanging silks. I loved it, but I was sure the old, plain-bonneted Quakers would turn over in their graves at all this pomp. Emma's face was flushed and her eyes shone, almost as if she were crying. I dismissed the thought. She was a bit too cynical and worried about bowing to lamas to be crying now.

Thongchen horns rippled the air with wide-throated blasts, powered by monks on the roof. Their sound rumbled in my chest. As I looked toward the source of the sounds, I saw hundreds of wooden beams in parallel, cobalt lines with a patch of bright yellow between each pair. I watched a monk pass a large bowl of tsampa, tossing a little in the air as an offering. Icy drafts chilled my arms, making me wish I had a monk's habit in which to wrap myself.

Dorje and Rinchen were both fully engaged in their prostrations, their oiled black braids glimmering in the light of the butter lamps.

Emma reached over and squeezed my hand. I had a memory of sitting in the Quaker meetinghouse—thrilling in being next to her, away from our parents—during her first time going with me. Our thighs had touched as we sat, awkward, both facing front. A light patina of sweat brought the smell of her hair right into my nostrils. With my heart throbbing, I sought her hand and was shocked by its warm, velvety feel. Her pale hand responded, not with the chaste pressing of palms together, but the *interlacing of fingers*. An exquisite tingling coursed from my hand to secret places. I felt drunk. I could scarcely breathe.

With gregarious Emma by my side, I made the acquaintance of several Friends that day, and their welcome was kind. We returned the next week. The week after that, I went alone, and Genevieve approached me and asked, "Where's your sweetie this week?"

My heart squeezed with glee that someone called her my sweetie. "Uhhh . . . she isn't feeling well," I lied. I couldn't keep the smile from my face for the rest of the day. That was how we found a place where we could be ourselves together.

I looked up and saw that Dorje and Rinchen had finished their prostrations. I turned to look at my wife. Her eyes were closed and her brow furrowed as if in concentration. She didn't look quite right, and just then she grabbed her hair up near the roots in both her hands, pulling it this way and that to release her tension.

Dorje walked to the back wall, and I tapped her arm.

As Dorje led us to the road so we could all continue toward Dawa's monastery, not one of us noticed the eyes that watched with suspicion our mixed-race party.

Emma

"What happened to you in there? Are you all right?" Gerald demanded.

"Of course." My voice sounded like metal.

"I saw you crying, Em."

"I'm fine," I insisted, but my voice trembled just a tiny bit.

He studied my face. "Are you having me on? I swear I saw tears on your face."

"What's the big deal?" I rolled my head around to loosen my neck muscles.

"Well, you cry about once a decade."

I rolled my eyes. "If I wanted to talk about this, don't you think I'd bring it up?"

"Ouch. I see. You're not going to tell me, then."

We passed a beggar man with only one brown tooth as we walked behind Dorje and his family. We were on our way to the river for a picnic. Dorje was fingering his ever-present *mani* beads as we walked.

Gerald's lips pressed together, and then I felt bad. "Okay, I'll tell you. I had a deep moment in there," I said in a mocking tone.

"Did you? What happened?" His lips curved into a smile.

"It's stupid," I mumbled. "I felt my dad's presence, sort of saying . . . this is silly, Gerald."

"Will you bloody well tell me already?" His eyes widened with irritation.

"Okay, it was like he was telling me why he came to Tibet. I mean, there was no voice. I just sensed it. I looked around me and it was gorgeous, and there was incense hanging in the air and it was actually holy—whatever that means—and it just hit me why he couldn't get it out of his system."

Gerald smiled. Love was in his eyes. "I'm glad for you, Em."

"Look, my dad's still not off the hook."

"And you can keep him there as long as you wish." The smile on Gerald's lips was gentle. He was beautiful, even with his overly large nose. His full, sensuous lips balanced it all out. It humbled me, seeing his beauty, and reminded me to settle down and be grateful in this moment.

"So, my eyes did tear up. I was feeling forgiving towards him, and I told him that I surrendered my pockmarked heart to the whole thing. And that's it." I tried to keep my voice hard.

Gerald grinned. "Remarkable."

He kissed me, and I was glad to close my eyes so he wouldn't see that there was more I hadn't told him. I'd started feeling trembly on the way there, when little Champa took my hand. It made my throat hurt. He took my hand as if it belonged to him. I walked along unbelieving, thinking he'd taken it by mistake. But he didn't let go the whole trip. His hand was so sweet in mine. He did other things to charm me. Marching around stiffly in imitation of a Chinese soldier he saw on the road. Showing me a small, stuffed animal he'd named Aba.

Why would a child want my hand? The hand of Emma, the infertile freak. Biology or the Guy Upstairs had decided I wasn't going to have children in my life. So having Champa embrace me made me a weepy mess. I hoped I could pull myself together once we arrived at Dawa's monastery.

Before we reached it, I asked Dorje how long Dawa had been at the monastery. I expected him to say a year or two, but he said Dawa had been there since he was six years old! Dorje must have seen how astonished I was because he quickly explained that this was a customary age for children to undertake such a life. He added that this was how children in Tibet received an education, and that not all of the children even within the same family had that opportunity. When I asked if any other schools existed they could attend, he shook his head.

During the entire discussion, Rinchen held her head high. Then she told us that Dawa was more than a monk; he was a lama.

"What does that mean exactly?" I asked.

"He is a teacher, a priest," she said, beaming.

"He has just begun his time as a teacher," Dorje clarified, his chest broadening. "The older lamas started training him early for that because he showed a lot of promise from the beginning."

"I cannot wait to meet him!" Gerald told them, and I nodded enthusiastically.

Indeed, my whole being was tingling in anticipation of the chance to meet and really talk with someone who'd dedicated his life to a spiritual pursuit so wholeheartedly.

When I actually met Dawa later, I noticed that he appeared how I would imagine Rinchen to look as a man. They had the same full face, but instead of braids like hers, he had the close cut of a monk. His irises were a burnt brown, and his eyes were wide open to the world. He chased Champa around outside the monastery and grabbed him and tickled him until Champa was too tired to go on. Dawa had much more energy than I expected from a monk, especially a lama!

We all sat next to a stream and feasted on lamb and pea noodles and fresh radishes that were so spicy they bit back. I felt full, not with food, but with belonging. I had the odd thought that if we were back in the States, we'd be at our annual family picnic for Independence Day, Abby and Eddy's attempt at fitting in with the "Yanks." But in all these family gatherings I'd experienced, I'd never felt such a fullness of belonging as I did today with Dorje's family.

Dawa's eyes were joyful, but when I told him how Champa had been aping a communist soldier on the way there, he changed. His face fell into angry lines and he became quiet. "So Champa is getting used to the Chinese being here," he said tightly.

Rinchen's voice was stern as she answered, "We are here to celebrate and spend time together, Dawa, not to talk about the Chinese. Besides, we bought a special butter *torma,* so the gods will protect us."

I couldn't help thinking, weren't monks supposed to have equanimity no matter what happened? Didn't he have faith since he was a monk?

Champa came over to me holding a flower in his hand. I swallowed and accepted it. Rinchen seemed grateful for the distraction. Dawa adjusted his robes over his left shoulder and said to Gerald, "Champa likes your wife. He wants her to be his aunty."

"I'd like to be a *mother,*" I heard my voice say. The words jumped out like a little toad.

Gerald snapped a shocked look in my direction. This was something I would *never* say. I wouldn't even let *him* talk about it.

Dawa asked, "Will you have children, then?"

I took a big breath and held it, wishing I'd kept my mouth shut. "I can't," I said in a low voice.

The burnt-brown eyes looked right into mine. He said nothing.

I sat there wondering what in the world was happening to me.

Dorje

"You are Dorje Thondup?"

I did not recognize the voice, speaking to me in Chinese. I was outside tending to a sore on the shoulder of one of my yaks. I turned around. "Yes," I answered, bowing.

He smiled and bowed. He wore the soldier uniform I'd seen on the hundreds of soldiers who had arrived in the past months. He was thin and taller than me, but I noticed most that his eyebrows seemed too large for his face. They looked like the thick fur on the yak next to me. I must have been nervous because I had the silly thought that they might crawl away like two furry creatures.

"Come into the house and have some tea, please," I told him.

"Thank you," he said warmly.

I let him into the gate of the courtyard. As we walked toward the house, I felt two things: my heart was beating fast, and I also had a strange liking for this furry fellow. His eyes seemed as if he had nothing to hide.

We walked into the house and Rinchen looked up. She stared hard at Comrade Wei with the glassy, dark eyes of a she-bear. Then she stood still, sniffing at this stranger.

"This is my wife, Rinchen."

"It is wonderful to meet you, madam, and see such a proud laboring family." He bowed, and she bowed slowly to him, never taking her eyes from his face.

I said to her, "Is there some tea for Mr.—"

"Wei. *Comrade* Wei," he corrected, but his voice was kind.

"Yes, I just made some." There was a knife behind my wife's words.

We sat down at the table. He sat straight, and I wondered if he was a bit nervous as well. He began, "I've come to you because of your special connection to the motherland."

"My—what?"

Rinchen brought our bowls of tea. Then she went into the altar room to show politeness. However, I knew her she-bear ears were listening from the other room.

"Your connection to China. We heard that you speak Chinese?"

"Yes, my father was Chinese," I answered carefully.

"Well, there is much work to be done here, and we need a person who speaks Chinese and who can communicate with the Tibetan proletariat."

"The what?" His big words confused me.

"The proletariat. We need someone who can help us liberate our Tibetan brothers." He smiled as though he were giving me a gift.

I was so puzzled that I stayed silent. My heart was knocking in my chest and I wondered if he could hear it.

"I can see you don't really understand the opportunity we're offering you." The eyebrows hopped around on his forehead. "We want to take you to China."

There was a gasp from the altar room. Suddenly it was hard for me to breathe.

"We want to take our most important new comrades to China, to show you how Chairman Mao has opened our eyes, and how the working class is leading us to a perfect society. China is becoming strong. We are renewing our glorious Chinese heritage, bringing back the real names of our cities, not the names given to them by imperialists.

"You see, Dorje, we were invaded so many times, we became weak. We listened to our oppressors, who said they were superior while they took what they wanted from us. Chairman Mao will not let this happen again. And he won't allow imperialists to take over Tibet, either."

My mind was a blizzard with snow flying everywhere and everything white before me, and my not knowing the way to step next. Who was this Mao fellow? And the "oppressors"? I remembered his saying there were imperialists in Tibet. I knew of no one who seemed like that. "Imperialists? What does this mean?"

"The Japanese, the Europeans. The Europeans came and built their own places, restaurants, and hotels, in *our* country. Do you know, the Europeans put a sign in a park in Shanghai that said NO DOGS OR CHINAMEN? And the Japanese." He made a noise like a snorting horse. "They took over our country for seven years—made us carry identity papers. They forced our old men and women to kowtow to them. We lost our dignity, Dorje, but Chairman Mao has liberated us. And we will educate you and liberate *you* from your chains."

"My chains?"

"Yes! You work hard, but *who* benefits from your labor?" His voice was angry, and his fists went toward me, then upward as he spoke of benefit.

I decided to guess. "Rinchen?"

The eyebrows flew upward and Mr. Wei laughed. "You have a good sense of humor, comrade! Anyway, we'll leave in two weeks," he said in a friendly tone. The eyebrows bent down seriously over his eyes. "This is a trip that will open your eyes and change you forever."

I could not sleep that night. My head was full as with the buzzing of a thousand insects. I spent most of the night in the altar room praying for wisdom. Why was it so important for me to go there? If I did go, would I return home safely? What would they do to me if I did not go? At the end of his visit, Comrade Wei had said seriously, "To refuse to go would not be wise, Dorje. You could be labeled as a black hand."

Because I did not like his serious tone, I decided to make a joke. "A black hand? Is this a bad thing? I have black hands only when I labor very hard!"

He looked around nervously. Then he touched my shoulder and added quietly, "My friend, a black hand is an enemy of the Communist Party, an enemy of liberation. We do not joke about such things. To me you can say anything. But this is not true of all comrades. So you must learn to think and speak correctly. The day is coming when you will be grateful to be a friend of the Communist Party."

I gazed at the face of the Buddha on the altar. Rinchen walked into the room and began to speak before she even sat down next to me. "It's not right for you to go, Dorje. I don't understand why you are even considering it."

"Comrade Wei says I must understand communism."

"Why? Will it help you accumulate merit for a good rebirth? Will it make you a better trader or a better father to your children?"

"No. It is not like that."

"Then what good is it?"

"He said *it would not be wise to refuse.*"

"And what does this Mr. Comrade know of wisdom? He's not even a lama. So the Chinese will be upset with you if you don't go. But what can they do to you? Report you to the regent? Frown at you?"

"Rinchen, I have been hearing that you do not want them as

your enemy. Anyway, I'm going to see Lama Norbu tomorrow so he can perform a divination about this decision."

"Aha. And you will feel better when Lama Norbu tells you not to go." She stood up and left the room as if the decision were already made.

I stared at the Buddha's face, but it gave me no answer.

＊

When I reached the monastery the next day, I asked to see Lama Norbu. While I waited for an audience with him, I went to my son's room. When he saw me, he jumped up, grinning. We touched foreheads and I pulled out the sweets Rinchen had wrapped in a cloth bundle for him.

"Mmmm. My most favorite! But you didn't come here just to give me sweets."

"I came to see Lama Norbu." I paused. "I've been asked to go to China by the People's Liberation Army."

Dawa's chin dropped and he stood still as a rock. He shook his head.

"It would be four weeks in China to see what the Communist Party is doing there."

"Why?" Then he answered himself in a stunned voice. "Because you're half-Chinese. They want you to become a collaborator." His voice trembled, as though I had delivered the news of a family member's death. His face tightened with anger. "Oh! Why they won't leave us alone! What are you going to do, Pa-la?"

"It will be all right. I'm here to ask Lama Norbu to perform a divination."

"Hmm." Dawa did not sound comforted.

"And I will have my son, a lama, say prayers for me." I smiled at him with affection, trying to ease the fear in his eyes. "Dawa. For centuries we Tibetans have gotten along with the Chinese, and we will continue getting along with them." Now I was speaking with a confidence I did not really feel.

A young monk entered Dawa's room and told me, "Lama Norbu will see you now." When I entered Lama Norbu's room, Dawa followed me. He asked permission to sit in on the divination ceremony, and Lama Norbu nodded. I did three prostrations and presented him with a *khata* and a bag of dried peas. He smiled and asked us to sit down. I told him my difficulty.

He said, "We will roll the dice and the numbers will guide us."

He began the ceremony by reciting prayers over the dice. He rattled the dice in his hand, then let them fall on the table before him. Doing this several times, he wrote down the numbers. Then he consulted the scriptures in front of him to interpret their meaning. Finally he looked down at me, saying, "Dorje Thondup, the divination has indicated that you are to leave the land of snows and travel to China."

"What?" Dawa's voice cut through the air.

There was silence. Lama Norbu looked over at Dawa with a deliberate gaze. My son's outburst embarrassed me. I told Lama Norbu quietly, "Thank you, *Rinpoche*. The gods have spoken." I lowered my eyes to show my respect and confidence in his words, but my stomach felt like a churning river.

Dawa begged, "*Rinpoche,* I appeal to you, please repeat the divination."

Lama Norbu smiled compassionately at my son. My son's inability to keep himself still—even his mouth—seemed to be well tolerated in the lamasery.

Lama Norbu prayed, rolled the dice, and recorded the numbers again. When he finished, his words were slow and deliberate. "The divination has indicated the correct path for you. You are supposed to go to China."

My son gave a shocked exhale of breath. He exclaimed, "How can this be? How can it be *good* for my father to go there? Something terrible could happen to him. *Rinpoche,* you have heard the rumors about what the Chinese are doing in eastern Tibet!"

The older lama nodded. "We do not always understand all of the steps of the path before us."

My hands were sweating. It was true, I did *not* understand the steps of the path before me.

"Will you not perform the divination *one* more time?" my son asked respectfully with hands brought together in supplication. "I promise to accept the answer."

I put myself in the place of Lama Norbu and felt great caring in his heart. When I looked at my son through the old lama's eyes, I saw a young boy with small hands clinging to the cloth of his father's *chuba*.

So, while Dawa and I waited anxiously, Lama Norbu performed the divination again.

Then he shrugged. "The result is the same. You are supposed to go to China."

I looked over at my son. His hand was covering his mouth. His eyes were wide and frightened, but he replied in a quiet, defeated voice, "I accept this answer."

I sighed and stared at the floor with sad eyes.

Dorje

To be a friend of the Communist Party. Comrade Wei's phrase went round and round in my mind. I could not believe that this man had come to my door only two weeks ago, and now we were riding horses to the Chinese border. As we went, we gathered more Tibetans, whom Mr. Wei called "comrades." He called me Comrade Thondup, and I wondered, did his calling me this make it so? Was I becoming a comrade simply by sharing his company? And why had the divination shown I should be on this journey? My *mani* beads circled my wrist, and I wondered what he thought as I used them to recite my prayers. So far he hadn't said anything, although I'd seen him watching me.

I brooded on a disturbing memory: Dawa's face, wet with tears, as he said, "Pa-la. You know I will pray for you. But there are Tibetans fleeing. They say that anyone who gives the communists any trouble, the next day he is gone. Disappeared. So, Pa-la, do what they say and keep quiet. Please promise me."

"I will, Dawa. That is my way." I had taken both his hands and held them as I spoke to him.

My horse stopped to nibble on some grass, and I felt that this animal was my only friend. Out of all the Tibetans on this trip, I was the only one who spoke Chinese. So Comrade Wei chattered to me, especially when he was tired. He told me much about himself.

This morning as the sun rose, I asked him, how did he join the communists?

"Ah, comrade, that's a good story," he answered with the kind of grin men give each other when they are sharing cups of chang. "There are few people who *really* understand the *hope* of the revolution. But I do." He pointed to his chest, and his eyebrows hopped upward. "Can you guess what I used to do before the revolution?" Without waiting for me to answer, his words danced on. "I used to pull a rickshaw! I was a human beast, and here I am now. One of Mao's shining soldiers." His right hand traveled from his feet to his head, and he sat tall on his horse. "A Party cadre saw my suffering and brought me to Party headquarters. They told me I didn't have to be a rickshaw puller anymore—I could be a revolutionary!" His eyes bulged with excitement. "I walked out of headquarters in this uniform that very night!"

His face went dark. "As a rickshaw beast, what meaning could my life have? But now I'm changing the world, Dorje! So I become furious when I see someone laboring for another's benefit!" His voice moved down to a sad whisper. "And in Tibet I see it everywhere. The old women carrying water up hundreds of stairs for the lazy lamas who don't lift a finger!" Now his voice rose up. "The poor peasants—laboring with no hope, as I did—giving a portion of their crops to the landowners, knowing they'll never own land themselves!" Bubbles of spit flew from his mouth. "And the monasteries own so much—how they take advantage of the people in exchange for mumbling a few prayers for them!"

He turned to me, his brows a heavy line. "Do you not feel the proletariat's anger yourself, Comrade Thondup?"

I blinked, trying to think of an answer. "You speak of the anger of—"

"The poor people who have no hope. But don't worry, Dorje,

you're part of Mao's army now. Together, we'll throw the monks out of the monasteries"—he made a violent tossing motion—"and into the fields, and let *them* see how it feels to break their backs laboring."

Picturing what the communists had planned for people like Dawa, I felt the blizzard blowing inside my head again. I asked doubtfully, "But do the Tibetans seem happy you have come to Tibet?"

"I don't worry about that, Dorje, because they are ignorant. They don't see their chains, so how can they be grateful for their liberation?" His voice was light, so light, in contrast to the heaviness of my heart.

How deeply the communists misunderstood us! A Tibetan separated from his religion is not a Tibetan. The communists did not know with what joy we carried water for our lamas or gave them food from our fields. It was our souls' longing to do this. These acts of humility were the ways in which we stored up merit for the next life. If they took away our opportunities to do this, what would we do? They would be damning us to lifetime after lifetime of suffering, being reborn endlessly in the lower realms, as animals or demons.

I did not understand this idea of "oppressors." We were each given our place in the world by our own karma, which was the result of our actions in previous lifetimes, so what was this about oppressors? Our place was not determined by our oppressors. To take the "lazy monks" and throw them into a field to labor for our food, this would *guarantee* us a terrible rebirth! The communists could not see the wisdom and compassion of a being like Lama Norbu, who willingly returned to earthly form to help all sentient beings. Simply looking into the joyful eyes of such a bodhisattva could wash away one's suffering.

Still, Comrade Wei's wild eyebrows and waving arms showed me his sincere desire to eliminate suffering in the world. I wanted to tell him about our ways. Over and over he asked, "You work hard, but who benefits from your labor?" And so, one time I answered, "Does it matter who benefits? For us, to benefit other sentient beings is the greatest privilege, and the richest opportunity for us to accumulate merit for a good rebirth in the next life."

With a generous smile he said, "There they are, Comrade Thondup! Those exact thoughts, *they* are your chains."

I was stunned. The communists would have a difficult time persuading my countrymen that this way of thinking was a set of chains! I even thought, well, this revolution would never happen in Tibet. The Chinese would grow tired of trying to change our ways, and they would go home. Then I remembered Dawa's warning about people disappearing, and a shiver went through my whole body.

~

In Qinghai we got on the train, and I began to feel tense. All the hours of our train ride, I waited for someone to break the silence. It was not a peaceful silence. I closed my eyes and tried to put myself into the shape of it. But it had no definite form—it was like the always changing shape of a swarm of bees, flying above our heads, and everyone pretending they were not there.

Gray-blue Mao suits were everywhere. Whenever we stopped at a train station, the people walked by, each looking like a puffy blue stick with a pale, tired face stuck on the top.

We arrived in Shanghai, our destination, in the evening. Hundreds of the blue-stick people were shuffling through the streets with their heads down. They spoke in low voices with eyes going from side to side, always watching and wondering, is anyone listening?

Mr. Wei brought us to a political meeting called *thamzing*. He told us this meant "struggle session." I wondered what the struggle was about. As we entered, he explained to our group, "A struggle session is socialism in action, something we want to bring to Tibet as well."

An old man sat on a chair in the front of the room. He wore a Western-style suit that looked as if he had been wearing it for many days. A dark blood spot was on the right collar of his white shirt. He was bent over in his chair. He reminded me of a wild dog I'd seen in Shigatse, a dog that walked cautiously on its four paws with its back curved up in fear.

We found chairs right in the front and sat down. A young woman in a Mao suit walked to the front of the room. She had two short braids. A smirking man announced, "Our young comrade has evidence proving that the old man is truly an enemy of the people."

As she began to speak, I looked at the old man and put myself in his place. I felt in his heart a mix of affection for this girl, and also the hope that she would take pity on him. He gazed at her meekly. She had the small features of a hummingbird, and the paper in her hands shook as she read from it. Something about the old man heading a company where grain had been milled for the socialist government.

Then she stopped, looking down at her paper. Cries came from around the room. "Get on with it!" "Send *her* to a labor camp too!" Someone shouted, "Long live Chairman Mao!"

She opened her mouth but said nothing. I could see her white teeth. She closed her mouth again and straightened her back into a pillar of ice. As she stood over the old man in his chair, she bowed until her head almost touched his. Then she opened her mouth and spat at him.

He flinched, and I did also.

The spit landed on the right side of his mouth. He left it and let it slide down his chin. His eyes grew sad. His chin trembled. Tears were in *her* eyes also as she looked at him, so I thought perhaps the ice pillar in her back would melt. Instead, she straightened. She pointed her finger and stood over him, shouting, "He stole money from the people! He set the milling prices high so he could profit from the state! He hates Chairman Mao! He's a foreigner-worshipping capitalist sucking the blood out of the people!"

The old man shook his head as he looked at the cold humming-bird destroying him with her sharp beak. Then he said something I could not believe. "Do not do this, Granddaughter."

She screamed back at him, "I'm no longer your granddaughter!" Her voice quivered like the furious beating of a little bird's heart. I imagined a sharp knife poking through feathers. I turned to Comrade Wei. His face was a mask as he looked at me out of the corner of his eye. That told me it was true. This girl was denouncing her own grandfather.

I glanced over at my Tibetan companions. Their faces showed confusion, alarm. They didn't know she was condemning her own grandfather, but they did not need to. To see her standing over her elder, allowing her head to be higher than his, this was enough to sicken them. All our lives we were taught to put ourselves below others in importance. This thing they called struggle was the opposite of everything we believed.

The hummingbird was finished. The man's sentence was announced by a cadre. "This capitalist dog will go to a labor camp in the countryside to learn about honest labor from the peasants!"

We got to our guest quarters after midnight because the *thamzing* continued for so long. Although my throat was dry like dust and my bones ached cold and tired, I could not sleep that night. I wanted to vomit out all I had seen, to scrub my skin and even my mind.

As I lay on my mattress and stared up into the darkness, Lama Norbu appeared. His eyes glowed like tiny stars in a vast sky as he looked at me.

I understood then why it was my destiny to come here, along with the other Tibetan men with me. We had to see what the Chinese were planning for our country.

～

It was morning. My neck hurt and my head felt like one of the vibrating cymbals the lamas hit in their ceremonies. My heart beat in my chest like the running feet of a frightened horse. The sleep sounds of the others made me wonder, how could they sleep after what we had seen last night at the *thamzing*? I imagined walking over to Comrade Wei's mattress and falling on my knees before him, saying, *Take us home now. Please.* But I was too afraid to even beg for such a thing.

During our morning tea, I heard the same swarming silence that hung dark above all of China, I was certain. We walked like dumb sheep through the streets of Shanghai with one cadre in front of our group and Comrade Wei in the back. He kept talking in his hopeful voice, and now I did not understand him at all. I recited prayers silently and pictured Champa's sweet smile. *Om mani peme hung. Om mani peme hung.*

Soon I began to feel like Dorje again.

As we walked on a Shanghai street, something up high moved. I looked up above, and my feet stopped moving. A man in a Mao suit stood on a balcony four stories above my head. He walked to the railing of the balcony, and his stomach leaned against it. He unbuttoned his jacket. His face held compassion and a wild look of joy. I saw something written on the shirt he wore under the jacket, but I could not read it. He lifted his right leg over the railing gracefully, as though he were dancing. Then he shifted his weight onto the toe of that foot on the shallow ledge outside the railing. He put both hands on the railing, and slowly the other leg followed, ending with his standing on both toes on the ledge. He spread his arms wide and stretched out his fingers. Now I could read what was written in red paint on his shirt: I DO THIS FOR THE PEOPLE.

I put myself in this man's place and felt my toes resting on that thin ledge. I sensed how he wanted the entire world to see the words on his shirt—that he was dying, *dying to tell the truth.* That his body was so filled with lies it was like a wound dripping with pus. That he had become so small and ashamed from his kowtowing to the Party that this one act was all he had left. That as he stood on this ledge, his chest felt as wide as the entire earth, shaking with relief and with joy and regret that stabbed like a thorn.

He lifted up his head, and in a voice that tore from his chest, he shouted, "*This* is liberation!" As his toes sprang from the ledge, I sucked a breath into my chest and felt I had taken to the air with him. The rawness of his throat was my own. The blue jacket widened as his body went horizontal, and the two sides of the jacket flapped against his arms as he fell.

The sound of his landing, facedown in the street, was so short. It had passed before I could think. Then, in the next moment, blood made a red pool around his head. I stood, not breathing, as if a large rock pinned both my feet to the ground. One thing I noticed: quiet. There was not even a gasp. *People in China have become too frightened to even gasp.* I saw the people's eyes, first looking at this body, then looking all around, wondering, who has seen me here? Instantly everyone rushed away.

My Tibetan heart awoke as I stared at the body. I was so sad for this man who had condemned himself with the worst possible karma. He would pay for this act with lifetimes of agony. Tears warmed my eyes as I gazed at the shining black hair on his bleeding head. I quietly recited prayers for his soul, for its journey in the *bardo. Om mani a peme hung . . .*

Then a hand was on my arm, and Mr. Wei pulled me so hard I almost fell down. He hissed, "Where have you *been*? Come quickly! You cannot stay here, Dorje!"

I let him pull me wherever he was going because I could not think or walk on my own. After a few minutes of his pulling and my stumbling, we were on another street.

"What were you doing?" he demanded. "We could not find you!"

"I . . . I am sorry."

"It is very dangerous to watch a counterrevolutionary act like that!" Out of his mouth came a heated whispering that scraped against his throat.

"Why?"

"That was a *protest suicide*! We are not supposed to watch protest suicides!"

I was confused. "You mean other people have done . . . suicide also?"

"Yes! There have been waves of them. But you're not supposed to watch, or the cadres will think you're a sympathizer!"

"But I don't understand." Tears were in my voice. "You said this revolution is . . . what the people want."

"They don't . . . always know what is best for them." The words came out in a voice that did not sound certain. Then, defiant, he added, "You cannot get lost from the group!"

I blinked at his anger, then looked all around me and back at him. "But, they are so . . . unhappy, so frightened." I wanted to cry.

In that moment, it was as though I had caught him hiding. His eyes shifted first one way, then another, and then they settled on me. Eyes that were naked and heavy with sadness.

He whispered, "I know, Dorje. Perhaps there are . . . excesses. I don't understand all of it." He stopped as though he were waiting for an answer.

I could hardly speak. "But . . . this suffering—"

"I *see* the suffering. I do. But I know the Party is trying to do something *good*. To end suffering that has lasted for *centuries*. To take someone like me, a rickshaw puller, and give my life more purpose than to be a pulling beast. It's not a perfect movement, but the *end is* perfect."

He so wanted me to understand. His eyes were watering.

"But my friend, when does the end come?" I whispered.

He did not answer.

Part

Two

Emma

It was a basket of pea noodles that led to our ruin. They sat in dried bundles with a green tint like my eyes. Having been stiffened to immobility by drying, they looked innocent there in the marketplace as they rested in an oxblood-colored basket.

They *were* innocent, those noodles. So was Gerald, so was I, and even the boyish communist soldier who tripped on the basket and overturned it. Even *he* started out innocent. My heart tells me that.

We were walking through the local outdoor marketplace, breathing in dust and smells of unwashed bodies and letting the sun caress our shoulders. We held hands and savored that we'd now been in Tibet for four months. I tried my Tibetan with a stumpy-looking woman who looked to have only four teeth in her mouth. *How much for the seven brass altar bowls?* We were shopping for Dorje and Rinchen, wanting to express our gratitude in a gift for them. Unsure if it was the right gift, we ambled on, unaware that each step brought us closer to catastrophe.

Such simple trust flowed between our hands, trust that the world was gentle and the universe benign. That trust burns now, like a hot stone in my chest. I noticed the uniform of the Chinese soldier who happened—it really *was* just chance, I think—to be walking ahead of us. We stayed a cautious distance from him, but near enough that I saw the back of his neck, shaven closely on the nape up to where his coal-black hair stubbled out from under his cap. The fit of that uniform outlined a strong back, with lines that hinted at its owner's youthful vanity. He couldn't help it that he had a back like that, and that it filled him with a pride that showed in the thoughtless scuffing of his boots. The right boot snagged the twig weave of the basket and turned it on its side. He reddened with shame at his clumsiness—he looked so young in that moment—but then his features hardened. His jaw muscles tightened, and in his mind a trace thought passed, something about how he should be, I think, and that shamed him more, a thought about the dignity of soldiers and being in charge. He hesitated and even reached his hand toward the basket in a caring impulse to right it again. Then he pulled his hand back and looked down his nose at the noodle lady's frightened eyes and felt his power.

He could walk away. That's what I read in his shoulders thrown back.

Gerald's mouth fell open from surprise as the basket tipped. He pushed a hand through his blond curls and waited to see what the soldier would do. He looked at the noodle lady crouched there, and his brows drew together with concern. She had started to stand to save her noodles, but then she froze in a half-bowed position under the shadowy eyes of the soldier. He scuffed away with elaborate casualness, kicking up clouds of powdery dirt. Then Gerald and the lady merchant moved as one, bending low to gather the noodles, him with lips pursed together in a *sorry* shape, sky blue eyes looking up into hers of almond.

My gaze was drawn back to this soldier because I felt on my prickly skin his eyes, which had become small and sharp as he watched Gerald from twenty yards away, eyes that watched as my beloved picked up the basket, blew the dust off the noodles, and handed them back to the lady, who bowed and smiled gratefully. After smoothing her hair, she reached into her other basket of clean noodles and grabbed a fistful of them. Shyly she took my husband's hand, turned it over, and placed the pea noodles in his open palm. The smile on his face was gracious and amused. I could see by the way his ears moved slightly, pulled by the skin of his neck and Adam's apple, which worked up and down in silent laughter. Surely he was thinking, *Thank you, but we hate peas.*

The youth looked down at his boots for a moment, feeling shown up, I think, by Gerald's chivalry, brown eyes recording this suspicious interaction between white foreigner imperialist and native proletariat. Then he placed his hand on his hip and pulled his pride from that strong back of his, standing as erect as a door-frame. His eyes locked on mine, dead on. I felt at first motherly, wanting to smooth those ruffled feathers he carried inside, until I sensed the cold from him, a cold that spread across the twenty yards and into my limbs up the back of my neck and rested there like an icy clutch—his desire to trample us utterly with his finely dusted boot.

And he could, I realized.

〜

We had tucked ourselves into bed and slept warm last night. I had stuffed my marketplace misgivings into some obscure backwater of my mind. *Why did I do that?* We'd slept spooned together, nestled under the comforting weight of our indigo wool blanket. Gerald's nose and ample lips rested against my neck.

I should have known. I *did* know—I saw the warning in that soldier's eyes, felt the twinge of hairs standing up. We could have left in the dark of night. We could be climbing a mountain pass, already on our way out of Tibet!

Now, I sit in our house and bring my fists up to pound my ignorant head. It's eerily still and so empty I feel goose bumps on my arms.

We went to the river this morning, Rinchen and me and Champa. He hopped over rocks while she and I beat the clothes and rinsed them in the river. We laughed at him, hopping like a frog, then running like a deer. We walked back with cold, heavy clothes in our arms. She sang a song about a snow leopard, and her voice was deep and dark like baker's chocolate.

We came into her courtyard. Her singing cut off abruptly. The door to her house was open. We looked at each other uncertainly. When we reached the door, she told Champa to wait outside with me. She went in. I heard a muffled cry. I stepped one foot inside the doorway, still keeping Champa outside with my hand pressed against his chest. A knife was thrust into the hardwood of the table. It held in place a large poster of Chairman Mao's fleshy face. Rinchen called, "Samten? Samten-la!" I heard her feet crossing the doorway, the scrape of her boots as she ran to check behind stacked bales of hay. "Samten!"

I put my hands on Champa's little shoulders.

"*Tashi delek,* Emma." Over the low wall of the courtyard I saw Dorje arriving. He said, "Samten isn't here, Rinchen. I think he went to the market to buy meat for our trip."

"No, Dorje! The communists were here—they left a knife and a picture of a Chinese man on our table!"

Dorje's eyes focused inward. "Ama-la! Where is Ama-la?"

He led both of them rushing into the house, past where I stood with Champa. But nothing had dawned on me yet. I was merely concerned for my friends.

Dorje sprinted into the altar room. "Ama—" Then a pause in which I heard the air pushing out of his lungs. Then, hushed with dread: "Ama-la."

"Stay here," I told Champa. He blinked his wide brown eyes. I walked over to see what Dorje had found, hearing Champa's steps shadowing my own. Ama-la was seated in profile, with her legs tucked under her, behind the altar, partially hidden behind a waist-high Buddha statue. Dorje touched her wrist where prayer beads were coiled. He searched for a pulse, but the stillness of her body was unmistakable. Her left shoulder was slumped against the wall next to her. Her mouth hung open with a lax jaw. Her eyes stared forward.

Then I heard Dorje's pained voice: "'*Eh Ma Ho!* In the center is the marvelous Buddha Amitabha of Boundless Light . . .'"

The prayer for the dead.

Gerald! I felt pins in my flesh. Even as my feet raced for the door, a part of me already knew what I didn't want to know.

That he wasn't there.

A tiny, old woman bumped right into my chest as I hurried out Dorje's doorway. Her voice was reedy with tension. "They took him, and the other one also."

Rinchen leaped from the altar room. "What?"

"Samten they took, and the white man also."

"Who took them?"

"The Chinese."

I sprinted out of the yard, crossed the dirt road, and threw open my gate, running inside.

The door to the house stood open. The Mao poster lay on the table, stuck there with a knife. The air was still as a morgue.

I stood like a glacier, staring around me. Feeling this moment like a punishment I'd known was coming. Seeing in my mind the hateful eyes of the soldier looking at Gerald yesterday.

I heard footsteps behind me, then Dorje was beside me. He touched my arm, then led me to his house. He talked to all of us, talking that I took in as though hovering on the ceiling. "Mr. Wei will help us," he soothed. His voice was smooth, and I found myself thinking that this was how he gentled horses and yaks, with this melodious voice. "It is simply a mistake. I will explain to him, and the communists will release both of them."

He left to go find Mr. Wei. I shuffled blindly back to my house, then huddled on the bed. Tears dropped onto the blanket, making dark raindrop dots. I shut my eyes, scrunched my body into a tight ball, afraid to hope, afraid to breathe.

Dorje

I rushed to the communist headquarters, wishing my feet could go faster. I thanked the gods who sent me to China in their wisdom, for otherwise I would not know Mr. Wei, and then I would not know what to do. Sweat ran down my face and my *chuba* was soaked from my perspiring. My legs shook with fear, but I forced myself to remember Wei's kind face. I prayed he would see that taking Samten and Gerald was a mistake.

As I ran, guilt burned in my chest. I went all the way to China, and when I returned home, did I take my family to a safe place? Did I alert my neighbors that their loved ones might disappear? No. I did none of this. How could I be so stupid? Like an animal without the power of speech. I was someone who watches the avalanche falling and does nothing to dig out those who suffocate under the heavy snow.

Guru Rinpoche, if it pleases you, let me atone for my failings.

I hurried to the back door of the communist compound. My throat was as dry as sand. A trapdoor was at the level of my eyes. After we had returned from China, we came to this door, Mr. Wei and me. He knocked and the trapdoor opened from the inside, and two eyes filled the little, square opening. He said, "News of the revolution." They let him in.

With a shaking hand I knocked at this door. With a squeak the trapdoor opened. I whispered, "News of the revolution . . . for Comrade Wei."

"I don't think so." The eyes squinted suspiciously.

I swallowed back fear. "Please, I'm Comrade Thondup, to see Comrade Wei."

"He's not here." A flat voice like a frozen river.

Sweat dripped under my arms. My mind was blank. I asked, "Where is he?" My voice cracked with fear.

"He was found to be politically unreliable."

I did not understand these words. My heart sped faster in my chest.

The trapdoor man continued, "He was caught growing vegetables for his elitist palate, so he was sent back to China to reform his thinking. I will bring Commander Liu."

The trapdoor closed. I stood like a stone, hearing my breath in my ears. In the back of my mind a red thought flashed.

Run. Run now.

SEPTEMBER 15, 1954

Gerald

It happened so quickly. How could life change so fast?

I was helping Samten in Dorje's courtyard. He was behind me, stacking the supplies he and Dorje needed for their trip.

I was sitting on the ground sewing up a hole in a wool sack when I heard a muffled voice behind me. I turned and saw two Chinese soldiers hauling Samten out of the courtyard. They'd clamped a hand over his mouth. I opened my mouth to cry out and suddenly felt a cold gun barrel pressing against my tongue. From behind me, they pulled me up by my collar and took me by the arms, pulling me out of the courtyard. They dragged me toward a truck several hundred yards away. I saw Samten already in the back of another truck. His hands were tied behind his back. His eyes were round, unblinking with terror. I felt a sharp point in my back, and hands pushing me up onto the truck bed.

A soldier pointed a gun to my head and pushed me down to a sitting position. I couldn't see Samten anymore. I visually checked my house, praying that Emma had not got home yet. There was no sign of her. I thanked God she was still away washing our clothes in the river.

The engine roared to life and my heart jumped in my chest. The truck lurched forward. As we drove away, I watched the house get smaller. We turned a corner and then I couldn't see it anymore.

I looked around me. The truck bed had tall wooden planks along its sides, and no back. I could jump off. I peered through the window into the cab and saw narrow eyes looking right back at me. Eyes that already knew what I was thinking.

What about Emma? Would they come back later and get her too?

The engine whined as the truck rumbled down the road. We headed toward the big road that led to Gyantse and the capital. I unbuttoned my shirt collar. I couldn't get any air. There was sand on my tongue. The air was thick with exhaust, as if I were inhaling it straight from the tailpipe. Through the cab window I saw the two soldiers laughing. The one on the passenger side held an automatic with the barrel tilted up to the windshield.

Two Tibetan men were in the back with me. One, in a clean brown *chuba,* looked quite young, maybe sixteen. He wore two braids tucked against the two sides of his head, gathered into a topknot. He had a straight, noble nose and enormous eyes that give him a naïve appearance. He gazed at me with a glazed look as he held the sleeve of his *chuba* over his nose and mouth. Next to him was an old monk, thin with sunken eyes and leathery skin. He had a round, placid face. The stubble on his shaved head was pure white.

His eyes were closed and his lips were moving.

The floor of the truck bed was stained with blood. I swallowed, chilled by the sight. A strand of prayer beads jumped and rattled each time we hit a bump. I wondered what had happened to the one whose hands once held them.

I prayed. *Please, God. Be with me. Do not abandon me.*

The truck hit a bump that heaved us upward, and I landed hard on my tailbone. I jumped from a gunshot sound, only to realize it was the truck backfiring.

The minutes passed, and I felt a dreadful helplessness. I saw my house in my mind. Felt it slipping farther away. I wondered if Emma had reached home yet, and what she'd do when she found I wasn't there. My heart was racing. *I pray they only want me and Samten. If this is my last day on this earth, Lord, please—keep her safe.*

I gazed at the young man in the back with me. He had the terrified eyes of a caged rat. He stood up on wobbly legs and walked to the back of the truck.

The old man spoke. "Don't jump off—I saw them shoot a man who tried that." The young man sat down and the monk closed his eyes again. We passed a town, then another town. On and on the motor whined, toiling its way over the road, which was muddy in places from the tail end of the monsoon. It seemed my heart had been pounding for hours. Dread sat like a brick in my stomach. Each time I looked at the sun, it was a little lower in the sky, until its slant baked the hillsides a golden brown. We rode on a gash sliced through this brown carpet.

I couldn't help thinking of how Emma and I had celebrated being in Tibet by walking through the Shigatse marketplace just the day before. And now I was here.

The truck began ascending a mountain pass. The slope steepened sharply and the three of us slid toward the back of the truck. The old monk's eyes popped open. We grabbed hold of the wooden planks along the sides. The old man lost his grip, fell to his belly, and began sliding headfirst. I reached for his robes, but they slipped through my fingers. His body slid off the back edge. The young man and I gaped at each other, unsure what to do.

Before we could move, the truck stopped. The soldier on the passenger side stepped out and tossed his cigarette with an irritated flick of his fingers. He scowled at us, and his cross mood frightened me. The two of us in the truck bed walked slowly to its back edge, not wishing to agitate the soldier. I caught his eye and pointed to myself, motioning that I wanted to get down and help the old man. The soldier's eyes narrowed, and he stared at me suspiciously.

The old monk lay facedown, moaning. His right arm was pinned beneath him. I stood still, uncertain, then pantomimed once more that I wished to get down. Finally the soldier nodded his assent. After descending, I turned the monk over carefully. His face was covered with dust, but his eyes were bright. Once I'd helped him to stand, I told him in Tibetan I was a doctor. He held up his arm for me to examine.

The soldier watched us warily. He lit another cigarette and sat down on the bumper.

The arm had a crooked appearance. I ran my fingers over it and felt a break in the bone. "Your arm is broken," I told the monk. "I can fix it, but it will be painful."

"Thank you," he replied, a smile lighting his face. He turned to the soldier and explained what was happening. The soldier rolled his eyes and pointed to his watch, but continued to smoke his cigarette. I asked the young man to come down and hold the monk around the waist. Grasping the old man's hand, I pulled. He grimaced. When I released his hand, the arm was straight again.

In searching the ground for a tree branch to use as a splint, I took a step away from the truck. The soldier stood instantly, pointing his rifle at me. I raised my arms to show him I knew he was in charge. He lowered the rifle. *Best to abandon the idea of a splint.* Slowly I walked back to the monk and touched the long piece of red cloth draped about his shoulders. Beneath this cloth was a fitted, sleeveless garment that covered his chest. "May I?" I asked, tugging gently at the cloth. He nodded. I ripped a long strip from it to use as a sling. As he squinted against the pain, he watched me through the small slits of his eyes. He wore the hint of a smile as if he actually enjoyed the sight of me tearing up his robes. He rubbed his arm and winced. I wrapped his arm with the cloth, tying the two ends around his neck to make a sling. His brown eyes looked into mine. "Thank you."

"Don't move your arm," I told the monk. He nodded and covered the broken arm with his other one.

The soldier tossed his cigarette at my feet, and I glanced up at him to gauge his mood. He looked nothing more than bored. He motioned with his head for us to get back in the truck. The younger man helped the monk climb up, and I pulled myself up. Now we sat close together. The soldier muttered some word over and over as he walked to the cab.

The old man's ashy eyebrows rose. "I'm Lama Tenzin. There is compassion in your hands, and you speak Tibetan very well," he said kindly, smiling.

Smiling back, I bowed my head to him. "Thank you. I'm Gerald. I'm visiting from America."

"My name's Lobsang," the young man said.

I nodded at him. "Gerald."

"What was the soldier saying?" I asked. We started to slide toward the cab as the truck descended the hill.

"*Latseng,*" Tenzin told us. "He called us 'garbage' in Tibetan." He said this calmly, as though reporting fine weather.

Lobsang gave an offended scowl. "I didn't know he said *that*!"

"Oh, don't bother to be upset," Tenzin said, tipping his head lightly to one side. "It brightens his day to insult us."

Lobsang asked, "But what are they going to do with us?" His voice was tight as a bowstring.

"Take us to the prison. Feed us horrible food. Question us—how do we feel about His Holiness Kundun? Try to make us confess our crimes." Tenzin sounded tired, even bored.

"What crimes? I haven't committed any crimes!" Lobsang exclaimed. "They came to steal my father's farmland, and now he's by himself because they took me."

"Oh, you don't have to have a crime. They'll make one up for you. If you disagree with them, then you have incorrect thoughts. So then they are kind enough to reeducate you." Tenzin sighed, giving us a sad smile. "I'm sorry you're both here. It will be difficult for you."

"But why did they take me?" I asked Tenzin. "I'm not even from Tibet."

"Ah, but you're an American. So of course that means you're a capitalist." He gave me a wry look.

My mind reeled with imagined horrors of what they'd do to a capitalist.

His brows lifted, Tenzin commented, "Not many foreigners in Tibet."

"My wife and I came here." Simply mentioning her brought a stab of pain.

"Is your wife all right?"

"I—I don't know." My throat tightened. "I hope so. She wasn't home when they came for me."

"So I'll pray for her safety." Tenzin's voice was warm.

Lobsang sat with both hands tucked into his *chuba,* his eyes large and worried. "I don't know what my father is going to do. I won't be there to make his tea and his lunch." His lashes were long and his nose straight and thin, while his lips were as full as a girl's. He was like a delicate china cup, and thinking of him in the thick, clumsy hands of these soldiers filled me with dread.

Sadness twisted in my throat and spread down my chest. There was a silence. I looked out across the landscape, and the truck bed vibrated as we rode on.

We stopped at a small village after the sun abandoned us. Lights glowed yellow in the windows, making me long for home.

They ordered us out of the truck to relieve ourselves. Insects lit up like tiny flames as they fluttered before the vehicle's headlights. The snapping of dry grass beneath our feet penetrated the quiet as they prodded us back into the truck. When we sat down, they turned off the headlights, and darkness fell like a thick, black liquid. A soldier stayed to guard us. We burrowed together with Lama Tenzin tucked into the warmest corner.

My worries gnawed at me like animal teeth. I worried about how they'd treat us in the prison, or that we'd freeze to death in the back of this truck. It seemed so long ago that Emma and I had camped in the icy winds on our way into Tibet. Winds that caused my nose to tickle when the mucus froze and melted with each in- and out-breath. The sky hung over us like an enormous cold sapphire, making me feel small. My empty stomach rumbled. I fell asleep and dreamed of finding my own body frozen stiff.

Dorje

"You want to wait until the communists take us all away? Well, Champa and I are leaving!" On the last word my wife brought a soup pot down on the stove with a loud crash.

"Calm yourself," I told her.

"Dorje, I can't believe you! We *must* leave. They took my brother and Gerald in order to send a message. The Chinese do not want Tibetans to associate with foreigners, and we did! How can it be that you went all the way to China and you don't understand why this has happened?"

"How did you learn all this, Rinchen?"

"I've heard whispers in the market among the women. Because I love Emma and Gerald, I hoped that nobody knew they were here, but obviously the Chinese have been watching us and they saw us with them. So we *have to go.*"

"But what about Ama-la? We can't leave her body here with no one to bury it properly."

My wife shook her head back and forth quickly, her eyes like those of a spooked horse. "No! We will have more people to bury than her if we stay here."

I sighed, knowing from the heaviness in my shoulders that my wife was right. "All right. I will ask Lama Norbu to have her buried properly, and we will leave during the night." I walked out the door to find our neighbor Yeshe. It was a relief to breathe the air outside, to be away from the avalanche that had come into my home. I did not want to ask him because he enjoyed excitement, even that caused by misfortune, far too much. But there was no one else. A few moments later, he rode away on his horse to bring Lama Norbu. The sky was as dark as Chinese ink.

When I returned home later that hour, Champa was dragging a bag of *tsampa* out the door. Rinchen was packing tea bricks and dried meat into a sack. "I can't believe we're still here now." Her voice was as sharp as a needle. "Perhaps I should be saying the prayer for the dead for my brother, but I don't know where he is. And if we wait long enough, maybe Lama Norbu will be saying prayers for the dead for our whole family!"

"Rinchen! Stop!"

She blinked. Then I saw the shaking of her chin, the only sign she was ready to cry. It pulled at my heart like a vulture tugging with its beak. I wanted to put my arms around her, but she turned away. *Don't touch me or I'll melt onto the floor,* her back said.

I went into the altar room and gently picked up Ama-la's body. "*Om ami dewa hri.* I am so sorry, Ama-la." I put her in bed and pulled her quilt up to her chin.

Champa came and took my hand. He studied Ama-la's face. "She looks asleep, Pa-la."

"This is the prayer you must say until Lama Norbu arrives, Champa. *Om ami dewa hri. Om ami dewa hri.*" His child's voice recited with me.

My face felt heavy as I walked into the courtyard. Rinchen was tying a bag onto a yak. "I will get Emma so you can start dying her hair," I told her.

"Quickly," she said.

Without asking Emma's opinion, we had decided she should

come with us, for the communists would surely be back for her too. To keep us all safe as we traveled together, we decided that Rinchen would try to make her look Tibetan. But when I told Emma, she shook her head at me. "I can't leave Gerald here. I have to look for him!"

"Emma, I cannot help you with this—we can begin searching once we reach Kathmandu."

"Just give me a horse, and I'll go look for him myself!" Her hand flew in the air as if to show the path of her search.

I felt like a crazy sheepherder trying to stop a sheep from leaping off a cliff. "Are you going to speak with the communists yourself? Will you talk to them in English, or will you be learning Chinese? Even I do not dare talk to them, and I speak their language." My tone was not gentle, but I had to make her understand. "It is not safe here for us. How will you help Gerald if *you* are taken by the communists also?"

Tears leaked from her eyes. "Don't ask me to leave him here."

"I'm not *asking,* Emma-la. You are coming with us." I took hold of her arm firmly, as when I tie the feet of a sheep. She did not resist.

By the time Yeshe arrived later with Lama Norbu, Rinchen had already begun her work on Emma's hair. We all bowed to Lama Norbu.

He asked, "What is happening, Dorje? Yeshe was so worked up I couldn't understand what he was saying."

I invited him into the altar room. "The communists came to our house. They took Samten. Ama-la—well, that is why I sent for you, to say prayers for her as she journeys through the *bardo.*"

"Oh, Dorje, I am sorry," he said quietly. "But what happened to her?"

"I think the fright of their visit stopped her heart."

"Ah, the poor creature. But your wife was packing. And what is she doing to the foreigner's hair?"

"She is trying to make her look Tibetan. We are leaving for Kathmandu. My wife, she wants to leave tonight."

"You're leaving Tibet?"

"Yes." I lowered my eyes, as I was embarrassed that we had decided without seeking Lama Norbu's guidance. Perhaps he would be angry with me.

To my surprise, he answered calmly, "I understand. So you will need me to bury your mother."

"Yes, if you would be so kind." I could not bring myself to look in his eyes.

"I'll take care of her for you. And I'll pray for you and your family. You will not be the first to leave Tibet."

I held my breath as though he had handed me a secret I didn't want to know. When I looked at him, his eyes were sad. He murmured, "Go and make your preparations."

I bowed to him gratefully. He went into Ama-la's room.

In the kitchen I found Emma still sitting on her cushion, looking dazed. Yeshe sat next to her, gazing at her hair. His eyes glowed. "Dorje, come see what your wife has been up to!"

Rinchen scowled at him, and I hoped she would control her tongue.

"She was braiding the American's hair, but it didn't work, so she said, 'This hair is like yak hair, or maybe it's like a sheep?'"

I looked at my wife. "Rinchen, why are you making such a problem? Just braid it!"

"Just braid it, you say? I cannot believe this hair. I put the yak butter on it to tame it, and the waves became bigger, *more* disobedient than before!"

"You see, Dorje?" Yeshe laughed. "Your wife is in a state!"

Now Yeshe was irritating me as well. Turning to Rinchen, I ordered, "Braid it, or wrap her head in a cloth!"

"I can't believe I have this hair to work with and two men telling me what to do."

Emma stood up suddenly. "Just give me the cloth and *I'll* do it!"

Her loud voice made me jump. It became suddenly quiet in the house. I had to let the two women be alone. "Yeshe, can you help me get the yaks ready?"

"Oh. Sure."

As we left, I heard Rinchen say, "I'm sorry, Emma-la. Let me finish your hair now."

Emma

With my scalp still sore from Rinchen's hair ministrations, I walk into our house for the last time. Go to the stove and press my hands to the iron surface. It's cold, and that makes me cry. I wrap my arms tight around me. My only real blanket, Gerald, is gone. Opening the top drawer of the bureau, I press one of his white cotton undershirts to my face. It smells like his sweat and river water. I pull it on and hug it to my ribs, then wrap my *chuba* over it, assuming my disguise for a trek I cannot bear to make.

The mirror on top of the bureau reveals the blankness in my eyes. Eyes that still can't believe what happened. *Maybe they'll bring him back in a few days. They just want to scare us into leaving Tibet. I should be here when he gets back.* But I have no choice. I can't look for him alone.

I stare down at my boots. For walking out of Tibet again, without him. How in the hell could that be?

At the kitchen table, I sit down to write him a note. Moonlight, austere and lovely, enters through the window and fills the outlines of a window shape on the floor. The moonlight is a bridge between the normal day that began with Gerald warm-spooned against my body in our bed, and the frigid abyss I'm about to step into when I walk out the door.

But not yet. I pull in a deep breath and set my pen to the glow of white paper before me.

September 16, 1954

Gerald, my love,
If you find this note, then maybe God is merciful and has brought you back to me. I am desperate enough to pray that God or someone is protecting you. Dorje has convinced me we have to leave, because whoever took you will probably be back for the rest of us. We're going to Kathmandu, and as soon as we arrive, I'll be drawing blood and raising hell to find you. Please remember, I hold you in my heart, and in the Light. I pray we'll see each other again, and soon.

I love you forever,
Emma

As I put the note in an envelope and hold the paper to my cheek, sobs shake my chest. I push love into the envelope, thrust in more than will ever fit, then leave it sitting lonely on top of the bureau.

Then I walk out the door.

～

Before dawn we stepped out of Dorje's courtyard into the chill breeze. The wind stung my eyes like sharp icicles. I walked against it, watching Rinchen's boots in front of me.

Walking away from our house, the cozy nest that had sheltered all our love and hopeful imaginings—all we'd dreamed of for years—I felt as if I were dying. And that I wanted to. I walked in a tunnel, darker and more frightening than anything else I'd ever known.

Terrifying thoughts played across the tunnel walls. *They're holding a gun to his head . . . pulling the trigger. His pale curls stained brown with dried blood. His wrists are shackled to a wall, and his eyes, starving, look at me.*

Inside me was a desolation like the moon. This was the worst day of my whole life.

At midday we stopped for butter tea and tsampa near a hillside cave. At the opening of the cave, Rinchen built a fire out of dung chips and sticks she'd picked up along the way.

I sat on a rock watching, feeling like lead.

She pushed the plunger up and down in the tea churner, then poured me some.

Champa handed me a little dough ball of tsampa, with big brown eyes that forced me to eat it while he watched. My little protector. I put it in my mouth and sipped the rich tea. I let the hot mixture dissolve some of the dough in my mouth, then forced the lump down my throat. Touching his head, I rubbed his hair, feeling humbled by the loving heart of this little Buddha.

Gerald

It was a long night of howling winds in the back of the truck. I slept only in short patches, often waking with a start. The air chilled my earlobes, making them ache.

At daybreak my stomach growled loudly. I sat up and Tenzin smiled at me. "Ah, you are hungry," he said.

I was embarrassed. "Excuse me. Yes, I am. Very hungry."

"They won't feed us until we reach the prison, my friend."

Lobsang was sitting up. He looked as though he hadn't slept at all. His delicate eyes had grown shadows beneath them in one night. "Where is this prison?"

"In Lhasa. It isn't far now."

We got the nod from the soldier to disembark and form our line to do our business again. Then he prodded us back in with the butt of his rifle. Seeing him poke Tenzin in the ribs, I felt angry, but Lobsang was enraged. Lobsang grabbed the rifle butt and pulled it away from Tenzin's side. Then he stood holding it, glaring at the soldier. It would have fired right into his face, but he seemed not to care.

I held my breath, waiting for them to blow his head off.

Carefully I stepped forward and placed my hand on Lobsang's arm.

"Lobsang, let go. It won't help us to see them shoot you in the head."

He blinked and seemed to return to his senses, allowing me to pry his hand from the rifle butt. I helped him sit down on the truck bed. The soldier looked up at him and made a whistling noise while shaking his head, then walked away.

As the truck started forward, I didn't know what moved my body more, the trembling coursing through me or the jostling of the ride. I took Lobsang in my arms and felt his chest heave with sobs. He seemed no more than a small boy in my embrace.

As we rode on, Lobsang fell asleep in my arms. After a long while, he awoke and stood up. Over the wooden sides of the truck, I glimpsed the distant figure of a girl gathering yak dung from the ground and placing it in a basket on her back. A normal day, for her. I glanced at Lobsang. He was watching her too, with longing in his eyes. His young skin was flawless. Had he fallen in love yet or been with a girl?

Holding his slinged arm carefully, Tenzin lowered his eyelids and breathed deeply. After a few minutes, his face relaxed and he opened his eyes.

I asked him, "Why are *you* here? You're a monk, what could they have against you?"

"Oh, we monks are their favorites! This is my third arrest. To them I am dangerous, a very bad boy. 'Religion is poison'—that's what they say. They keep bringing me back to get rid of my poison, but it never works." He smiled wryly.

Lobsang asked, "Then why do they let you go at all?"

"I don't know. Perhaps they need a rest."

Lobsang laughed nervously. He seemed as confused as I was by Tenzin's good humor. The old man continued, "From my *gompa* they have now taken seventeen monks. They come when we sleep. I'm lucky. Most of the ones they take never come back."

I swallowed. Sweat rolled down my sides from my armpits as I imagined the fate of those others. Lobsang stared at the floor with wide eyes that made me think of my brother.

Tenzin looked at us both, suddenly serious. "I'm sorry. I don't mean to frighten you. But don't worry. I have survived already two times in prison, and I will recite one thousand prayers of protection for all of us."

"What happens to the ones who don't come back?" Lobsang asked.

"They get sick, or they don't have enough to eat, or they are mistreated. But there is no worry for them. The ones who denounce other prisoners or His Holiness Kundun? It is for *them* that I worry. They get released, but their karma is very bad." Tenzin shook his head sadly.

"I'm surprised to see an American in the back of this truck," he observed.

I snorted grimly. "I am too."

"So you have been living in Shigatse?"

"Yes, the regent there gave us permission."

"I've heard of America," Lobsang said. He reached over and touched my curly hair with curiosity, his eyes owlish.

We all noticed the nomads at the same moment. Silence fell among us. Standing at the side of the road was a grimy man, covered with years of campfire soot and Tibet's fine dust, and next to him a woman in a black *chuba,* the colored stripes of her apron dulled to gray from years of living in the soil. They stood with fear in their eyes and their tongues sticking out in the Tibetan gesture of respect, watching the wheels of the monstrous truck approaching. They'd probably never seen one before.

I envied them that they could stand freely. Yesterday, my day had started in the most normal way. The yak chips crackled in the oven fire. The clean smell of soap filled my nose, its velvety softness on my fingers as I lathered my face for shaving. Emma held her hands over the stove, her auburn hair curling over her shoulders. I closed my eyes tightly, wishing all of the present away.

When I opened them, I saw Tenzin's lips moving, already at work on those one thousand prayers. Lobsang hung on to the wooden side of the truck. He stared forward so intently that I stood up, curious.

We pulled up to a huge cinder-block building in an ugly utilitarian style. It was a drab gray with bright green lettering. Below the Chinese characters I saw the more shapely Tibetan script. Four guards stood motionless in immaculate olive uniforms.

Lobsang's face went white. Our truck joined a line of large vehicles. With grunts and pointed rifles the soldiers indicated we were to get down and stand in single file facing the morning sun that slanted from the east.

And that was where we stayed. As the day came to its boiling point, the sun braised my skin like a hot skillet. Tibetan sun feels as if you're right up next to it staring it in the face. Sweat ran in rivulets down my face and neck. My tongue stuck to the roof of my mouth. We stood until the sun blazed down in singeing vertical rays. A man next to me fainted, and a soldier dragged him inside the building. I heard cries from inside a moment later.

When the sun was at my back, I heard shouts in Chinese. The line began to move into the building like a doomed centipede. Passing through the glass-and-metal double doors, my heart seized for a moment as if it were being squeezed in a vise. The air inside was cold as a cave. Although it was a relief from the heat, I shivered uncontrollably.

Tenzin walked in front of me. Two guards fell in on either side of him to escort him. One held a gun in Tenzin's back while the other held the lama's arm. The gun-toting guard looked all of seventeen, with a long, thin face that brought to mind a turnip with hair. He walked ramrod straight and looked from side to side with suspicious eyes. The other guard was much older with the bulges that come with age.

The older guard smiled at Tenzin and spoke to him in Tibetan. "You're back, Grandpa Tenzin. We missed you."

"How's your wife, Lin?"

"She's fine."

I could scarcely believe my eyes and ears. Why did this frail little monk need two armed guards to escort him? The older guard knew him. What had he done when he was here before to inspire such simultaneous caution and affection? I watched this bizarre, quite everyday conversation carried on at gunpoint.

The younger guard stepped up so he was even with Tenzin, still pointing his rifle in the old man's side. He gave the older guard a prune-faced frown, but Lin didn't notice.

Tenzin turned to the new guard and said in Tibetan, "I have not met you yet, my son."

"I'm a son of Mao, not your son, *latseng*."

Tenzin smiled at him. "I am *latseng,* and when I'm dead, I'll feed the birds."

The turnip-faced guard scowled at Tenzin as if he were a lunatic and jabbed the rifle a little farther into the lama's side. Lin stopped suddenly and stepped toward the other guard. He brought his face within an inch of the younger guard's nose and pressed a finger into the skinny chest. His words were like shark's teeth. I didn't have to understand Chinese to sense the reprimand occurring.

Then the three went back into their previous formation. Lin muttered to Tenzin, "Young cadres. Think they own the world."

❧

We stopped at a cell, and the guards pushed us inside. Although my heart raced as I crossed the threshold, I was relieved to be with Tenzin and Lobsang.

I stared around me. The walls were cinder block, stained brown in spots from blood or feces, I couldn't tell which. Nothing was in the cell except a bucket in the center. No beds, no blankets, no sink for washing. A simple wooden bucket.

I heard a loud command in Chinese. I turned around and saw a guard standing in the open doorway, eyeing me impatiently. He motioned that I should move to the other side of the room. On trembling legs I walked over to the spot he indicated. The floor there was red with blood. He yelled at me again, and I finally understood he was ordering me to sit. The sadistic glint in his eye told me he wanted me to sit in the blood simply because it would disturb me to do so. After hesitating, I settled into the pool of blood, shuddering as the cold wetness seeped through my trousers. I rubbed my arms to halt the crawling of my skin. The guard slammed the wooden door closed, and it echoed in my mind long after he'd left. The sound of the end of hope. My head throbbed, the pain piercing my eyes like two swords. My mouth was dry and pasty.

With a nervous eye toward the door, I moved out of the blood puddle.

My cellmates and I sat in silence for a time. Tenzin's fingers worked over his prayer beads, and Lobsang paced back and forth. I closed my eyes because his fear was infecting me.

A little later came the scraping noise of metal on concrete. Through a low hole in the wall, they pushed in three tin bowls. Lobsang grabbed a bowl. I took two bowls and handed one to Tenzin.

In the bowl was something I didn't recognize. As I stared at it, Tenzin explained, "A *momo* and *thukpa*. Just enough so you'll always be hungry."

He saw Lobsang opening up his *momo* looking for meat and said to him wryly, "There's nothing inside. Dough all the way through."

It had been so long since I'd eaten that I was past the stage of hunger pangs, but my mind was dull in a way that told me I needed to eat. Each of us drank every drop of liquid from our bowls after eating the *thukpa* because we were so thirsty.

Out of the tiny window high up in the cell wall, I saw that the sky had gone to black.

As the hours passed, the cell got colder. I folded myself into a ball against the chill radiating from the cinder blocks. The cold seeped into my back where it touched the wall. Tenzin sat next to me with his torn robes wrapped tightly round him. I heard him snoring. The hours of that first night stretched on forever, as long as the Great Wall of China. I was exhausted, but I couldn't sleep. My eyes kept checking the window, hoping for the sky to lighten soon. Lobsang played the same game.

He turned to me and mumbled, "I was supposed to get married tomorrow."

"You were?"

"We were preparing for the ceremony when we heard a shout outside. And so we went out, my *apa* and I." He looked at the floor, his eyes moving as if he were seeing it again in his mind. His face resembled that of a sad doll, so perfect with his eyes framed by dark lashes. "I didn't want them to take my *apa,* that's why I tried to fight back. He's very old—he couldn't survive this." I listened to the young man's whispering voice as he said, "I hope *I* can."

Near dawn, we heard screams. The back of my neck bristled. Whereas Tenzin merely looked around curiously, Lobsang and I stared at each other in terror. The cords of his neck stood out, and all I could think about was how utterly different this dawn was from what either of us had expected forty-eight hours earlier.

Dorje

After traveling for half a day, we stopped at Dawa's monastery to say good-bye to him. After we arrived, I went into the assembly hall and stood watching him. He had not noticed yet that I was here. He was sprinkling red sand in a small mound on the corner of a mandala. Even when he was a child, I liked watching him before he noticed I was there. As a baby he would sit in Rinchen's lap like a little man with his brows close together, concentrating. He looked that way again today holding sand in his fingers. He had eyes like Rinchen's: large and dark like a night sky.

My throat was sore and I felt sad. My chest was heavy with the knowledge of what Dawa did not yet know: that his favorite uncle was taken, and that soon we would also be going away from him to a place far away. I tried to forget my thoughts by sensing my son's heart. It was peaceful, with strong, slow beats.

It has hurt Rinchen's heart to be away from her son with those eyes like hers. On the day we sent him to the monastery when he was six years old, she stayed busy with extra cooking. That night I found her crying in the kitchen. She pretended she burned her finger, but I knew it was not so.

My son glanced up and saw me looking at him. He set down his sand quickly and ran over to me. He embraced me as if he were a child again, but the force of his arms around me reminded me he was not a child anymore. "Pa-la! You are here! This is a good day."

"We are all here—Rinchen and Champa also."

"They came too?" His smile was wide, then it dropped. "What happened?"

So fast he goes. Dawa is like my name, Dorje, which means "thunderbolt." I had wanted to keep him going slow in our talk, but thunder goes as fast as it wants.

"Your uncle Samten was taken, Dawa."

"Taken? What do you mean?"

"The communists took him."

My son's face darkened to the color of blood. His jaw muscles tightened. He looked away from me, trying to hide how angry he was. "Do you know where they took him?"

"No. And there is more. Dawa . . . we are leaving Tibet to go to Uncle Tinle's house in Kathmandu. It is no longer safe for us to stay here. We are certain the communists are watching our house because they are suspicious that we were friendly with the Americans."

Dawa's mouth fell open. He sat down on the corner of one of the benches where the monks sit for chanting. He put his head in his hands and sighed.

I touched his wrist. "Also, Ama-la died."

"What?" He swallowed with his eyes wide.

"I believe she became frightened when the communists came to the house. And one more thing—they took our friend from America."

"Emma? They took a *woman*?"

"No. Emma is with us. They took Gerald. He and Samten were together when they were taken. So we're here to say goodbye and to ask for the blessing of our son, the lama. We want you to recite prayers for our safety."

My son did not respond. He stayed completely still.

"May we have the blessing from you? And your prayers, Dawa?"

"I—" He stopped. Other words were in his mouth, but he did not say them. His mind seemed far away. "I will, Father." His voice was tight, as if he were being strangled. "But I don't think my prayers will help you."

"What?" I laughed, trying to bring a smile to him. "This is what a lama says?"

"I am not a good lama." As I was about to ask him what he meant, he said, "I'd like to see the rest of the family now. They are outside?"

"Yes. Let's go."

As we stepped over the high wooden threshold to go out, I stared at his back. I felt a storm inside his body. I smiled at him when we stepped into the warm sunlight, letting him know it was all right, but he wouldn't look into my eyes.

Rinchen and Emma were squatting on the ground, and Champa was running around them in circles, tapping them on their heads as he went by. "Pa-la," he exclaimed, "Emma has taught me an American game called dukdukoose! See?"

Emma laughed, "Champa, you cannot tap both of our heads at the same time. Only one of us can be the goose!"

Dawa walked to his mother. They touched foreheads and embraced. "My son, the lama! And so handsome!"

"Oh, Mother!" Dawa shook his head.

Dawa and Emma bowed and touched foreheads. "I'm so sorry about your husband," he whispered.

She pressed her lips together, then mumbled, "Thank you."

He stepped back formally, as if it were too disturbing to see the sadness in her eyes. He played with the *mani* beads wrapped around his wrist, then said, "Please come inside and share *tsampa* with me."

We ate lunch together, speaking little. In the evening, we went to the monastery's guesthouse. Emma went to bed even before

Champa, as if she could not wait for sleep. After Champa went to sleep, we drank tea with our son in the guesthouse kitchen.

He set down his bowl. "I would like to come with you," he announced.

Rinchen's eyes popped wide as a lizard's. "What? You are a lama! You stay in the monastery."

"I am wondering if I could do more to help Tibet from outside the monastery."

Rinchen shook her head fast, and her lips set up firm in her face. "No. You have a task, to pray for all beings in the world. This is your destiny! Lama Norbu said so!"

"But terrible things are happening in Tibet!" Dawa was a pile of dry sticks, and Rinchen was a flame.

"If bad things happen in our country, it is because we have not followed the wishes of the gods. If we have had too much pride, then we will learn from our sufferings. You cannot simply decide, 'Oh, I've grown tired of being a lama, I guess I'll leave the monastery'!"

"Mother, I recite prayers all day for the future of Tibet. And what is happening? The Chinese come and destroy our monasteries! I want to go to university. I want to learn about the world—it's changing, and we Tibetans know nothing about it."

"University?" I heard myself saying.

For once, my wife was unable to speak.

I talked in a soft voice. "Rinchen, I have also been thinking, maybe it is not safe for Dawa to stay here. So please, we must all calm down and try to understand each other."

"The gods will protect monks in a monastery," she told me, as if it were the most obvious thing in the world. She turned to Dawa. "By going to university, you will save Tibet?"

His voice rose like hers. "Tibet will be ruined by its own ignorance!"

The fire between them burned, and their cheeks were the bright color of radishes. Even though I was frustrated with my wife, I sensed that she felt her life slipping through her fingers like sand. She stood up and left us.

My son pushed the air out of his mouth, fast and hard. Then he looked at me. "Pa-la, I'm not the only monk who feels this way. There are four of us who talk about what is happening to our country every day. For centuries we Tibetans isolated ourselves, and now most people in the world don't even know we exist. Maybe they could help us, but not if they don't know who we are! And also, *we* do not know anything about the world. One of the monks secretly brought in a wireless so that we can hear news of the world. There is talk on the wireless of other places, and I have no notion of where these places are or what is their significance. Now China wants to destroy our ways and take our land, and we have no way to stop them."

"Dawa, His Holiness Kundun will guide us and protect our country."

"Can His Holiness do that? Does he know about these other places? He is just a boy."

To doubt His Holiness in any way is not something Tibetans do. To hear my son speak in this way—I could not accept it. I looked into the glowing ashes of the cooking fire because I did not know what to say.

"Pa-la, please don't be angry. My heart is the same. Only my mind has new ideas."

"Yes, Dawa. But these ideas are very strange to me. They are not what I expected you to learn in a monastery!" I smiled at him.

He said in a serious way, "Thank you for listening, Pa-la. I need to tell you that I have decided to go. I'd like to go with you, but if Mother doesn't allow it, I'll go alone."

"That is exactly what your mother said to me yesterday—'I would like to go with you, but if I can't, I'll leave Tibet without you!' You and she are the same, and you both make my head ache!"

I grabbed his ear and gave it a little pull to show him my love.

"I am still your father, Dawa, and now, for my sake, I am sending you to bed."

"Pa-la, I'm happy to obey you. Good night." He laughed and we both stood up. He put his arms around me to embrace me. Then he walked away toward the monastery.

The next morning, Dawa left with us. He and Rinchen walked side by side, but they did not look at each other.

Emma

Ten days since we left, and I haven't slept. I look for Gerald constantly, even though I know I won't see him. My heart thumps through each panicky day and night. My legs prickle with restlessness, but I'm too exhausted to walk up a hill.

It is drier here, with the plants getting smaller and squatter as we move westward. Despite the fact that we're just emerging from the wet season, I seem to be drying up like the shrubs, cringing into a smaller, fearful form. The entire skin of my body is parched like the soil, dried up and cracked open. Crawled upon by bugs that bite at my mind with bloody images of what might be happening to Gerald.

From what I've heard, he's either in a labor camp or he's dead. I just want to see him, put my hands on his face, stroke his hair.

Rinchen feels sorry for me. She sends me out to gather yak chips or has me churn butter tea, even though I'm totally clumsy at it. I can see in her ample shoulders that she carries the same loss I do. She speaks little, and there is heaviness in her movements when she wipes Champa's brow or ties her *chuba*.

Dawa moves his fingers over his prayer beads as he walks, and I hate him for that because I can't pray. The words turn to cement in my mouth. How can you pray when you just want to curse at God and everything that moves? Not that I was any good at praying before this happened, but now would be the time to get busy praying. What would Gerald do if the situation were reversed? He'd pray, oh, you bet he'd pray. My companions must wonder, being religious Tibetans, Why doesn't she pray for Gerald? *Screw it. I'm boycotting God. This whole thing confirms my deep fear that the world is a sick place full of hateful people who don't give a goddamn about anybody but themselves, and that life is a sick joke.* It feels ridiculous to pray. Prayers don't do anything, and we're way too stupid in what we pray for and shouldn't be in charge of anything anyway.

The other day I tried reading psalms for some comfort, but they made me want to scream. *And the sun shall not smite thee by day, nor the moon by night.* They read that psalm at Daddy's funeral. The minister went on about God protecting us from all harm as we all stared at Daddy's casket. I sat in a cloud of evil thoughts, wondering in a farcical kind of way, Is Daddy seeing how insane this is, us sitting before his *casket* listening to promises that God would protect us from all harm? If death isn't harm, then *what the hell is?*

The only thing that keeps me going is Champa. He holds my hand all day on the trail. He senses my despair and so he has tied himself to me, probably worrying I'll leap off a cliff, given the opportunity. It's unbelievable that he's actually able to make me laugh at times. He'll push his chest forward and proclaim, "Today we'll see nomads and eat *tsampa* with them," or, "Today we will see many sheep." And he'll be right; we'll have gone for days with nary a sign of sheep, and on the day of his prediction, behold, there are sheep.

I think incessantly about death, not being, falling into a forever sleep. Leave me like a carcass on the trail, I want to tell my companions. But then Champa looks at me with serious eyes, even as one of his fingers picks his nose, and I'll feel this absurd impulse to laugh. I rest my eyes on my little protector's head and keep plodding.

Gerald would want me to have faith. Well, this is the absolute closest I can get, to keep walking and keep holding Champa's hand.

Gerald

A bucket is in the center of the cell. The piss pot. We have to do our business in front of each other. It's a humiliating ordeal to squat over that bucket, although we each avert our eyes from whoever's using it. What's worse is that it stays with us for days, reeking and overflowing until one of the guards brings a prisoner in to empty it.

Every day we have work detail. There's actually no real work to do, so the guards make up work for us. We dig ditches and then refill them from an hour after sunrise until sunset. On my second day of digging, my skin came off on the shovel handle. The handle turned red as blood dripped down. The guards laughed under the heat-lamp sun, saying, "Now the bourgeois rulers are humbled— sweating like peasants." Now that I've been here for three weeks, my palms have the beginnings of calluses.

Shortly before lunch today Tenzin fell to the ground. I went to him and felt his wrist. His pulse raced and his face looked pale. A guard came over to us and pushed me away from him. There was the dull sound of boots against Tenzin's ribs as the guard kicked him. I felt a searing rage, but did nothing. Tenzin opened his eyes, and another guard helped him stand. They left him leaning precariously against his shovel. My arms reached out toward him, but I let them drop to my sides. I hated myself for that.

I gazed at the puffy dirt beneath my shovel and heard a low voice beside me. "We're all wondering why they put you in the cell with Lama Tenzin. The whole prison wants to know." A man stood to my right. I looked at his face, braced for his anger that I hadn't protected Tenzin. But his expression was pleasant; only my guilt was convicting me. "Don't worry; he'll recover soon. He always does." The man had wiry forearms that showed his veins. He kept digging as he talked and scarcely glanced at me so the guards wouldn't detect us.

"How does everyone know him?" I asked.

"Perhaps because he has been here so many times, but really it is his strength and his compassion. No matter how they beat him, the light of compassion never leaves his eyes. I once saw him put his hands on the very guard who had just finished beating him, granting the guard blessings. There were tears in Lama Tenzin's eyes for the guard. Many prisoners pass messages asking for Lama Tenzin to recite prayers for healing from their beatings, and these prisoners always heal."

I looked at my companion blankly, feeling suddenly deluged with the good fortune of being in the same cell with Lama Tenzin. "I don't know why they put me with him."

"Lama Tenzin is a legend here," the man said, smiling at his shovel. "Even the guards love him."

"Yes—I noticed that."

"They're animals when he's not here. Lama Tenzin was in my cell the last time he was here. It was a great blessing." The man put his hands together quickly in a *mudra* at his chest, then flashed them back onto his shovel handle. "You must have wonderful karma," he added seriously.

I pondered what a strange thing this was to say. He continued, "He smiles at them kindly while they interrogate him. Some guards are infuriated by this; others avoid him because they're afraid of the bad karma they will earn by beating him. Last time he was here, they sent him to solitary. That was a mistake. The entire prison rebelled. We banged our bowls on the cell doors and screamed all night long, and some of the Khampas even went to the bathroom and then threw their *kaka* at the guards! We made such a terrible noise they couldn't stand it, and the Lhasa residents and monks complained to the government in Beijing. They took him out of solitary, and then they sent him out of the prison, just to get some peace." The man chuckled and shook his head. Our talk ended abruptly when he saw a guard eyeing him.

That night, the cold seeped through my clothes and chilled every inch of my body. I dreamed of Emma, and her eyes were sadder than I'd ever seen them. When I woke up, the piss-pot stench floated to me in the dark and I remembered where I was. But I was certain that her hand had graced my cheek in my sleep. My hand went to where hers had been and I held it there.

As the days here become weeks, a deadness spreads inside me. The screams don't crawl up my back as far as they used to.

~

They brought Lobsang back into the cell this morning from his first interrogation. His right eye was a bloody red ball with a black dot in the middle. His arms were spotted with purple bruises. He stared in front of him like a mannequin. The hairs on my arms stood up.

I went to him and examined his eye and his bruises. But I was helpless without my medical bag. My throat tightened with tears at seeing someone so young who might lose the use of his eye. I didn't want to frighten him, so I merely said, "Just leave your eye alone; it will heal."

That night we three sat together in silence. "They'll come for you too," Tenzin told me. "You must think of what to say to them."

"What is it they want?"

"They want you to be their trained monkey. To say exactly what they want you to say, to spit on whomever they want you to spit on, to denounce your cellmates." Tenzin paused. "They'll push bamboo under your fingernails and tell you to write a confession of your anticommunist thoughts and actions."

I asked, "But don't some of the men simply lie to save themselves, write a confession they don't even believe? Where's the victory in getting you to lie?"

"If you confess, whether you are sincere or you lie, they are controlling you. They'll say you're a spy or a missionary, or that you were spreading anticommunist ideas among Tibetans."

Lobsang spoke. "You *have* to lie. I tried to tell them the truth and look at me."

"I—don't think I can. It's against what I believe. Against God."

Lobsang made a snorting sound. "So is your god more important than your life?"

I looked at Tenzin. His eyes were sad, disturbed by what Lobsang had said.

"What kind of god allows them to do *this*?" Lobsang pointed at his eye. Then he started to laugh, a sickening half-crying sound. His bloody eye watered and then he shuddered with silent sobs. Tenzin put a hand on his shoulder.

The old man looked at me and said quietly, "Do not ruin your chances for a good rebirth."

Lobsang laughed again, saying, "It's too late. We're already in the realms of hell."

I asked, "Can't I explain, I'm not a spy, or a missionary?"

Lobsang spoke with tears in his voice and a bitter smile, "They won't listen! I told them that my *apa* and I are good to the peasants! We give food to anyone who comes begging. But the guards beat me until the room went black."

Tenzin looked at me, his face grave. "Even as they torture you, pray for them, because of the karma they're creating for themselves."

I wondered, *What does the bamboo feel like, forcing underneath, tearing nail from flesh?* My mind shut like a vault. No. I couldn't believe they'd do that to me.

But what if? I didn't know what I was made of.

Dorje

Each day we stop for *tsampa* when the sun is right overhead. We sit in a circle around the cooking fire, Rinchen and Dawa and Emma and me, while Champa plays outside our circle. When we sit in this way, I feel I am all four of us. The frown of my wife's lips tells me that she is still upset with me for disagreeing with her about Dawa, but I can also feel she has been enjoying him. Dawa hunches over his *tsampa* as though he has lost all that he loves.

Then I feel myself sitting in Emma's place, and inside her it is dark and cold. All winter, the snow covers the Himalayas, and in the spring the snow melts and water drips down into the valleys of my country. Emma stands like a frozen mountain. Her pain comes from her like the water drips off the mountains. On and on it drips. She has a lot of pain.

Champa has been playing the clown on our trip, making animal faces at Emma to cheer her. He's delighted to act the part of any animal and have her guess which one. It is a special prize to him when he acts out an animal she cannot guess because she doesn't know Tibetan wildlife. Then he plays the schoolteacher, standing tall and instructing her on all the animals.

Champa also helps her climb the hills. This week she walks slowly, as if she carries heavy stones inside her. Rinchen has given her extra meat for the last three meals, but still Champa must push her up the passes.

My wife has an idea why Emma is weak and tired. These are the things of women. They pass beneath my nose as quietly as spiders, but she sees them.

Yesterday Emma apologized, "I'm sorry to be so slow, Dorje. It must be the altitude."

Rinchen smiled, like a secret, and whispered to Emma, "You're not sick. You're going to have a child. I had a dream."

But Emma did not smile. Her face colored and she said, "No. I'm *not* having a child," with a voice as hard as a stack of bricks. She stood up and walked out of our circle.

I knew Rinchen's mind was twisting Emma's answer around, trying to make sense of it. She asked, "Why would she not be happy? I don't understand these foreigners. I burned incense between my legs to draw a soul into my womb. We all do this to bring this blessing into our lives. Did Emma not say she wanted a child?"

Dawa and I did not answer, embarrassed to hear her speak of these things of women. He picked up a stone and tossed it.

My wife insisted, "She is pregnant."

I said nothing, because even though I do not understand the things of women, one thing I do know: Rinchen's dreams are always true.

Emma

Rinchen is driving me insane. For the past four mornings, she has approached me as we're packing up to leave. "I had another dream! You're going to have a child, for certain!"

There is not a bloody thing she could say that gets under my skin more than that.

She keeps on. "Our children will play together!"

I appeal to Dorje with a look, widening my eyes like a lunatic on the brink. He shrugs helplessly. Rinchen moves closer to me with a stubborn grin on her face. "You're lucky to have this good news!"

I make an elaborate show of plugging my ears to her.

She stands there with head cocked to one side, eyebrows scrunched, perplexed. "Don't you *want* a little baby?" She holds her arms in a cradle position and swings them.

"Enough!" I cry, thrusting my arms at her. Then I'm running away from them all, over the dry dirt. I fall to my knees and hug the ground, grabbing fistfuls of dirt, punching at the earth. I push my cheek into the rocky soil, smearing dust into tears. My stomach shakes against the earth with each sob.

After a long time, I roll over onto my back and lie spread-eagled gazing at the dome above. Tears run back toward my temples and into my hair. The sky is a bleached blue. A rock pokes me between the shoulder blades.

Time slows.

Eventually, I sit up and run my fingers over my braids.

Dorje sits cross-legged a hundred yards away. He's letting me be, not looking at me. The wind moves the sleeve of his *chuba*. I get to my feet and walk toward him. After I reach him, he stands up and drapes a red woolen blanket around me. "I'm sorry," I tell him. He nods as though I didn't need to say it. I listen to the in, out of my breath, feeling the itchy warmth of the blanket as we plod back to camp.

～

I'm hiding inside my tent. Four days have passed since my out-burst. Rinchen and I haven't spoken to each other. I should apologize, but I can't bring myself to do it.

I've needed the silence. Silence and privacy, because I've thrown up every single day at least once. I've even considered whether Rinchen's nocturnal imaginings might be on the mark. What I used to eat daily, I can't even contemplate without feeling sick, and my breasts have blown up like two prize squashes. So either I'm really losing my mind or another immaculate conception has occurred. *Except that the last time Gerald and I were intimate was not that long ago, so it is possible . . .*

Do not get your hopes up.

I once threw up a bunch of peas when I was seven. My father had fed them to me one by one, and although I abhorred peas, I would've eaten anything because he was paying attention to me. He'd just returned from a four-month-long trip, so I was drinking in his smells of cologne and old books. After lunch we went to a park and watched ducks from inside the car. He told me their quacks showed God's sense of humor. I loved that.

He rolled his head around in small half circles, gripped the wheel, and turned to face me. "Muffin."

I stared ahead because in that instant I knew exactly where this was going.

"I'm not sure what to say here."

"Just say it, Dad, you're leaving again."

The dash clock ticked loudly in the silence.

He'd pulled me in a little further with each pea. Each mushy ball I swallowed seemed like a promise that he'd stay this time. So I threw up. The vomit splashed on the dashboard and onto the cream-colored leather seat between my legs, and I was glad.

"Don't be embarrassed, Muffin. We all get tummy problems. It'll come clean." He reached into the glove compartment, searching for napkins.

Hope is for imbeciles.

But now, on a mountain in Tibet, the part of me that specializes in stupidity is still thinking, *I haven't gotten a period in . . . how many weeks now?*

The queerest feeling spreads through me. I stop breathing.

Oh, now, that's just so dumb to even consider it.

But.

Gerald

I hear the clink of keys and it starts my heart speeding. The clinking gets closer, and the three of us look at each other. I hear the lock turning, and the cell door opens. It's unmistakable that the three guards are here for me. They take hold of my arms. As we emerge into the corridor, a guard is on each side of me and one in the back.

They bring me into a small room with hospital-green walls. The air is unnaturally cold. They sit me down on a chair with a table before me. Then they retreat behind me, standing against the wall, as if they're waiting for something or someone. I sit on an icy metal chair. My legs shake. My forehead is sweaty and my palms stick to the table.

A portrait of Chairman Mao is on the wall, his round face blown up as large as the table in front of me. A rusty hook hangs from the ceiling. A length of rope coils in the corner. Parts of the rope are stained the color of rust. Of blood.

There is gooseflesh on my arms. I hear a guard shifting from foot to foot behind me. Turning round, I see a brown smudge the size of a head on the wall.

I try not to imagine what's coming. *Dear Lord, may Your words be my words. The Lord is my light and salvation. Whom shall I fear?* I say it to myself over and over. It is a small comfort. I'm not convinced.

Time passes achingly slowly. Prepare yourself, Tenzin had said. *When we depart from truth, we separate ourselves from God. Help me, Lord, please.*

A thin man with a cane enters. His lips are a slit like a snake's mouth. A scar crosses his right cheek. He sits down in the other chair, erect. Chairman Mao looks over the man's shoulder. Another guard enters and stands behind the first man's chair.

I hear my heart pulsing up into my ears.

The thin man speaks to me in English. "I am Comrade Han. It is simple. If you confess, tell us who your collaborators are, then we will release you." He purses the snake lips. "Why are you in Tibet?"

I swallow. "I came to learn about Tibetan religion."

"You came all the way from America to learn from these backward people?" He laughs.

I bring my gaze to his face, blinking. My mouth is dry, my tongue like sandpaper. His eyes shine black like a crow's. He strikes the table with his cane. I jump, my nerves like shattered glass. Then he's up from his seat, thrusting his face into mine, shouting, "We're liberating Tibet from foreigners like you!"

I pray for Light. "Umm . . ." My voice cracks. "I'm not here to interfere, or spy—"

He pushes in close to my face. Shouts, *"Incorrect answer!"* Places the tip of his cane against my soft belly. And thrusts.

I can't breathe. Hands grab me from behind. The scratch of rope being wound around my wrists, binding my hands behind my back. Someone pulling the rope up. My arms stretch upward, trussed behind me like a bird with bound wings. Fire shoots through my arms into my shoulders as the guard pulls the rope higher. Other hands lift me from the chair. All my weight hangs from my hands tied behind me. My feet dangle above the floor. Screams. Coming from me. Then I'm alone.

A trickle of saliva pools in my throat. I cough. Black closes in on my eyelids.

I feel hands on my hips, lifting me. My feet touch the floor, my arms drop and searing heat shoots down my shoulders. My legs collapse under me. They unwind the rope and my arms fall to my sides, burning like flames. The room darkens and I feel myself blacking out. They drag me back to my cell. My heels thud against the floor. The cell door opens, and they throw me inside.

Tenzin crouches over me, sad eyes tucked into his kind face. Tears are on Lobsang's face as he looks at me. A sob lies in my gut. I can't move. Tenzin and Lobsang put their hands under my back and move me to the corner. Tenzin sits down next to me. He pops each shoulder back into its socket. My throat is raw. I look down at my hands. My wrists are engraved with rope marks. Skin branded red. Robed arms close around me.

Dorje

We have reached steep hillsides and trees heavy with leaves of deep jade. Champa points to them, saying, "Look! They're so big!" He is excited to see trees larger than his imaginings, but the green only brings me sadness. It means we are near Zhangmu, where we must say good-bye to our Tibet and feel it pulled from our bodies. It is only the second time I have ever left my country, and my feet do not want to walk away from it. Maybe we will never see it again.

I imagine us returning in a few months and walking through the gate of our courtyard. Our sheep coming over to nuzzle us, as if we never went anywhere. But when I look at Dawa, whose eyes see farther than any of ours, I feel it will not happen that way.

With each step, I can see the border sign more clearly. I look at each of us, and each seems to be crossing in his or her own way. Emma has the look of faraway in her eyes. Rinchen grabs Champa's hand and runs on quick feet that say, *Soon we will be safe!* Dragged alongside my wife, Champa makes it a game, hopping over the rocks and jumping up to hit leaves with his hands.

I look back at Dawa and Emma, and I catch a moment between

them. Dawa's face sags like wilting cabbage leaves. Emma gives him a smile that says, *I'm trying to be brave too.*

I have been giving thanks to Guru Rinpoche for the great blessing of having my son with me. If we had left Dawa in Tibet, how could I have peace? At any new report of Tibet's troubles, I would be worrying for his safety. My mind does not want to imagine such things.

During our trek I've been frightened because we left without a lama's blessing, and worse, we left on an inauspicious day. We did not do the simple things that any wise person would do to prepare for a trip. Each time we have gone up a mountain pass, I've been certain we would be punished for our pride.

So now I say to my wife, "We have almost finished our journey, and there have been no demons to bother us."

"Do not say this, Dorje. The journey isn't finished."

Such a pessimist! I only want to hear happy things, so I say, "Perhaps because we have a lama with us, we are protected." I smile at her.

"A lama who's fleeing a monastery! I don't think that gives us protection. Besides, you shouldn't say these things, or the gods will think we're proud."

"You make your mind small when you think just one way, always the same way. The world is not the same as before, Rinchen. Even His Holiness might not stay in Tibet! I heard this from a trader on the trail. His Holiness was in India, and He consulted an oracle to see whether it was safe to return to Lhasa!"

When I see her shocked face, I regret what I have said. "I'm sorry, Rinchen."

She doesn't hear me. She walks ahead on the trail with her head low.

As we cross into Nepal, I can almost hear a door closing behind us.

Emma

Last night when I went to sleep in my tent, it was like any other night on this godforsaken journey. Except that last night, I finally gathered my courage and felt around in my satchel. I looked at, smelled, touched, what I had of my husband. His white cotton shirt. I'd stuffed it in my bag prior to leaving. He'd worn it the day before his capture, and it carried his scent—a sweet, leathery spice in the fabric, even in the mandarin collar. The fibers had touched his chest, his back, the sinews of his shoulders. When I drew my fingers across the weave and pulled the scent into my lungs, I was touching him, sensing him. I lay down with my face nuzzling the shirt, like a child with a stuffed bear.

I wanted it to stay just as it was, untouched by what came after. Before capture and after capture—my life is divided along that border. But already the shirt was absorbing those things that came *after*. A smudge was on the shoulder where I'd dropped it yesterday while rummaging through the bag on the trail. I wanted to keep hold of *before,* but *after* was already covering it like a layer of dust.

Four weeks now. It was one month ago that they took him. It

was a horrifying realization because of all that could have happened to him already. . . . I sat up quickly and hit my fists on my head again and again, to forget my thoughts. Grabbed a button on his shirt and scraped it hard across my forehead, back and forth. I wanted the pain, wanted to bleed.

My husband was supposed to carry me through anything life could throw at me. A stabbing, searing pinch came within as I imagined what life might be—no, not just temporarily, but maybe forever—without him. Living the rest of my life alone.

I had a dream that night. In this night vision I was lying on a soft bed with pillows and a fluffy comforter, and on the side of my bed were two women: Rinchen and Genevieve. Rinchen was feeding me a warm soup, holding a wooden bowl to my lips, and Genevieve was stroking my right hand, murmuring comforting words. I lay there glowing against the sheets. I fell into a doze, then I felt a warm weight on my chest. It moved up and down with my breathing. When I woke up, still within the dream, I looked into the eyes of my own child lying on my chest. They were Gerald's eyes, a stunning clear blue.

When I woke up from this dream, I looked down to find both hands on my belly. Then I laughed, and my hands shook on my stomach. I said out loud, "God, you have a truly absurd sense of humor." Only in Tibet, where lamas levitate, where a woman once pointed out to me a goat that she insisted was the reincarnation of her father, only in this barren place could *I* conceive a child!

I felt different. *Really* different. This whole new world was about to open up to me, a world of burp cloths and tiny fingers and soft skin against my cheek.

But it was more than that. I felt humble. This is not a feeling I've had often in my life. It was a good sensation, as if I were a kid, standing next to God, and he had my hand and I could just relax and stop worrying about everything. For the first time since Gerald's disappearance, I didn't feel alone. God was right beside me.

This was a lot for me, the scoffer, to take in. The scoffer within sneered, *Is it God's presence or madness?* But another part of me, a new part, answered, *You've always thought God lived in Gerald and Genevieve. So why can't he live in you too?*

I was also sad because I wanted to run to Gerald and drop the news on him like a fabulous bomb. I wanted to see him dance, unable to contain himself.

When I came out of my tent, it was still dark, and the dawn air was cold on my face. Rinchen was packing our belongings on one of the yaks. I walked up to her with a grin on my face, and when I stood before her, I put her hands on my stomach. Her eyes widened.

"Rinchen, I had a dream! I'm having a child!"

She smiled, then threw her head back and laughed. We wrapped our arms around each other. She held me for a long moment, and a few tears leaked out of the corners of my eyes.

I nearly danced across the Nepalese border when we crossed it today. A sweet memory came to me. I was twenty-two, fresh from my graduation from Smith College, back at home for the summer, and Gerald was home in between his first and second years of medical school. Our parents were away for the day, and I had spent the day in the kitchen, kneading bread and rolling out pie crusts for blackberry pies. One baking project wasn't enough.

Gerald had asked me to marry him under the mulberry tree in the front yard.

My fingers kneaded the bread dough, working it first gently, then furiously, until it was hard as an overdone steak, thinking it would give me an answer if I squeezed it hard enough. Then, as I rolled out the dough for the pie crust, an idea lit my brain. I would leave it up to the dough. My father had told me that Tibetans sometimes made decisions by putting the two options in two pieces of *tsampa* dough and spinning them clockwise in a cup before a statue of the Buddha. I grabbed a piece of scrap paper from the counter, tore it in two, and wrote two outcomes about marrying him:

It is right to marry him!! and *It is wrong to marry him.*

I balled up each piece of paper and walked over to the dough. From the flat piece of dough I'd rolled out, I snatched a lump from the corner and broke it into two wads. As I placed the paper into the center of the second piece of dough, Gerald walked into the kitchen.

He looked at me quizzically. "Are you putting *paper* into the pies? Yum." He smirked. "Can't wait to taste that."

"No, I am not. I am using a deeply scientific method, taught to me by my father, to figure out the answer to an important question."

He grinned. "And what question would that be? I wonder."

"None of your business, Geebs. It is a matter of grave importance, and very private."

He wrapped his arms around me from behind. "So you're going to figure this out by baking pieces of paper?"

"Yes," I replied, very dignified, stepping deliberately away from him.

"Deeply scientific, indeed." With that, he rushed me, grabbing for the pieces of dough I was holding. He was fast. Before I knew it, he'd unrolled both of my wads of paper and was spreading them out on the counter. "Aha!" he exclaimed, triumphant. "Just as I suspected!" Then he adopted a Svengali voice, saying, "Ah, but my dearrrrr. Ze ansah is alrrreadeee decided. Zat is clearrrr."

"Oh, is it?" I retorted, hands on hips, enjoying him.

"But of courrrse! Look at zee opshons. On zee *no marrying* opshon, vee haf a period. On zee *marrying* opshon, vee haf two exclamation points. It is clearrrr vat opshon you vant!"

"No, it's not," I said in a shaky voice. "I don't want to mess this up, Geebs. Your—our parents are going to kill us."

"Well, then we'll just have to educate them. There is nothing scandalous about this—we are *not* related to each other! Look, they'll be reasonable. Just let me do all the talking."

"That goes without saying."

"I know, but will you actually *do* it?" He raised an eyebrow at me, in a way I liked, an exasperated way that was also filled with his affection for me. He liked that I had guts. He just didn't always like the way I spilled them all over people.

On the Nepali trail, I heard the plodding of three goats going by, prodded by their owner. Their hooves thumped against the dirt, reminding me of the clunking sound of our feet, Gerald's and mine, on the stairs later that same afternoon of the balls of dough. I convinced Gerald we needed a divine blessing on our decision on whether to get married. We placed the two wads of paper into the balls of dough and set them in an amber drinking glass. As we were about to shake them, we heard our parents' footsteps on the front landing. Up we went, two steps at a time in a giggling racket, to the attic to complete our divination. Out of breath, we lunged like children hiding some creature we'd brought into the house. The glass turned frosty-looking in Gerald's sweaty hand, then we burst through the attic door, and Gerald tripped and nearly dropped the lumps of dough. Finally we sat on opposite sides of Mother Kittredge's travel trunk, with our feet tucked beneath us.

"We'll shake them, and we'll open the one that lands on the left," he suggested.

"Fine, let's get it over with. I can't take this." I covered my eyes and told him, "You do it," praying for the right heart to keep the commitment I might be asked to make: to be with him, or be apart. I couldn't hurt someone so precious, with eyes like the sky. Either we'd be together forever, or we'd have to stay away from each other to stand the pain.

He shook the glass. The larger ball fell to my left. He snatched it up in his hands and unrolled it.

I didn't have to ask what it said. He was jumping up and down, and the floor vibrated with joy. He danced around the attic in exuberant circles.

These happy thoughts carried me now until the day we reached

Kathmandu. I was completely unprepared for that city, although I'd been there only months before. The trails of Tibet were so quiet and pensive that they had stilled even *my* agitated mind. I didn't notice this until we entered the frenetic buzz of the city: merchants shouting, "Come in, take a look," sari-clad women selling tea at stalls, a cow snoozing undisturbed in the street as cars careened around it, the smell of burning paper and car exhaust in the air. It made my head pound.

Dorje's uncle and aunt, Tinle and Pema, welcomed us warmly into their home. They gave me my own room, for which I was deeply grateful. Tinle and Pema's children had only recently moved into the modest three-bedroom house on their own, so we were fortunate indeed to receive their hospitality. As I lay on the mattress with my arm over my eyes, my feet throbbed within my boots. The cries of vendors traveled through the closed shutters, but even so, I dropped into a sleep of fifteen hours and woke up from the pinch of my boots around my swollen feet.

Gerald

I lie in the same spot where I've been for days. My shoulders burn as if they were branded. I touch my wrists. Dry brown scabs cover where the ropes were.

Tenzin looks over when he sees me stir. "Are you all right?"

"I'm alive." My voice is flat.

"Both you and Lobsang. They took him again for interrogation. You suffer so much."

"What about you? They do the same thing to you."

He looked at his blackened fingernails. He'd lost two of them already, never to grow back. "For me, it's not so bad. I liberate my mind. It travels, flies over hillsides while they do their mischief to my body. So I'm not there."

"That's how you get through the torture?"

"All lamas know how to do this."

"Can you teach me? I've never been so afraid." I pause, feel tears coming to my eyes. "And I hate them."

"That is natural."

"Lama Tenzin, I'm a Quaker. In my religion, we say love your enemies, pray for those who mistreat you. But now . . ."

"You want to kill Comrade Han."

I hesitate. "Yes."

"That is the ignorance within each of us. It causes suffering. You must meditate; it will make your mind free."

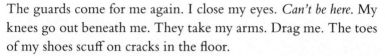

The guards come for me again. I close my eyes. *Can't be here.* My knees go out beneath me. They take my arms. Drag me. The toes of my shoes scuff on cracks in the floor.

They leave me in the room and I wait at the table, alone. I put my forehead on its cold surface. Look up. The hook leers at me.

I conjure Emma's face. *Courage, Geebs,* she says, a crease between her eyebrows.

Don't be here. Take your soul to music. The icy table becomes a keyboard beneath my fingertips. I dive into Rachmaninoff. When I see the hook, I blink it away.

Movement in the hall. My fingers halt.

Comrade Han steps into the room, the interpreter behind him. Sweat drips down my right temple.

His gaze rests on my fingers. I hear the contempt in his tone, even before the interpreter translates. "Your fingers play pretty melodies on the table, imperialist dog?"

He walks around behind me. My shoulders turn to stone, waiting for the cane. His breath warms my left earlobe. He says in a whispering hiss, "Even in prison you take leisure time. Living on the necks of the peasants."

He grabs my hair, yanks my head back. Jabs my groin with the cane. Tears leak from my eyes. A gasping sound. He walks around to stand in front of me. Unbuttons his Mao suit and pulls out a red book. It hits the table with a loud thwack. "Read this, foreign devil. It tells you what to write in your confession." He slams down a pen and paper on the table. "You'll stay in solitary until you write it."

He goes to the doorway and turns around. He says, smiling, "Enjoy your ten fingers." Then he steps into the hall.

A terror chill shoots down my neck to my toes. *What does he mean about my fingers?*

My ears follow his tapping steps. Two guards take my arms. We pass my cell. I hold my breath as they bring me to another block of the prison. I stand before a steel door. They push me inside and it shuts tight.

It's darker than a moonless night. I can't even see shapes as I edge one foot forward, then the other. The smell is familiar: the metallic scent of blood, damp stone, and shit. On trembling legs, I lower myself into a sitting position, resting my back against the wall. I hug my knees to me and rock and breathe. My eyes are wide as portholes and totally blind.

After several minutes, I stand. I need to find the bucket. With one hand on the cement wall, I walk bent at the waist, searching with hands and feet.

No bucket. *No bucket! Am I supposed to sit in my own piss and shit? For God knows how long?* Finally I shuffle to a corner and piss on the floor. I walk along the wall to the next corner, then the next one, and sit.

After what seems to be hours, I drop into a dreamless sleep.

When I awake, Emma's face comes to me. I'm so sad. As if a hand were squeezing my throat hard.

I whisper prayers and hear them echo back at me. Empty.

Emma is before me, and her white skin glows from her collarbones up to the waves of her russet hair. I ache to touch her, to feel her soft yielding curves beneath my fingers, to smell her, lose myself in the wildness of her. When we lay together, a fierceness burned in her. It flushed her skin and she gave herself to it, pouring her body, her mouth, the silk of her hair, over every inch of me. She would bite my flesh, gently at first, then harder, moving to the tender flesh of my stomach, down to the inside of my thighs, until I could bear the exquisite pain no longer. Then I would pin her beneath me and watch her mouth curve upward as I took possession of her, hearing her cries blend with mine.

My body pulses with the thought of her, even in this cell. It is ready to take her this minute. I think of whether to relieve my own desires, but a sob shakes me. I can't. It hurts too much to know that I may never possess her again.

How am I going to make it in the dark? How long will I be in here?

Time passes so slowly. Up to now, I've been able to keep track of the days, and I know it's mid-October, so I've been here for a month. But not being able to tell day from night will make me lose track of that, something that has been a lifeline to me. *Middle of October, 1954,* I recite again and again to the darkness before me.

At other times, memories come like a picture show in the blackness.

Mum telling me about another of Emma's scrapes. "Your sister had an altercation at school. Would you please talk with her?"

An *altercation*. Of course it was her mouth that got her into trouble.

"Perhaps you could tell your sister that slugging a little boy is not the done thing?"

"Oh, certainly, Mum," I'd say, secretly rubbing my hands together in anticipation of hearing what sassy thing she'd said to start the argument.

In my junior year, I began to feel strange and quiet around her. On Valentine's Day, she received three red carnations from a boy in her class. I started feeling crazy.

"Where did those come from?" I asked, my voice sounding snide.

"From one Tim Redfield," she pronounced distinctly. She was at the kitchen sink, cutting the stems with a paring knife on the bare counter. I stood beside her thinking, *Mum would have a fit.*

"He's an idiot," I mumbled.

"Oh, does this concern you?"

I was uneasy. "You know he's an idiot, don't you?"

Then she turned to me with a smile I couldn't read and asked, "Would *you* like one?" Her jade eyes were so inviting. I wondered whether she was being obnoxious, but then she took one of the red blooms and put it against the side of my neck.

I felt it, the petals and the green light of her eyes, down to my nether regions and beyond, and I struggled to keep my breath steady.

She looked into my eyes, her brows lifting just slightly. A question in her eyes. I didn't know what to do. I wanted a flower, but . . . what I really wanted, so much I could taste it, was *her.*

In the shadows of the cell, I touch my neck. I can almost feel the petals, cool like her luminous skin.

"I'll wrestle you for it," I'd said back then, hearing the tremble in my voice, and frustrated at my lack of nerve to declare myself.

"Geebs, we're a little old for that. Just take it." She had a faint smile on her face.

She took it wrong. Didn't get that I'd do almost anything just to touch her. I wasn't sure what she meant by it, but I took it. At the end of the week, I pressed it into my chemistry textbook and shoved the book behind all the others on my shelf.

I first looked into Emma's green eyes when I was ten and she was an eight-year-old in braids. We lay spread-eagled on the floor of my parents' parlor, head to head, separated by a scattering of marbles between us. From the moment she saw my set of marbles (they were initially *all* mine), her face flushed with her desire for more and more of them. She proceeded, with malice and wickedness, to win the better part of my marble collection. It was humiliating to be outshone by someone younger than me, and who ever heard of girls playing marbles anyway?

During Emma's stays, I discovered more of her surprising quirks. No doubt she'd developed these as a consequence of having no playmates or siblings, and, as my mother put it, "no feminine hand to guide her." One day she showed me what could only be described as a set of facial gymnastics. She could wiggle her ears, and dammit, I couldn't! She could raise first one eyebrow to a quizzical height, then the other, alternating back and forth. It was maddening! I spent many harried nights lying in bed twisting my face this way and that, but I simply could not imitate the fantastic contortions of her face. My brows only worked in complete sync with one another. Up, down. Up, down. The merely fascinating led to the bizarre when I saw her crossing the left eye and then the right, moving each eye independently. I approached her each day after school wondering what humiliation I might suffer, but always finding at the end of the day that we'd done something I'd never tried before. My school chums were insulted when I'd scurry home to be with my eight-year-old friend who was *only a girl after all*. A cute spitfire of a girl, I might have added, and a spring breeze blown into the musty closet of my sheltered life.

Thinking about her makes me miss her more. Her proud, full forehead that looks smaller when she's afraid. But I can't stop. I'm so lonely I fold myself down against the wall and escape into sleep.

Emma

My first mission upon arriving in Kathmandu was to reach the American embassy and start them searching for Gerald. So, after sleeping like the dead, I wiped the sleep out of my eyes and scrubbed off the travel grime in the one bathroom we all shared at Tinle and Pema's house. As I dressed in a skirt kindly provided by Pema, I could hear Dorje preparing for a similar errand this morning. He was heading for the Chinese embassy to begin the search for Samten. He gave me a sad smile with his brilliant teeth as he headed out the door.

I set off on my swollen pregnant woman's feet toward the embassy. The walk was a sad reminder of the time I'd spent here with Gerald before we'd ever ventured into Tibet. We'd been here for months polishing our Tibetan. We'd gotten used to Nepali ways, their fatalistic sense that whatever will happen is just going to happen, so you might as well sit and have some tea and maybe even laugh about it. In them was none of the hard-driving need to master the world I'm so used to seeing in my own countrymen. Just a friendly *"Namaste!"* with a bow attached and hands pressed together at the chest, the throwing of trash out the window because everybody did it, shopkeepers tossing water into the street to cut the dust on the crumbling roads, and the grinding sense of impotence that the country's poverty would ever change, that the beggars would ever be fed.

Now I was here alone, seeing the filthy hand of a child stretched out to me for alms as I walked. I felt vulnerable, and I worried my ankles would swell more from all the walking. After an hour and a half, I pulled open the heavy door of the embassy.

The air smelled different inside, devoid of all the musky scents of bodies and spices and dirt I'd been inhaling for the past several months. Antiseptic, like cleaning agents. It shocked my nose, but calmed me as a reminder of the superefficiency with which my country would set this situation right. A clerk took down my information. I sat and sat in the waiting room, occasionally grabbing fistfuls of my hair and pulling it to relieve my frustration. After doing that and resting my hands on my belly for two hours, I saw the clerk come back to the waiting area.

"Mrs. Kittredge? You'll see Mr. Bausman—he'll be handling your case."

I stood up and grabbed my purse, ready to run into his office and spill my story.

"Oh, you'll have to come back in a week. He's on vacation until first November."

I wanted to scream, but I said through tight lips, "My husband may be in a Chinese labor camp. When someone's standing before a firing squad, you don't sit around until so-and-so gets back to save them, because they might be *dead*."

"I'm sorry," the clark said airily. "The appropriate forms have been filed, but we cannot proceed without Mr. Bausman." He turned around and walked back to his desk, leaving me standing like a clenched fist. I glared at him. He hid behind the piles of paperwork on his desk.

So much for efficiency. I stomped past his desk and out of the office. *Son of a bitch.*

Unconsciously I felt my belly. *Okay, wait. It can't be good for the baby to hear—or sense—that I'm cussing. I'll pray instead. All right, God. Give me patience, now, goddammit!*

Dorje

When Dawa is especially angry, he becomes quiet. You notice this because it is one of the only times he is quiet, except when he is meditating. When Dawa was quiet for many days this week, I watched him to see whom he might be angry with, but I saw nothing.

So I invited him to walk to Boudhanath Stupa, hoping he would tell me something. It was a warm day, which was strange. In my country we would have been beginning our months of the coldest nights of the year, when the windows become white with frost. But now, as we walked toward the *stupa,* the air was mild on my skin. First Dawa and I did a *kora* around the giant white shrine, turning the prayer wheels at its base as we walked. Doing this always brought me warm feelings of home, seeing the women with bright silk blouses under their *chuba*s, and everybody walking around in the same direction, like fish pushed by the water of a clear river. After completing our *kora,* we walked near the shops surrounding the *stupa.* Dawa still wore his monk's robes, but I do not think he liked to wear them anymore. He adjusted the material around his shoulders with annoyance.

I asked, "Dawa, are you upset?"

He took a deep breath, then sighed. "Oh, Pa-la!, I can't hide my worries from you, no matter what I do! I've even been trying to stay by myself, so that you won't also have a heavy load in your mind, like I do."

"Yes, but I see these things." Then I waited to see what he would say.

"I'm impatient. *So* impatient." He hissed the word as if he were cutting it with a knife. Then he stopped in his place. He led us over to a stone wall, and we sat down to lean our backs against it.

"I want things to be different. I can't accept that the world is becoming a place that feels wrong. Our country, and everything we've always believed, is dissolving, like the salt in your tea. Everything they taught me at the monastery, I don't know if it's right anymore. The oldest lama at my monastery, everyone there loves him, he's so gentle and he has a strong mind. Before you came to the monastery, I went to tell him my worries about the communists. I asked him, should I try to commit myself even stronger to my studies as a monk, or should I think about escaping, out of Tibet?"

Dawa looked at me. "Do you know what he said, Pa-la? He told me that our ways have been the same for hundreds of years, and we have learned to trust that if we stay in our monasteries, recite prayers, and make sacrifices to the gods, the Chinese cannot harm us. But perhaps this time it is different. Then he said that each man must make the decision for himself, what is right for him to do, to stay in Tibet or try to escape."

Dawa's words became quiet whispers. "I couldn't believe it, Pa-la! Everyone goes to Lama Tsethar for advice, and he *always* knows the answer. That night, I had a terrifying vision in my sleep that I was walking, but I didn't know where I was going. My only thought was to find the monastery. If I could find it, I would feel safe again. In the distance I saw it, so I ran as fast as my feet would take me. But when I got there, it was a ruin. The Chinese had exploded it with things they dropped from the air above.

The roof was gone. I ran inside to the place where Lama Tsethar had his quarters and found him lying on his mattress. There was a large stain of blood on the mattress, like a perfect mandala around his body, the same color as his robes. His mouth and his eyes were open, but when I put my head to his chest, it was silent. Then I woke up. This was the dream I had two days before your arrival, and when you got there, I was ready to go."

"So this dream made you decide to come with us?" I asked.

"Not only this dream. When I awoke, I couldn't erase the dream from my thoughts, as if it was a vision of what is to come in our country. I talked to one of the other monks, and he had heard reports that the communists want to get rid of the monks especially, in Tibet. So then I felt that my dream was a warning."

"Are you still afraid, even here?" I asked.

"I am, but not for myself. Every day I wonder whether the communists have reached my monastery yet. Mother doesn't understand this—she's so angry, thinking I've committed a great error. But even someone as wise as Lama Tsethar *did not know what I should do*—how can Mother be so sure? I didn't steal away in the dark! Before I left, Lama Tsethar put his hands on my forehead, blessed me on my journey, told me to take all of the spiritual practices I have learned, to guard them in my heart and teach them to others, so that even if monasteries are destroyed, these practices will never be lost. I feel it's my karma to be in this place, but I don't know if I'm still a holy man."

The noise of hundreds of people was around the *stupa,* but while my son spoke, I heard nothing but his voice. It was full and smooth like tea, and I felt so much love for him.

When we first brought him to the monastery, I doubted he could be a monk. I never spoke these things to Rinchen or Lama Norbu because they said it was his destiny to be a lama. But he was not serious or disciplined to sit still even long enough to finish his dinner! How could he sit in meditation day after day and receive instruction from the older lamas?

But today, I could see how wise he had become! His vision was as wide as the sky. I sat beside him helplessly. Finally I whispered to him, "You *are* a holy man, Dawa. You feel the suffering of all sentient beings."

"Thank you, Pa-la," he said, looking down, and his eyes were shiny with tears.

I had no wisdom for him because everything he had told me was the truth.

Gerald

I look around me, hear skittering noises, invisible in the pitch dark that surrounds me at night in my solitary cell. The darkness is so gloomy it feels solid, like oak doors on every side. At times it's suffocating, but then the skittering of some tiny creature penetrates the solid, and I feel it dissolve into cold air. Other times, I welcome it, the cloak the night gives me—it lets me pray on my knees and commune with my God in safety, free from the judging eyes of the guards, who pronounce that "religion is delusion."

I'm so lonely. I miss Tenzin and I worry about Lobsang's tender young soul.

These skittering sounds, caused by the creeping of some creature across the damp stones of my cell, bring me comfort. They assure me that another being lives purposefully, even in this place that is so without purpose for me. My dreams for my life have faded into shadows, but even so, a little form, perhaps an ant, scavenges for his family. He strides in a grand mission through this wasteland. I imagine him and fancy that I walk with him, in a small form of myself, following his mincing steps, and watching from behind as he saws at a piece of dough from my dumpling with his steely jaws, then lifts the booty onto his shoulders. He teeters this way and that with his burden, then marches on.

Something good is happening right here in my cell, I tell myself. With this table scrap I've given, he will feed sons, daughters, cousins, aunts, and uncles. *Do such filial relationships even exist in an anthill?*

Meanwhile, my imagined companion leaves, heading for home. He's small enough to wedge his shoulders through the cracks between cinder blocks in the walls. This is no prison to him. He can go home, and I'm certain at times our roles were reversed, and then I have a boyhood memory, one that stings now, of neighborhood boys whose friendship I tried to win by doing wicked things that little boys will do. I see in my mind's eye an anthill, much like the home to which my ant companion is now returning, and I see myself and my boyhood chums stamping our feet in an orgy of power, killing as many of those small creatures as our feet could. I smell the minty scent of paste, lifted from our homeroom, and watch as we poke a Popsicle stick smeared with paste into the opening of the anthill. We spoon it into the mound from the plastic tub. That day we collapsed its tunnel walls and stopped them up with paste, turning the anthill into a prison. Surely, that day, some ant was in much my same predicament, trapped inside walls.

Then I notice how time has passed and wonder whether my mind doodlings serve any purpose. Will I grow wiser here in the dimness, or will I lose my mind? To ground myself, I place my hands on the cold stone beneath me. I get an image of myself leaving the prison, stooped and graying with my eyes in a perpetual squint against the glare of reality. Horrifying.

No day or night to tell me how much time has passed, but I've learned to figure it by the tray they bring once a day. The scrape of the tray slot opening, then the tray entering the cell. I eat the doughy dumplings (all dough), slurp the broth, then spend the next hour using the calories I've taken in reciting the date, the year.

November 1, 1954, which means I've been in this prison for approximately six weeks.

How long? Or maybe—forever? I shake my head to clear it, wiping my face with my filthy hands. But my head feels like a Christmas globe, filled with water and plastic speckles of snow. No matter how much I shake it, the contents stay the same; they simply float down to a new place.

Emma

The first day of November came, after what seemed like an eternity. As I had no desire to squirm my way through the appointment, I went early to use the ladies' room, as all pregnant women do. Mr. Bausman greeted me in the waiting area at nine o'clock. I was astounded. He looked so much like Gerald that I wanted to reach up to his tall shoulders and squeeze him to me. But I looked at him again, saw he wore glasses and was as tall as my husband, but with very proper posture. Gerald's shoulders stooped a bit, as though he were bending over to listen to you, which I loved. All these thoughts swirled in my mind as Mr. Bausman led me to his office.

"Now let's get right down to it, Mrs. Kittredge," he said as I sat down. "I've looked over the file. Now can you tell me how it was that your husband disappeared?"

He didn't know this already? "He was captured by the Chinese."

"You saw them take him?"

"No, but a neighbor did." It was *so* hard to keep the contempt from my voice.

"So you believe he was taken by the Chinese."

"The neighbor *saw* the Chinese take him." *Here we go again. What, do you have yak dung for brains?*

"Oh. Let me get this down."

Yeah, you do that. He scratched out notes on a piece of scrap paper. At least ten separate piles of paper rested on his desk, with notes on all of them. A marble stand had slots for two pens. The right slot was empty, and the left held a small, faded American flag tacked to a broken wooden stick. "So, what's the next step?" I asked impatiently.

"Hmm?"

"When do you send in the commandos?" I tried to make it sound like a joke, but it didn't work.

He gave a slight smile, stopping when he saw my serious expression. He took off his plastic-rimmed glasses, pulled out a shirttail, and rubbed the lenses. "Not so fast, Mrs. Kittredge. Let me ask you . . . any chance he simply walked away?"

I didn't understand the question. "What?"

"You know, sometimes people disappear, and we find out later"—his hands traced a large arc in the air—"they wanted to— they made themselves disappear."

I jammed my mouth shut. If I'd opened it, his head would have been in my jaws. My eyes bulged and my head shook quickly. I squeezed the armrests on my chair, silently praying. *God help me, or I am going to get violent, and I need this guy's help.*

"Oh. Well." He leaned back in his chair, grabbed his suspenders. "Well, we'll study the situation and determine, based on our policy, what the best course of action is."

"Could you possibly be any more specific?" A thick lacing of sarcasm was in my tone. "What policy?"

"With other countries, we use our policy to determine how we proceed, but with Tibet"—he shrugged—"there isn't any official policy."

"With all due respect for the embassy's experience in these matters, what I *need* to hear, given that my husband may be being *tortured,* is that the United States will do everything in its power to rescue him."

"Oh. And of course, the United States *will* do everything in its power to rescue him."

Convincing, to quote me my own words. Lord, I'm going to tear him limb from limb.

"You see," he mused, "with Tibet these days, it's really quite tricky. Who's in charge? China? Tibet? And really, it hasn't come up, because there aren't any Americans over there. We've been trying to appear neutral. So, we have no official policy about Tibet."

"Do you perhaps have a policy about protecting the lives of American citizens?"

"Of course." His arms went broad again. "We will do some checking around, we'll sniff this man out . . . one way or another," he said with little conviction. "But let me just say, you might want to go to the Chinese embassy, see if they'll help you."

I couldn't believe it. He wanted me, as a private citizen, to talk to Chinese-embassy officials? "Won't *you* be contacting them?"

"Well, we've got a hands-off approach with China right now. See how things play out, strategically. Off the record, I'm just telling you that you should go yourself."

"A hands-off approach when there's an American citizen who's been abducted? What the hell good is that?"

He sat blinking. I was reminded that to restore his dignity, he could crush me. Or worse, ignore me. Then I felt a strange sensation. A burning in the pants, as Quakers called it. I was supposed to make nice and get out of here, now. *Is that you, God, telling me this?*

I stood up abruptly. "Thank you very much. I appreciate your time," I said mechanically. "When can I check back with you, to see how the search is coming?"

He blinked again, apparently surprised by my swift change of course. "Hmmm. I'd say . . . give it a few weeks. No—make that three weeks."

I've been walking around the house singing! I got a call from Everett Kingsley. He was one of the first people I'd contacted upon arriving back in Kathmandu because he was one of my father's associates, and Gerald and I had spent time with him here as we were preparing for our trek into Tibet. He lives on the outskirts of town, having retired from his post as a British diplomat a few years ago. His voice over the phone was warm and excited. "Good morning, Em. I've had an inspiration. We can try to locate Gerald by radio."

"What? How?"

"I must confess I'm a bit ignorant about the question of radios. But a few years back there was a dreadful story about the Chinese taking two Englishmen prisoner in Tibet. They'd been hired on by the Tibetan government to establish two radio stations there. I don't know if the system is still operational with the Chinese taking over, but if it is, perhaps we could connect to someone who can look for him there."

"My God, that's brilliant! Do you think it would work?"

"It's certainly worth a try. If we could just find someone to send a message, perhaps it would be picked up on the other end in Tibet. I'll make some inquiries."

"I am in awe of your mind, Kingsley. Thank you."

"I'll get right on it."

As I hung up the phone, my jaw hung open. Who would have guessed they'd have radios in a place like Tibet?

Dorje

After Dawa and I returned from Boudhanath, I decided to talk with Rinchen again about our son. I have to talk to her a special way during difficult times or she will not listen.

I tried to explain to her what our son had said about even Lama Tsethar being unsure what to do.

She answered loudly, "Don't tell me even the lamas are confused now! The whole world is something I can't understand! How many pilgrimages have I made, Dorje? Every meal I cook, I spend in prayer for my family. But now brothers disappear, we're forced to leave our home"—her voice made choking sounds of crying—"and my son goes against his destiny, thinking he is the best judge of what the gods want!"

"Rinchen, you raise your voice like you are angry, but I know you are just afraid. And I am afraid too," I said in a voice so quiet.

"Is there some error we have made to bring this to our lives?"

"Nobody seems to know."

Then her expression changed to disbelief, as if a new thought had come to her. "I don't understand, why did this lama not try to divine an answer to Dawa's question? How could he let Dawa go without knowing what is the right path?" Her eyes pushed out against her eyelids.

I shrugged my shoulders. Now she seemed angry at Lama Tsethar, but at least she was not upset with Dawa anymore. Relief came to me. I told her, "Please, be gentle with him. He's very worried, and he knows how angry you are."

She sighed with frustration. "I am his mother. I will talk with him."

Everyone in the family has been affected by our leaving Tibet, even Champa. He usually keeps us laughing through the day. Yesterday, I saw him sitting on Rinchen's lap. Although he is seven years old and big for her lap, he looked like a small, sad boy. He asked, "When are we going home?"

Then Rinchen, who always wears the same face, started to cry. To hide this, she turned away from him, but he twisted around to get a look at her face and exclaimed, "Ma! You're crying!"

Her voice was flat like glass. "No."

But Champa knew. He leaned back onto her chest, as if he did not know what to do. The air is heavy in this house with everyone missing home.

The only happiness we have is from a blessing we have received: Rinchen is pregnant. Aunt Pema cleans house and cooks with special vigor because she is excited about the little one. Later today, Rinchen will tell Emma about this blessing. I can already hear my wife saying to Emma, "You see, I told you our children will play together! Now you will know that I am always right."

My wife is *not* always right, but I will certainly not be the one to correct her!

Gerald

The voice of my body is running on a rough trail. Like a wash-board. I'm clinging to the edges of this raft I'm on. When I woke up—day or night, who knows?—webs had been spun across my eyes by some malevolent spider. Crusty eyelashes. Or was it from crying? I scratched at my eyes. Rubbed away the crust.

Sleep is gone. A lifetime ago. No comfort there. Last night Chairman Mao came to visit. He brought two things with him. A pair of pliers and my wife. He opened her mouth and gripped her front tooth with the pliers.

"Your confession!" He grinned. "Now." He knew he had me.

I went to my knees. My legs shook, but Emma was calm. So oddly calm, with warm tears on her luminous cheeks. I knelt before her and caught one of her salty tears in my mouth. My tongue held it as if it were her heart. Then I took off my clothes. I folded them sadly and handed them to the Chairman.

"I confess. Take my flesh. Eat it. Set her free." I was on my knees before him now. Putting my arms around his legs and holding them tight. *Please.*

Then they were gone. I thought he would leave her here, but

he let her go, I guess. Someone screamed. Scratching came from the cell next to me—nails on brick. Blood is on the wall, but my eyes are closed. Was it me? Scratching?

I don't know whether she was here. I hate that. For hours I've been trying to reason it out. Would they bring her here? How did they know she was my wife?

She didn't do it. I did. Let her go.

My brain is eating itself as fuel. My trousers are falling off my hips. An insect voice is in my head. Buzzing. They're inside my head. They keep me awake. In the backyard there were cicadas— in the summer—and they buzzed when the cars drove by. They're nesting up in my head now. They keep me company while they eat. I laughed this morning when one told me a joke. It hurt my belly, and my hip bones stuck into my arms when I laughed. It became a hurting, a crying feel. My ribs shook, my back bones rattled against the wall behind me while I laughed.

I'm going to do it. Tell them about what I did. It was wrong.

I called out to them and pounded my knuckles on the door. They opened it, and in the Light I saw the face of God. Blinded. *It hurt so much, Lord. Help me do the right thing.*

Then I walked, felt a hand on my arm. It tugged me. Then two hands pushed me into a chair. I was lost, but now was found. The steel of the chair under my thighs. I curled up in it. *Please be nice, chair. I will be good.*

The man with the cane came in. He smiled. His nose flared. The chair seemed to be rocking. It was me rocking. I crawled down from the chair. Looked up at his black eyes. My body trembled like a moving train.

I had to confess. "I did it. I killed them, all of them! I liked it. Their bodies were small and frail, and I counted them." *I'm so grateful he's giving me a chance. Thank God.*

He looked down at me. A frown. "Who? Who did you kill? The workers? Your servants? What did you do to them?"

"All of them. *I* did it. I was evil."

"How many did you kill?"

"There were hundreds, thousands, of them. The entire ant colony." I was crying, on my knees. Holding his legs, as I did the Chairman's.

"What? You're confessing to killing *insects*?"

He hit me in the face with his cane. I flew back. The wall hit my head.

Then the pressing, the red rage. Scorching flames pressing inside my skull. Wanting out. Wanting to burn his flesh.

"This man is insane! Take him back," he spat out the words.

The hands on my arms. Scuff of my heels dragging. A door shut behind me.

An old man in red robes. *I know him.* He put his arms around me. I fell asleep.

There's more food here in my old cell. The guards love Tenzin, so they bring him extra portions, and he shares with me and Lobsang. I'm so grateful I cry when they bring it. By my just looking at Tenzin and Lobsang, the tears well up. It's pathetic to be grateful in a cell that reeks of shit, but I am deeply grateful to be back with them. My family.

Even when I was in solitary, I worried over Lobsang as if he were my son, and even now the hollows in his face fill me with dread, like seeing a china cup with cracks running through it. He's gotten dysentery. After he eats, cramps rack his body and he lies moaning, so now he doesn't want to eat. Tenzin feeds him as if he were a small child. As sad as it is to see the shape my friends are in, I need to be here with them because it matters to them whether I live or die. It does me good to hold Lobsang as Tenzin feeds him, and to serve God in the only way I can, by caring for these two men.

I cannot see myself, how I look now. I wonder if anything is left of the things Em has told me she loves about me. She'd wax on about flawless skin, and the softness of my curly hair, which now feels like straw to my fingers. My skin falls off in large flakes.

Other times my mind wanders to Dorje, remembering the grace with which he carried himself, the hopefulness of his broad chest—a chest that took in life as large gulps of air, undaunted by life's sorrows, anticipating joy and sadness with equanimity.

When I was in my solitary cell, I couldn't sleep, but now I can get at least *some* sleep. It depends on the nightmares and the night sounds. When the nightmares visit me, Tenzin puts his arms around me while I sleep. I would never have let a man comfort me in the past. But now it's like having a father with me. He has tied 108 knots in a piece of string to help him recite his prayers. No matter what he's doing, digging ditches or being interrogated, he prays. Seeing him again was a shock. The bones in his arms stick out. His fingers tremble more than before as he prays from knot to knot.

He told me how I was right after I got out of solitary. "There was a demon inside you when they brought you back. Your mind did not belong to you. I was worried."

"I was starving and so lonely in that cell. Don't ever let them send you there, Tenzin."

"They're losing patience with this old monk. Don't worry. I'm ready to pass on when it's time. When that day comes, I'll recite prayers to help me on my journey through the *bardo*—the place in between—and then my soul will be reborn."

"Do you want to die?" My voice shook.

"Wanting only brings suffering. If I die, it's my time. If I don't, I must accept more time here."

"I want to live so much. I want to see my wife. I want everything. Sometimes I even want"—I can hardly say it to this holy man—"revenge. I can't stop wanting."

He smiled gently at me and laughed. "If I were younger, I would want like you do."

"You *must* want to leave here, with how they treat you." I

looked at his fingernails. They were swollen and crusted with blood.

"Yes, they're still putting bamboo under my fingernails," he answered when he saw me looking at them. "My fingers would like to leave this place," he mumbled, smiling.

"How can you stand it?" I shuddered. "How can you not want to kill them? I don't even know how you're surviving. I'm still young, but even I can't live on lumps of dough and watery soup."

"There's a lama secret you should learn. I have been trying to teach Lobsang too. When there is no food, you must eat the air."

"What?" I was certain I'd misunderstood him.

"Yes. It feeds your body if you drink it."

"Drink? What do I drink?"

"When there is not a lot of food, you must eat the air."

"How do you do that?"

"You pull the air into your body, down far into your stomach when you breathe."

An impatient sigh escaped me. I wanted blood, and he wanted to teach me how to eat air. But I owed him so much that I did as he asked. Then he told me, "Hold it there, all the air, and now let it go out your mouth." He waited for me to exhale. "Now keep going."

He watched me breathe down deep, holding the inhaled breaths so that my body could "feast" on them. After several minutes of this breathing, my hands throbbed with warmth. My anger settled, didn't pulse so hotly. There was more space inside me.

~

I stand in the field, my hands wrapped around the neck of my shovel. I have the shovel in a lethal grip. A dream hangs over me from last night.

He has his hand on my bottom lip, pulling it until it's tearing away from my gums. With his other hand, he has hold of my hair. He's pulling my head back with it. I've got one hand on his, the one he's using to pull my lip. I'm prying his index finger loose, bending it back. There's a pop. He loses his balance momentarily. That's all I need to rush him, push him back toward the cinder-block wall. I hear the crack of his skull against the wall—the bizarre sound makes me think of a coconut. A seam of red forms in his hair. It thickens and darkens to the color of a wet brick. Then an ecstasy swells in my chest: I've done it! I've rid myself of him. Satisfaction like molten tar runs through my veins. It flows deep into my belly. I sever his head, throw it onto the dirt. My fists pummel that serpent face until it's swollen blue. Then I grind his skull beneath my boots.

When I awoke from the dream this morning, my hands were balled into fists. My jaw ached and the base of my head throbbed. But my body was revved with sadistic pleasure. A glow of carnage; a violence that lifted me like a sweeping joy. I still wanted his blood, to hear the crack of that skull, to feel the jolt of it in my hands.

I shoved it into a corner of my mind then. But now as I stand in the field, the hands around my shovel grip Comrade Han's neck.

I feel sick. *Dear God, what is happening to me? Love your enemies, pray for those who persecute you.*

The scabs have dried and fallen off my wrists, but some marks will stay forever. My body remembers what he did. The ropes around my hands, the twisting, searing, snapping feel as my shoulders popped.

What was it like to have a peaceful mind without a snake sliding through it? To feel love? Tenderness? To give my Emma caresses? To feel I could show my face in the world? These days, I can't even imagine it.

Emma

I asked Dorje to babysit me today while I went to see Mr. Yuan, the Chinese ambassador to Nepal. Dorje gave me his customary wide grin as he said yes. I wondered how he could smile like that, with such brightness. He'd been to the Chinese embassy before, filing papers to find Samten. I asked him to come along and keep me in line, what with my temper and my hormones. In hindsight, I don't think he was up to the job.

Mr. Yuan was about my age with cropped black hair. He wore a fashionable Western suit and a poker face. He opened the drawer of his desk and extracted a legal pad. My heart leaped with hope that finally someone was going to get the details down and start the search.

"When was the last time you saw your husband?"

"It was September fifteenth, on the day they took him away."

"And when did you enter Tibet?"

"Umm . . . five months prior to that date, in May."

"May I see your passports?"

"Yes, of course. This is mine, and here is my husband's."

He opened them slowly and fingered them in a way I didn't

like, with skepticism and a frown on his face. "There is nothing about Tibet on these documents."

I blinked, then put on my best patient voice. "Yes, and there wouldn't be, would there? They don't give visas, as you know."

"So you are saying you and your husband entered Tibet *illegally?*"

Uh-oh. I hadn't anticipated this line of questioning. I'd been so certain of the righteousness of my case that I hadn't considered someone else could see it any other way. I told him, "There's no way of entering legally, but we got permission to be in Shigatse once we arrived."

"Do you enter a man's house and ask his permission afterwards?" He raised his eyebrows like a principal questioning a disobedient child.

"We got permission from the *garpon* of the province."

"And you have that permit with you?"

"Well, no. Things don't work that way there. It was a verbal permit."

He nodded knowingly. "So you and your husband invaded a province of China illegally, your husband was then arrested, and now you're asking for my help to save him?"

"My husband was *not* arrested. He was—captured, like a prisoner of war!"

"Except that the United States and China are not at war, are they, madam?" Triumph was in his voice.

I looked at Dorje. His disapproval of my approach was all over his face. His normally erect posture was a bit hunched.

"The People's Liberation Army is there to help Tibetans, especially to protect them from foreigners who insist on crashing their borders. Perhaps your husband started an altercation with a soldier or mistreated the Tibetans in some way? Does he have a temper?"

"My husband is a pacifist!" I heard that I was raising my voice, heard how ridiculous it was to be yelling at him about being a pacifist.

A clerk opened the door and directed a disdainful glance at me. Mr. Yuan wore the expression of an indulgent parent and instructed me, "I would ask you, madam, to please keep your voice at an appropriate level." The clerk closed the door.

I mumbled an apology and took a deep breath. Dorje's alarmed face told me I'd been walking in a blizzard without any boots on. He'd begun fingering his *mani* beads in earnest while I was talking. I closed my eyes and thought of Genevieve, trying to muster her peaceful ways in myself. *God, I'm just not . . . able to do this. You have to do this for me. I'm completely bungling this, and it could cost my husband his life.*

"So then, you believe that your husband was taken by soldiers out of sheer . . . malice?"

"I'm sorry for my impatience earlier, Mr. Yuan. I know this may sound strange, but I think a Chinese soldier had followed us home the day before."

"Did you see this soldier following you?"

"No, I just had a feeling." I looked him in the eye. "You know when you have a feeling?"

Silence. One eyebrow lifted as he looked at me. He continued, "Above all, you have no proof that your husband ever entered Tibet, and so this story sounds more like American anticommunist propaganda than a legitimate claim."

He didn't care. He wasn't going to do anything. Something snapped inside me, fast and tight like a crocodile's jaws. Some other person within me emerged. I stood up, then went down on my knees. My voice was deadly quiet and sincere. "Mr. Yuan, I'm here for the child I'm carrying, who may *never* see its father." My face quivered, and tears fell down my cheeks. "I'm not a communist, not a capitalist, just a woman. I don't know if you have any children of your own, or a wife, but when you go home tonight, think of them tucked safely in your house, and what you would do if you didn't know whether they were dead or alive."

I sat down and looked at my lap. After a moment of silence, I lifted my gaze to Mr. Yuan, and he didn't look like a stone, quite, anymore. He studied me, looking troubled.

Finally, Dorje broke the silence. "Mr. Ambassador, please do not take offense," the mellifluous voice soothed. "Perhaps you understand . . . that women, when they are with child"—he placed his hands on his stomach—"they are very emotional."

"I see that," muttered Mr. Yuan without taking his eyes away from me.

Dorje stood and bowed. "We appreciate your time and assistance." He helped me up from my chair.

The atmosphere in the room changed, and the ambassador's tone became conciliatory. "I would like to be of help, Mrs. Kittredge. Before you go, let me say one thing. I think it is important that you *consider your story very carefully.* That is the only way I can help you." He pronounced the words slowly, looking from me to Dorje and back to me.

Then Dorje glanced at me with a look that pleaded, *Let's go.* I walked out without seeing. As we left the building, Dorje handed me my purse, and I realized I had left it in the office.

We headed home on foot. I went over and over the interview, and the more I thought about it, the more hopeless and furious I became.

"Dorje, my religion asks me not to hate people, but I despise that man enough to wish him dead." A tremor was in my voice and tears stung my eyes.

"Emma. You misunderstand," he said, his voice patient. "He *was* trying to help you. He was telling you how your case will be seen by the Chinese government, with no proof, only a set of accusations that make them lose face. And"—Dorje lowered his velvety voice—"I could feel he was afraid."

"You say the strangest things sometimes," I muttered, irritated and hopeless.

Dorje stopped me by grabbing my arm. We stood in the street, and I felt conspicuous. "Emma, you must try to understand Mr.

Yuan." I'd never heard this sharpness in Dorje's voice before. "The Chinese do not say things the way Americans do. If they want you to do something, they do not tell you to do it. They say it in a soft, polite way, as he did at the end of the meeting. It was a suggestion that you change your story. But he did not *tell* you to do it. That is not the Chinese way."

"I don't care if they have some polite way of speaking while they imprison my husband! I *hate* the Chinese—do you understand me?"

He lowered his eyes and squinted as if he was in pain. Finally he said, "Emma, I *am* Chinese." Then he quietly tucked his hands into his *chuba*.

Oh, God, pull my foot out of my mouth, please. "Dorje, I'm *so* sorry. I'm not in my right mind. You and Rinchen and Champa, and now Dawa, you're my family. I love you all."

"I know this, Emma." He nodded, but pain was still in his brown eyes.

I was deeply ashamed, but I still found myself building a little corner for Dorje. He was a good Chinese person, but I despised the rest of them. I asked, "Any news on Samten?"

"No." He stared down at his feet.

~

I'm a fly on its back with one wing, buzzing around and around in little black circles, helpless since seeing Mr. Yuan. But there is hope. Last night Kingsley telephoned me at Pema's house.

"Emma. Kingsley here. I've got news. I've found a Tibetan fellow named Sangye who lives here in Nepal, in Pokhara, and he was trained as a radio operator by the Brits when they were running radio stations for the Tibetan government. When the Chinese came, they took him and the Brits as prisoners of war, but Sangye escaped. He doesn't know whether there's any radio equipment running in Tibet anymore, or whether the Chinese have control over it. But he said he'd transmit messages, in the off chance someone might hear them."

"But won't the Chinese hear his messages?" I asked.

"Well, yes, but he doesn't use words, you see. He'll be communicating via code. Back before the Chinese arrived, a handful of Tibetan radio operators used a specific code based on Tibetan language to transmit state secrets between Tibetan cabinet members. The Englishmen didn't even know the code. He doesn't know what became of all the radio operators. If any of them are left to hear his transmissions, they're the only ones who could decode it."

"When can he start?"

"He already has! No one has acknowledged his signal yet, but he's going to keep trying, every day."

After hanging up, I was floating on air, but with pinpricks of anxiety. I couldn't sleep.

This morning I went to the telegraph office and sent two wires.

TELEGRAPH OF NEPAL
TO GENEVIEVE RUMBLE 303 HIGH STREET MIDDLE-
TOWN CONNECTICUT UNITED STATES STOP FROM
EMMA KITTREDGE STOP KATHMANDU NEPAL STOP
GERALD IN TIBETAN PRISON STOP I AM WITH CHILD IN
KATHMANDU STOP DESPERATE SITUATION STOP I AM
WORKING TO LOCATE HIM AND GET HIS RELEASE STOP
PLEASE COME STOP

I also sent a telegram to our parents, trembling all the way through the writing of it. I heard each word the way I knew they would, as a personal indictment of all the trouble I'd caused. If not for my encouraging of Gerald's fanciful ideas about travel and flying lamas, I'm sure Geebs would have settled down as a nice family physician with a levelheaded wife who would probably have borne him three children by now.

We'd had a simple Quaker marriage ceremony. There, we didn't have to hide our exuberance. A tiny corner of me was sad that our family wouldn't join the celebration. In the months before, Genevieve had suggested we present the question of our marriage during Quaker meeting to seek clarity about it. She was the only one who knew that we'd been raised together and that we still lived under the same roof with two uneasy parents. It was no scandal to her, and she assured me that Quakers did not abide by the judgments of society, they abided by the Light. It was good to think of her now, and of the meeting clerk's gentle hands on ours as he gave us its blessing. We were married three months later in the meetinghouse. Genevieve stood up for me, and for that special day she abandoned her gray garb and wore yellow.

A little being inside me was now making swimming motions, paddling with this hand or that foot to find the comfiest spot, which was often jammed somewhere beneath my rib cage. All my reminders of this small being were invitations to hope. I'd thought I knew exactly what would happen in my life—that I'd never be a mother—but I was wrong.

Dorje

I have started a job and I am grateful. It is a blessing to go out of the house each day and have the opportunity to accumulate merit, and to be able to contribute to Tinle and Pema's household. I am working as a translator at a medical clinic in the heart of the city. The clinic has no Tibetan doctors, so the patients and the doctors cannot speak to one another without my help. I love this work because I can serve my people in an important way. Many Tibetans now arrive in Kathmandu exhausted. Many of them have nowhere to go, and all I can do is send them to the camp for refugees. But with so many Tibetans coming, this camp is becoming crowded.

Yesterday I saw a young girl, about six years old, with an infection in one of her toes. It was winter when she and her family fled Tibet, and the mountains can be quite harsh, so this girl got frostbite while she was walking the high, snowy passes with her family, fleeing from the communists. I felt sad for her, to be so young and to have to lose a part of her foot. She had big eyes, and a gap between her two front teeth that gave her a delightful smile.

I explained to her family what the doctors had to do. The

mother bent over and held her stomach and landed in a chair, as if what I had said knocked her down. The father stood up extra straight, trying to be strong, but if I had even breathed on him, he would have fallen over with grief. I told them she would still be able to walk in some way, but not with good balance as before. Finally, they calmed themselves and told their daughter what the doctors said. She cried for a few minutes, then pulled her head up and said solemnly that she was ready. I told her they would give her something to take away the pain. I held her hand during the procedure and recited prayers unceasingly to Guru Rinpoche, asking him to have compassion for her. She was so brave, lying on the table, but a tear ran down from one of her eyes.

When I meet people like this little girl, I am reminded that I should be brave also. Especially with Dawa. He seems more disturbed with each report we hear of events in Tibet. More and more of us are fleeing our country, many people are killed—and the monks, especially, the communists punish the monks more than anyone else. Perhaps the communists know the mental strength of the monks and fear it. Each time Dawa hears a report on the wireless, he paces around the room, shaking his head, making his hands into fists. He is so angry, every day he is angry.

This morning, I was pulling up weeds in Uncle Tinle's vegetable garden and Dawa was helping me. We had the wireless pointed out the window so that we could hear the world reports. As usual, the news about Tibet was bad. Dawa turned off the wireless and cried out, "I wish I had never left! What can I do here, so far away? My brothers in the monasteries are being attacked, killed, and there is nothing I can do! I should be there!"

He sat down heavily in the dirt. I came over and sat beside him.

"What would you do to soldiers with guns?" I asked.

"I would take a stand against them."

"And they would kill you."

"Perhaps I would need weapons of my own," Dawa responded quietly.

Weapons? This is my son the monk, speaking of weapons? Dawa used to save all of the insects when Rinchen cleaned the house. He would take a stick and gently lift a spider from its web, then carry it with love to the outside of the house. This is the way all children in my country are taught, to not take the life of any being. So I wondered if I had heard my son correctly. "Dawa, what did you say?"

"I said, perhaps weapons are needed," he answered, his voice deadly quiet.

"Now you do not sound like a lama. What do *you* want with weapons?"

"The communists have no respect. They force monks to take guns and shoot each other, just to make them suffer, to make the monks break their vows against killing before they die. They do unspeakable things to the nuns." He placed his hand on his heart as he spoke. "How can people like that understand anything but guns?"

I simply stared at my son.

"The communists are taking over, Pa-la. Maybe forever. Our way of life, our songs, our foods, our language and the way we live—it is disappearing, dying. Don't you see that?" Dawa was breathing faster. "We cannot allow them to do this."

"I thought you came here to receive an education. Now you are speaking of guns?" I shook my head. "I do not understand you."

He stood up, and so did I. He paced back and forth in the space between two rows of green beans. "Pa-la, I don't understand myself. Each day I change the way I think. I contemplate what is the way I should take, and I decide I should study, learn about the world. But then the reports I hear—they drive me out of my mind." He held his hands to his head. "I *must* do something. This is a problem we've never experienced. Perhaps it requires a *new* solution."

"*Killing* is your new solution? To feel you have the right to take another person's life from them? What pride you have in your heart, Dawa!" My voice was rising, but I could not stop it. "I have been trying to help your mother understand that you want to learn outside of the monastery. And even though she is a stubborn woman, she is working very hard to open her heart and her mind so she can accept it. But these ideas—I do not know where they came from!"

He was looking down at his feet. His face was red. "There are other monks who think as I do." He sounded steady, but full of feeling.

My voice was still loud. "And what would Lama Tsethar think?"

"Lama Tsethar is probably *dead* by now!" My son screamed this, then he sat down on the ground and sobbed. His whole body trembled, and I was reminded of how he cried when he was just a young boy. Back then, the sight of a tear on his cheek made me cry along with him. This is how I felt now, seeing him. I sat next to him and laid my arm across his shoulders. He turned to me, and I put both my arms around him while he cried into my *chuba*.

After a long time, he became still. Then he wiped his face with his robes. "I am sorry I shouted at you, Pa-la. It was wrong of me."

"You are still my good son, Dawa. But please, think carefully of this lifetime, and your rebirth into the next."

～

The next morning I got up off my mattress, feeling cold. It was winter, but my heart also felt chilled, as if something was not right. I walked through the house. The voices of Pema and Rinchen came from the kitchen, as they were getting started on the day's cooking. When I got to the kitchen table, I saw a piece of paper, folded over. On the outside it said, *Pa-la*.

I unfolded the paper.

Dearest Pa-la,

I'm sorry I left without saying good-bye to the family. Please ask them to forgive me, especially Mother. I'm confused, and I believe I am bringing you and Mother many troubles. It is better for me to go away at this time.

I'm going to stay with a friend and his family outside Kathmandu. It isn't far away. I still have my plan of going to university, after I complete the studies necessary for me to be accepted and find a job. My friend Ngawang is helping me prepare for my studies. He says perhaps we should go to India to study later.

Don't worry about me, Pa-la. Your words of advice stay in my heart. You and the rest of the family are in my mind, and I recite prayers for you each day. I will write to you as soon as I'm settled.

Your loving son,
Dawa

My son left without saying good-bye? He told me not to worry about him, but why did he feel he could not be with us? We could help him calm his mind and decide the right way for his life. The way he was acting *did* make me worry about him. I could no longer predict anything he would do. Now my heart felt even colder, as if someone had left the door wide open to let in icy winds.

I sat down on a cushion. Rinchen was right. The world did not make sense anymore. We lost our home, we lost the way the snowy mountains looked outside our window when the sun shone on them, and now we had lost our son too.

A certain day came to my mind, when we were in our home in Shigatse. We were gathered around the warmth of the stove, and all of us, Rinchen, Champa, and me were listening to a lama joke Dawa was telling us during a visit from the monastery. A pot of noodles was boiling, and Rinchen was tossing garlic into the pot. It smelled so full, and safe, like a thousand other times she'd cooked the same thing. I wanted to be there again. Was our home still standing? What about the yard outside, where Champa drew pictures with sticks in the dirt? Were those pictures still there? When he was a baby, Rinchen had bathed his round, little body in a small tub out in the sun of this yard. My chest was hurting, all the way up into my throat. I brought my teeth together to hold back my crying, but I could not.

Gerald

I'm ready to die. I've never wished for it before.

They took my finger.

They brought me to the infirmary, as though I were sick. The large room was packed with beds, all of them filled. I went like the docile lamb I've become in the four months I've been here. They put me in a hospital gown and took my boots and clothes. I wouldn't lie down; it would make me feel too helpless, and anyway I wasn't used to being on this side of things in an infirmary. The floor chilled my feet as I sat on the edge of the bed.

A doctor came to see me. He went through a rather deliberate drama, pretending to examine my index finger.

His hair was loose. It fell into his face as he looked at my finger. He made disturbed sounds in his throat, then looked at me expectantly. He was waiting for me to respond with an anxious look. But I didn't because I'm a physician and I knew my finger was perfectly sound. He tucked his hair behind his ear, then told me they'd have to take it off, so sorry, there was nothing they could do.

This cannot be happening. I stared at him, paralyzed, my heart thudding in my chest. After a minute of staring at him I heard myself say in a low voice, "What are you going to do with it?"

He was startled by my question. "I'm sorry?"

"What do you need it for?"

He shifted his weight from foot to foot. "We're doing this for your good. Chairman Mao cares about the well-being of all."

My voice came out sharp as a nail. "Look, I'm a doctor, and *I know you're not doing this for my good.*"

He fiddled with his stethoscope. Pushed his glasses up on his nose. Avoided my eyes.

A man approached from behind him. Whose face I recognized all too well, with its thin lips and crow eyes. Comrade Han. He stood next to the doctor. He raised an eyebrow and cleared his throat.

"Good morning, Comrade Han," the doctor said in a shaky voice.

"So is it as I thought? What's the diagnosis?"

The doctor stood gazing at his shoes, still fondling the stethoscope in his hands. Then he replied, "Yes, Comrade Han. Of course you were right."

I saw a drop of sweat rolling down the doctor's forehead. Comrade Han walked away. Still gazing at the floor, the doctor whispered, "Don't worry, we use anesthesia—"

"During all of your torture procedures?" I deliberately did not join him in whispering.

His face paled. He swallowed, still looking at his shoes.

I caught his eye. Held his gaze insistently. Like a target. My voice was low, intimate. "Will you keep it please? My finger? Take it home with you."

He stared at me. "You're crazy." He shook his head back and forth quickly. He wanted to run from me, I could tell. Looking at me sideways, he sneered, "Why would I do that?"

I still held his gaze patiently. "To remember. So you can remember what you've done."

His eyes widened in his face, and he turned and left swiftly.

I felt a strange calm, a resignation, an odd sadness. I understood what Tenzin had said about karma, about how souls are destroyed in places like this. Mine and theirs.

I knew why they were taking my finger. It was Comrade Han's revenge on me for blithely playing the piano when I was supposed to be terrorized down to a puddle.

In that moment, I felt myself let go. Of trying to live. No point in going on.

They tried to find what you loved the most.

And kill it.

～

There's a bandage around the stump. It throbs, but when Tenzin saw it, he told me I was lucky. "I've heard of them cutting off people's arms," he said. When Lobsang saw what had happened, he sat with his big eyes like moons in his face. Then he stood up and banged his fists on the wall while he wept.

Tenzin tells us suffering is what prepares us for enlightenment. Mostly I'm too tired, too despairing, to care.

But he is teaching me to meditate, and I suffer less. Meditation lets me watch my own suffering, like floating above clouds. Sitting in the cell, I cup my hands together, palms up. Ready for escape. I hear things—the drip of water coming into the cell, the fidgeting of my companions, Tenzin's breathing and my own. At times my thoughts stop, and I get a glimpse of a still inner pool and I can hardly believe it hasn't dried up.

As I sit with my eyes closed, I see and feel what they've done to me here. Or I hear the screams of others from outside my cell. And then I'm shaking again.

I want to run from the scenes in my mind and from the screams. But Tenzin says not to: "Let them be there. They are only thoughts, and thoughts are only illusions. They are not what is happening in this moment. Even when they tortured you, it was a moment that came into being and then passed from existence. All of your torturers are dying; they will pass into another existence, as you will. Everything is impermanent. As I speak to you, the walls of this prison are crumbling into dust. Your body is passing away with each breath; your body is not *you*. The torturers try to hurt you—and they believe they do—but that is their illusion. Do they hasten the death of my body? Perhaps. Why should that concern me? My body is returning to dirt as it once was. They want to play in the dirt, like bored, unhappy children."

At times I get to a place within as vast as the sky—a place I know the torturers cannot reach. Where God dwells in me. Only a place that vast and empty could hold God. All the sounds of my life become one—my screams and the snap my muscles make as one of them rips, intermingled with sounds of Bach's strings—his feeling and mine stirring into one—agony overlaid with exquisite peace. Traveling through a violin string into that hollow space of God within me. God holds it all—the vibrating resonance of a cello string, the blood spilling from my amputated finger. I lie in His hand in the emptiness of silence. In that moment, I go on.

Emma

Yesterday Dorje and I went to the fruit stand to buy some mangoes for Rinchen. She wanted to make a Nepali fruit-salad dish she learned about from our neighbor. He needed my help picking them out because most Tibetans know little about fruits and vegetables.

He picked up a mango and handed it to me. "This one, what do you think, Emma-la?"

"Dorje-la, it's green and hard as a baseball."

"It's a lovely green," he said, smiling, but his smile was weak. His heavy brow told me he was preoccupied.

"It is lovely, but I told you to look for the red color and a mushy feel." I knew what was bothering him. I picked out three mangoes and handed them to the vendor. "Any word on Samten, Dorje?"

He sighed. "It is not good. They will not tell me where he is, they just say he has committed a crime."

"A *crime*?" I was incredulous. "What crime?"

"A crime against the people, they say. But they won't tell me what it is."

I swatted a fly away and groaned. It sounded more like a growl.

The vendor weighed the mangoes using counterweights and two scales. Flies hovered and landed incessantly on the oranges and mangoes in the stand.

Dorje said, "The Chinese say Samten is a citizen of China and has broken its laws."

"Oh, and I'm sure his crime was 'having an American standing next to him.'" I handed the vendor a velvety rupee bill. "I'm sorry we brought this on your family, Dorje."

"I was already their target because I speak Chinese. Anyway, we cannot change the will of the gods."

"You think the Chinese invading is the will of the gods?" I was instantly in a rage.

"I don't know." He sighed, looking defeated. "Maybe it is."

Sometimes Dorje's passivity *really* irked me. I wanted to round up a posse and go back into Tibet with guns slinging, although Gerald would have hated such a violent thought. I was about to express this when I felt a light tap on my shoulder. Turning around, I saw a welcome face: Everett Kingsley. He tipped his hat to us. "Hello, Emma."

I grabbed his arm. *God is looking out for me and Gerald.* "Oh, Kingsley, thank God it's you! I tried to reach you, but your housekeeper said you were away. We had a disastrous meeting with the Chinese ambassador. Oh—have you met Dorje? He's a dear friend." Then, smiling at Dorje, I added, "Although, since fleeing Tibet together, we're more like family. He and his wife have sort of adopted me."

Dorje smiled, and he and Kingsley exchanged bows.

"Oh, so this is the fellow. Any friend of Emma's is my friend as well," Kingsley said warmly. "We go way back, Emma and I, because I knew her father."

"So you are like family also—like an uncle?" said Dorje. "Emma has many relatives."

"Yes." I grinned. "All adopted ones. But so far, they've been the closest to my heart." They both smiled back at me. "But as I said, our meeting at the embassy did not go well."

"Emma, you must meet with Mr. Yuan again. Have patience," Dorje cajoled.

Kingsley's eyes were warm. "Are you free for tea? Perhaps I could be of help."

I looked to Dorje. He nodded encouragingly, so I said, "We'd be delighted."

When tea was served in Kingsley's parlor, I sat through a short minute of niceties, then pushed right into my worries. "So, can I tell you what happened with Mr. Yuan?"

"Of course. I know him by reputation. A decent fellow," Kingsley said between sips.

"Well, he was *not* decent to me. He spouted some nonsense that Gerald and I were imperialists trying to take over Tibet! He's not lifting a finger to find Gerald."

Dorje stared rather deliberately into his teacup.

I motioned to Dorje with my thumb, saying, "He seems to think I offended the ambassador and botched the whole thing."

Dorje corrected, "I did not say that. But you must not insult the one who can help you."

"Don't *tell* me you insulted him?" The horror in Kingsley's voice was palpable.

"He insulted *me*! He treated me like a criminal! But I suppose that's not the point."

"Emma, now you'll pardon my frankness." Kingsley expelled air from between pursed lips. "You Americans go crashing about flexing your muscles, so to speak, expecting the world to submit to your will. That simply is *not* how it is done. Now, please, Emma, try to imagine life for a man like Mr. Yuan." He paused. "If you lived in a country pervaded by suspicion, where people denounce one another to the Communist Party for personal gain, how would you react to someone like you? Someone who shouts at you? Offends you?"

Kingsley leaned forward in his chair and pressed his hands together for emphasis. "Know your enemy, my dear. What are his daily concerns, and what does he want in his life? Until you can answer these questions about this man, you will never gain his help. Remember this: the one who appears to be your enemy could in reality be your friend."

"That is what I think, Emma," Dorje chimed in. "I can tell he is a good man."

Kingsley continued, "The most important ingredient you must have is this: respect. Treat him with respect and let that respect be sincere."

Oh, please, I thought. But I kept my mouth shut.

"Emma." Kingsley's tone was disapproving, fatherly. "Listen to me. One of these fellows was sitting next to me at a pub one night. I couldn't fathom why he'd be at a pub, but there he was, having a pint and looking as though the world had given him a good working over. Soon enough the brew had loosened our tongues, and a sorrier soul I have never met. He absolutely despised the communist government, and he obtained his post with the precise aim of escaping to the West! Only by denouncing friends did he even procure the post here. Pitiful, really."

Dorje interjected, "This is what I saw when I went to China. The blank faces—like Mr. Yuan's face. I felt his fear."

"So I'm asking him to practically risk his life in order to help me?" I was overwhelmed with desperation. "Then it's hopeless! There's no one who's going to want to risk that!"

"I do admit the picture is rather bleak, but you mustn't give up. I'm merely pointing out that all of you, you, Gerald, and Mr. Yuan, are caught in the very same web. And now, I must insist that you eat something, both of you."

The little one kicked me as if to say, *Feed me.* We dined on a spread of roast beef, new potatoes, and green salad. I was grateful for Kingsley's care. As we ate, Kingsley began talking about the Chinese again. "You know, Emma, the Chinese are not entirely paranoid—the U.S. does have agents seeking intelligence in Tibet."

"Huh?" I had no idea what he was talking about.

"Spies. The CIA."

"What? How do you know that?"

"I pick up intelligence of my own in the pubs about town. I've seen droves of young American men, talking about their training in the mountains of Colorado, you know, to acclimate to the altitude, and they've got their orders to head for Tibet."

"How do you know they're spies? Surely they don't admit to it?"

"No, but you don't think they're here on holiday, do you? They're CIA operatives."

"What possible interest could they have in Tibet? At the American embassy, they told me the U.S. doesn't even have an official policy regarding Tibet."

"Yes, that's the party line. But they're in Tibet watching China—you know, the Red Menace and all that."

"My God. What a cauldron Gerald and I jumped into!"

"Not a cauldron, my dear. Rather more like a Cold War."

On the walk home with Dorje, I found my mind working at untying a last knot. "You really don't hate them, do you, even though they took Samten? How do you do that?"

"Hate is a waste of life." Dorje shook his head. "We are here to accumulate merit in this lifetime, to be reborn to a better existence in the next life. If I have hate in my heart, I lose my merit, as if I'm throwing away riches. Why would I do that?"

He made it sound so perfectly logical. Why was it so hard for me?

Kingsley and I went to collect Genevieve at the airport today. He found us some chairs, then promptly dozed off. Lulled by the rhythm of his bearlike snoring, my mind traveled to my memories of Genevieve.

I poked Kingsley in the arm. "Her plane was due at four o'clock. What's going on here?"

"Emma, nothing ever goes to plan in Kathmandu, least of all at the airport. It's quite possibly the most disordered place on earth." He patted my hand gently, smiling. "She'll be along shortly."

This airport was a torment for me as a pregnant woman because the restrooms were horrendous. Better than Tibet, mind you, but still requiring that I wrap a scarf over my nose to keep from vomiting from the stench.

Then a door opened, and there was Genevieve, shuffling in my direction. She stopped and set down her suitcase when she saw me. The first thing out of her mouth was "Oh, yes!"

I nearly squeezed the life out of her, then stood back and looked at her. She wore an ankle-length, khaki skirt with matching jacket cinched at the waist and comfortable flat shoes.

"You're taking a look at my getup, aren't you?" She beamed.

"Yes. You look fabulous!" I squeezed her again. Hanging from her arm was her trusty vinyl handbag. "Did you use your little booster on the plane?"

"Oh, yes, sometimes. When I needed one of the stewardesses, I'd sit up on it so she could find me." Genevieve reached a hand toward my middle. "Oh, let me feel that belly of yours, see if the little fellow will give me a kick."

No kick for her yet.

"Genevieve, this is my dear friend Everett Kingsley. Retired diplomat, friend of my father, and most of all, knight in shining armor. He's been looking after me."

"Delighted to meet you, madam." Kingsley was incurably old-school, so formal.

"Oh, goodness, call me Genevieve," she said with a swatting motion.

"Genevieve it is, then." He picked up her suitcase, and we walked to his car. Kingsley had generously offered us the cottage behind his house. I looked forward to her mothering me, to being there, just the two of us, and eventually, the little one with us.

I looked at her silvery head and sighed. *She is my mother. She is my home.* If there's a way to move a mountain on this earth, it will be with her veined hands.

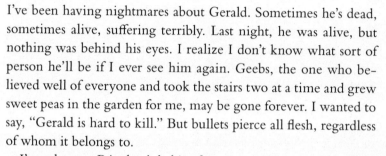

I've been having nightmares about Gerald. Sometimes he's dead, sometimes alive, suffering terribly. Last night, he was alive, but nothing was behind his eyes. I realize I don't know what sort of person he'll be if I ever see him again. Geebs, the one who believed well of everyone and took the stairs two at a time and grew sweet peas in the garden for me, may be gone forever. I wanted to say, "Gerald is hard to kill." But bullets pierce all flesh, regardless of whom it belongs to.

I've taken up Rinchen's habit of praying while I cut vegetables or yak meat. *Chop. Chop. Please, God, watch over my love.* Rinchen says prayers to accumulate merit. If I pray, can I exchange my merit for the life of my husband? I don't care what happens in my next life, if there even *is* one. He needs to be with me in *this* life, and despite my praying, most of the time I honestly don't care what God's will is about it.

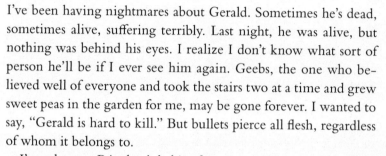

I returned to the embassy to see Mr. Yuan, and Genevieve was with me. Her little hand radiated its warmth on my arm as we walked in together. She gave me a Bible verse to repeat to myself as preparation for the meeting. *Let the words of my mouth, and the meditation of my heart, be acceptable in Thy sight, O Lord.*

We were shown right into Mr. Yuan's office. When he came in, his face told me everything. It did not brighten as he asked, "How may I be of assistance to you today?"

What do you think we're here for? To chat? Squelching my anger, I pushed out the words, "I appreciate you meeting with us. We're here to ask how the search for my husband is progressing."

A crease formed between his eyebrows for just a second. Then he replied, "Oh, I believe there has been a misunderstanding, madam. Since you provided no proof that your husband ever entered Chinese territory, we have been unable to begin a search."

His words knocked me over as if I were a sapling. I let Genevieve herd me out of the building after she said good-bye to him. Once at the cottage, I went to bed with the blinds drawn, stewing in a black storm cloud, and stayed there for four days. Genevieve came and fed me like a hen dropping food to a chick.

On the morning of the fifth day, I woke when the baby kicked. A peaceful silence spread through my arms, legs. Sitting up, I sensed its source, a white-hot stillness in my gut. I was two sides of a blade, both ice-cold and white-hot, all at once. As I breathed out, my throat tightening around the air as it passed, I heard the hissing power of it as it left my body. This power lived in the sinews of any wild animal, and it was in me too. I was a little frightened by the teeth of it. Nothing Christian about it, nothing noble.

Just *hate*. And there, in that fire of revulsion, was the power to move. To get out of bed. To walk down a street, to feel, in pulsing waves, my abhorrence of every Chinese man who passed and embrace it. It was warm inside me, like other passions. Pulled all of me together and held me tight, like a lover. Painted the gray world where I'd been living in crisp black and white. Us. Them. Simple.

Dorje said hate is a waste of life. Ha. Hate is getting me up in the morning.

Amen.

Dorje

Champa and I are on our own this morning. Uncle Tinle is away in Pokhara, and both Rinchen and Pema have gone to Emma's house because she is about to give birth. Early this morning, Kingsley came to Pema's house to tell us Emma's time had come. He had brought a car to drive the women to the house. I asked him into the dining room while he waited for them. He sat down and looked at his watch.

Both my wife and Pema gathered up blankets to keep Emma warm, and Pema brought a pot of beef broth for Emma so she can stay strong during the birth. They looked like two confused rabbits running around, with Pema shouting, "Rinchen, get the blankets! I'll get the food!" and Rinchen saying, "Pema, get the food! I'll get the blankets!"

Rinchen prepared many things to help Emma have her baby in the Tibetan way. She had incense to light when she arrived at Emma's house to keep away the evil spirits that could harm the baby. And Rinchen had formed some yak butter into the shape of a fish with two eyes. Then I brought this butter to have it blessed by a lama, who recited a mantra over it two thousand times, then blew the energy of those prayers into the butter. Rinchen will bring it to Emma so she can swallow it headfirst. I do not know how she will convince Emma to swallow the fish because Emma thinks that yak butter is "disgusting." But Emma said she would like to have her baby in our traditional way, so she will have to swallow it. Emma can be stubborn, but she is no match for Rinchen, especially when my wife is in charge!

Champa and I hid in the hallway, trying to stay out of their way. Champa was a little afraid at first because he did not understand what was happening. I told him quietly with our backs against the wall, "It is all right, Champa. They are excited because Emma's child is coming, so they are running around like rabbits. But they are happy." Then he looked up at me and laughed each time one of them ran past us.

From my place in the hallway, I peeked into the dining room. Kingsley was pacing. Not knowing what else to do, I offered him tea.

"Oh goodness, no, Dorje!" He smiled. "You're very kind, but we do have to get going."

"Yes, of course. I will do my best to get them ready."

Kingsley started to laugh. "Looks as if you'll need a few dogs to herd the sheep."

I grinned at him. Then Rinchen ran into the dining room. "We have to go! Right away! Let's go!"

"Indeed," Kingsley said, still smiling at me. He and I carried the blankets, the broth, the incense, Rinchen's herbs, the yak butter, *tsampa,* the churner for butter tea, and many other things to the motorcar waiting outside.

When I saw how many things they were bringing, I asked Rinchen, "Are you moving in with Emma forever?"

Rinchen looked at me as though I were an annoying child.

Kingsley did not say anything while we packed the car, but his one raised eyebrow told me he did not understand the way Tibetans take care of a woman when she is giving birth.

Then they drove away. Kingsley promised to send his driver back for us to take us to Emma's house too. I would have to be there later, after the baby was born, to give it a blessing. Emma had asked me to do this in Gerald's place. I was so moved I felt tears in my eyes, so I told her, "There could be no greater honor for me than to do this, for Gerald." As I bowed to her, I felt sad that Gerald would not be there.

A few months ago, I was surprised when Emma had told Rinchen and me that she wanted to have the baby according to our traditions. She had said, "My husband is still in your country. This is the closest I can get to him right now." My wife had a big smile on her face because she was so happy Emma asked her to be the midwife. Even so, Emma will have an Indian doctor in attendance as well.

Champa and I waited in the garden in front of the house. I was showing him some of Uncle Tinle's vegetables, and I found myself feeling sad. In my last conversation with Dawa, he had cried between the rows of green beans. The beans had already been harvested, and I had still not received a letter or visit from my older son.

I was staring at the empty rows when Champa tugged at my *chuba*. "What happens when a woman has a baby, Pa-la?"

"Well, her stomach gets very big. Have you seen how big Emma's stomach is?"

"Like the belly of a giant Buddha!"

"That is the child inside her, getting bigger. Then it gets so big that it is ready to come out and join us."

"But how does it get out if it is so big?"

"Oh. There is a special passage that it takes in the woman's body, and this passage can stretch, so even a big child can come out."

"It *stretches*?"

"Yes, like your yakskin boots. They start small, but they grow bigger so your feet will fit into them."

"This is the way I was born too?" His eyes were the size of plums.

"Yes, your mother also stretched to let you come out."

He was thinking it over with a serious face.

I explained, "When we get to Emma's house, I do not want you to be afraid. This stretching, it hurts a woman a lot, so she sometimes cries and yells. These yells can be—very loud. But that is how it happens, the way life is born."

Champa started hopping between the rows. I sat down, feeling tired.

In a few minutes he came back to me. "When are they coming? We are going to miss the whole thing."

I laughed. "Oh, I don't think so. These things take a long time. It may not happen today, even."

Later, I was excited for my son as we rode in the motorcar to Emma's house because this would be the first time he was old enough to be aware of what was happening in the birth of a child. Although Rinchen had had one birth since Champa was born, he was still too young to understand it. It would have made him sad anyway because the child did not survive for more than five days.

When we arrived, Kingsley opened the door to welcome us into Emma's little cottage. Emma's moans were loud, and Champa looked at me with scared eyes.

I reassured him, "It is fine. She is all right. Your mother is taking care of her."

He grabbed my hand, and we walked into the living room of the cottage. Kingsley invited us to sit down on the couch.

"Why does it smell like lemons?" Champa asked.

"That is a tea of herbs that Rinchen is giving to Emma to drink, to help her labor," I said.

"Can I taste it?"

"No, you silly boy! You are not giving birth! It will make you sick." He is such a curious child!

"Is the boy all right?" asked Kingsley. He didn't understand because I had been speaking to my son in Tibetan. Kingsley was being a good host.

"He wants to taste the lemon birthing tea they are giving to Emma," I told him.

"Oh, that won't do," said Kingsley, chuckling. "Here, my boy, have a sweetcake instead." He passed a plate of sweets to Champa.

Pema opened the door to Emma's bedroom. Emma was in a long flannel dress, pacing around the room, hands on her belly. Genevieve was holding Emma's arm, supporting her as she walked. Then Rinchen closed the door. Pema asked me to warm some butter to rub on Emma's belly. I was happy to be doing something because it seemed funny to sit with Kingsley and Champa and me all staring at each other.

I brought the melted butter out of the kitchen and tapped on the bedroom door. After Pema took it, she asked me to churn some butter tea for Emma. Walking back to the kitchen, I was amazed that Emma was having so much yak butter in one day!

When I came back into the living room, Kingsley was sitting on the edge of the couch next to Champa, and they were playing with a toy on a string.

Champa's eyes were bright. "Pa-la, it's a yo-yo!"

"Hope you don't mind," said Kingsley.

"No, not at all. He loves this toy," I said.

"Watch me!" Champa showed me how it went up and down on the string.

Emma's cries were getting louder and closer together, so I knew she was at the time when she was pushing the baby out. I heard my wife commanding, "Push now! Push!" and Emma screaming, *"I am pushing!"*

Sometimes I cannot believe that these two women are friends!

After a terribly long time of this shouting and grunting, it became quiet. None of us in the living room said anything. I wondered at that moment if everything was all right with the baby, or were they cutting its cord and cleaning up? I stood up to knock on the bedroom door, but as I was approaching, Pema opened it. She was smiling. Everything was fine.

She invited all of us into the room. Emma had the baby at her side and a smile on her face. Her hair was stuck to her forehead from her perspiring, and her face was red.

"Emma has a baby girl," announced Rinchen, her face beaming.

Emma's eyes were wet, but her smile filled her whole face.

A dark man in white Indian silk stood up. "You're Dorje? I'm Dr. Patel. Your wife is a talented midwife. Perhaps she has found a new profession?"

I have rarely seen my wife stand so tall as in that moment, but she said humbly, "It was a simple birth, with a good mother." But still my wife was in charge. "Now you need to give your blessing, Dorje."

My heart was full, wishing Gerald were in the room with us. I took the baby in my arms. She had a lot of blond hair for a newborn baby, and her skin was pink. She looked strong and healthy. I felt she would stay with us for a long time, and I was glad for Emma.

Looking into the baby's blue eyes, I spoke tenderly to her. "Dear child, you are born from the hearts of your mother, Emma, and your father, Gerald. May you live to see one hundred autumns, may you overcome all ills, and may your life be filled with love, joy, and good fortune."

Emma was crying now, but she still had a smile on her face.

"I've also asked Genevieve to give a blessing," Emma said, sniffling.

I passed the baby to Genevieve, who said, "Little one, you surprised us. You showed us that God has plans we can't know ahead of time. You are a living miracle. May you know how you've blessed us already, and may your heart be full of the Light and love of God every day of your life."

Emma looked at my wife and proclaimed sternly, "Now, I

know that your tradition is that a lama should give the baby its name. But I've already chosen a name for her."

Rinchen frowned, and I wanted to tell my wife to relax.

Emma continued, "I'm naming her Rinchen, after you. One year ago, I didn't know either of you, but neither I nor my little bundle here would be alive today if not for you and Dorje."

Oh, this was amazing! I had tears in my eyes, but my wife could only stare at her feet. She does not like to show her emotions, but we could all see that her face was becoming red, and tears were leaking out the sides of her eyes. I wanted to say to her, *No reason to hide what is already on your face, Rinchen!*

Finally, she looked at Emma and said, so low you could barely hear her, "Thank you."

Next, Rinchen brought saffron to the baby and stamped the syllable *dhih* on the baby's tongue, to bestow wisdom on the child. Then she touched a bit of yak butter to the baby's nose and put some on her tiny pink tongue as well, to give her a long, healthy life.

Then the women made us leave the room so they could collect the afterbirth. We would bury the afterbirth in the next few days, saying prayers over it.

As I touched Champa's head on the way out of the room, my heart was full.

Gerald

Yesterday, they took us out to the fields. Tenzin leaned heavily on a shovel he carried. Lobsang stood near me, talking to himself and rocking. Tenzin and I have been watching him closely because he has taken to picking up large rocks and hitting himself in the head. He seems to have decided that killing himself is his only escape from here. The other day he made a four-inch gash in his forehead. I wound his head up tightly with some cloth from Tenzin's robe to stop the bleeding. Hope is faint that the wound will close; it's more likely that it will become infected and not heal properly. Just thinking of it makes me feel heavy and defeated.

But today in the fields, the strangest thing happened. A thing so hopeful I can scarcely believe it. I stood near the edge of the field removing a rock from the ground with a hoe when I had the odd sensation that someone was staring at me. But not one of the guards. Not even from the direction of the guards. From outside the field. When I turned around, I saw a man standing there, looking right at me. A Tibetan man in a brown *chuba* with a gold-and-turquoise earring. Not a poor man.

I checked again, and although he'd turned to the side, he was still looking at me. He seemed to want to talk to me, but that would be dangerous with the guards watching. I made my way toward him slowly, digging up rocks along the way. I started a small pile of rocks near him so I'd be able to approach him again and again, depositing what I'd dug out of the ground. He knelt down and made a great show of removing one of his boots as though a pebble were bothering his foot. Finally I was within fifteen feet of him. After a quick glance up at the guards, he removed a piece of paper from his boot and placed it under a rock. He looked at me for a split second, then swiftly walked away.

I dug my way over to the edge of the field, checking the guards as I went. No one seemed to notice he'd stopped there. As I got closer, my head throbbed. My heart pounded. By the time I lifted the hand-size rock he'd placed over the paper, my mouth was dry.

Turning my back to the guards, I unfolded the paper hastily.

Hello,
You are Mr. Kitrech? Your wife stay with Mr. Khingly in Katmandu.
They look for you. Very worry about you. He try get you free. I come
back soon. I say prayer for your helth.
*   Sonam*

I read it and read it and read it again, looked up to make sure no one was watching me, and read it yet again. It simply could not be—like a visitation from another planet. But he mentioned Kingsley—by name. In Kathmandu. My legs trembled with adrenaline, with happiness! My Emma was safe and they had found me! How in God's name did they find me? Hallelujah! I fell to my knees and kissed the ground as though it were God's very face. Through the rest of my work detail, tears coursed down my face.

When I woke up the next morning, I thought I'd dreamed it. But when we went out into the fields, I saw the man again, this time in a maroon-colored *chuba*. He was taking care to not be recognized. Again I dug my way over to him, acting as nonchalant as I could manage, given that I wanted to run over and jump the fence and beg him, *Take me to Kathmandu now!*

He looked over at the guards, then reached into his *chuba* and swiftly removed a black object. I couldn't tell exactly what it was until I heard the snap of him taking my picture. Then he walked away again, leaving me with my mouth hanging open, legs wobbly with joy.

Once I finally got to sleep that night, I slept in hope, like a snug cloak.

Part
Three

Gerald's image first appeared in the tiny darkroom of Sonam's friend Derge, whose noble status and wealth afforded the leisure of travel and dabbling in photography as a diverting pastime. Once the photo became its undeniable, proof-establishing self, it was carefully wrapped in the Nepali paper so prized by Derge— the very man complicit in writing the note Gerald had held in his trembling fingers the day before, feeling as if the sky had opened and rained manna from heaven upon him. Derge fashioned a smart-looking package with an envelope addressing the missive to *Mrs. Kitrech, in the care of Mr. Khingly, Katmandu, Nepal.*

Derge and Sonam enclosed the missive in a wool cloth and tied it with cotton string. Then they set to thinking about how it might best be spirited all the way to Kathmandu. But although they thought and thought, it seemed rather impossible. They themselves could not deliver the missive, as business and family matters tied them to Lhasa.

After a bit of dust-gathering, the letter and the address of its destination were carefully placed into the hands of Puntso, a merchant friend who regularly made the trek to Kathmandu. Puntso then tucked it into the yakskin satchel he slung over the back of his horse. The little wool package jiggled and rocked back and forth as Puntso's horse trotted along the paths leading out of Tibet. Along the way it witnessed many a meal within the yak-hair tents of nomads and survived a withering storm with whining gales and slanting sheets of rain.

Once the bearer trotted into the Kathmandu valley, he unpacked his horse and lay his exhausted frame down to rest in a cousin's warm bed for two days. The missive lay forlorn by his bedside, as Puntso had forgotten his promise to Derge that he would deliver it straightaway. However, one morning as he was ruffling through his belongings in search of his *mani* beads, he came upon the little package entrusted to him. The string had dulled to a gray-brown and the wool was worn at the corners. He sat down and scratched his scalp, suddenly and uncomfortably aware that he'd misplaced the address to which he was to deliver the package. He searched all of his belongings, scoured his room, checked the satchel he'd once placed on his horse. In vain.

Then he remembered Derge mumbling that the package pertained to something American. As luck would have it, Puntso had an American acquaintance. *I'll give it to Edward Carolan and my duty will be done,* he thought. Happily unaware that Mr. Carolan hailed from Ireland, Puntso set off to find this bohemian fellow who seldom bathed and smoked *bidi* cigarettes on a Kathmandu street corner.

Mr. Carolan was happy enough to accept the package in one hand while shrewdly combing his beard with the other. Although the Tibetan man had asked him not to open the package, Mr. Carolan's eyes could not resist a peek. Just one little peek.

When he saw the fancy Nepali paper envelope, he thought he'd stumbled onto the source of a lifetime of *bidis,* but once he opened the sealed envelope and saw the photo of a half-starved man with a bandaged hand, he tossed it to his feet in disgust. It lay there all morning, with *bidi* ash falling on it. Mr. Carolan couldn't have been entirely heartless, however, because before he ducked into a dive to stuff a Nepali lunch of *dhal* and rice into his mouth with his *bidi*-stained fingers, he tucked the package into the back pocket of his threadbare trousers. Why would someone send a photo of a half-dead man? he wondered. As he ate, he placed the photo next to his heaping plate of *dhal*. The man in the photo looked skeletal, hungry, to Carolan. He felt the tremor of something dimly familiar and terribly bothersome: a conscience. The conscience instilled in him by the nuns of St. Joseph's Parish School in Dublin. The conscience he'd traveled thousands of miles to escape rose up and smote his chest with a profound, perspiring anxiety. But what was he supposed to do about it?

After a sweaty night in which Mr. Carolan was visited by all manner of unwelcome nuns brandishing rulers and raised eyebrows, he cursed the little package and decided to be rid of it at once. He wanted to give it back to the Tibetan man, but he didn't know where to find him. So he spent his *bidi* money on a *tuk-tuk,* ordering the driver to take him to the next best thing he could think of, the Tibetan embassy. Whereupon the driver turned round and gave him the arched eyebrow Mr. Carolan had seen in his dreams, saying to him, "No Tibetan embassy, only Chinese."

Irritated at being corrected by a *tuk-tuk* driver, Mr. Carolan replied, "I don't give a fancy fart whose embassy it is, just take me there." Whereupon, the package bearing Gerald's heart-stirring photograph landed in the hands of Ambassador Yuan, who tossed it heedlessly onto his desk on his way to the washroom.

SEPTEMBER 20, 1955

Emma

I'm out walking in Thamel, the shopping district, which teems with tourists. Rin is back at Kingsley's cottage with Genevieve, where we've been staying since Rin was born. I'm taking my time, breathing in Kathmandu—the sweet rotting-fruit smell, the exhaust, the sweat of bodies heated by sun. I'm leaving tomorrow, going back to Connecticut with Genevieve and Rin.

It was difficult to decide to leave. I've simply been so unhappy here I can't stand it anymore, and I'm running out of money. Kingsley has hinted that he'd be willing to be my contact with the Chinese embassy because he apparently thinks my presence might become an irritant to Ambassador Yuan. How will it feel to go home? It's hard to say, but I want to make a settled home for Rin, not be staying in one place after another.

I need a gift for Rinchen and Dorje to thank them for saving my life, my child's life, and helping me to go on, to even imagine a life after Gerald's disappearance. I want to give them a *thangka*, a painting done by monks on silk, of the goddess Green Tara, one of the few female emanations of the Buddha whom Tibetans worship. On one day of our journey we stopped at a small monastery in western Tibet. Rinchen saw hopelessness in my face, so she told me, "Pray to green Tara." She showed me a mural of the goddess in the monastery and said with enthusiasm, "Look how she's sitting, with one leg in half lotus and the other with her foot on the ground. Like she's ready to get up and help you right now."

Rinchen. Her solid body is a pillar of strength and optimism. Her brother had been taken away by communists, she'd lost her home and country, and her son had left his monastery, but still she was telling me that Green Tara was ready to get up and help *me*. When I think of her and Dorje, I realize I now have two more people in whose eyes I see God. I'll miss Dorje's broad, hopeful shoulders along with his constant praying. And with Rinchen, I'll miss her solid arms hugging me, as if she'll never let me fall.

I stop for a moment and lean against the brick wall of a shop, ignoring the shopkeepers hawking their wares in my direction. That's when I see the old woman. She's bent nearly double with a back ailment or deformity, I can't tell which. Her long black hair is matted into a rat's nest, and her dress is covered with years of grime. She holds her hand in front of her, begging. She has such a patient expression on her face, waiting on the charity of others.

As she walks by, I try to become part of the bricks that support my back. I don't want her to see me. Seeing her makes me cry because she reminds me of another day. During the time before. That day, Gerald and I stood at a dried-fish stand. A mound of mushroom-colored fish was before us. Small fish, no longer than five inches each. Thousands of dried-up eyes stared up lifelessly from the scaly, misshapen pile. While I was repulsed and the stench made me gag, Gerald was fascinated. He asked the vendor question after question.

How do they taste?

Like a fish.

How do you dry them?

In the sun.

Where are they fished from?

From the water.

I stood shaking my head restlessly, sweating in my cotton shirt. Before we'd even reached the stand, I'd had enough of Kathmandu. Enough of nearly being run over by *tuk-tuk*s, of being accosted by shopkeepers, of being asked for money by every dirty waif in the street, of seeing half-starved female dogs who'd had so many litters their teats hung nearly to the ground, of witnessing a three-year-old girl picking through roadside trash for food. The suffering here was overwhelming and, finally, deadening.

Gerald's curls were dripping with his sweat, but on he went with his maddening fish exchange. That was when I noticed the hunchbacked woman waiting off to the side. We'd given her money twice already, first when we were watching the funeral pyres burn at Pashupatinath Temple, then again in a marketplace. The last time we'd seen her, Gerald and I had joked with each other that we'd run away if we saw her again. When she noticed me looking at her, she put out her hand.

I was about to say "Help" to Gerald when I saw him bite the head off a fish. I yelled at him, "Geebs, what are you doing? That is sick! I swear I'm going to—" Vomit choked off my words. I threw up in the street. The vomit splattered onto the hem of the hunchback's dress, but she didn't step back. Her outstretched hand didn't retreat.

It was starting to rain. Suddenly I had to escape. Then I was running, away from the fish, from the hunchback, from the shame of my own vomit.

Gerald caught up with me, panting and smiling broadly. "You all right, Em?"

"I'm fine now, as long as I don't see another hunchback or dried fish!"

"We're being stalked!" He giggled.

"By the Hunchback of Kathmandu!"

We laughed a hyena cackle until our legs went weak under us as we ran all the way back to our hotel, up the stairs, into our room, and collapsed on the bed. It wasn't that we didn't care. It's just that after a while, you can't. Your heart hurts and you can't stand it and then you're doubled over with it.

Today, the hunchback makes me sad, remembering those earlier days. When we'd just started our adventure. Full of hope. Not like now, when I hear nothing—no word from any embassy, no response to our radio transmissions. Nothing. There's no point in going on here. I've felt this way for months, ever since my last meeting with that coward at the Chinese embassy. I've held on anyway because leaving feels like defeat. Five days ago, on September fifteenth, marked a year to the day that Gerald disappeared. It is a blessing that I didn't know then that a year later I still wouldn't know his whereabouts. If I had known it, I might have taken my own life and Rin might never have been born.

I'll say my good-byes tomorrow morning. I'll touch foreheads with Rinchen and kiss her new baby, Lhamo, born a few months after Rin. I'll bump foreheads with Dorje and Champa with a lump in my throat. Kingsley will drive us to the airport, and I'll feel I'm closing a chapter—one I don't want to close. Not without Gerald. Leaving without him is like dying. Once we reach Connecticut, my home that'll never really feel like home again, Rin and I will move in with Genevieve.

Rin has given me the brightest moments of the last several months. She's unaccountably happy, with a smile full of pink gums. It's an instant of grace I don't deserve, the way a laugh bursts right out of her. She pulls me into her world each moment with her tiny, soft hands. Genevieve raises an eyebrow at her, until Rin reaches and touches her finger to the eyebrow and babbles some goofy, joyous garble. Rin will get me through.

SEPTEMBER 24, 1955

Dorje

Today I received a letter from Dawa. I was so excited when I saw the postmark from India, where he has been taking classes for the past several months. He has not written us much. Even when he was living at the monastery we saw him more than we do now.

It is not simply the distance that separates us from our older son. For some reason he has not told us, he holds his heart away from us ever since we left our country. I worry about him finding his way. His life is a mystery to me. I cannot picture where he eats his meals or where he sleeps or what kind of people he has for friends.

Rinchen will not talk about it because she becomes too upset. She only talks about our new baby girl, Lhamo, and does not want me to speak about Dawa. I took his letter from our postal box hoping for good news. Even seeing his handwriting, so sloppy because he is always in a hurry, made me feel glad. Perhaps Dawa would tell us a little more about his life, and my wife would begin to talk about him again.

I leaned against the garden gate as I opened the envelope and read the letter.

Dearest Pa-la,

I hope that all members of the family are well, especially the new baby. I apologize that I haven't written more.

My studies have been going well, and I've met some other Tibetans. This is the reason I'm writing to you, to let you know I'm going back to Tibet with two of the men I've met. I know you won't understand my reasons, but our country needs to be defended from the Chinese. Tibet is our mother, and I'm willing to give my life to save her. My friends and I have discussed this issue for months, and we've made our decision to join the resistance in Kham province. I want to make it safe for all of us to return to our country, forever. Please try to understand.

I write this letter as we leave and will write to you again when I've arrived in Tibet. As always, I continue to recite prayers for the gods to protect all of you.

Your loving son,
Dawa

I slid onto the ground and put my head in my hands. It was as if a stranger had written a letter telling me of my son's death.

He was gone, my son. He was gone.

I could not move.

I sat. A neighbor walked past. There was the sound of a bee in the garden. A man rode by on a bicycle that squeaked.

I had to get my son back. But how could I do it? How could I even find him? He would be killed. What did Tibetans know about war? About battling Chinese? The Chinese had airplanes, guns, and millions of men in their army. We had swords, rocks, maybe a few guns.

I shut my eyes tight to erase the images I was seeing of my son being killed. My body was shaking. I sat in this way, watching people go by, for a long time.

How would I tell my wife? To tell a mother who has carried a child in her body—your son has gone to fight. He will certainly die. I stood up, and my legs trembled as I walked into the house.

Rinchen was sitting in the altar room with Lhamo. Our little girl was watching as her mother lit a stick of incense. A smile was on Lhamo's face as she looked at the statues of the Buddha.

I thought I would explain it slowly to my wife. Perhaps I could ask Pema to take Lhamo into the kitchen for a while. But when Rinchen saw my face, she asked, "What is wrong?" She saw the letter in my hand, and she blew out the match she was holding. Then she walked over to me. "What does our son say?"

"How did you know—"

"What does he say?"

"He is going back to Tibet."

"Back to the monastery?" Her voice rose hopefully.

"No." I stopped.

"What?"

"He's joining the freedom fighters."

She covered her mouth with her hand and ran from the room, then upstairs. I walked over to Lhamo and knelt beside her. Together we listened to the wailing coming from upstairs.

SEPTEMBER 27, 1955, (MIDDLETOWN, CONNECTICUT)

Emma

The sound of the telephone jars me out of sleep. The clock reads 3:18 A.M. The faint outlines of my room in the dark remind me of where I am. Connecticut, not Kathmandu.

I pick up the receiver and say a tentative hello. My voice is small, frightened.

"Emma? Kingsley here. We've found him!"

"What? Where? Is he okay?"

"Yes, he's all right. He's being held in a prison right outside of Lhasa, *and,* I have a photograph of him, which establishes his location."

"Oh my God! How in the world did you get it?"

"That's a bit of a long story, but somebody must have heard our radio transmission." His voice is cautious.

"Wow! I'll be on the next plane!"

"There's no need for you to come—"

"I *have* to see that photo!"

"Well, all right then. You're certain you want to turn right round and come back after scarcely a week at home?"

"Kingsley?"

"Yes?"

"Why do you even ask? I'm coming!" I slowed myself down to say, "And—thanks a quadruple million."

"You're welcome. Good-bye. Call me when you arrive so I can fetch you."

"Thank you, thank you! Goodbye."

I stood up on my bed, then jumped off, crying, "Yes! Thank you, God!" I ran down the hall and banged on Genevieve's door. "Wake up! You're not going to believe this!"

I heard a muffled "My goodness" through the door. She opened it and stood there with her long, braided hair hanging like a silky rope.

"They've found Gerald! Kingsley has a picture of him in a prison in Lhasa!"

"Oh my!" Genevieve grabbed me and squeezed me in a way I didn't know she had in her.

"So I'm calling the airline now to get a flight! You don't mind watching Rin, right?" I was calling out to her as I raced back into my room and began throwing clothes into a suitcase.

She came and stood in the threshold of my door, her veined feet bare on the cold floor. "Now, honey, don't you think you should get a flight *before* you pack your bag?"

I stopped for a second. "Right. Okay."

She walked over and handed me the phone. "You'll need this," she said, chuckling. "Now where are you going?"

"To Kingsley's place in Kathmandu."

"Oh, ye-es." She intoned it the way I loved and stood there with her crooked smile, in which her top and bottom teeth didn't meet quite right, her jaw tensed with glee.

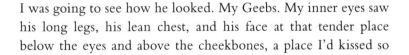

I was going to see how he looked. My Geebs. My inner eyes saw his long legs, his lean chest, and his face at that tender place below the eyes and above the cheekbones, a place I'd kissed so often, and the corners of his mouth that turned up when I called him Geebs.

The plane ride was turbulent, but not from the plane. Inside me a cyclone was swirling. What would it be like to see his picture? I was trying to prepare myself for the worst. He was always so thin. My insides hurt when I thought of his being hungry, or hurt. I hoped the Chinese were afraid to mistreat him because he was an American, but I also knew they might not give a damn about that. A shiver ran through me.

But now I finally had *proof* that he was in Tibet. No one, not even that cold good-for-nothing at the Chinese embassy could tell me, "Your husband was never *in* Tibet." I was ready to harangue Mr. Yuan: "You've stood in my way at every step, but not anymore! You told me you needed proof, but you never dreamed I'd actually be able to *produce* it!" I wanted to slap his cold, arrogant face. To shock him speechless, glasses slipping down his nose.

God forgive me for hating his guts, but I can't stop. Even in Connecticut, if I chanced to see someone with straight, black oriental hair and almond-shaped eyes, I only saw *him.* Then I wanted to hurt someone, really do some damage.

Jeez, Emma, that's really sick. Calm down. Kingsley would tell me to get hold of myself. I could see myself jumping across Mr. Yuan's desk to do some real damage to him. *God, help me out here. I'm turning into a horrible bigot.*

Kingsley seemed preoccupied when I arrived. He had the look of a doctor about to tell his patient grave news. I knew that look. Gerald had worn it a few times.

"You're looking well, Emma. I trust your flight was bearable?"

"I was barely there, I was so lost in worrying and hoping."

"Well, that's certainly understandable," he answered sympathetically.

I grabbed his arm. "What is it, Kingsley, what's wrong?"

"Nothing is wrong, Emma. Now let's go and get you settled in your cottage."

We squished into a taxi so small it looked like a clown car. Kingsley sat with his head bowed because it hit the ceiling at every bump. The ride seemed endless, even though the driver was careening around the city at frightening speeds.

Once we'd set down my suitcases in the cottage bedroom, Kingsley clapped his hands together. "Now then. You really should lie down and have a nap."

"Kingsley, what is going on? You're treating me like I've got a hatchet over my head and I'm the only one who can't see it! Why are you being so . . . overly hostlike?"

I instantly regretted my tone. He was so English, and I was so abominably American. Cut to the chase, lay it on the line. He was too well mannered for that. I guess he was used to me by now because he stayed calm. He said, "Well, at least let me offer you some tea."

"Tea would be delightful. And then, the photo."

"Very well. I'll make some tea, and you shall have your photo."

"Thank you, Kingsley."

I walked into the bedroom and surveyed the queen-size bed with the ruby-colored coverlet. The smell of slight damp was familiar, bringing back the worried heaviness I'd hoped to escape when I'd left Kathmandu less than two weeks earlier. How hopeless I'd been then, but now, I reminded myself, we knew where Gerald was! I looked at the wall at the foot of the bed where there was a landscape painting of rangy hills in earth tones of mustard, with white sprinkles of snow on them like sugar. Lying down on the bed, running my fingers over the cool silk, I permitted myself a moment of unbounded hopefulness.

Kingsley arrived with a silver tea tray. I jumped off the bed and hurried into the living room. My eyes were drawn to the envelope on the edge of the tray. He handed it to me hesitantly. "Now, prepare yourself, Emma. He's clearly been through . . . a great deal."

"I know, I know." I grabbed the envelope impatiently. With a deep breath, I pulled out the photo.

And stopped dead. My hand went up to my mouth. My body turned to wood.

He looked so . . . *old*.

My beautiful Geebs was now an old man. His hair had thinned. The honey color had faded to a dull whiteness that hung limply on his head. No waves were in his hair. The gentle cheekbones that had graced his face were now angular, jutting outward. But worst of all were his eyes. They were frightened, wide and staring.

Kingsley put a hand on my shoulder. "Now, Emma, I know it looks rather tragic."

"*Looks?* It *looks* tragic?" Tears fell down my face, landing in my lap. My chest folded onto my lap, contracting with sobs.

"I'm sorry." He handed me a handkerchief he'd brought in on the tea tray.

"I don't know this man." I choked out the words, shaking my head and pointing to the picture. I wiped my drenched face with the handkerchief.

"I know. He looks dreadful—truly he does. But the point is that this photo clearly identifies for us where he is. Do you see the sign in the right-hand corner? It says, in Tibetan *and* Chinese, *the name of the prison*. Dorje said he had heard of that place. It's obviously a well-known location."

I was suddenly bone-tired. As I lay back on the couch, I mumbled weakly, "I'm sorry, Kingsley. I'm just, all of a sudden—"

"Exhausted. Now is the time for rest. We'll talk again tomorrow."

Without taking off my clothes, I slipped under the ruby coverlet and escaped into sleep.

I woke up when I heard a light tap on the cottage door.

"May I come in?" It was Kingsley's voice.

"Yes, come on in."

The smell of fresh scones drifted over the coverlet into my nostrils along with the bitter scent of scalding black breakfast tea. He knew very well what would get me out of bed.

I slowly pulled my reluctant body out of bed and went into the living room. "Sorry. I must look like a cat just dragged me in."

"Oh, don't bother about that, my dear. We need to discuss how we're going to proceed from here. I took the liberty of setting up an appointment with Mr. Yuan tomorrow, and I strongly advise you to allow me to speak with him myself."

"If you think that's best, then of course. Although I *was* relishing the look of shock on his face when I gave him that photo!" I spat out each word.

Kingsley opened his mouth to answer, but hesitated.

I couldn't help adding, "He was so smug, thinking I'd never be able to prove Gerald was in Tibet."

Kingsley's eyebrows went up. "Oh . . . I think you've got the wrong end of the stick here. The photo came *from* the embassy."

"Oh. So Mr. Bausman finally did something to earn his keep?" I sneered.

"Not the American embassy. The *Chinese* embassy."

I stared at him as if he'd grown another head.

"Well, in truth, the photo came from Mr. Yuan himself . . . in an unofficial capacity."

"What do you mean? What was *he* playing at?" I said suspiciously.

"He was playing at being a decent human being! He arrived at my doorstep on a rainy night, having ridden a bicycle, and he was hunched over trying to disguise himself. In fact, he seemed quite panicked that I happened to be standing out on my porch and he couldn't simply find a dry spot for the envelope and leave it there. Of course, I recognized him instantly from my years in diplomatic service."

I sat on the couch with my mouth hanging open.

"He handed me the envelope, then immediately pushed off and disappeared round the corner. For the longest time I couldn't figure out how he found me, but then I saw your last name on the outside of the envelope. He wanted *you* to have it, and this was the last address he had for you."

I sat stupefied for a long moment. "I can't believe it. I can't even breathe. I'm going to cry." The tears obligingly started. "Kingsley, I am the biggest fool . . . you have no idea the murderous thoughts I've had for that man."

"I daresay I can imagine." He smirked.

"I completely misjudged him! How could I be so blind, so completely off the mark?" I struggled to catch my breath.

"You apparently made quite an impression on him, a woman clearly with child, her husband having disappeared. It's a tragic circumstance. He must have felt that."

"But I thought . . . he felt nothing. He came on a bicycle in the rain? I can't believe it." The tears were rolling in cascades down my face now. "He must have been terrified someone would recognize him."

"Well, we now have an advantage, and I submit to you that we should use it wisely. As I said, I believe I should go see him myself, if you don't object."

"How could I object? I'm an imbecile." I laughed through my tears. "I put it in your capable hands."

A day later, Kingsley arrived breathless from seeing Mr. Yuan. He sat on the couch heavily. "The meeting was not encouraging, Emma. However, I believe the ambassador was absolutely on the level about what needs to be done."

"I thought he couldn't speak freely."

"Yes, well, once I referred to my background in diplomacy, he understood that we could speak in a sort of code. I made not one reference to the photograph. I told him I was seeking information about a hypothetical situation and asked him how the Chinese government might view such a case if one had proof that someone was being held in Tibet against his will."

"And?"

"This is the dismaying part. He conveyed to me that proof did not in fact make much difference in this case because 'that person' was being held for committing a crime."

"*What?* What crime?"

"Crossing Chinese borders without permission and spying for the U.S. government."

"This is absurd!"

"Emma, let me finish. What we must do is this: Go above the heads of *all* embassies. You simply *must* convince some important people in *your* country—I mean, politicians—to put pressure on China to let Gerald go. And for that task, the photo will be invaluable."

I felt hopeful. But helpless too. Was that possible?

Gerald

Is that him?

That's what I asked myself when I saw him. Before I received the news he had for me. I smile, unable to believe how my life is now changed. Going over it in my mind, I shake my head in disbelief and laugh giddily to myself.

Sonam. Sonam. Before I saw him again this morning, that name reverberated through my mind thousands of times. I looked and looked for him for weeks, mistaking other passersby for him.

This morning when I saw him, I watched him approach, with my head down, hoping desperately. He walked slowly, looking down at his feet. He had a yak with him, prodding it with a stick. The animal stopped and the man bent down. I saw his face, saw him look my way, using the yak's legs to stay out of view of the guards. He smiled for the briefest instant, such a big smile—and now I know why, because of the news he had for me—then stuck his hand in the fold of his *chuba* and pulled something out. Placed it under a stone. My hands were shaking, half with fear that we'd be caught, and half with hope.

I took my note out of my pocket. On the paper they gave me to write my confession, I'd written to Emma instead. I stood with my back to the guards, hoe in one hand, and my other hand clasping the note I wanted Sonam to take with him. If he could get a photo out of Tibet, why not a note for my Emma? I unfolded it against my chest. I held it there for a second, hoping he'd see it. He nodded, a barely perceptible tilt of his head. Then he walked away with his animal companion.

I waited several minutes to let Sonam get away, my pulse hammering in my ears. Our task today was weeding, so I pulled up weeds as I inched over to the spot where he'd left my treasure. After tucking his note into the cuff of my sleeve, I set my note under the stone and hoped he'd pick it up after we'd gone back inside the prison.

My breathing came shallow and fast, my heart thudding like the up and down of a sewing machine needle.

When the guards gathered together to smoke, I opened the treasure he'd left for me.

Hello,
Your frends say you look thin. They still try help you. They say tell you keep strong so you can see your daughter, born 5 May, 1955. Your daughter name Rinchen, wife say tell you is mirakle.
Sonam

How many minutes passed before I remembered to breathe? Staring at a spot ten feet away, I could not, could not, believe what I'd read. Read it again and again. I figured out the months and read again that Emma said to tell me it was a miracle. Then my eyes widened as if they'd pop out of their sockets, as if my hair would fall out from sheer happiness, my arteries would burst, my teeth would erupt right out of my gums, because it was just *too* amazing!

I had a daughter. My every muscle was glowing. I had a *daughter.* I had a daughter. I laughed from somewhere down in the soles of my beat-up boots up through my giddy jaws and streaming out the top of my head. Laughing and hoeing, because I'd remembered where I was. Even my internal organs were shouting, "*I have a daughter!*" I couldn't believe nobody else heard it.

When we got back to our cell, I told Tenzin and Lobsang. The old monk's smile for me was enormous. He asked, "Now you want to go home very badly, don't you?"

"Oh, yes, I do." Tears sprang to my eyes.

"A child is the most precious blessing. I will say prayers for your family and this Sonam."

"Yes. I'm worried about how he may have risked himself to bring me this news."

"He will be fine. He has accumulated great merit with his kindness."

Dorje

In the seven weeks that have passed since receiving Dawa's letter, I have watched my wife grow sadder than I have ever seen her. Sad about everything. So distressed that she doesn't oil her hair and put it into braids each day, just leaves it however it falls. When she cooks, she cries that she isn't in her old kitchen. Her tears fall when she talks about her brother. She worries about Dawa's soul, that if he involves himself with killing as soldiers do, he will destroy any merit he has accumulated in his life and have a terrible rebirth. Other times she frets over what the Chinese are doing to Samten. We have learned he is in a laogai prison camp, a different place from where Gerald is being held.

One afternoon Uncle Tinle and Aunt Pema were at the table with us, and we were having our midday *tsampa*. Lhamo was taking a nap, and Champa was playing out in the garden after finishing his food. Rinchen was silently crying. She had a lot of tears—they were dropping into her bowl of *tsampa,* and it was becoming soggy. We all stopped eating, but nobody said anything. Pema and Tinle and I looked at each other with wide eyes. Pema asked, "Rinchen-la, why are you crying?"

My wife left the room and I followed her into the bedroom. She lay on her back, staring at the ceiling. The tears still came from her eyes, dripping down.

"What is the matter?" I asked.

"I should be happy. I have a new baby. But I have awful dreams."

"About Dawa."

"Yes. And I don't live in my home anymore. There are so many people in Kathmandu. There are no mountains. Everything is different; I want things to be as they used to be."

I wanted to ask her something. I took a deep breath. "I have been thinking. I could go back to Tibet and try to convince Dawa to return with me."

She sat up fast. "Now you want me to live without a *husband* too?"

"No. No. I just want to—bring Dawa back."

"What if they put you in prison? Then what will I do? You cannot do this!" She cried even harder. Tinle and Pema and Lhamo could surely hear her, even in the dining room.

"I just want to do *something*."

"There is *nothing* to do." Her voice was angry, but not at me. She was angry to lose so much, so I put my arm around her. I felt her sadness as my own. Kathmandu does not have enough space for all of its people. In Tibet, we always had enough space. In my old house, sometimes the only sound was the wind blowing outside the windows or sheep bleating in the courtyard. When the snow fell and I stood outside under the white sky, the whole world stood quiet. I would go back inside to warm myself with butter tea and listen to the silence.

At Tinle's house, we hear the noise of peddlers and bicycles and motorcars going by outside, and I cannot find peace. Tinle tells me the quieter places are outside the city. Perhaps Rinchen would be happier there.

Some days she lies on her mattress and no one, not even

Champa, can convince her to get up. On those days I pack Lhamo on my back and take her and Champa to the marketplace. They love to see all the bright colors and smell the vegetables and fruits. In the market, Champa enjoys being the schoolteacher. He picks up each type of fruit and holds it up to Lhamo's face to tell her what it is. Of course, she just wants to put the fruit in her mouth and taste the new thing she has found.

So Kathmandu is a sadness for me and my wife, but for Lhamo and Champa, perhaps it is simply a new taste.

Emma

"Now, Emma, remember: honey attracts more flies than vinegar."

"I know," I say, sounding like a teenager answering her mother.

Genevieve adds, "I only say it because I know you're spitting mad." She squeezes my hand kindly to ease my digestion of her comment. She has on her crooked black-rimmed glasses for our session of letter-writing. Technically it's not the glasses that are crooked, it's her face. One of her eyes is slightly higher than the other.

When I got back to the States in early October, she and I stepped up the letter-writing campaign we'd begun months before. Every night, a new member of Congress. In my chest there is a rush of affection for this tiny woman who writes letters that move mountains. All her life she has written bushels of letters to congressmen about everything from child labor to women's suffrage, and she even once wrote to the president about the Indian question. Her letters are like her prune cakes: they go down easily and get things moving.

For instance, due to Genevieve's letter-writing, I now have the ear of Senator Jonathan Squibb. It was months ago when we first sat down with her Smith-Corona typewriter and I watched her draft a heart-wrenching letter to Senator Squibb. I'm not sure whether he actually did anything back then, aside from assuring us he was doing all he could. However, we recently sent a copy of Gerald's photo to the senator, and since that time he has really stepped up to the plate. He has written two letters to high officials in the Chinese government and has even received an answer. Their response was exactly as Ambassador Yuan had predicted: Gerald had committed crimes and was serving his sentence. Even though I should have known that would be their response, it still made my head pound with rage when I heard it. How could I deal with a government that fabricates whatever it pleases?

When I got this news, I felt obligated to share it with Abigail and Edgar. Since returning to the States, I've seen them three times. The first two times they doted on Rin. Abby had stitched a handmade doll for her, and Edgar bounced her on his knee. We drank tea in Genevieve's parlor and had sugary conversations about the weather, and I complimented Abigail on the roses she brought. Still, the stiff way Edgar held his body told me that underneath his politeness lay something darker. Whatever it was, I was sure I'd see it today during our third visit.

Their dining room smelled of burnt toast. I delivered the news as gently as I could. Afterwards, Edgar's face was set in a permanent scowl. Abigail sat primly next to him on the couch, keeping her diplomatic gaze on the floor before her.

I told them, "I want you to know this is very complicated. The Chinese are accusing Gerald of a list of crimes."

Edgar spoke in a steely voice, "Well, there's been a mistake then. The senator will clarify the situation, and then they'll *have* to let him go."

"You don't understand." I hesitated because I didn't know how much to tell them about how fanatical the communists could be. Abigail and Edgar assumed that this could all be worked out rationally. "China's a cauldron. People get thrown into prison for believing the wrong things or for not worshipping Chairman Mao ardently enough."

Edgar was glaring behind his glasses. The lenses magnified his eyes so he looked like an angry bug. Abigail's gaze wandered around the corners of the room.

I continued, "They do thought control, brainwashing, in these *laogai* camps. I've heard if you don't tell them what they want to hear, or bow down before a picture of Mao, you'll be . . . punished."

Abigail's eyes were wide and she was blinking rapidly. During a long pause she laid one hand on top of the other in her lap, trying to compose herself.

Edgar's stiff upper lip was getting stiffer by the moment. Taking a deep breath, he said, "You'll pardon me speaking my mind, Emma. You are . . . our daughter. But what I will never *begin* to understand—if these Chinese are half as—unbalanced—as you say, is"—he cleared his throat in a professorial way—"why you insisted on deliberately putting our son, well, in their path. I *simply* cannot—" His mouth snapped like a turtle's when he spoke the word *simply*. He frowned, then stood up and left the room.

I thought I knew how Edgar's sentence should end: *I simply cannot—forgive.* He couldn't forgive me. He blamed me. I stared down at my hands, tears filling my eyes, and I willed them not to run down my cheeks because it seemed selfish for me to cry in front of either of them.

Abigail sighed, then said softly, "You'll have to excuse Edgar. First he lost Tyler, in a manner of speaking, and now—"

I waved my hand to stop her. "I understand how he feels." My face was frozen.

"We don't hold *you* responsible, Emma." She was lying. Otherwise she wouldn't have bothered to say that. She wanted not to blame me, but she did anyway, and so did he.

And so did I. Me, the one who saw what was coming and then

promptly forgot all about it. Tears spilled onto my cheeks. Abigail offered me a handkerchief. I didn't want it, but realized she wouldn't stop offering it, until I took it.

"Thank you." I lifted it from her hand. She left the room and I pressed it to my face. Rin crawled over to the couch where I sat. As I closed my eyes, more tears leaked out. I felt the light pressure of her two little hands on my skirt at knee level. Opening my eyes, I saw her entire face stretched into a gummy grin as she looked into my eyes. I picked her up and held her gratefully, amazed at her love for a selfish woman like me. After gathering our belongings, I quietly let us out of my childhood home.

&

I was grateful to return to my real home, the one I now shared with Genevieve. She was an endearing sight with her sleeves rolled up, hair pinned up in a bun right on top of her head. She took Rin and put her in her high chair with a small bowl of batter.

"Ah, you're going to teach Rin to make prune cakes too? Recruiting a new helper early," I said, smiling. Tomorrow Genevieve would go to the prison and continue her hand-holding of WWMMs, as she called them: Women Who've Made Mistakes.

"Oh, ye-es," she purred. "Tomorrow's the day. I'll miss having you with me."

"I really wouldn't be of any use."

She turned from the counter where she was stirring the batter in a bowl and raised a quizzical eyebrow at me. "Now how could that be?"

"I am a woman who's made an unpardonable mistake." I started crying again.

She came over to me and put her hands on my arms. "There's no such thing as an unpardonable mistake, dear." We sat down at the kitchen table and she brushed a lock of hair out of my face. "What are we talking about, anyway, honey?"

I looked up at the ceiling and sighed heavily. "Oh, just luring Abigail and Edgar's son into a hotbed of communists."

"*You* did that?" A faint trace of a smile was on her lips.

"Yes! *I* did that!" I said bitterly. "*They* seem to think so—and I guess I agree."

"Oh, hogwash! You answered a call. The Spirit was goading both of you to go to that place for years! Plus, as I remember it, it was Gerald pushing to go there in the beginning. I don't suppose you remember that, do you?"

"I don't think—"

"Don't contradict me. I'm your elder. My memory may be a little patchy sometimes, but this I remember. You weren't particularly interested at first when the promptings started coming to you and Gerald in meetings. And wasn't it me"—she pointed a finger to her chest—"who said to you, 'Don't ignore the promptings of the Spirit'? So I guess I'm to blame too, eh?"

I rolled my eyes at her, but smiled weakly.

She rubbed her flour-covered hands together briskly. "It couldn't be that *God* is in charge of all this, could it? On Thursday, it's Thanksgiving, and you're going to sit at the table and thank God for only the good things in your life. And then you're going to blame *yourself* for the bad things. Because that's *your* department, eh? Hmmmph. You're overestimating your superpowers here, my dear."

I smiled through tears. She held me while I let out a few sobs. Then she stepped back and looked up at me, still keeping hold of my arms. "Honey, every place I ever went on God's errand wasn't a place where reasonable people go. But we Quakers aren't reasonable people. We go where God leads us, and then we wait humbly to see what's needed. Maybe you're thinking it would have been more holy to stay at home and put your feet up on the couch?"

I couldn't help but laugh. "No," I admitted, squeezing her hand.

I'm standing in the foyer in my nightgown. The mail has been pushed through the slot in the front door. An air-mail envelope has Kingsley's fine handwriting on it, and I reach my hand to it, a smile on my lips. I can't wait to rip open the envelope. Kingsley had called last week to tell me he'd got a letter forwarded to him through Ambassador Yuan.

A letter from Gerald.

I carefully open Kingsley's envelope. The inner envelope is still sealed, and my first name is written across it in a hand I don't recognize. I press it to my chest, then open it.

Em –
It's Geebs. I am alive, in prison in Lhasa. I love you. Kiss my daughter for me.
  Gerald Kittredge

Tears roll down my face. At the left corner of the page is the faint smudge of a thumbprint made by the dirt rubbing off his fingers onto the paper. Smiling, I kiss the smudge.

He knows Rin has arrived. Even though he's never met her, he loves her. Best of all, he sounds as if he's all right. The handwriting is shaky and large, as if done with the stub of a dull pencil. *I hope he's all right.* He was himself enough to write *It's Geebs.* The man I love is still in there. And he loves me. He doesn't blame me; he loves me.

I read it over and over, aloud and silently, in a chair, then on the couch, then at the window. Rin touches it with her little fingers. My nose sniffs it, but it doesn't have any particular scent. I tuck it inside my dress next to my heart because I can't get it close enough to me. I thank God for this letter over and over.

But does God make these things happen? I don't want to think that God put Gerald in prison in the first place. Genevieve told me she thinks God made us extraordinary and flawed beings, set the world to spinning, and left us in charge. She said, "Sometimes humans make the world a mess. Get busy fixing it."

~

Thanksgiving. I sit at my dining-room table with Abby and Eddy, Genevieve, Rin, and Tyler. The second Thanksgiving without Gerald. A sad silence makes the clinking of forks on plates seem coarse and loud. It reminds me of the quiet we had at the dinner table growing up, broken only by Edgar's well-meaning but intolerably boring lectures. No matter what my age, I still feel like an unruly child around them, testing their last shred of patience.

Genevieve's chewing her turkey with her mouth open and squishy sounds are coming from between her teeth. I giggle inside, enjoying how she can break the rules because she's a sweet old lady. Abigail and Edgar probably find her barbaric. Seeing her food turn inside her open mouth as she chews, like beans in a coffee grinder, brings a smile to my lips.

"I got a letter from Gerald," I say quietly, hoping no one's going to go off the deep end.

"What?" Edgar says. I expected him to be shocked, but the harsh lines of his face make him look annoyed.

"It came in the mail yesterday," I hurry to say. "Well, it's very short. Probably he didn't have much time to write it. Maybe someone was watching him—"

"Go on, never mind about that!" Edgar interrupts. "What did it say?"

"That he's alive, and he knows about Rin. He asked me to kiss his daughter for him."

"May we see the letter, Emma?" It's Tyler. It has been months since I've heard him say a single word. His voice is gentle, his eyes suddenly alive.

"Of course. Let me get it." I go up the stairs to retrieve it from my bedroom, stopping on one of the steps to take a deep breath. When I return, silence has blanketed the room.

I hand the letter directly to Tyler. He reads it quickly, then passes it to Abigail, who takes it hungrily from his hands. Edgar leans toward her and reads it with her. It's quiet. I can't read Edgar's expression. His eyebrows are pulled together. "Hmmmm," he says. "Well, that's wonderful. Wonderful. He seems sound enough. Although I daresay I don't understand this 'Geebs' business."

I look at him as if he's lost his mind. How in the world can he focus on that one little thing? How can he not be moved to hear his son's words?

Genevieve's eyes sparkle. "I suppose Gerald likes being called that. Like a nickname between two lovebirds," she says through her crooked grin, as if it can barely hold her joy.

"Hmmmph" is Edgar's only comment.

Abigail studies the food on her plate, her lips quivering. My fists clench under the table. I look at Genevieve again to remind me to have charitable feelings, but she's picking her teeth at the moment. Her glasses have again gone askew on her face. I shove a piece of turkey in my mouth to muzzle myself.

Years ago, Genevieve's first words to me were about my strong back, but hers is even stronger. People say Quakers are too idealistic, with our complete avoidance of violence, but Genevieve is the most practical person I know. She had the idea of getting the press to cover Gerald's story, so tomorrow we're making the rounds to every newspaper office in the vicinity. Between Rin's cute face and Genevieve's mesmerizing firecracker eyes, I'm sure we'll have some success. After that, we'll come home and sit down at the typewriter to roll out a letter to the president of the United States. All in a day's work.

> If we were to save only our bodies and nothing more from
> the [concentration] camps all over the world, that would not be
> enough. What matters is not whether we preserve our lives at any
> cost, but how we preserve them.
> —ETTY HILLESUM,
> a Jew killed in Auschwitz in 1943

NOVEMBER 29, 1955

Gerald

When night falls and the air blows in cold through the cell window, Tenzin sits in meditation pose and Lobsang sleeps. I pray for my daughter. Love feeling the word *daughter,* the way the two consonants come to life against the roof of my mouth. The hardness of them makes me stronger.

I pray to be released. The ache to be gone from here has never been so strong now that I've spent another Thanksgiving here. Every sinew in my body recoils from the walls around me because I no longer feel this is where I should be. I want to grab the piss pot and hurl it across the room and watch the shit run down the brick wall. My mind conjures vivid fantasies of shooting my way out of here with the spicy burn of gunpowder in my nostrils. Now I want to write a confession. To lie.

I've failed God. I despise my enemies instead of praying for them. Now I want to take the coward's way out: confess, like an ignoble rat.

I know Emma and Kingsley are trying to free me, but the

Chinese are so unreasonable. They have me—why should they give me up? They've accused me of preposterous crimes. Inciting counterrevolutionary activity among Tibetans. Forcing my religion on the masses.

I've been on my knees asking God to help me to be brave. To be loving in the face of hate. I've tried to suffer nobly, and to follow in the footsteps of Christ and of my Quaker brothers and sisters. To stand against what they do here—stand *against* being dehumanized, speak against one human being hanging another from the ceiling until his hands go blue. Speak against it to the death. I have wanted to be part of that voice.

Early on, I so wished to resist, with all my strength. I didn't know whether I'd survive, but if I did, I wanted to leave here as myself, as the soul God made me, maybe with cracks running through me, but still . . . the me God intended. Not their puppet.

The moon peeks through the cell window and I think of returning to Emma. My left hand clasps my right one, my remaining fingers like thin pencils, and I consider how my hands have wanted to strangle Han's skinny neck. Not strong enough to love my enemies. I've given up on looking for the seed of God in my interrogators.

I'm not sure whether Emma could respect me, knowing I've failed so shamefully. On the other hand, maybe she'd hate me if I didn't do everything possible to return to her and our child.

I have a child. I don't know the right thing to do, but I know what I *want* to do.

What was my daughter doing in this second? Sucking her thumb? Taking a nap? Crawling on the floor? Trying to stand with my Emma's steadying hand? Taking her first taste of a squashed banana pressed into her tiny mouth by Emma's fingers?

I could no longer ignore *the question*. It rattled me, poured restless energy into my legs. The question, Lord, was this: *Was my will to tell the truth worth missing those moments?*

Denying my daughter a father? Making Emma raise a child all alone?

Was it worth Emma's worried evenings and tormented dawns, wondering how I was, and if she'd ever see me again? I put my hands over my mouth and whispered into them, *Do You have an answer for me, Lord?* I'd said I wouldn't confess, wouldn't bear false witness. *But if I did, Lord, who would be harmed? Can You answer me?*

I pictured my daughter growing older without me, until she reached that second in time when she passed the place where her heart could bond with mine—when she was five? Six? Seven years old? Then it would be too late.

Is that not a sin, Lord? To abandon her to the world in that way? Are my convictions not just a little self-important when measured against that? Your commandment to not bear false witness—is that not a bit small compared to her soft hand curled into my open palm, her cheek against my chest as she falls asleep on my lap? Do you have an answer for me, Lord?

The only thing I was accomplishing by staying here was giving Comrade Han something to do. Someone to torture so he could prove his loyalty to Chairman Mao. My hands balled into fists as I thought of him.

What if I wrote a confession? Would I be lying if I said I tried to turn Tibetans against the invading communist forces? Even if it was only Dorje who heard me criticize the Chinese? Would I be lying if I admitted I'm guilty of being a capitalist? Was it a lie that I'd unfairly benefited from the labor of others? Wasn't it true that my country's continuing wealth was originated by means of slave labor? That wasn't a lie.

If I did confess, what was the guarantee they'd actually release me? They promised, "Confess your crimes, and we'll release you." Or was it really, "Confess your crimes, and we'll execute you for them"? I didn't know what happened to people who confessed. They got more food, more privileges, then they disappeared. Were they dead, or had they been released?

My hands touched the cold floor. I wondered how, or if, I'd survive another winter here. Leaning my head back, my newly gray hairs touching the gray cinder blocks, I thought of staying here and, in that moment, decided I'd rather crack my *own* head open on cinder blocks than stay. I'd rather be dead.

So I didn't sit in silence and didn't seek the Light. *I* decided. Even if they killed me, I had to try a confession. Then I had to work desperately hard to make them believe everything I'd written.

I had to do it.

I prayed God would pardon me if this was a sin.

NOVEMBER 30, 1955

Dorje

The night is glowing with the lights of the city outside my window. Rinchen and Lhamo are asleep in the bed beside me. In the quiet of the house, I hear only the rhythm of my wife's snoring. This is the time when I find myself thinking about important things: sometimes sad things, sometimes things that make me feel fortunate. I am missing home tonight, but I am also getting used to where I live now. In the spring, Rinchen and I and the children will move outside the city.

I go over to the window and push it open. American music travels on the night air, a foreign sound. But Tinle and Pema have made us feel at home in Kathmandu, even though the stink of the motorcars is so bad the Hindu women cover their noses with their saris.

When you must leave your own land, you begin to feel the world is larger than before. Especially in Kathmandu. When I walk in the streets here, I hear languages I do not recognize, some with soft words like Hindi, and some that come from a hard place in the throat, like German. When I go with Tinle, I am always asking him, "What was that language?"—after each foreigner passes us on the street. There are dark people, darker than Tibetans, like the Bengalis, and people so pale—more pale even than Gerald!—who are from such places as Denmark or the United States. I think to myself that Dawa was right, I have no idea where these places are! Far away, or close? How would you travel to arrive there?

Champa has started going to school. He comes home from school with books that have pictures of the whole earth in them. All of the countries are drawn on the page, so you can see how far away some places are! I was astonished to see how far Emma and Gerald traveled to come to my country.

Champa loves to learn. At first he did not want to go to school at all, and back in Tibet he thought he would never go to school because he did not go into the monastery. So a few months ago, when Rinchen and I told him that he was going to start classes, he went crying into another room, saying, "I want to go home!"

We followed him and both of us sat down with him on the floor. "This is our home now, Champa," I told him gently.

"That's not what you said when we left our house! I left Aba there because you said we could go back!" Aba was a little stuffed-sheep toy with black plastic eyes. We had left so quickly that none of us had remembered to take it along.

"I am sorry, Champa, but we are going to stay here," I told him. "At least for now, because it is not safe to go back."

He looked down at the floor with his lips quivering. Tears rolled in two lines down his face. If he only knew how much Rinchen and I wanted to go home too!

"No one will take care of Aba. He'll be so lonely, he'll die." Another tear rolled from Champa's right eye, and he looked straight at me.

"Aba is not alone. The gods are watching over him. They will send a little mouse or a spider to come and visit him in the house." I put my arm around my son's shoulders.

Then Rinchen added, "We will recite prayers for Aba so he will not be lonely."

"But I still have to go to school?"

"Yes," I insisted.

"But then *I* will be lonely! I will miss you! How can you send me away?"

"What do you mean? We are not sending you away."

"You sent Dawa away to school," he wailed.

"Champa, that was a monastery. This is a school where you study during the day and then you come home. You have dinner with us!"

"Oh." That stopped him. His eyebrows pushed together as he considered. "Every night I sleep at home?"

"Every night," I promised.

"What if I don't like it?"

"You will like it. There will be other children like you and a nice teacher and many books."

I felt funny telling Champa what it would be like to go to school because I have never been myself. My son would learn things that were strange to me and Rinchen. I wanted him to learn these lessons, but would it feel odd, as if we were in two different worlds?

Also, I do not want him to lose our old ways. For centuries, we have kept our gods happy by showing our respect in our festivals, reciting prayers, hanging prayer flags. Would Champa understand how important these things were with his mind full of new ideas? I had already seen what happened in our family because of Dawa's new ways, and I did not like it.

Rinchen, she is a deep thinker, especially when she hears something disturbing. She does her thinking all day as she churns butter tea, cooks, or washes the clothes. The other day we heard reports on the wireless of some of the things the Chinese have been doing in Tibet. They are building roads for motorcars, and we Tibetans never even used anything that had wheels because the gods forbid it. The Chinese are cutting down trees in the southeastern part of Tibet. You can see the bodies of all the trees lying dead on trucks heading to China. When she heard these things, Rinchen stopped her weaving in the middle of a row of thread, just dropped it on the floor, and went outside. From then on it was her mind weaving, trying to understand the meaning of these events. Later in the evening, she was clicking her jaw while she thought, like a yak chewing grass he finds on the ground.

The next day, she came to me three times in one morning. Each time she had butter tea in one hand and a question in the other. In the early morning she said, "The gods are testing us to see if we'll be loyal even in a new situation. That's what is happening to our people, Dorje."

These things she says do not sound like questions, but I know she is asking what I think. The problem is, I try not to think too much. If I spent my day wondering about things as much as she does, my head would snap open like a dried-up pea pod.

The second cup of butter tea came with her saying, "The gods are teaching us a lesson because we became prideful." She stood there with her hands on her hips while I sipped my tea. I was giving my tea a lot of attention. Then I said, "Delicious tea, Rinchen. It is really good." She frowned at me impatiently and walked out of the room.

When she brought the third steaming cup in the late morning, I was outside in the garden. This time she said, "I have the answer now. I believe the gods have abandoned us because we let the Chinese into Tibet. The thirteenth Dalai Lama gave us the word of the gods that this is forbidden."

I looked at the brown soil on my hands and realized I was upset. "How could we stop them, Rinchen? We did not invite them in! How could the gods be angry with us for that?"

"They don't seem to be protecting us, do they? We must have failed in some way!"

"You should go to a lama to answer these questions! I am a simple trader—ask me about salt or wool or routes over the mountains! You think too much, Rinchen—your mind is like a monkey jumping from tree to tree all day long!"

She rolled her eyes. "I have a husband who doesn't care what happens."

"No, you have a husband who has wool between his ears and wants it to stay that way!"

She tried not to smile, but I saw it anyway, and then she shook her head as she walked into the house.

~

Sometimes I think about Samten. It is strange because sometimes I envy him because he is still in my country and I am not. When you do not have your country, you notice that the way people talk and even the smells are not the same. When I drink masala tea as the Nepalis do, it makes me lonely. I start to think, *Are my ways of thinking the correct ways?* When I put myself in the place of all the strangers around me in the street, I become aware that they see the world differently, and they think *they* are right. Such as the American I saw on the street the other day. He was in a fancy suit, walking very straight, with his nose in the clouds. He seemed to be thinking he was more important than me. In Tibet we are taught to think of others as more important than ourselves. So who has the correct way of thinking?

I knew I would learn about Nepal, but I did not expect to learn more about my own country. Tinle says that Tibet is a rare thing. He claims that in other places people do no prostrations at all, and that some people do not believe we are reborn—that we live just one lifetime, and that we must learn all our lessons in that short time! No butter lamps, no Buddhas even—and no striving to accumulate merit. What then is the purpose of one's life?

The longer I live outside my country, the more I learn that Tibet is unlike any other place on the earth.

NOVEMBER 30, 1955

Gerald

I'm holding a pen. It's slipping between my sweaty finger and thumb. With Thanksgiving done, and what will be my second Christmas here lurking in three weeks, I feel my body standing on a cliff, and I'm about to move. To pick up my foot, place it on ghostly air, and plunge. I'll never be the same once I write these words. I won't be able to take them back.

I tell myself, *Lift that foot, touch the nothingness, and step into it. Leap toward your daughter's face.*

I, Gerald Kittredge, declare that I am guilty of wrong thinking and wrong action. I have been an enemy of the people. Because I was born into a life of privilege in capitalist United States, I developed wrong thinking from a young age. In my schooling, I was taught that Communism was wrong. Other people's labor provided me with food to eat, clothes to wear, toys to play with. It is only during this time with my comrades here that I have learned how badly I was taught in America. I have learned that my bourgeois American ways caused suffering for others.

While I have shivered in my cell here, I have felt the physical suffering that the proletariat must endure each day. I have felt his empty stomach, empty because of rich men exploiting him. I suffer gratefully, giving thanks to my comrades and to Chairman Mao.

After crossing the borders into Tibet without China's permission, I spread imperialist ideas among the impressionable Tibetan masses and criticized the actions of the Party in Tibet.

My fingers are stiff with cold when I lift the pen from the page. What if the communists take me at my word and put me to death?

I tell myself I have to take that chance. To see my daughter's tiny fingers.

It was wrong for me to impose my counterrevolutionary thinking on Tibetans. What if this isn't enough for them? What if they make me prove that I've changed? What if they try to force me to denounce someone? Droplets of sweat collect above my lip and on my back, although the air is cold enough for me to see my breath in the cell. Where do I draw the line? Have I already crossed it? No doubt they will ask me to denounce Tenzin. That I could not do. No matter what.

What if they'll never believe me? *No. Stop worrying. Get down on your knees, man, and play the game to the stars. Figure it out.* What do they want, more than anything? They want to see the American on his knees. They want to hear me despise my country and extol theirs. Fine. I'm no patriot.

I was infected with the disease of imperialism from a young age. In America, I was taught that communists were ignorant fanatics. Now I realize my country is the ignorant one. Before I was rehabilitated, I spread anticommunist thinking to my countrymen by criticizing the Party's actions in letters to my friends in the United States. For this, I am deeply sorry. My reeducation has been an opportunity most Americans never get to be shown the right way of thinking. I thank

Chairman Mao and all those who have shown me the errors in my thinking.

I signed it. Dropped my pen on the page and sighed with relief. *God forgive me.*

➤

After delivering it, I sat shivering in my cell. Not from cold, but from the horror of what I'd done. My Quaker brothers and sisters, they'd be sickened. But Emma, what would she think? I wished I knew. Then again, maybe I didn't.

I couldn't get warm. What would come next? Would I be asked to struggle against Tenzin or Lobsang? I ground my knuckles into my eyes to erase the image.

When I'd delivered the confession to Comrade Han, the slit mouth spread into a broad grin. He stood over me as I sat in my chair, the proud schoolmaster beaming at the good little boy. He touched my shoulder and purred, "Good work, Comrade Kittredge." Then he dismissed me. I felt sick.

He'd move up several rungs in the Party for breaking the American. As I was being escorted out, I saw him reading the confession with raised eyebrows. A look of surprise, then suspicion. Then as they walked me back to the cell, I wondered, *What are the Chinese going to make of this? Will they trust that they've really broken me after all the time I resisted them?*

Back in the cell, Tenzin greeted me with a smile. I sat down and felt a cold spot on one half of my backside. My trousers got torn on a piece of metal, and the hole has grown. It told me I was wearing out. Maybe the best thing was to throw in the towel.

I didn't tell Tenzin what I did. I was too ashamed. He would never make the choice I did. How could he understand?

I did it for my daughter. Because I'm a father. Although I kept telling myself that, I felt like a traitor already.

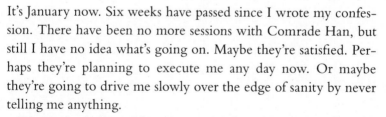

I confessed again. This time to Tenzin and Lobsang. Told them I lied, that Comrade Han broke me. It was so hard to say it.

Tenzin was quiet. I went on babbling, trying to justify myself, glancing from Tenzin to Lobsang and back.

Lobsang looked defeated. He shook his head and said, "But you are a *strong* man."

"No, I don't think I am."

"You are a strong man, but even you confessed. What hope do I have?" Despair lay heavy in Lobsang's words.

I was ashamed down to my boots and so sad to have disappointed him.

"Does he have your heart?" Tenzin asked quietly.

"Who?"

"Does Comrade Han have your heart?"

I thought about it for a long moment. "No. He doesn't." That I knew for sure, like knowing my heart was beating because I could feel it.

"Who has your heart?" Tenzin's tone was patient, inquiring.

No hesitation. "My daughter has my heart. And Emma."

Tenzin said nothing more. I didn't know what he meant—if I was being absolved or asked to examine my soul further. Lobsang pulled his knees to his chest and rested his head on them.

It's January now. Six weeks have passed since I wrote my confession. There have been no more sessions with Comrade Han, but still I have no idea what's going on. Maybe they're satisfied. Perhaps they're planning to execute me any day now. Or maybe they're going to drive me slowly over the edge of sanity by never telling me anything.

It's strange because I have more reason to hope now than ever before. I'm better fed—all of us are—than when I first got here.

There's no more Comrade Han, at least for me. And yet I think that just opening the possibility of release in my mind is driving me mad.

The meditation that Tenzin taught me is making me aware of the illusions in my mind. I see that each eternally long day I live now is really the same length as any others I've lived.

Tenzin tells us that each day of life leads to death, then rebirth. He says, "For Tibetans, every day is an opportunity to prepare for death. We can escape the endless cycle of death and rebirth. We can eject our consciousness straight out of the body and become liberated from suffering."

"Eject our consciousness?"

"Yes, this is the practice of *Phowa*. In the very last second of life, you push your soul right out of the top of your head. But you have to practice so you can do it when the time comes, or your consciousness may leave the body through your bowels. Then your journey through the *bardo* is more difficult, and you may be reborn in one of the lower realms."

I can't imagine such a thing, so I don't say anything. As much as I'd like to take such a long view, I see now that being a father ties me to the earth. I used to want to be liberated from my earthly body. But now, I don't want to go sailing in the clouds of nirvana.

I want to see my daughter's face and feel her milky skin.

Emma

"Mrs. Kittredge? This is Senator Jon Squibb." His voice wheezed through the telephone receiver that Monday. It had been five months since I'd heard from Gerald. "I wanted to call you personally—"

"What's happened?" I burned with fear and impatience.

"I got a letter regarding your husband. They're considering releasing him."

"What? Really? They said that? Oh my God. That's fabulous! When?"

He pulled in a wheezy breath. "Well, they said—now, let me explain this carefully—the letter just said they may release him."

"May? Meaning what?" Now I was snapping at his heels for answers.

"Meaning they're considering it," he said noncommittally.

"Well, when are they going to decide?"

"There are some problems to work out first. Would you like to come by my office later this week, say Thursday afternoon?" His words were measured and deliberate.

"Certainly." My skin prickled. "He's all right, isn't he?"

"He's fine. That's not the issue."

My heart was throbbing out of my chest. "Then what is it?" I was so impatient I wanted to scream, *Tell me!*

"We'll talk about it Thursday." His tone was firm. "See you then."

Thursday finally inched its way into the present, and I sat in Squibb's waiting room with Rin on my lap and Genevieve beside me. I was surprised when Senator Squibb himself appeared to show us into his office. He was shorter than me and large around the middle. After we'd arranged ourselves into chairs in his office, I noticed that skin bulged over the edge of his shirt collar. He poked a finger under the collar to tug at it. He looked nervous.

"Well, isn't this the lovely family," he said in a sugary voice.

I smiled some sugar back to him and held Rin proudly, hoping she'd tug at his heart. He reached out a hand for me to shake. "Jonathan Squibb. Call me Jon."

"Emma Kittredge, and this is my daughter, Rin, and my friend Genevieve Rumble."

"Isn't she a lovely little girl!" he cooed.

"She looks just like her daddy," I piped in hopefully.

"Well," he began, "I have to say what an honor it has been to be involved in this case. "

Has been? This was sounding like a departing speech. He tugged at his collar again.

I couldn't wait any longer. "And so, what did you want to discuss with me?"

"I have good news, Mrs. Kittredge. We've gotten a tentative agreement from the Chinese to release your husband on May fifteenth."

Genevieve exclaimed, "Why, that's wonderful!"

Although my heart was jumping out of my chest, I sat quietly, my eyes boring into Squibb's forehead, waiting to hear what the issue was.

He saw my serious expression and cleared his throat. "The letter from the Chinese said something about Gerald being—a communist."

I laughed bitterly. "They lie continually. What's the problem?"

"Well, this isn't going to play well with Senator McCarthy and the American public, for me to secure the release of a known communist."

I felt searing heat in my head, as white-hot as a flashbulb. "This is insane! Pardon me, but my husband is the victim here. He's not a communist! He is a Quaker, in fact, with strong religious convictions. He would never, ever, ever become a communist."

"Well, I'm asking because they said he wrote a letter of confession, or something that says he's seen the light and now he's a communist."

I wanted to screech at this ignorant man. *Breathe. Do not foul this up, Emma.* I reminded myself that Americans didn't understand that the communist movement in China and Tibet was somewhat like the Crusades. The communists were happy to see people drawn and quartered if it meant they might embrace the correct ideology. Every last person they could count among their fold, even if those people were lying, was another moral victory.

I kept my voice low, hoping the senator couldn't tell that I was ready to spit. "I can assure you that Gerald would lay down his life for his Christian faith. You can tell the public *that.*"

"I don't want him making any pro-Red statements that'll be unfavorable for me," he mumbled, his breathless voice sounding like the gutless weasel he was proving himself to be.

It took every ounce of my self-control to not explode. "After the Reds have held him in prison for several years, I don't think he's likely to make pro-Red statements, do you?"

"Mrs. Kittredge, the Chinese want a press conference. They want me to go over there for a photo opportunity with some of their officials, and they want American press covering the story." His eyes darted around the room and his hands flailed around helplessly. As though I should save him from this awful fate by telling him, *Oh, okay, then let's just let my husband rot. We absolutely can't harm your reputation.*

"They sent me this." He handed me three large photographs of pages someone had written. "Ma'am, those are photos of your husband's sworn statement that he's a communist."

I swallowed hard, my hands trembling. *It's falling apart, I feel it.* The handwriting was shaky, as if written by someone with a tremor, but the shapes of the letters were distinctly Gerald's.

"I'm sure you can see the problem for me, Mrs. Kittredge."

I was breathing fast and thought I'd faint, thinking of what they might have done to get him to write this. And to make his hand shake. Seeing my face, Rin started crying. I handed her to Genevieve, who began walking her around the room in her arms to calm her.

"You have to get him out of there," I said, my voice like a feather.

"I can't do that, ma'am. I'm sorry, but I can't go over there and shake hands with a bunch of Reds in order to free someone who's publicly proclaimed he's a communist. Mrs. Kittredge, you know I have a conservative constituency, and frankly, I don't think you appreciate my position here."

Me, me, me. My position. His words rang in my ears like a mosquito, making me want to bang him over the head until I saw blood and lots of it. "Oh, I see it with perfect clarity. You, with your tail between your legs!"

"All right, Emma," said Genevieve in her quavery but determined voice. "Now young man, you've made yourself clear. But if you're not going to do this, then you need to help us figure out how this deal with the Chinese can be done *without* you."

He sighed, all put-upon by these females in his office. "I believe I've made it perfectly clear, ladies, that I will not be having any more communications with the Chinese." His wheezing breaths were getting faster. "I can't do that."

"Not can't. Won't," I spat at him.

But Genevieve was minding the details. "Have you told the Chinese no?"

"No. I haven't told them anything. I *no longer communicate with them.*"

She smiled straight into his acid tone. "Can we have your word you won't make a move until you've given us time to figure out something? We can't let this chance pass, and there may be another way to make this happen." She turned to me and said, "We'll take it to the Quaker meeting and have the whole meeting hold this problem in the Light."

He raised his eyebrows sheepishly. "That's fine, Mrs. Rumble. I'll give you the name of the contact and you'll have to take it from here."

"Very well," said Genevieve in a businesslike tone. "Good day, Senator."

I plodded out of the office behind my two companions. As she shuffled along on the sidewalk, I heard Genevieve mutter, "Lily-livered buffoon."

That Sunday, Genevieve and I left Rin with her grandparents while we went to Quaker meeting. After sitting down, I felt desperate and stirred up during the silence of worship.

A little voice prodded me to stand up and ask all members to hold Gerald in the Light. The muscles in my legs tensed, eager for me to stand up. Then I was on my feet, mouth open to speak. "Please. Hold Gerald in the Light." My voice shook. Tears trickled down my cheeks. "All of us, right now. I feel he must be suffering so much in the prison, and now the Chinese have forced him to write a confession that he's a communist. I know he would not write that unless they were doing something to . . ." My throat closed on the words. I sat down and wept as quietly as I could, aware that all eyes were on me.

Genevieve's hand was on my arm to steady me. After worship, we had introductions. A balding man introduced himself as Arnold Lichter, a member of the Philadelphia meeting who had just moved to Middletown. When the announcements were over, Mr. Lichter walked up to me. He extended his hand, and I shook it hesitantly. "Arnold Lichter. I felt so moved by what you said."

I sighed and gave an abridged version of Gerald's ordeal.

When I'd finished, I saw he was smiling. "I've got Senator Aronson staying at my house. He's an old family friend. Maybe he could help you."

"Jacob Aronson from Pennsylvania?"

"The very one. Heck, he's been wanting to give those red-baiters a kick in the pants for years now—since '47, at least! I'll go home and talk to him about it. Can I call you on the telephone?"

"Yes! I'll write down my exchange for you." My heart sped up, hoping.

<hr />

A week passed. Every time the phone rang my heart jumped. What was taking so long? I should have asked Mr. Lichter for his number.

On Saturday afternoon, I scrubbed the floor with Rin. A brush for her, a brush for me. She played with iridescent soap bubbles. I scrubbed a tile. She scrubbed the sofa. The toilet. The drapes. I scooped her up and blew a raspberry on her cheek. She shrieked with laughter.

The phone rang. I picked up after one ring and heard Mr. Lichter's pressured speech. "Senator Aronson wants to meet you at my house tomorrow morning."

"Just tell me how to get there."

The next morning, I stood on the doorstep, ringing the bell. The air was crisp and sweet with spring blossoms. This time, I wasn't going to waste any time. I was going to pin Aronson down one way or the other, today.

"Ah, Mrs. Kittredge." The senator stood in the doorway and motioned me in. He was as tall and elegant as an English walking stick, with gray sprinkled around his temples. "It's a pleasure to meet you. Please come in."

"Thank you for making time to see me!" I was breathless. My backside had scarcely touched the paisley couch when I said, "Well, after what Mr. Lichter told you, does this sound like a situation you'd be willing to involve yourself in?"

"Tell me exactly what you'd need from me." He sat with hands clasped over his stomach, looking calm.

"I need you to fly with me to Tibet, shake hands with some communist bureaucrats, and say cheese for their cameras. They're trying to lure an American statesman over there so they can pretend they have our blessing. Are you up for it?"

He hesitated, squinting doubtfully.

I pressed on. "Just so there aren't any surprises, you might be called a communist sympathizer for doing this. But, Mr. Lichter said you might be willing to brave that. I have here for your perusal my husband's so-called confession that he's a communist. Undoubtedly extracted by means of torture."

My hand trembled as he took it from me. He kept his eyes on me.

I explained, "The Chinese are getting heat from the United Nations for invading Tibet, so this is the Chinese attempt at public relations, or propaganda, if you will. If they can show pictures of themselves shaking hands with an American delegation, they're hoping it will stop the flak."

"So they're going to have press there?"

"Theirs. And we are to bring our own."

One eyebrow shot up at that, then his brow furrowed, as if something had occurred to him. He glanced down at the photos of the confession. "Can I have time to think this over?"

"Well, not much. The meeting's in three weeks, and we'll need travel papers."

He put glasses on and read Gerald's confession carefully. Then he looked up, amused. "So Squibb thought your husband was a Red, from this?"

I nodded.

He chuckled. "That makes sense since he's never spent any time behind enemy lines."

I didn't know what Aronson meant, but I was hoping this was a good sign.

"I did," he said. "I was a POW. Captured by the Germans. I won't go into what that was like—you probably remember hearing the stories."

I swallowed, not wanting to remember. "Yes."

"My point is, I would have said, signed, or done *anything,* including chewing off my own foot, to get out of that prison camp." Pain and humor were in his voice, a mix that made him seem unutterably wise to me at that moment.

"How long were you there?" I said quietly.

"Eight months. Sounds short, but I'm still trying to wipe it out of my mind."

I looked into his eyes. "Imagine almost two years."

"I am."

Our eyes locked, and then I felt that he understood, all of it, understood it in his bone marrow. He said, "I'll call you tomorrow morning."

I stood up, not wanting to take any more of his time, and reached out my hand. "I don't know how to thank you for—" I was suddenly undone with a wash of tears. A few sobs shook me and I struggled to contain the avalanche of feelings brought on by looking into the eyes of someone who'd been where Gerald was. Through my tears I mumbled, "I'm sorry."

"It's all right. I understand." His face was sad. He squeezed my hand warmly, rather than shaking it. Then he showed me out.

"Looks like a green light on our mission, Mrs. Kittredge." Aronson's voice held a smile in it, one I could hear through the telephone.

I held my breath. "You're certain?"

"Absolutely. I'll have my secretary arrange it. We'll have to charter a plane, arrange for some press folks to go with us. I'll need to talk with the Chinese to confirm."

"I'll give you the contact information," I said, speaking through the lump in my throat. "Senator, may God repay you for your kindness." My voice was thick with feeling. "You are assured a place in heaven for this!"

Dorje

Kingsley came to visit this morning. I had never seen him so excited. He is normally a quiet man who taps softly on your door and waits until you invite him in, then he steps in slowly and removes his hat. This morning he strode through the doorway right after knocking, and his hair was sticking out sideways when he took off his hat.

"He's going to be released!" he said. "I've heard from Emma. Gerald is going free!"

"Oh! Thank the gods!" We were inside the doorway, two grown-up men, jumping up and down with our hands on each other's shoulders as though we had drunk too much *chang!* My wife came to see and stood covering her mouth, looking at us and laughing.

"They are letting Gerald go free, Rinchen!" I told her.

She smiled and put her hands in *mudra* to mumble a prayer. Then she was silent, and I knew she was thinking about Samten.

I pulled Kingsley into the kitchen so Rinchen could serve us some butter tea. Then he told us how it was that Gerald was going to be freed.

That night my heart was sad like Rinchen's, but I was thinking of Dawa. In his latest letter from inside Tibet, he and some other members of the freedom fighters were going to Lhasa to save it from the Chinese. I have never heard him have so little hope.

He is one who must have a purpose in his life. I always thought he would find that easily in a monastery, with so many wise men to guide him. But he is a restless young man, even more restless than I thought. And so sensitive—for him to see his people hurting is a lot for his heart to bear.

I sat up in bed and looked at my family sleeping around me, Rinchen cradling Lhamo in her arm, and Champa rolled up into a tight ball close by, the way he always sleeps. I imagined saying to Dawa, "Come back with me and I will help you find your way." But I am his father, only a wool trader, and he does not listen to the words of even one like Lama Tsethar anymore. Why would he listen to me?

I got up and took the latest letter out of a drawer. The writing on the envelope was strange. Some words had letters with soft edges and others had points like knives. The letter seemed to hold all of his emotions, sharp as needles and raw as yak meat drying in the sun. I picked it up. It was cool in my hands, not hot as I had expected. The paper inside was folded in crooked lines. I opened it to read.

Dear Pa-la,
We are moving our forces to the holy place. Dordrum is dead. A bullet pierced his heart and blood flew from his mouth. I wanted to help him die in peace so I whispered the prayers in his ears, but he died so fast, I don't know if he attained the liberation. I cannot see how to die in the right way when shot with a bullet—there's no time. This life of fighting—maybe it's not so natural. My soul is heavy—I think I failed

*my friend when I asked him to join the resistance with me. I don't want
you to worry, but I have no one else I can tell these things.*

Pa-la, I so wish I could see your face.

Your loving son,

Dawa

So—I had to show him my face, I thought. I had to see him,
hold him, get him to return with me. Gerald will be set free.
Why cannot my son be freed?

Kingsley gave me this idea today. When I told him Dawa was in
Lhasa, he asked me if there was anything I would like Emma to take
to Tibet for my son. Tonight I thought, *I wish she could take me!* Even
though I do not want to bring more trouble to our family by taking
this risk, Dawa is in great danger as an enemy of the Chinese.

I shut my eyes in the darkness, trying not to see images of what
happens to Tibetans in Chinese hands. With my bare feet on the
cold floor, I walked slowly into the altar room. A butter lamp
painted the room the color of gold. On the altar was a gold statue
of the saint called Padmasambhava. His eyes were large and open
enough to see things we cannot see as humans. I prostrated myself, then stood, lit a stick of incense, closed my eyes, and asked
him to grant my prayer for my son's safety and to show me the
correct way. When I looked at him again, his eyes stared back at
me. I could not see an answer in them yet.

Tomorrow I will talk to Rinchen. Padmasambhava will answer
my prayer.

~

I spoke to my wife early the next morning as she was serving me
my butter tea and tsampa. Right away she answered, "It is right for
you to go to Dawa." She would not look at me and held her back
stiff, as if saying this took great effort. "He needs your help. Because you have a good intention, the gods will watch over you."

I was shocked. She had forbidden a trip earlier when I had

asked her, so I answered her playfully, "What has happened, Rinchen—have you grown tired of your husband?"

She smiled at my joke, but only a little. Then she took my hand, still keeping her eyes down, and said, "I love my husband for his big heart that wants to protect our son." Then she finally looked at me. "I'm afraid, but what can I do? Live in this fear forever? No! We will pray for you every moment you are away."

I squeezed her hand. "Dawa is calling out to me in his letter. He knows he has made a mistake. But he needs his father to order him to come home. This he cannot do for himself."

"And when you go, you will tell him that his mother also orders him to come home!"

I was delighted to hear her commander voice, and I teased her, "That will certainly make his decision for him!"

~

My journey began two days later, when I caught a ride to the border of Tibet on the back of a Nepali man's truck. I was stuck between two chickens in cages. The one on my left was light-colored, and the one on the right had dark reddish brown feathers, the color of dried grass on a hillside at sunset. The light one fell asleep, but the other one stared at me. Perhaps she could tell I was admiring her feathers because she turned her head to look at me with one eye and then the other. I stopped admiring her colors because she did not seem to like it, then I started dozing off. To be truthful, I fell asleep so I would not smell the chicken stink on both sides of me. Every few minutes the dark hen would lean my way and peck at my sleeve, just to remind me not to bother her. I would look at her and say, "You are the one staring at me! I am sleeping. Look, my eyes are closed."

This sleeping and pecking continued for hours. I could not understand what was bothering her. At one point I even reached into my *chuba* and got some of the bread Rinchen had sent with me and fed it to the hen as a peace offering. But she only took it as an invitation to peck at me more. Finally, I stood up and leaned against the rails of the truck to get away from her. Still, each time I turned, she was staring at me.

I gave thanks in my prayers, thinking that perhaps the gods had sent this little chicken to distract me from my worries. She did her job well because I soon recognized we were close to the border.

In that moment, I could hardly believe my good fortune. I was about to enter Tibet. My home.

The truck stopped right before the border. I jumped off the back and walked up the road toward the bridge that joined Tibet and Nepal. Below the bridge flowed an enormous white river fed by the land of snows. From this bridge, the road, cut into a series of switchbacks, lay on a magnificent steep, green hillside. On the Nepali side were hundreds of shanty houses made from whatever materials their creators had found on the road. On the Tibetan side of the hill were hundreds of square, Chinese-style buildings.

I would wait until nightfall to cross the river beneath the bridge at a place where I could climb over boulders. It was treacherous, as the boulders could be slippery. As I waited, I recited prayers. *Protect Rinchen and Champa and Lhamo. Watch over Dawa, he is not on the right path.*

After sunset, a half-moon hung in the sky. There would be light to guide my journey, but not too much. I walked a distance away from the bridge to a thick cover of trees. The wind blew against my back, shuffling the leaves and pushing me toward Tibet. In my hands was a tall, strong stick to help me balance in the white storm of the river water. The boulders were wet from splashing. As I was wearing shoes I'd bought in a Nepali trekking shop, I did not slip. I crossed the river with prayers in my mouth. From here, I climbed the steep hill, staying away from the switchbacks and under the cover of trees. My boots made soft crunch sounds on the rocks. I turned my prayer wheel as I walked to make my feet silent to the ears of any border soldiers.

For the next few hours I climbed the hill and prayed *Om mani peme hung* with each four steps. I picked up my feet carefully to be as silent as a snow leopard.

The sound of an engine came from behind me. I dropped to the ground and froze like a lizard about to be attacked. A Chinese army motorcar approached. It came so close that I saw the dirt beneath the driver's fingernails. Would the driver see me?

The motorcar passed by and I breathed again.

After much climbing, I finally reached the top of the hill, and I felt safe enough to stop and thank the gods for my safe journey so far. Taking the pack from my back, I dropped down and put my chest onto my country's soil. My heart wanted to beat against it. I gave thanks to all the Buddhas who helped me return to the skin of my mother. Kissing the ground, I was happy when the dirt stuck to my lips. My tears fell onto the soil and I wanted them to stay there. Always.

The rest of that day I walked. Around midday, a nomad family invited me into their tent to share tea and *tsampa*. Inside their tent woven of black yak hair a fire was burning, and a hole in the top of the tent let out the smoke. Although it was hard to breathe in the smoky tent, the warmth of the fire soothed me.

There were four of them, a mother and a father and two children. They were dirty from living out on the hillsides. The woman offered me yak meat, and I accepted it with thanks. I wanted to ask them about what had been happening in my country, but I did not speak their dialect. We sat and smiled at each other. Their younger child was about Lhamo's age, with a filthy face and just a few teeth. She pointed at them with her finger. Her hair was long enough that it stood up in parts as Champa's hair used to do when the air was dry. I missed him.

They invited me to sleep in their tent with them, so I spread out my bedroll. I left quietly as the sun was rising, after giving them a gift of some turquoise beads I had brought with me. The woman was putting the beads in her hair as I left.

As I kept walking each day, I saw the land change before me. The snowy edges of the peaks reached toward the sky. I said to myself, *I am in the land of snows again.* As an offering, I left a silk *khata* I had brought from Kathmandu at the top of the highest pass. In the days that followed, I watched for signs that I was nearing the cities. It was strange that there was now a road, wide enough for a motorcar.

Chinese guards were directing crews of Tibetan prisoners as they worked on the road. I walked past with my head down, afraid the communists would stop me. The prisoners were moving big rocks. First they picked them from the ground with tools, then two or three people would lift them up and put them on the side of the road. They worked slowly because they were wearing chains around their ankles. A road sign said FRIENDSHIP HIGHWAY in Chinese and Tibetan.

As I walked on the Friendship Highway, built by the sweat of Tibetan prisoners, I wondered what old Comrade Wei would have said about it.

Also, I was thankful I have been living in Kathmandu. To see the skin of my mother torn and scraped by tools and the wheels of trucks was a lot to bear.

Later I saw a truck filled with monks and could not believe it. Why would monks ride in something with wheels? They would know it is forbidden. Then the truck came closer to me, and I started my prostration to show them respect. One of the monks began shaking his head at me, calling out, "No bowing, don't do it!"

I froze, not believing what I had heard. For thousands of years, we have been bowing to our monks to show respect, but this monk kept shaking his head at me. A communist soldier was driving the truck carrying the monks with their red robes and no smiles on their faces. Among them was a taller lama whose face was as red as his robe. It was blood, running in a line from his forehead down to his neck. I understood then that the other monk did not want me to bow because maybe I would also be beaten.

Tears warmed my eyes and fell down my cheeks. I sat down on my pack on the side of the road. The dust from the truck's wheels stuck to the tears on my face. To not bow to a lama and to see monks treated like criminals made my stomach sick.

Tibet, my Tibet. It was gone.

For a long time after the truck passed, I simply sat. I thought of Rinchen. She had wanted to come with me. On the day when we had planned my return to the land of snows, she had had the glowing fire of memories in her eyes. Now as I sat on my pack, I thought, *Like the cooking stove is the heart of the house, Rinchen is the heart of our family. She is how your hands feel when they hold a bowl of soup—the ache of your cold bones and her seeping into you slowly.* But the things I was seeing on this journey would break her into pieces, and they would scatter into the corners of the kitchen. No way to put them back together.

I wanted her to keep our old Tibet alive in her mind. I would talk to Dawa and tell him, no bad stories of Tibet in our house. He could tell his bad stories to me on our journey home.

In maybe half a day's walking I would reach Lhasa. I longed to feel at home somewhere, but I told myself it would not be home. It would be different. Even from the people on the road I could see the difference. Their faces were closed, the way we close and bolt a door in a snowstorm.

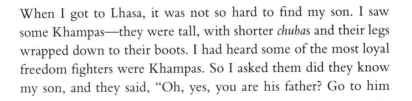

When I got to Lhasa, it was not so hard to find my son. I saw some Khampas—they were tall, with shorter *chuba*s and their legs wrapped down to their boots. I had heard some of the most loyal freedom fighters were Khampas. So I asked them did they know my son, and they said, "Oh, yes, you are his father? Go to him quickly, he is not well. We have taken him to Sera Monastery. They're hiding him there as one of their monks. Go now!"

When I reached Sera, a young boy, younger than Champa, led me to a small room. In this room a thin man was lying on a bed. I wondered why they'd brought me to him because he did not look familiar, but then I looked again. It *was* my son. I could see the bones in his wrists. His eyes were closed, and his lips were dry and cracked. Never had I seen him so pale.

A monk about Dawa's age sat by his side, holding a bowl of tea to my son's lips. "You're his *apa*? I'm Tharchi. I was with Dawa when he was injured."

"What happened?" I was shaking. Dawa didn't move. *Did he know I was here?*

"He got a bullet in his shoulder. The monks removed it, but the wound isn't healing. He hasn't been eating for two weeks now. But he will drink tea if you feed it to him."

He offered me the bowl, and I took it. "Why doesn't he eat?"

"It was after his friend Dordrum was killed. He started to look very sad. He wouldn't eat, wouldn't even talk. We don't know what to do with him—he cannot come with us to fight when he is so weak."

"So you're not a monk?"

Tharchi looked down at his feet. "I was, once. This is the first time I've worn my robes in quite a while." Then he stood and left the room.

Dawa opened his eyes just a little, as if it took all his strength. I felt an aching coming from him, but not a hurt of the body. Of the heart. I took his hand. "Little *bö*, can you say something? You must talk to your *apa*, you know. It is disrespectful not to."

"Good to see you, Pa-la." His voice was a whisper.

"As your *apa*, I am ordering you to eat some food."

"I cannot eat. My life is . . . wrong." He started to cry, and his hands trembled. I pulled him to a sitting position and put my arms around him. He leaned against me.

"Do you think it is right for you to starve yourself?"

"Dordrum did not have a favorable death. So he won't have a favorable rebirth. Why do I deserve a favorable one?"

I did not know what to say. "Perhaps you chose the wrong path, Dawa, but now you are choosing to stay on it?"

"I deserve nothing better."

"What about your destiny? This is how you spend the precious days of your life?"

"Pa-la, I have killed. His brown eyes were clear, naked. I have felt the pleasure of killing, of the hate inside that you let flow out into your finger that pulls the gun's trigger." He stopped, shutting his eyes tight. "And you take from your enemy his life. He looks at you as he dies . . . and his eyes boil you alive in your skin . . . because you cannot hide from him.

"My friend Dordrum killed too. So he died with his terrible karma. I watched him die. I held his hand, thinking I should recite the Bardo Thodol to him to help him attain the liberation. But I didn't, and I don't understand why.

"I saw the Chinese kill a woman who was with child, and they took the baby out." His eyes filled with tears and he closed them tight. "And then they split it open, like they did the mother. The baby died slowly. . . . I am still seeing this.

"And they took one of the nuns who was protesting in the street, and on her private parts they put—" He stopped, shaking his head, because he could not say it.

"All right, my son. It is all right." I held him close to me. "Rest now."

Gerald

I'm just rotting here. It has been six months since I confessed. My daughter's first birthday was two days ago, and I still haven't met her. No more torture sessions. But they haven't told me anything. I had a tender little shoot of hope back in January, but it's all dried out and brown now. Meanwhile, the hills outside the cell window have gone the opposite way—from frozen brown to lush green.

The mind games of the Chinese are a torture in themselves. Sometimes I've thought I'd rather be beaten or hung backward by my hands than get on my knees and spew out a bunch of lies and then find out, oh, that was just another trick.

The worst of it is, Tenzin is starting to break down. For the past few weeks, he hasn't been able to get up on his own to go out on work detail. Lobsang and I have had to help him walk and not make it too obvious. The Chinese take the frail ones and shoot them in the back of the head. The other day I helped Tenzin back to our cell after work detail. As I settled him on the floor, he said, "It's time. I'm dying, my friend."

My head shook back and forth. "No. We're going to help you. You'll be all right."

Lobsang's owlish eyes opened wide with fear.

Tenzin seemed as though he hadn't heard me. He never stopped looking into my eyes. "I am deeply content to begin my travel to a new place. I have been preparing my mind for this time all of my life. When I am in my transition, please don't let them disturb my body."

I did not want to hear this. Lobsang was softly crying. He crouched in a corner, looking overwhelmed to the point of another episode of laughing and crying.

"If it's necessary, take my body to Sera Monastery," Tenzin instructed.

"If it's necessary? What do you mean?"

"When the time comes, you'll know what to do. Lobsang will help you."

"But, how can we—take your body?" We could sooner promise him a trip to the moon. Did he realize we were still in a prison? Was he delirious? I looked over again at Lobsang, to see if he was hearing this, but he was shaking his head as if he could make this go away.

"Lama Tenzin, we're in a *prison*. I can't take your body to a monastery!"

"I request this of *both* of you." He touched my arm and whispered to me, "But I think it will be you, Gerald, who gets out of this prison first, so I am asking you."

It hit me in the chest like a hundred knives—I didn't want him to leave me. How would I survive without him? And Lobsang, how would he cope? I couldn't breathe.

"When I begin my transition, I won't answer when you speak to me. My body will lose its power. I will be in the bardo. You will pray for my passage to be smooth, and Lobsang will say the words of the Bardo Thodol to help me in my journey. You'll see the signs to tell you how my journey is going."

"Signs?" I asked.

"I'll push my consciousness out of the top of my head. It will travel and hopefully reach the celestial spheres. When that happens, my skull will expand. Blood will come from my nose. When you see these signs, you will know I have reached Amitabha." A blissful smile spread over his face. "On the eighth day, my body will be ready for burial."

It sounded so final it knocked the breath out of me. But I wanted to do this for him. I placed my hand over his. "I would be honored to do this." My throat ached.

"You and Lobsang will help each other."

I hugged him. His arms felt like two sticks of tinder wood. And he smelled different. It was a smell I knew, a sour spoiling odor. The odor of decay, of the body shutting down. Tears spilled down my face. He knew it was his time, and I knew it too.

〜

It's the middle of the night, and Tenzin is in meditation pose. I no longer hear his breathing. He's completely still. *How will I know for sure when his spirit has passed out of his body?*

Lobsang has escaped into sleep. I've never seen him sleep for so long. Though I'm terribly lonely, I don't have the heart to wake him, bringing him back from his one escape.

As Tenzin travels, I go out of *my* skin. I feel so terribly alone. I'm pacing, then sitting. Then pacing some more. I can't sleep while I feel him slipping away next to me.

What will my life be like here without Lama Tenzin? I can't think of it. What will I do when I figure out he's really dead? I know what his wishes are, and I promised him. But what if several days pass? The guards will notice, and the body will start . . . breaking down. It's May. I can't count on cold temperatures preserving it.

There's nothing to do but pray. *Lord, please bless your servant Tenzin. Bring his soul to a peaceful place. And as for me, only You will get me through this.*

Eh Ma Ho!
In the center is the marvelous Buddha Amitabha of Boundless Light,
On the right side is the Lord of Great Compassion
And on the left is Vajrapani, the Lord of Powerful Means.
All are surrounded by limitless Buddhas and Bodhisattvas.
Immeasurable peace and happiness is the blissful pure land of Dewachen.
When I and all beings pass from samsara,
May we be born there without taking samsaric rebirth.
May I have the blessing of meeting Amitabha face-to-face.
By the power and blessings of the Buddhas and Bodhisattvas
of the ten directions,
May I attain this aspiration without hindrance.
Bodhicitta, the excellent and precious mind—
Where it is unborn, may it arise;
Where it is born, may it not decline,
But ever increase higher and higher.
—PRAYER TO BE REBORN IN THE BLISSFUL PURE LAND OF AMITABHA

MAY 7, 1956

Dorje

I stayed with my son for the rest of the day yesterday, then I lay down next to him to sleep for the night. He spoke into the dark many times, but his words did not make sense. I did not know what to do, so I tried to feed him some butter tea and some *thukpa*. He still will not eat much, even when I order him to eat. In the early morning, he had some *thukpa* broth, but soon after he lost what was in his stomach.

I told my son to rest, not just his body. His soul was tired. He seemed to have experienced many lifetimes of suffering during his time in the rebel army. I could do nothing to take this from him. In the middle of the night, something in him slipped away. He did not recognize me anymore. I found the abbot of the *gompa* and asked him, would he please have all of the lamas recite prayers for my son?

A few more hours passed. The lamas began droning their prayers.

I have always put myself in another's place, to understand how others are feeling. But in these moments with my son, I did not want to do this. I am like a man who walks in the snow without shoes—there is nothing to cover my heart.

When I held my son in my arms, and all I felt was darkness inside him . . . I looked for the light in his eyes, and it was gone. I have never felt such a piercing darkness. In my mind I heard the words, *Your son is dead.*

The monks laid his body out on the bed. We recited prayers. *Om ami dewa hri.* My lips could hardly say the words.

I held my crying in my chest. If Dawa's spirit heard me, it would disturb his journey through the *bardo.* You see, I felt that my son was not following his destiny, so I could not feel any joy in his passing.

I still wanted the chance to convince him. To tell him he should come back with me to Nepal. Leave the freedom fighters and go to university. I wish, I wish I would have said something more when I still could. Something. To change his mind.

I ached to go out into the cold air with the young Dawa, before we sent him to be trained at the monastery. I wanted to watch him wobbling through the snow after he learned to walk, reaching his small hand into it and putting his tongue out to taste it for the first time.

I longed for our old life in Tibet, when we felt safe. When we didn't even think about every little thing we did every day, that maybe . . . we would never do again.

Even though we gave thanks for what we had in those days, still we did not pay attention. Not enough.

Dawa has left me. I feel as alone as if I were wandering in the Himalayas. All I can do is pray for him and wait here in Lhasa for his burial, worrying about how to tell Rinchen.

I think of her brown eyes, her brows slanting down sadly on her face. Before I left Kathmandu, she brought me tea and stood next to me as I sat on my cushion. She said, "Dorje-la, it would be a special blessing for me if you would try to see Samten."

"I do not know if the communists will allow this."

"Please."

She does not usually ask for things; she gives commands. And she is not often quiet in her asking. She knew it might not be easy for me to visit Samten. I smiled at her gently.

She returned my smile. "Perhaps after you find Dawa, you can go together to see Samten."

I took her hands. "Rinchen, I will see if it's possible."

The monks chant the Bardo Thodol for the safe passing of Dawa's soul, the only journey he will be taking. Dread is in my stomach as I step out of the room where I have been staying in the monastery. Two young monks are playing with sticks, jabbing them at each other like swords. I sweat in my *chuba* as I cross the inner courtyard.

Lama Sangye, the abbot of the monastery, walks down one of the corridors to the assembly hall. I walk after him. *"Khenpo?"*

He turns around slowly. "Yes?"

I bow, then do a prostration. When I am standing again, I say, "I hope I am not bothering you?"

"You're Dorje Thondup, no? I heard your son has begun his journey."

"Yes. And for him to begin his journey in this monastery, it is a great blessing. May I ask you a question, *Khenpo*? It is my brother-in-law. They are holding him at a *laogai* prison camp here in Lhasa. Do you know how I might find him to visit?"

"Oh. I'm sorry." Lama Sangye shakes his head quickly. "It is . . . difficult. The Chinese have taken some of our monks, and they won't let us visit them. In fact, one monk who tried to visit was taken prisoner himself. So it is quite dangerous."

Oh, let me do this one thing for Rinchen. "But, *Khenpo,* my whole family, we have moved to Kathmandu, and now I have the good fortune to be here for this short time—"

He shakes his head again, his face grave. "It is not safe. I would advise you against it."

"I see." I bow to him again. "Thank you, *Khenpo*."

I turn away quickly. A bursting inside my chest goes up my throat. I hold it inside as I hurry to my room. After shutting the door I lie down heavily on the bed, feeling helpless as I listen to the monks droning next door. My mind goes to my wife's face and the way it will sag like a branch covered in snow when she sees that Dawa is not with me. And Samten is still shut away with no one to comfort him. I turn onto my belly and cry into the mattress, hoping no one can hear me.

My delight in death is far, far greater
than the delight of traders at making vast fortunes at sea,
Or of the lords of the gods who vaunt their victory in battle;
Or of those sages who have entered the rapture of perfect meditative
absorption.
So just as a traveler who sets out on the road when the time has come to go,
I will remain in this world no longer,
But will dwell in the stronghold of the great bliss of deathlessness.
—Longchenpa
fourteenth-century Dzogchen master

Gerald

I hear the rain pounding away on the prison roof. Rain as thick as a wool blanket. The monsoons are starting early. It's so dark it's like night. Tenzin's just a shadow in this dim cell.

He hasn't moved for two days. This moment doesn't feel real. I stand outside of it watching.

I put my hand beneath his nose and feel only cold. No warm breath from his nostrils. I walk to the corner and tuck myself into it. Then I cry without a sound, wanting only to disappear, wanting my heart to stop.

Lobsang sees all of this. Then he stares straight in front of him, his eyes glazed. His face never moves as his tears come down.

After his tears, Lobsang begins reciting what he knows of the Tibetan Book of the Dead to help the journey of Tenzin's soul. I feel a swell of pride seeing Lobsang bravely putting aside his feelings to honor Tenzin with these words. His body hasn't been moved because the mud outside has precluded work detail. The old monk would be pleased.

Several days have passed. It seems we've been shut in our cell for a week. The cloud cover has been so heavy I could hardly tell day from night. With Tenzin's body still here, it feels like a tomb. Sometimes I pray for him in my own words, sometimes I try to join Lobsang as he recites prayers. I drift in and out of sleep, hearing the whisper of Lobsang's prayers in my ears.

But now, even before opening my eyes, I know something has changed. A dim light penetrates my eyelids. I open my eyes. The sky glows with the light of dawn.

My gaze wanders to my left to check on Tenzin.

He's not there!

I see a pile of red monk's robes where he was sitting.

Oh, dear God. His only wish was that he not be disturbed, and we let him down. God knows what they did to his body. "They took him?" I ask Lobsang.

He shakes his head slowly. He's sitting erect, his neck stretching like a beatific flower to the sun. He wears a peaceful smile.

I've never seen timid little Lobsang look so at ease. *Why isn't he upset?*

He says in a hushed voice, "Lama Tenzin has attained the body of light."

"*What?*"

"His material body dissolved into pure light." Lobsang's eyes are as bright as a sunrise. He smiles. I wonder if he's gone over the edge.

I'm blinking fast. My brain is blank. "What do you mean? The guards must have taken him in the middle of the night."

"No, they didn't. No guards have entered the cell."

I look at him. "A body does not—disappear into thin air!" I hear in my voice that I'm angry. *He's dead, the guards are probably desecrating his body, and I'm in the cell with a psychotic Pollyanna.*

I want to object, but something in Lobsang's face stops me. He *really* believes this. And he has never been one to believe much of anything.

I'm speechless. *I am open-minded, but—I'm a man of science. A doctor. He's not going to tell me that bodies dissolve into light.* I hold my head.

Lobsang says, "It *is* rare. It's also called the rainbow body because there are brilliant colors—I saw them last night while you slept. Only the holiest souls with the purest consciousness can attain so perfect a liberation."

I'm sitting with my mouth hanging open. *I'm in Tibet. Things happen here that . . . the rest of the world does not understand. That I don't understand.*

I look at Lobsang again, unable to comprehend the complete transformation that has taken place—in Tenzin, *and* in Lobsang. He senses my doubt. "You would have heard the guards enter the cell."

I pause, letting this sink in. "Yes."

"And you would have heard them take his clothes off. He was right next to you."

Could I really have slept that hard? No. I would have heard them open the door. I would certainly have heard them moving a body.

Then I notice Lobsang is pointing to the place where Tenzin once sat. Lobsang is smiling. He continues to point until I realize he wants me to touch the robes.

No. I don't want to.

I look at the red fabric. My heart beats loudly against my sternum. I pause, waiting for something to happen. Then I watch as my left hand lifts off its resting place on my knee. It travels slowly, until it is less than an inch from the robes. My pale fingers tremble against the red fabric. The fabric is cold against my fingertips. I pick it up and hear a small rattling sound on the floor. My hand recoils, startled.

Scattered on the stones are several oval, whitish objects. Parts of the objects are grayish black. Then I recognize what they are.

Tenzin's nails.

The ones I've examined once a week or more often, worrying over the infections he got from the bamboo torture. He lost two of his fingernails completely—they never grew back. Eight fingernails are in front of me, and ten tiny toenails as well.

I shudder. My fingers still hold the fabric. I look at it closely and see white strands.

His hair.

"Only the nails and hair, the impurities, stay when a person attains the rainbow body," Lobsang says. "He left that, and he left something for me. I don't know what it is"—here Lobsang's wondrous eyes well up as they often do—"but it is peaceful." He points to his chest. "Here."

My mind is still reeling with this information. I look at the nails and hair more closely. There's no blood on any of it. No blunt ends to suggest the hair was cut. Nothing to suggest that his hair or nails were extracted or taken against his will. On the floor is the prayer string of 108 knots Tenzin wore around his wrist.

I'm numb. I find myself staring at the floor, gazing at the hair, the nails, the string, then staring at the floor again.

Lobsang sees my face and says, "It's hard to believe. But it's a wonderful thing for Lama Tenzin."

"I feel sad he's not here with us." I'm selfish. As empty and lonely as a cave. Ashamed that a teenager has more poise than me in this situation.

Lobsang nods. "Yes, I'm sad too." His eyes water again, and a sob shakes out of him.

I close my eyes. I don't want to think anymore. My body tugs me down, down, down into an empty sleep. A sleep that blots out the world.

I dream I'm in a desert. I think I know how many miles I need to walk to get out of that desert, but more sand keeps accumulating. The desert grows and grows. There's no one else. I sit down in the sand and rub it into my hair. I rub the bare skin of my arms raw with fistfuls of sand. Then I sit for hours and feel the sun crisping the skin on the back of my neck and my arms. The vicious sun will bake me into a pile of ash. Nobody will know.

Oh, God, where are You?

Our bodies are what we are most attached to. That's why
offering one's body carries the greatest merit.
— *TIBETAN MONK*

Jesus took some bread, and after a blessing,
He broke it and gave it to the disciples, and said,
"Take, eat; this is my body."
And when He had taken a cup and given thanks,
He gave it to them, saying, "Drink from it, all of you;
for this is My blood of the covenant,
which is poured out for many for forgiveness of sins."
— *MATTHEW 26:26–28*

MAY 15, 1956

Dorje

It is the day of my son's burial. The abbot of the monastery came
to comfort me this morning. He had shining eyes that reminded
me of Rinchen after a pilgrimage. When she returns, hers are like
candles in a dark room. He told me death is a joyous thing, but I
do not think I could ever feel joy.

"Do not worry about your son's soul," he said. "Dawa was a
lama, so he accumulated much merit in this lifetime. He would
know the ways of *Phowa* to help him send his spirit to the pure
lands in his next life. And the astrologer determined your son has
the chance to be reborn in the higher realms."

"Thank you, Khenpo." I bowed deeply.

Since speaking with him, my mind is split in two. Part of me feels peace, feels it on my skin like when I close my eyes and tip my face up to the warm sun. This part rejoices that Dawa will be reborn in a high place. But another part of me, Dawa's *apa,* is cold as a hermit's cave in winter, with winds that wail all night long.

I am not a hermit. Some gain merit by living a lifelong meditation: no speaking, only chanting, reciting prayers in the shelter of their caves. They are unattached to the things of this world.

I am not one of them.

My heart beats with my son inside it, attached to its walls, like the blood in my veins. Dawa is in my heart, my blood, my skin, my tears, my tongue. The air in my lungs is Dawa air.

Many times each day, my body talks to him. My heart beats out the words: *I will not see you again in this life. My love, my adorable, gentle one with hands that moved in prayer, my firstborn, the one who came first and stayed—how can it be that I will not see you again in this life? How can it be you're no longer my son, whose head I kissed, whose face I washed, whose six-year-old feet walked bravely away from me to go to the monastery? How could I give up those precious years back then, thinking I would know you, have you for a long life?*

If I could start your life again, I would never let you go. I would hold you so close, with shaking arms, that you'd suffocate.

I can't breathe, my son. You have taken my breath with you. I can't eat. I can't sleep. Your mani *beads are all I have. I can't get them close enough to my heart—closing my eyes at night holding them to my lips, knowing they carry your prayers and the oil of your fingers.*

I lie in bed thinking of the last time we spoke, when you said, "Pa-la, I have killed, and felt pleasure in killing." My whole body shudders each time I think of it.

How could my gentle son say those words? How could those hands that once calmed a sheep, that could feel the pain of another, that were pressed together to receive the blessed waters from Lama Tsethar each week, how could those hands take a life?

I have not been a real apa *to you. I did not guide you, did not love you enough. I thought I would always have you in my life, and that you'd care for me and Rinchen as we grew old.*

I'll never forget the moment when I saw your purple wound. I knew then; in your eyes it was clear that you knew you were leaving me. I could not even speak, doubled over, my heart splitting into pieces of glass.

I failed you, my son. Now I want to put my head, my whole body, under the ground, but nowhere is low enough to put myself, to beg your forgiveness.

I let you wander the world with your mind in confusion and despair. Why should you have any bad karma for this? My next life should be spent in the lower realms of ignorance, as the lowest animal form, to atone for how I failed you.

There is a knock at the door, and I hear the abbot's voice. "It is time."

I walk to the door with a body of lead. My feet do not want to go.

I open the door. I walk down the corridor toward the rear of the *gompa,* chanting prayers for Dawa's soul, focusing on my lips. *"Om ami dewa hri . . . Om ami dewa hri . . ."* My mind hides inside my skull, as though wrapped in thick wool. Yet my senses are so clear. Chanting fills my ears and I smell butter lamps burning. The gods painted on the wall seem to move as my shadow hits the wall. Some bare their teeth in a terrifying way. I press my arms closer to me. Painted on these walls are all the delusions and horrors Dawa faces on his journey.

Then I bump into something—a small boy in monk's robes. He bows to me and smiles. His eyes are startlingly joyful and ringed with thick, black lashes. He says, "I will show you to the abbot." He takes my hand. My heart glows from the feel of his warm hand.

I realize I don't want the abbot. I want this boy.

It is as though the young Dawa is with me, completely restored. This boy's simple nature, his smile, are a comfort. I say to him, "Come with us to the burial, little *bö.*"

He smiles again, showing the pink gums above his teeth. "If Lama Sangye allows."

I bow to the abbot when he joins us, and he lets the boy stay with us. Five other monks come along as well. Soon we are like a line of pilgrims walking out the back of the *gompa* and up to the charnel grounds. One of the monks carries Dawa's body on his back. It is folded as it once was when my son was born, and it is wrapped in white *khata*s.

At the top of the hill is a gathering of stones. A few of them are quite large, almost the size of a person, and flat like a table. A wrinkled old man with gaps in his teeth smiles at us. He wears a burgundy *chuba* with a red belt and a dun-colored cap with flaps that could fold down over his ears, but he wears them in the up position. It is quiet except for the mumbled sounds of prayers and the flapping of prayer flags.

My little friend is at my elbow and points to the man in burgundy. "That's the *tomden*." Then the boy hands me a small juniper branch. The scent of incense and juniper hangs in the air, as well as smoke from a small fire tended by one of the monks.

I feel grateful that Dawa will have the privilege of a sky burial. It is another chance for him to gain merit by offering his body as food for the birds.

The *tomden* removes the silk *khata* scarves wrapped around Dawa's body. The wind catches the white silk of one of the *khata*s. It floats for a moment on air, fluttering. I think of Dawa waving at me; my lips part in a sad smile.

Your young body is naked now. So frail and helpless. I want to cover it with my own.

They lay your body out on the tomden's *flat rock. He walks over to a patch of grass where he has left his enormous sword, the length of a leg. His hands close around the handle and he lifts it, then carries it closer to you. He raises the sword. I hear my breath in my ears. I close my eyes.*

Om ami dewa hri . . . om ami dewa hri . . .

I watch my feet dart forward toward the tomden—*to take you from him, but I hold myself in place. I must let this sacrifice come to pass.*

. . . Om ami dewa hri . . .

I fall to my knees as the sword splits your belly open, exposes all of your flesh, so you may give your body. My son, may this sacrifice bring you the merit of many lifetimes.

The tomden *invites the vultures, saying,* "Shey, shey." *The vultures cover you, and I can no longer see your body.*

The young monk motions for me to add my juniper to the purifying fire as an offering.

The abbot speaks. "This is the supreme sacrifice, to give one's body for the benefit of other living beings after the soul has risen to Amitabha, the realm of Infinite Light. It brings great merit."

The *tomden* approaches the vultures' circle. He cuts off the arm and leg bones and throws them to the birds with a kind smile. He picks up a stone mallet. I close my eyes and hear the sound of him crushing the skull with a stone. He pounds the rest of the bones until they are powder.

The little monk says, "He mixes the bones with *tsampa* for the birds." I know these things, but I let the little *bö* speak because he is proud of what he knows. His voice comforts me. "Lama Sangye says every Tibetan should see a sky burial at least one time in his life." The boy smiles. "If we look at what's waiting for us, we won't waste our lives."

The little *bö*'s robes rest lightly on his shoulders, and I want them to be Dawa's shoulders. I want the shaved hairs to be my son's hairs. I long to touch that head again, to bump our foreheads in greeting and see my son smile back at me, saying, "Hello, Pa-la."

The *tomden* is finished.

I can no longer see your body that I washed, hugged, kissed, tossed over my shoulder to hear your cries of delight. I cannot see the lips that pushed out your joyous laughter.

I will not worry for your soul, Dawa. I'll never forget you, my firstborn. My boy with the delicate heart. My gentle teacher. My serious one, who had lines on his brow the day he was born.

My dearest son, be blessed with liberation. May you be free of all suffering. Fly high in the bodies of the birds.

Gerald

The dark week of rains has finally come to an end. In the dreamy rays of the late-morning sun, the cell door opens. Comrade Han is coming toward me. He grabs my arm. I stand up, trembling.

He looks round the cell. "Where's the old man?"

Lobsang answers in a voice that's surprisingly strong, "He died, and his body was liberated."

"Liberated?" Han makes a snorting sound. He stops, looks around again. His lips tighten into a disturbed line. Letting go of me, he steps into the hallway, yells for a guard to come. "Where's the old man?"

"The monk? He's in the cell," the guard answers in the corridor.

"No, he's *not* in the cell!" Han snaps. His eyes burn as if he is looking for someone to kill.

The guard appears in the doorway and peers inside. "He was here . . . earlier this week." His face looks blank.

"Well, find him!" Through clenched teeth Han hisses, "We do not lose prisoners here." He grabs my arm and pulls me out of the cell.

He's going to kill me because Tenzin disappeared. He thinks I'm in on it.

He leads me toward the interrogation room. *God help me. No no no no. I can't do this, Lord. Take my life from me. I don't have the strength. He's going to interrogate me about Tenzin's disappearance. What the hell am I going to say?*

Wait a minute. We're not stopping. We're passing the room. Oh, shit! What does this mean? My heart is banging out of my chest.

We continue down another corridor to places I've never seen in this prison. He brings me into a room with tile on the floor and the walls. The tile was once white, but now it's the color of dirty oatmeal, with dark brown smears through it—blood? My teeth clack against each other. *I am a dead man.*

Without turning my head, I look to see if Han's carrying a gun. Yes—in a holster around his waist.

"Take off your clothes," he spits out.

They put things on people—put things on their private places—I've heard about it from other prisoners.

His eyes have gone black and shiny as ice. Their coldness is even more terrifying than the raging look they had a few minutes ago in the cell.

I fumble with my shirt buttons. My fingers are doughy and stupid. I feel his eyes on me. My breath pumps through me like a bellows. I unfasten my belt. My pants tumble down to my ankles, the belt buckle clanking on the tiles. Beads of sweat roll down my temple.

A guard with thick jowls comes into the room carrying a large wooden bucket of water and sets it down near me.

"Wash yourself," commands Han, his iron voice bouncing off the tiles.

I look down and see a drain in the floor. I peek at the ceiling—my mind flashing to the gas "showers" of Auschwitz. Nothing is up there but white plaster.

The guard jabs a thick finger toward the bucket. A grimy

brown bar of soap is next to it. I bend to pick up the soap. I dip my other hand into the water. It is glacially cold, stinging my bony fingers.

My mind is pinpricked. Adrenaline-soaked. I try to scrub off the reeking prison smell. The guard and Comrade Han stare at me openly as I wash. My mind hovers, terrified. *Am I bathing just so they can execute me?* I try to read Han's face.

Another guard enters with a bucket and swings it toward me. I duck by instinct. The icy water stings my skin. I'm visibly shaking. The second guard then throws a pile of blue-gray fabric at my feet. "Put that on."

A Mao suit. Han grins, chuckling.

I step into the pants and pull them up. I pull on the Mao jacket and struggle with the buttons. My nerves are raw. *What happens now?*

Han takes my arm and leads me down the corridor. A soft cotton cloth falls over my head to cover my eyes. Tied tight at the back of my head.

Oh, God. Oh, God. This is it. They're going to shoot me. Please, God, be with me, walk with me. Bless my Emma. Take care of her, and our daughter. Watch over them.

My breath comes in short gasps. I start to black out. My heart thuds. I walk slower. A sharp prod in my back keeps me moving.

The sound of a door opening, closing. Warm sun on the top of my head.

Shot in the sun. Shot in the head.

Dear Lord, forgive me all my sins; may I know life eternal with Thee.

Walking, then he's putting his hand on top of my head, pushing me down and shoving me inside . . . a car. He's next to me in the car as it moves. I can smell his cigarette odor.

What the hell is going on? Where are they taking me? An empty, barren place where a gunshot will echo in the silence. Good-bye, Emma. I love you more than . . . I can't even say. Good-bye, my daughter, although I've never even seen your face.

The bumps in the road jostle my insides. I feel sick.

The car stops. I hear Han get out. The door on my side opens. His hand on my arm tugs me up.

"Raise your hands and put them behind your head," he orders from behind me.

I lift my arms in supplication to God. Put my hands on the back of my neck. Wait for the bullet. *Please let it be in my head.*

I'm coming, Lord.

The blindfold is lifted.

What I see before me can only be a fantasy. A thousand yards away, a silver plane with American flags on it rests beside an airstrip. I blink, but it's still there.

I glance backward. Still waiting for a bullet. But Han walks around to face me. Over his shoulder I see people near the plane. Some in Mao suits and some in Western clothing.

"Comrade Kittredge!" Han bellows.

My eyes jump back to the thin lips.

His voice is low, menacing. "We rehabilitated you. Give thanks to Chairman Mao."

This is an order. His gun waits in its holster.

Someone is waving in the crowd near the plane. But Han isn't moving. *He's going to shoot me in front of . . .*

Or he's waiting for me to obey. To be an insect under his boot.

Something dangerous surges in my veins, something *free* that wants to run to that plane, risk a bullet in my back.

The cavalry is here! I've seen an American plane, and I know it's here for me!

Pulling myself up to my full height, I say it. "Thank you, Chairman Mao."

Han turns and nods toward the plane. "Go," he orders.

I walk, then sprint, dashing toward it, still waiting for a bullet in my back. Voices surge upward from the crowd in front of me, cheering.

I can't believe this is happening. My heart pounds like a crazed drum.

I see a woman with wavy auburn hair, running toward me with her mouth open. Her hair is blown across her face by a chilly wind. She reaches to clear the hair from her face . . . in a familiar gesture so dear to me.

Our bodies collide, and she wraps her arms around me and she smells the same, the same, the same, ahhh, she's holding me, I reach to pull my belt tighter because I'm so thin, how can she still love me but she does even though I'm an old man and I'm blubbering. She's holding my face in her hands then squeezes me so hard I cough and finally my dead arms wake up and I crush her in a hold my arms have awaited for almost two years. I'm sobbing and she's sobbing and she and I touch foreheads like Tibetans and then mush our faces together and our tears mix together. She stands back and looks at me with eyes like the forest and says, "Geebs," and we lose our balance but we never stop looking at each other. Oh, she's so beautiful when she laughs.

MAY 15, 1956

Emma

Oh, my Lord, how can I say what I felt when I saw my Geebs again? The most exquisite joy. And the most soul-tearing agony.

Agony, because he looked worse than I could possibly have imagined.

He was *so* thin, bearded, and gray like a stern old saint with long hair. Those tender spots under each eye and above the cheekbone had sunk like pockets so deep I could have placed a coin beneath each eye and the coins would have stayed in place. His hair was a dull gunmetal color—gone were his gleaming honeyed waves. All my grief and joy washed up into my throat and sat there like a lump of cement.

He was my Geebs, but his gaunt form told me how much I'd lost, we'd lost.

There was a stump where his finger had once been. My throat clenched and my insides heaved upward.

This aged man, who was my husband. Yet his blue eyes still had light in them. I held him, cried into the godforsaken Mao suit they'd put him in, and felt his boniness and his trembling. I wanted to take it all into myself, wash it away, and I knew I couldn't. A sick, helpless feeling hovered in my stomach.

I ran my fingers through his straight, limp hair. His eyes looked so sad, as if he knew he wasn't what he'd been before. I gazed into the circles of blue and whispered, "I still see the Light in your eyes, my love. And I love you."

He smiled. The lonely boy, the lovely youth in him, and the man before me, all were returned to me. All that I loved and more.

"Ready to meet your daughter?" I whispered to him.

He grinned wider. Taking it in while it took his breath away.

"I named her Rin, after Rinchen, who delivered her."

His eyes filled with tears.

"Dorje blessed her in your name," I said.

He dropped his gaze down to his hands and looked so sad. His heart breaking over missing something that happens only once.

"Is—that her?" He pointed to her in the senator's arms, ten yards away.

"See the golden curls? Come on."

I took his hand, pulling lightly. He remained rooted to the spot, and I saw his legs tremble. "Are you all right?" I took his other hand in mine as well and stood before him.

"Yes, it's just I feel a bit more like a grandfather than a father," he said quietly.

I looked into his eyes and whispered, "It's going to be all right. I promise. You just need time . . . and food, and me to look after you. And . . . if you look into her eyes, *you'll know . . . you're her daddy.* Come on."

Aronson was already approaching us, but he'd slowed when he sensed Gerald's distress. We met him in a few steps and I took Rin in my arms.

Then, she and Gerald looked at each other for the first time. She stared at him openly, without fear or hesitation. Then she reached her hand up and grabbed his nose. He smiled with so much more than simple joy—as if he were seeing God's very face—the kind of joy that hunkers down into your throat and pushes tears out through your eyes.

For a moment they stayed that way, she still holding his nose with her small, silky fingers, as though leading a bull by the ring in its nose. The devoted fatherly beast she held would certainly have followed her to the ends of the earth! He swallowed a few times, breathing deeply. Slowly he reached over and took her in his arms. She settled in and scraped her fingers across his jacket.

I stood watching, all wet with tears. On the day of my death, this moment will be the one that flashes through my mind as the most precious I've ever known.

Gerald

My nose, so used to the stench of filthy bodies and blood, now rested against the head of my sweet daughter, who smelled of milk and apples in her silky, fine blond hairs.

I got confused when I saw all the cameras, until Emma explained the deal that had been brokered with the Chinese by Senator Aronson. Tables and chairs had been set up with a banquet of food that made my stomach clench with hunger.

The senator handled himself like a trained diplomat. He bowed when introduced to Mr. Loh, the Party leader, and asked Mr. Loh to tell him about the work the communists had done here in Lhasa.

The picture-taking was as communist and propaganda-conscious as it could possibly be. The three Chinese officials wore Mao suits, looking as plain as devout Quakers. They formed themselves into a tableau with the senator for the photos.

I told Emma, "I really don't want to have my picture taken."

She laughed bitterly, saying, "You think they'd want a picture of *you*—to show how they starved and mistreated you? Oh, I guarantee you they won't want *that* picture."

Her voice had a knife edge. I heard the bitterness born of her time of waiting. She must have seen something on my face because she said, "Oh, I've hurt you! I'm sorry."

"No—I didn't take it that way," I soothed her. "You're right about them." I couldn't stop looking at her, the graceful curve of her neck from her chin to her chest. The wind played with her hair and she wore a forest-green, belted silk dress with a gold locket I'd given her.

Her eyes flashed. "Well, don't worry, we're getting on that plane soon and leaving them all behind."

A few moments later, we were asked to sit down at a long table the Chinese had set out in the clearing surrounded by willow trees. The head of the Chinese delegation was going to make a speech. I sat at the table between Aronson and my lovely wife, with the wiggly weight of Rin on my lap. Several members of the Chinese delegation sat across the table from us. Mr. Loh stood behind a lectern while the two other communist leaders sat in seats on either side of it. Two members of the American press corps moved around the table snapping pictures.

I dimly heard the words of the speaker and then the echo of their interpreter: "We welcome you to the land of China. . . . We have taken our younger brother Tibet, a member of our family for centuries, under our communist wings. . . . We are spreading the peaceful revolution of equality to our Tibetan brothers, bringing them schools, medical care, and communal-izing their agriculture . . ."

I was listening to this mouthful of claptrap when I saw a communist soldier approaching, dragging a man in a *chuba* by the arm. The Tibetan man stumbled forward. When the soldier reached the lectern, he stopped abruptly. Mr. Loh halted his speech and watched as the soldier threw the Tibetan man to the ground. His face hit the earth. Some of the American men began taking pictures of him. The soldier spoke to Mr. Loh excitedly.

The Tibetan man looked up. The stocky build, the proud bearing, seemed so familiar.

It was Dorje!

Emma's mouth was agape, as mine was.

I didn't know what to do. There was a strange silence. Mr. Loh was blinking fast, looking nervous. I asked what was going on, to no one in particular, because I didn't know whom to ask. One of the Chinese men answered me in English, saying, "The soldier brought a—counterrevolutionary."

I sat for a beat in silence. Then I heard myself say, "No. He's . . . with us. He's supposed to . . . help us today, as an interpreter, with the reporters and . . . all that."

Emma's eyes widened with alarm.

Oh, Lord, what have I done?

The young soldier narrowed his eyes at me. "I see. So he must speak Chinese fluently?" His words were like a mocking song.

I cleared my throat. "Uh, yes . . . in fact, he does."

Dorje added in a quiet voice, "I speak Chinese because I am half-Chinese."

The communist officials did not reply. Mr. Loh was scowling.

The soldier narrowed his eyes, then said, "Ah, but in order to translate for *you*, he must also speak English." The soldier's voice was high and tense, and he was watching Mr. Loh's scowl. I realized the soldier was afraid he'd made a mistake. He was trying to save himself.

"He *does* speak English," I said carefully.

Mr. Loh spoke to the soldier in pointed words. Although he probably wasn't supposed to, the interpreter translated, "The American delegation has come to see that we are here to *help* Tibetans. Thank you for helping this man find the airstrip. Since he has fallen down, you will now help him to stand up. And I'm certain they need you back at your post now."

The soldier let the air out of his mouth with a trembling sound.

His eyes on the ground, he pulled Dorje up to a standing position, released his arm, and walked away.

In silence we all watched the soldier leave. It seemed no one knew how to go on.

Slowly Emma stood and walked over to Dorje. "Are you all right, my friend?"

He looked over at me and smiled apologetically. "I did not mean to cause you any trouble," he said breathlessly.

Mr. Loh approached us, his sallow, oval face looking like a disgruntled potato. He set his gaze on Dorje and said to him in English, "You've recovered from your fall?" It was more a statement than a question.

"Yes, sir, thank you," Dorje answered without skipping a beat.

"You will join us, then," Mr. Loh commanded, motioning for Dorje to take a seat at the table.

"Thank you," Dorje said, bowing. Then Mr. Loh walked back to the lectern.

Dorje turned to face me. I stood. With Rin holding my legs, we touched foreheads. Dorje sat down between me and Emma. Mr. Loh started a new speech from the lectern. They served us hot tea in tiny cups.

"What are you doing here, Dorje?" Emma asked in a low voice.

"I came to Lhasa looking for my son."

"You found Dawa?" Emma asked, excited.

"I did. But . . . I was too late." Dorje's eyes watered.

"What happened?" I was confused.

"I cannot tell you everything here. But he had a bullet wound in his shoulder that became infected. He died. Emma's face was stricken, and she covered her mouth with her hand. His burial was this morning. I felt so sad that I wanted to watch your family being reunited from a distance. I did not want to make problems for you, but then they saw me."

I'd been certain I would die today, but Dawa had actually crossed over. So young.

"It's fine, Dorje." Emma put a hand on his arm. "I'm . . . *so* sad to hear this."

I asked quietly, "How did he get a bullet in his shoulder in the monastery?"

"He was no longer there. He was . . ." Dorje hesitated.

"I'll explain it to you later, Geebs," Emma whispered.

"You have finally met your daughter," Dorje said to me, smiling.

I smiled back at him. There were no words.

Aronson reached over and shook Dorje's hand. "Nice to meet you, and to have your services available." He winked.

Mr. Loh droned on with a speech full of slogans. They were so familiar to my ears. I shuddered and thought of Comrade Han. I scanned the entire gathering for him. He was gone.

I was relieved until I thought of Lobsang, now all alone, and maybe being blamed for Tenzin's disappearance. Suddenly I felt ill.

Emma

As the speeches continued, I turned to examine my husband's face. He looked haggard, anxious, and sad. He had new habits. Twitching hands. He wiped his nose repeatedly for no apparent reason. He whispered to me, "I'm concerned about Dorje. We've got to help him."

I lifted my eyebrows, startled.

"He has known ties to Americans. That's why Samten was thrown in prison."

A terrible feeling of doom spread in my stomach, and then, anger. *No. No one's going to hurt my family.* "Geebs, we have Rin now—we have to consider things differently than before. It isn't just you and me we'd be risking."

"I know what they'd do to him, Emma." His eyes went to a place far away. "We're all together in this—boiling pot. What happens to him happens to me."

My insides felt as if I'd just jumped off a bridge. "What are you suggesting?"

"When we leave today, he's got to be on that plane with us."

Panic froze me. "You just got out, and now you want to risk *this*?"

"Emma." His voice was as pointed as a blade. "If we don't help him, I won't have a hope of sleeping through a night again for the rest of my life."

He'd never spoken to me in such a sharp tone before. It hurt. Dorje sat listening us with a pained, uncertain expression.

"I'm sorry," Gerald said softly.

I nodded. He wanted me to seek clarity about what to do. He was asking me to do *that* when all I wanted to do was run to that plane, tuck my family into their seats, lock the doors, and take off. Go back to my country where things were simple and everything smelled nice and there were laws. Forget Tibet ever existed.

I closed my eyes for a moment. And this is what I saw: my friend Rinchen in her kitchen, back in Shigatse. The image was so vivid I could almost smell the yak meat we were stuffing into *momo*s and feel the stringiness of it on my fingers. She was singing and rocking her body as we worked. She stuffed the meat into the dough. Her forearms were thick, sticking out of the rolled-up sleeves of her *chuba*. She reached up to scratch her cheek with her little finger. She had lines around her eyes and mouth. The lines were carved by smiling, by laughter that shook through her middle and traveled up through her mouth.

She'd lost two children, and she had smile lines on her face. She expected no different.

When I opened my eyes, I felt her close to me.

I felt clarity. Like a knife through me, damn it.

I leaned over to Dorje and whispered, "You're coming with us on the plane when we leave."

He started shaking his head. "No, that would not be wise."

Gerald said quietly, "Trust me, Dorje. If you're a friend of ours, you're on their enemies list, and you'll be in prison before night-fall."

Dorje looked down at his lap, his eyes blinking. I let Aronson know we'd be taking Dorje with us. He looked a bit concerned, but he nodded.

The speeches lasted for hours. My diplomatic façade had long since worn off. I was exhausted from listening to their lies. At last, Senator Aronson cleared his throat. He lifted his teacup and stood up. "I want to make one last toast before we depart to Mr. Loh and the entire Chinese delegation. May you have long lives and . . . great happiness. As we take our leave, I want to extend thanks, from each of us"—he extended his hand in our direction—"Mr. and Mrs. Kittredge and their daughter, Mr. Dorje, our interpreter, our press corps, and myself, for this informative and inspiring visit." We all drank a toast to Gerald's captors.

A few moments later, we stood up and made our way toward the plane. We started up the steps to the plane with Dorje sandwiched between me and Gerald.

"Wait!"

We all turned around. One of the officials approached us. He was young, with a face as sleek as a jaguar. The corners of his mouth turned down as he spoke to us in English. "We haven't seen any papers for this man." He pointed to Dorje. His eyes narrowed to suspicious points. "He did not get off the plane with you."

My mouth was dry as a desert. Gerald was wringing his hands.

"It is true. I did not travel on the plane with them," Dorje said politely. "But I came from Kathmandu, as they did."

"No, you're trying to escape. You have no papers."

Aronson stepped off the stairs onto the ground, motioning for the press corps to follow him. One of them removed his lens cap and began taking pictures. Aronson looked over at Mr. Loh, who was nearing the plane, and said pointedly, "Well, this is most surprising. Do Tibetans try to *escape* often?"

Dorje had been digging inside the sleeve of his *chuba*. He pulled out a small satchel. "No problem, sir. I have papers. Look." He removed several documents from the satchel. "My residence permit from Nepal. And also here, my identity card for where I work in Kathmandu."

After fingering the papers, the sleek young official frowned, saying, "These papers do not give you permission to enter China."

Mr. Loh looked at the photographer snapping pictures. He said, his gaze directed at the younger official, "We are here in Tibet as a kind older brother. And today, we are here in friendship with the Americans, to show them what we've achieved. There is no problem with this man's papers."

Aronson chimed in, "Oh, just a misunderstanding then."

Mr. Loh's face was tense. "Yes. We wish you a safe journey."

"Thank you." Aronson nodded.

We filed quickly into the plane. From inside, Aronson shut the door. And we all breathed again.

Dorje

I had to trust in my friends Gerald and Emma to get inside of the big-bellied bird to fly over the Himalayas to Kathmandu. Although I had seen planes, I had never been inside one. From the moment I stepped inside, I recited mantras for protection.

I had buried my son this morning, and now I was on a plane going to Kathmandu. My nerves were jumping with the miracle of escaping the communists.

I gave thanks to the gods for protecting me and hoped we would not be offending them by flying in this plane. We Tibetans never had planes because the lamas taught us that the air above our heads is the home of the gods. It is not to be disturbed, or they might be angered.

When I told Gerald and Emma my worries, they laughed. They told me they'd been in a plane like this several times, and that during the flying they usually fell asleep! This I could not imagine.

For Rinchen's sake, I hoped we would have a safe journey. Although I couldn't imagine how I would tell her the news about Dawa, I needed to be there to keep her in my arms while she cried and to love my other children as she went through her time of grief.

The noise of the plane was louder than anything I had ever heard. Even so, after a while I started to feel calmer. Outside the window were the mountains I've always worshipped, that have protected my people from outsiders for centuries. Now I was seeing them from the view of a flying creature. I could hardly breathe. I would have loved to share the moment with Dawa. He had such a thirst to understand how the earth really looked, and how far away this country was from that one. If he saw what I could see out the window, he would certainly not have been able to stay in his seat, even more than usual! Thinking of him made me smile, but tears came up from my heart into my throat. For the rest of my life I would have moments like this when I would think of him, again and again.

The senator sat next to the two men who had been taking pictures. I spoke to him. "Thank you for helping Gerald and me. It was brave of you. So this will be a big story in American newspapers?"

The senator and the two photographers all laughed at once. The senator clarified, "Oh, these guys weren't really taking pictures! They're just my army buddies."

One of them opened his camera. "See? No film."

I looked at Gerald, who sat with an astonished smile on his face.

Gerald and Emma sat holding hands tightly. They were staring at these same mountains. Gerald had tears on his face, and Emma sighed. Their little daughter was sleeping across both of their laps.

I didn't have to put myself in their place. Tears were on my cheeks too. But for me, a heavy question was sitting on my heart: *Will I ever return?* It squeezed my chest. My mind said, *Maybe, after some years. Perhaps if this journey goes well, I could come back with Rinchen and the family, through the air again.*

It seemed strange and impossible to travel on air, but then I remembered the power of Tibetan winds. They caressed the prayer flags, releasing the sacred words and carrying them to the heavens. We were floating over the mountains the way Dawa's soul did when the vultures accepted his sacrifice.

He would stay in Tibet. I was glad.

～⚜～

When we reached Kathmandu, it was already eight o'clock at night. Arriving again in this large city, I was assaulted by the stink of motorcars and screeching horns and the bells of bicycles.

Although I invited him to our house, Mr. Aronson said good-bye politely, saying he wanted to go to a hotel and soak in a tub of hot water. I thanked him again for his kindness as he got into a taxicab.

The four of us then stood at the place where we could catch our own taxi, and I told my friends, "You will stay at my house, of course."

They didn't move. Gerald looked at me with his eyebrows raised, and Emma stared at the ground. He said, "It might be better if you and Rinchen have some time alone."

I took a big breath, remembering what was ahead of me. "Please say prayers for us. What I have to do tonight is the worst thing I will ever do in this lifetime."

Emma looked at me with sad eyes. "Rinchen is a strong woman."

I nodded slowly.

"We'll stay with Kingsley," she said. "But we'll see you before we leave?"

"Yes, that is good."

"I'll be thinking of you, my friend," Gerald said, his hand on my shoulder. We all touched foreheads with each other, and even during my ride in the taxicab, I could still picture the concerned eyes of my friends.

When I stepped out of the motorcar, I stopped and looked at the house before going in. Yellow flowers bloomed in pots under the windows. They seemed to glow against the maroon paint. On the outside, the house looked as if it still held hope. Now I would descend upon it like a terrible storm.

I saw Rinchen move in the frame of the window. She saw me outside, and a second later the front door opened. She stopped where she stood. Her eyes locked on mine, frightened.

She looked for him and saw the empty space beside me. She knew.

I wanted to die in that moment.

Her eyelids closed in the slow way of someone who is fainting. The grief spread across her face, shutting her eyes tightly, pulling her mouth wide, as though she had been stabbed. The thin muscles of her neck tensed like strings, and she closed her fists around the fabric of her *chuba*. Her body folded until she was on her knees, bent over, bringing her fists down against her legs as her wailing tore into the night air.

O gods, be merciful. How can I help her? How could I fail her by not bringing our son back to her?

Her cries seemed to come from another realm, not from the chest of a woman. They slashed through my body. I hurried to her and put my arms around her, leaning my chest on her back, rocking with her. The heat of her body came through her *chuba* as her body moved with each sob. Her neck was damp with sweat, and her face was wet with tears. Her hair had its normal scent— the sweat of loving and tending her children and of spices.

I wanted to completely cover her. As I put my nose to her hair, I was reminded I had wanted to cover Dawa too when he told me about the terrible things he had done.

After a long while her crying changed to small moans in her throat. Still she rocked slowly, as though a baby were in her arms. My tears dried into lines on my face.

"I knew it . . . I knew it," she said through her tears. "I didn't want to believe . . ."

I waited a few moments, then asked, "Rinchen, what are you saying?"

She shook her head, still weeping with her chin shaking. "I knew. I knew it."

"You knew something happened to Dawa?"

She nodded as she rocked. "I did not want to believe . . . but then you came with the look of 'I'm sorry' in your eyes, and he's not with you . . ."

"How did you know?" My voice was filled with wonder.

"I had a dream . . . many dreams. I saw him . . . but I thought—"

"You *saw* Dawa?"

She wiped her face on her sleeve. "He came as an animal form."

I was hungry to hear what she had seen. Her head sagged low. "Shall we go inside?" I said, lifting her head by touching her chin.

"Yes." Her eyes were wide and blank. I wanted to breathe into her and bring light into her dull brown eyes.

She leaned on my arm. Like a child, she let me sit her down at the kitchen table.

"Tell me what you saw," I said.

"For many nights already, I've had dreams." She spoke in a voice smooth as a river pebble, her eyes like brown glass. "It was eight nights ago when I first saw a snow leopard. He was lovely, from his royal nose and silver eyes to the thick fur that covered him like a perfectly fitting snowy robe. He lived high in the mountains, and he was a fierce hunter, one whose heart tingled when he saw the blood of his prey. In his youth, there was always enough to satisfy his desire for a fresh kill. But then came a time of great suffering among the animal forms, and he noticed there were not many creatures for him to hunt. He often came upon the dry bones of animals who had starved to death."

She sat up and folded her hands in her lap. "So he went to the high places, to a great cliff. And he leaped from this cliff to the sharp rocks below. One of the stones pierced his heart." She put her hand to her chest, her face pulled down by sadness. "His belly split open; his organs were warmed by the sun. His blood spread onto the rocks and turned his snowy fur red and pink. All of the starving creatures of the mountains came and ate of him and were saved from death. In this way all the karma of his days of killing was purified, and his spirit floated up into the skies." Her voice was hushed as though she were seeing something unspeakably beautiful. Her eyes stayed on the same spot, completely absorbed in this image.

It was an astonishing dream—so close to Dawa's real life and death. Although I wanted to tell her this, I stopped myself. I could not tell her Dawa had killed as the snow leopard had.

She went on, "Several nights the leopard came to me in the quiet. I saw his shining eyes in the dark and heard the pads of his feet on the floor as he walked over to me. Lhamo and Champa were sleeping next to me, but I was not afraid for me or for them. I sat up and looked right into his silvery eyes." She let out a sigh. "He stopped and gazed at me, and then his image slowly faded. His body faded first, and his eyes—like two shiny coins— they faded last. Many times he came and went in this way. But a few nights ago, he settled himself down next to me as I sat. He lay his heavy white head in my lap, and I lay down and fell asleep feeling its warmth. When I woke up, he was gone. Since then, he has not returned."

I took both of her hands in mine. They were warm, but without life, as though the spirit had flown out of them. I sent a prayer to Padmasambhava, asking to take Rinchen's suffering into my own body and to send healing wind through my hands and words.

"It happened as your dream said," I told her. "His body was given for the benefit of the animal forms in a sky burial. A pure sacrifice."

"So he accumulated merit." There was hope in the high tones of her voice. "But how did you hear he had died?"

"I saw him *before* he died. I spoke with him."

She sat up, her attention pointed as a needle. "You *did*? How did you find him?"

"It was not hard. I saw some Khampas and asked them. They told me he was at Sera Monastery. The monks there were hiding him and caring for him because he was wounded."

Her mouth opened with concern. "What happened to him?"

"A bullet wound." I stroked her arms. "But he was peaceful. He had decided to come home to us, but then he couldn't because he was injured."

"He wanted that?"

"Yes, very much. But he was weak and already preparing for his death."

"If only I could have seen him." She dropped her gaze to her lap, and her mouth quivered. "I spoke to him in anger before he left."

"Do not worry about those things. He knew your love in his heart. He was at peace."

She sighed and I felt the warm air from her lungs flow over my hands that held hers. I added, "You know, he was happy to be able to die in Tibet."

With this story I painted over his suffering and his confession that he had killed, covering his death with tranquil golden colors. Beneath my wife's rough Khampa outside was a heart more tender than a lotus petal.

That night we fell asleep in each other's arms, with our children sleeping around us. I felt the favor of the gods—I was breathing in the same room with those most precious to me.

Gerald

Kingsley was so relieved to see me that he wrapped his stiff arms around me in a long embrace. He showed us into the cottage behind his home and had tea and sandwiches brought in. Then he left us.

There came the moment when I closed the door behind me. I leaned back against it and gazed at my wife as she changed Rin's diaper on the bed.

I breathed in the scent of the two of them—a powdery, clean smell like a bar of soap.

This morning. I'd seen a bar of soap this morning, the bucket, the dried blood smears on the walls, and the wet-concrete smell of the tiles. Comrade Han's face. I hadn't known then, scarcely nine hours ago, that this was the day of my release. That this evening I'd be leaning against a door, gazing at my Emma and my daughter.

Emma put out her arms to me. I went to her. We held each other hard until I was shaking from fatigue.

I tried not to breathe. If I let myself, I'd break down and it would all tremble through me like a spasm, and I'd weep and Emma would think I'm a lunatic.

Which wouldn't be far off the mark. The back of my neck tingled, as if someone were watching me, someone who knew I was no longer who she thought I was. I pushed the thought out of my mind.

She kissed me and we rubbed our faces against each other, getting to know again the curves of the other's face and neck. We moved onto the bed, lying on our sides facing each other and staring into each other's eyes. Rin crawled up onto the bed. She sat down on Emma's hip, wanting to be a part of it all.

"I'm really a mess," I muttered nervously. It was unnerving to let Emma look into my eyes, to possibly see all the mess behind them. My mind had been through a cyclone, with ropes and bamboo and hooks and slogans and screams all lying about in a rubble.

"We'll get you cleaned up. You'll be as handsome as ever," she said brightly.

I looked at her doubtfully. *I don't mean . . . on the outside.*

"Really. I've got everything: razors, toothbrush, toothpaste, soap, shampoo, dental floss, you name it, I brought it."

I gave her a smile as if those things *could* transform me, not knowing what to say.

She sprang up and opened the suitcase she'd brought. Then she came and stood before me holding something white, with an I-have-a-gift-for-you grin on her face. She held a snowy white oxford shirt, folded on top of tan trousers. The shirt was like the one I'd worn throughout my ordeal, but immaculate, unstained. As if when I put it on, I would be unstained too.

My stomach curled around a feeling of fear as I looked at the clothes. Changing my shirt wouldn't do it, and I didn't know how she'd understand that. I took the clothes and set them on the bed.

"I . . . uh . . . I'll need to scrub myself down a bit before putting on such a clean shirt."

"Great." She continued to grin and produced something else: a shaving kit, complete with soap, shampoo, razor, scissors, aftershave, toothbrush, and toothpaste. Then she pulled a chair around and ordered me gently, "Sit down. I'll cut your hair."

"How did you think of all this?" I asked, impressed and touched.

"It was Aronson's suggestion, actually. He had an idea of what you might need." She touched my arm. "He was a POW in World War Two, you know. That's why he agreed to get you out of there."

My jaw dropped open. But I was too overwhelmed to do more than sit numbly as she trimmed my hair.

When she'd finished with the shearing—and I do mean *shearing,* because she lopped off most of my hair and beard—she handed me a mirror. I looked cleaner, closer to sanity, except for my sunken eyes.

Fear still knotted up my stomach. Maybe she could shine me up like a new coin. I might even begin to resemble the former Gerald, the one who slept twelve hours at a stretch without waking, the one who ate food without thinking about every bite, the guy who thought that human beings were essentially good. But I was not him anymore. I felt so bad for her. She was being gypped by the impostor.

I grabbed the clothes and escaped into the bathroom. In the cottage's little claw-foot tub, I tried to scrub off every trace of what I'd been through. Then I spent a half hour brushing, flossing, and lamenting how bad my teeth looked.

Create in me a clean heart, O God.

I changed into the new clothes away from Emma's eyes. How wasted my body looked. I didn't want to shock her. The cuffs of my shirt seemed enormous around my small wrists.

When I returned to our room, she was chasing Rin around the corners of the bed, playing peekaboo with the covers. The room was filled with exuberant laughter. Although she stood and beamed at me, pain was in her eyes. She tried to hide it, but I saw it anyway.

I was stiff and frightened. I wanted to be close to her, but I needed to shield her from what she might see once I let her near me. "I'm going for a walk," I heard myself say.

She flinched and her smile faded. She wanted everything back to the way it was, right away. Who could blame her?

Offering her a smile, I said, "Just a quick walk."

"All right. Be careful." She nodded and smiled, and I turned and left quickly.

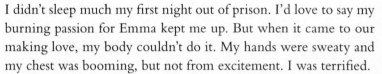

I didn't sleep much my first night out of prison. I'd love to say my burning passion for Emma kept me up. But when it came to our making love, my body couldn't do it. My hands were sweaty and my chest was booming, but not from excitement. I was terrified.

It was just too much. The only people who'd seen my withered body, unclothed, in the past two years . . . had made me ashamed. Had made me never want to be naked again.

We were kissing each other, our breathing coming faster, and it felt *so* good to touch her milky skin, her womanly curves again . . . and then I saw Comrade Han's face. It was as real and chilling as if *he* were suddenly in my arms instead of her. Low chuckles slithered out of his thin mouth. Because he knew. He knew it wasn't going to work anymore. I shuddered violently. I tried to look at her flushed skin and her eyes full of wanting and need. To breathe in her scent and stop shaking. But I pulled away, sitting on the edge of the bed, feeling her hurt eyes on my back.

She put a warm hand on my shoulder, and all I could think was that her fingers felt my stringy muscles pulled taut over creaky bones. She slowed down, caressing me, holding me. But, ashamed, hiding, lost somewhere in my fear, I couldn't find my way back to the moment.

After she fell asleep, I rolled myself up into the smallest wad of a human being I could and cried, silently, so she wouldn't hear how undone I was.

I felt as lonely as if I were in solitary again.

After the tears, I peeked over at her sleeping form. Who was this man in bed with her? She didn't even know. It was a skeleton lying beside her, who couldn't satisfy her as a husband, whose insides quaked, who'd compromised himself in ways she couldn't imagine. She still had the ideal in her head. Her young, vibrant "Geebs" who could feel joy, who wanted to consume every inch of her. Who wasn't afraid.

It was burning up inside me, this secret. But it wasn't really a secret; my body was broadcasting that something was wrong with me. She'd always been such a lonely thing, and she was lonely now, waiting for her man to come back to her.

If I were able to find that man, I'd gladly return him to her.

I didn't really know who was sitting in this cottage bedroom where my child had been born. I could begin to feel like my old self when she called me Geebs. But over the past nearly two years, I'd hidden myself away in some dark set of catacombs and I'd lost track of the key.

I felt her pulling at me, wanting me, but I didn't know how to get out of there.

Freedom looks so simple when you're in prison. You're sitting in a room with a bucket of excrement stinking up your nostrils, and you think wistfully that you'll walk out of that place and leave it behind you.

You don't know that it's *in* you.

Like a parasite lodged in your gut, eating you alive.

Was there some trail of crumbs I could follow to get back?

Speak plainly and honestly. That is the Quaker way. It felt like a hell of a cruel way, at this point.

I was still gazing at her sleeping face when she opened her eyes and said with a warm smile, "I thought I felt you looking at me."

I blurted out, "I'm not your old husband, you know."

She sat up, her face instantly serious. "How could you be?" Her words were slow and deliberate, like the steps of someone who slows down to walk beside you.

"No. I think you should know what you're getting, Emma." *She might leave if she gets the picture. But better now than later on.*

"I'm getting the chance to take you as you are, from right here, aren't I?" Her voice was surprisingly firm.

"I've done . . . I need you to know what I've done." My throat was tightening. "Maybe you wouldn't even be here, if you knew."

She sat up in the bed, rubbing her eyes. Then she folded her legs under her, holding her back straight. Her hair was a wild mass of curls around her face, adorable and distracting. She questioned, "We *have* to do this? Because whatever it is—"

I tensed my jaw. "I tried to stay strong, I thought of all the Quakers before me who were thrown into prison. You remember how I always wanted to suffer for my faith?"

She nodded. The curls bobbed. I wanted to touch them. But I plunged on in my resolve. "Well, instead, I wrote a false confession . . . I claimed to be a communist." My voice quivered uncontrollably, and I tried to steady it. I lowered my gaze to my hands. "I thanked Chairman Mao for rehabilitating me."

Her eyes widened, became like flames in her face. "Are you finished? I *know* what you wrote. I've read it, Gerald. Those bastards sent us a copy!" The flames filled with tears. "And do you think I give a damn? If you think"—she was shaking her head and her throat made a choking sound—"if you think that I would stand outside the bars of your cell and judge *anything* you did, anything, well, then, you need to get reacquainted with your wife, because you don't know her at all."

I sat down next to her, and we collapsed into sobs, leaning into each other. Rin After several minutes, broke it up by tugging on Emma's sleeve. Then Rin reached out a finger and pointed it at me. She gave me a grin with every one of her ten teeth.

"She's her own little one-woman show, isn't she?" I said to Emma, smiling back at Rin, while tears fell in two rivers down my face.

"Oh, yes, she earns her keep that way. I've needed someone to make me laugh."

The sounds of sniffling, of trying to compose ourselves.

"I'll bet you have," I said sadly.

I kissed my wife's freckled nose and then her lips, slow kisses and longer ones. I started to settle. A tiny glint of light was in my mind: maybe, maybe we could be together again, the way we were before.

She slid her hands under my shirt and up my chest, saying, "*You are my Geebs.*" In that moment of feeling her wanting, my heart fluttered up above the butterflies in my stomach.

A nasty voice started in again: *She still doesn't know who she's hanging onto.*

But I answered it, *No, she doesn't know all of me yet. But we're going to make a start at it.*

Emma

I'm standing at my kitchen sink, watching Geebs and Rin out the window. The scent of lilacs floats in on the humid summer air. My hands are soaking, motionless in the warm soap suds in the sink. My fingers are withering like raisins.

There's an ache where my throat should be. We've had one month of bliss together here at home—more than I deserve in several lifetimes.

I watch as he picks her up. Takes her to a rosebush—the kind with petals like a glowing sunset. She points to the thorns and says, "Hurt, hurt." Her expression is terribly serious.

He says, "Yes, they *can* hurt you." He takes her small finger and points at the radiant blooms. "But the flowers are beautiful." He brings her closer so she can lean into the blossom with her nose. "Smell that?"

She comes up for air and grins. "Mmmm." Still in his arms, she bends from the waist again with the abandon of a diving gull. "Mmmm!" Then she points at a thorn. "Hurt."

They've done this over and over for the past ten minutes. Geebs has the patience of an enormous, slow beast.

I cling to these moments like a shipwrecked sailor hanging on to the last piece of wood. I pray to God, *Can I trust that these people are mine to keep?*

Nothing is more terrifying than loving someone.

Reaching into the warm water, I grab for the next dish. My fingers close around a wooden bowl, and I pull it up, dripping water.

It's such a deep brown it's almost black. A carved bowl for butter tea I carried in my satchel out of Tibet. I smile, bring it up to my face, feeling the smooth, wet heat on my cheek.

I have this longing. For Tibet. I must be nuts. You'd think I'd retch at the very thought of it. But I miss the grace and gentleness of Dorje and his family. I miss seeing people bow to each other. Respect given and received. Now that I've tasted that warm respect, the air here feels colder than the land of snows. It was the first place where I didn't feel alone. It struck me one day in the temple near our home in Shigatse. Dorje had invited us to hear the monks chanting. We crossed the high wooden threshold and joined the flow of townspeople streaming toward the assembly hall. The rich sweetness of burning yak butter hung in the air. We joined a snaking line of several hundred Tibetans who'd come to do their *koras*.

We packed into that line, our bodies completely touching those in front and behind. A group of strangers in full body contact, but none pushing and none minding how squished they were. Despite the dirtiness of these pilgrims, I didn't feel squished either. I felt embraced. *As if we're all in this together. In life together.*

Didn't matter who I was. They let me be one of them. As we moved forward like one animal of a thousand legs, tears snuck out of the corners of my eyes. My heart could not be lonely among these people. We walked outside, where the sun baked my forehead. I thought, *This isn't the roof of the world. It's the floor of heaven.*

We went to Tibet wanting so much. Not just to be tourists, but to be touched, changed. And it changed us, let me tell you. It painted our insides a different color: the deep bronze of Tibetan skin, or the black of a moonless Tibetan night sky. Those colors seeped into us in a million small moments—as we sipped the salty richness of butter tea, listened to Dorje's delighted laughter, watched women prostrating themselves in the dust.

I hear Rin's shrieks of delight. Outside the window I see Gerald has now assumed the position of a beast of burden. He's on all fours and Rin is pouncing onto his back. He reaches behind his back for her, saying in the old Svengali voice I've always loved, "But I am ze Tickle Moan-stair, and now you are *mine!*"

Rin finds the joy in him and warms it until it melts all over her like soft candle wax. A smile pushes up through my throat.

I think back to the day in the marketplace when our ordeal began. I've often pondered what it was that got us into trouble, as I am now.

I've decided that it was Gerald's kindness. I still question God at times, wondering how He let such a beautiful soul go through so much.

Since his release, Gerald says he's afraid I won't love him anymore because of his confession to the communists. His "fall from grace." When he says that, I want to slap him. Thank God I don't do it. I tell him over and over, "Welcome to the human race, love."

After all, of the two of us, I've always been the mediocre Quaker, the leaky vessel for holding God's light and love. I've never been so good at it, but Gerald has been extraordinary. He's not used to mistakes and compromises and things that make your chest burn with regret, but I am.

He *has* changed. But what he never lost, even in the face of torture, is his kindness. Even with his captors all around him, he still refused to leave Dorje to fend for himself.

For that, I love him more than ever.

His kindness isn't the frail, fair-weather variety. It's a gritty kindness that grits its teeth in the face of torturers and still does what's right. It's the type that belonged to the Quakers who hid Jews during the Holocaust and ended up in the gas chambers themselves.

I've always had trouble believing the Quaker saying "There is that of God in everyone." I'm lousy at seeing people with loving eyes. My eyes have always been cynical, impatient, bitter. But strangely enough, after all we've been through, I find I believe that Quaker saying. And it's not an effort, as if I'm trying *very hard* to believe it. It's a knowledge that has grown in my chest, from the way strangers melt when Rin says "Hi" to them as we pass. It's a faith like a bed of flowers, watered by my husband's deep gentleness, and by Dorje and Rinchen, who protected me like their own kin, and especially by a Chinese ambassador who rode a bicycle through a rainstorm, risking imprisonment, to make sure that I got a photo of my husband.

These are the things that prove it.

There is that of God in everyone.

I look out and see morning sun bathing my husband's fine fingers as he cuts lilac stalks for my table. While on the plane home, I took his hand and squeezed it. His bones and skin pressed into mine. I felt Rin's gentle sleep-breathing against me as she napped on my lap. These were miracles I could feel in my flesh. I told myself never to take these sensations for granted again.

How can I possibly be grateful enough, mindful enough, to savor these moments as they deserve? I wipe down the sink, worrying over this while the bliss continues outside the window, passing right over my head.

Be silent. Pay attention. Take these moments, press them to your chest, and be silent.

Gerald

Emma has put a banquet before me at the dinner table, as she does every chance she gets. *I'm going to fatten you up, Geebs.* She's gone to tend to Rin, who just awoke from a late nap. We're drifting from summer into autumn now, even as the weather makes its last attempts at Indian summer. But in my mind's eye, all I see are snowy peaks in the mashed potatoes on my plate. The whole mountainous shape of them has brought me to tears. *Why do I sit before Himalaya shapes in my mashed potatoes and cry?*

I touch my fork to them, flattening one peak. It's an enormous dollop—a regular mountain range of potatoes. Emma's trying to bring me back from the brink. These potatoes are her caring for me. Light and fluffy, but they weigh on my conscience like boulders. Simply because *I* have potatoes now, and others don't. Lobsang doesn't.

Eating has become a *sin*. I've explained this to her, but she's too worried about me to pay attention to such talk.

Getting reacquainted with my wife is the strangest thing. All she cares about is *me*. But with every morsel of chicken divan and meat loaf and rhubarb pie, I see Lobsang's child-eyes, so big in the rest of his face. A face that grows thinner each day. Tenzin and I abandoned him. The last time I saw Lobsang, hope had filled those eyes. But how long would it last once he realized he was completely alone?

I'm eating my fill while he slowly starves. When I look at a chicken bone, I still see the shadows of his cheekbones and elbows and hip bones.

Emma can't possibly understand that. The gnawing feel of starvation. How can I describe it to her? It's like a small rat at first, nibbling at your fleshy parts, then a much bigger rat, chewing, devouring your muscles and thinning you down to lean ropes holding bones together.

The supermarkets here bulge with food. Friends and family—the ladies in Quaker meetings—are swept up in a hysteria of feeding me. I can't blame them. They want their casseroles and fried chicken and green beans to heal me.

I am eating, small amounts. And these folks are healing my body slowly, if only by force. But my soul that lived in that cell, well, I'm not sure if it has reached me here yet.

Shortly after we got back, I told Emma about Lama Tenzin and Lobsang. But it was impossible to tell her how much they meant to me. That Tenzin would live on in my mind and heart for the rest of my days. And that I came to love Lobsang as my own son. How much I wanted to shield him from everything that slowly killed us, day by day. I told her, "I have to help him. Then I can eat."

She balled her hands into determined fists and told me, "I'm just the person to show you how it can be done. Letters, Geebs. Letters mentioning Lobsang—and Rinchen's brother Samten—by name, letting the Chinese government know that someone in America is watching."

Every night after dinner, that's when we write them. And we're not the only ones. The members of Middletown Quaker meeting have adopted the Tibetan cause as their own. We've spent many

Sundays in "talking meetings" about what happened to me there. Some members cried openly as they listened to my story. Afterward, many came forward, saying they felt led to help. In the spring, a delegation of three Quakers from our meeting will visit Tibetan refugee camps in Nepal and India to find out what they can do.

Telling the Friends has been part of my healing. It gives some purpose to what I went through. At least we can make life better for the waves of Tibetans fleeing their homeland. When I get discouraged, Emma says, "Think like a Tibetan, Geebs. Each letter is an opportunity to gain merit. And you'd better eat, or you won't have the strength to lift a pen." She comes over and kisses me and strokes my hair.

I don't know about this idea of karma. What could I ever have done, in any previous lifetimes, to deserve such a loving wife?

~

It's one in the morning. Rin is crying. When I go into the nursery, she's sitting up in her crib, squinting in half darkness, looking forlorn and lonely as all the world. She reaches her arms up to me, and I pick her up with tenderness swelling up from my heart.

Probably she had a bad dream, and I know about those. Her cries awakened me from another nightmare that left me bathed in sweat. My heart breaks to think of Rin's little mind tormented even by childhood monsters, and I want only to protect her as my body shelters her tiny form in my arms.

I soothe her by turning in gentle circles until her eyelids droop to half-mast and she succumbs to a limp drowsiness. My swaying dance pulls her into the peace of slumber, and her breathing goes from the irregular cant of crying to the soft suspiration of sleep. Her head drops slowly onto my chest as I hold her, and I turn to liquid bliss.

I pad light-footed out of the nursery into the living room with her in my arms. With one hand I lift the needle of the phonograph onto the black vinyl disc. Bach's "Air on the G String" suffuses the room. This one piece holds everything, even this very moment: I am slowly dancing, shifting softly from one foot to the other, feeling her deepening breathing, my feet echoing the steady bass line of the cellos. The scent of my daughter's fine hair fills me. The silky skin of her tiny hand rests on my arm as I hold her. The ache of my arms is sweet from the exquisite weight of her, a weight that warms my chest. And Bach's air builds from peace to anguish to discord, two notes beating against each other in a chord that holds it all, the stench, the humiliation of nakedness, the hunger, all that I've lived through. They still overtake my mind at times, images of Han's slit mouth that intrude on the blissful sound of my daughter's light snuffling.

Tenzin taught me, let it be there, let your mind be exactly where it is right now. Be with your daughter's hushed breaths that smell like milk, and do not resist the visitations of your tormentor.

They are only thoughts, which are illusions anyhow.

Living with a mind turned against itself. I can't get it to stop. I can't shut Comrade Han into a little cell as he did to me. I've wondered sometimes if it's worth it to live this way.

But now, I do not wonder.

This is life, in its agony and in its simplest, most precious seconds, breaths, heartbeats, while we all still live.

Thanks be to God.

Epilogue

When the iron bird flies and horses run on wheels, the Tibetan people will be scattered throughout the world and the dharma will come to the land of red men.

—GURU RINPOCHE
(Padmasambhava), eighth century BC

NOVEMBER 1966

Dorje

The moon reaches a silver hand through the window and touches my face as I lie in bed. I close my eyes, but I cannot ignore this touch. So I stand up, wrap myself in sheepskin over my *chuba,* and accept the invitation of the moon. I open the door and step outside into the garden. Rows of green beans, radishes, and turnips shine in the blue light.

Oh, it is brilliant, this moon. I stretch my arms toward it, yawning.

I put my hands into my *chuba* for warmth. In there I feel the smoothness of paper, then sharp edges. A letter from Champa. I've been carrying it close all day since I first read it, because I miss him. After I read it to Rinchen, she sat for a long time, staring at Champa's picture from his university graduation. She gently put her finger on the photograph where Champa's face was. He is now another part of our lives that is too far away for us to touch.

I pull out the letter and unfold it.

Dearest Pa-la,

I hope everyone in the family is well. Please give my love to mother, Lhamo, Thubten, and the new baby. I've been praying this child will have a long and healthy life. I hope Lhamo and Thubten are being a good sister and brother.

It is such a blessing to be staying with Gerald and Emma! They have given me my own room in their home. It is strange to have an entire room just for me, and I told them it isn't necessary. But then Gerald told me that as a medical student, I'll need a quiet place to study. He insisted and even laughed, saying, "You'll see, Champa."

He is so kind, helping me with my anatomy homeworks when I have questions. He has told me he'll be my "personal tutor." I can hardly believe this is my life—going to medical school in America, with my own room and a tutor!

Emma takes very good care of me. She has been making my favorite Tibetan dishes. She says she doesn't want my studies to suffer because I'm feeling homesick. I'm so fortunate! How many other people come to stay in America and have a cook who was trained by their own mother?

The day I arrived, Emma brought me to their "dining room" and had me sit down in a chair there. She leaned forward in her seat with a big smile on her face and said, "Tell me everything!" She wanted news about our family, about the two children she hasn't met, and about Tibet. I told her everything I could think of. Of course, she already knew about His Holiness leaving Tibet. She said, "How are the people doing now that He is gone?" I had to remind her I've been a student in New Delhi for the past several years, so I haven't been to Tibet for a long time.

She said finishing my university studies at age nineteen was "quite a feat." And then of course she explained what that meant. With her, I'll improve my English very quickly! In fact, she'll only allow me to speak Tibetan for one hour a day—"You must master your English," she says. It's like having Mother with me, telling me what to do! But I know it's good for me.

The other day we were all at the dinner table, and Emma asked, "Rinnie, did you know that Champa was there when you were born?" Then Rin wanted to hear everything about her birth. I told her I didn't know, I was outside the room eating sweetcakes that day with my father and the Englishman.

I call her Little Rin, but she informed me, "I'm not little." I explained to her there's a big Rin who is my mother, and so there must be a little Rin too. Then she informed me, "I am already eleven years old and I climb trees." Since Gerald and Emma have an orchard behind the house, there's no end to the trees she can climb. She tells me, "I'm checking on the apples." She asks me to help her pick the apples when they are ready, but Gerald says, "Champa needs to study, Rinnie."

I am grateful to be staying with such a warm family because it's hard to get used to America, where everything is quick, quick, quick! Even quicker than the motorcars in Kathmandu. Everything here is so clean. Even the streets are clean. And all the events of the day run right on the clock. Gerald has been teaching me about the importance of being on time.

Each house here has only a small number of people. Not many children, and no relatives. Just the mother and father and children. And a television! Every house has the television.

I'm making friends in my classes. Mostly, I spend time with the students from India. Sometimes we gather at Gerald and Emma's house, and Emma cooks Tibetan food, and then she tries to learn how to cook Indian dishes from one of my friends. This is something that makes her so happy—she has a big smile for days after. She says she misses that part of the world.

I miss all of you. I'm hoping someday soon you can come for a visit.

It's time for me to get back to my studies. Please give my love and greetings to everyone.

Love,
Champa

I let the moon shine on the letter. The blue paper seems to glow in the moonlight.

Dawa. My son Dawa was named after the moon.

While Dawa was alive, I always wondered why Lama Norbu had given him this name. So fast he went through his life. He seemed to me much more like my name, Dorje, or "thunderbolt," which travels so quickly through the air. But tonight as I see the moonlight on my arms, perhaps I understand why, in this incarnation, his name was Dawa.

The moon shines from a great distance, but still we feel its light. It comes to us secretly in the night and talks to us in a hushed voice. Not like the sun, which shines on crowds of people in the day. When the moon finds you, it is the dark of night, while everyone else sleeps.

Always I spoke with Dawa in this way, only us two, after long absences. Just as the moon hides its face at times, there were dark times when my son's face was hidden from me.

I put up my hand, and I fit the moon into the rounded shape between my fingers and thumb. I turn my hand slowly and touch the moon as if it were Dawa's face. As my hand drops to my side, I shut my eyes and let the light paint my eyelids. Inside, I am peace and longing, a sweet and sad blend.

This moon also shines on the land of snows. It has been ten years since I have felt her soil beneath my feet. Twelve years since we have seen Samten, still being held in prison in Lhasa. By now, I thought we would certainly all be together again and have returned to our home to live. I told myself not to hold this hope, but I have held it as if it were air for my lungs. Seven years ago, when even His Holiness fled Tibet to live in India, I felt little air for my lungs.

My sadness is like an organ grown into my body now, always there. But as His Holiness tells us to do, I give thanks for my blessings. I pray for all sentient beings. And I tell myself, maybe Tibet is not just a place. There are things I miss that cannot be found anywhere else: the spring hillsides painted in green from the melted snowfall, the piles of *mani* stones along the sides of walking paths, hilltops where the only sound is the wind flapping the prayer flags. But Tibet is also the things I sense around me each day in Kathmandu: the clapping sound of hands brought together above the head in prostrations and the scraping vibration of prayer wheels turning. It is coral and turquoise woven into shining black braids. It is the pulsing clack, clack from the wooden looms of the weavers. It is Rinchen's prayers, mumbled as she beats the dirt from the carpets. *Om mani peme hung . . .*

Still I pray that someday His Holiness will return to Tibet. And then we will also.

I pray it will be soon.

AUTHOR'S NOTE

Since His Holiness the Dalai Lama fled Tibet in 1959, Tibetans worldwide have awaited his homecoming to Tibet as a signal that peace and security would return to that region. However, to this day, His Holiness continues to work toward a peaceful resolution with China from the safety of his adopted home in Dharamsala, India. A large community of Tibetans has settled there to be near him, and a democratically elected government-in-exile has been established.

Tibetans still living within Tibet remain subject to persecution by the government in Beijing. Over six thousand monasteries and nunneries have been destroyed by the Chinese since the invasion. For centuries, these institutions had been repositories of spiritual wisdom. Their destruction severely erodes Tibet's spiritual and cultural traditions.

For over fifty years the Chinese government has waged a campaign of terror against Tibetans (as it has against any of its own citizens it has deemed dissidents). This campaign has included imprisonment and torture and has been well documented by Amnesty International as well as many other human rights groups.

Throughout the prolonged Chinese occupation, Tibetans have striven to maintain their cultural identity and to practice the peaceful resistance modeled by His Holiness the Dalai Lama.

In peace,

Jeanne M. Peterson
March 2010
San Diego, California

If you would like to learn more about how you can support the Tibetan community worldwide, you may find the resources below helpful.

BOOKS

The Search for the Panchen Lama, by Isabel Hilton. W. W. Norton, 1999.

A Strange Liberation: Tibetan Lives in Chinese Hands, by David Patt. Snow Lion Publications, 1992.

My Tibet, by His Holiness the Fourteenth Dalai Lama of Tibet. University of California Press, 1990.

Tibet: Reflections from the Wheel of Life, by Carroll V. Dunham. Abbeville Publishing Group, 1993.

In Exile from the Land of Snows, by John Avedon. Alfred A. Knopf, 1984.

Orphans of the Cold War: America and the Tibetan Struggle for Survival, by Kenneth Knaus. Public Affairs, a member of the Perseus Books Group, 1999.

ORGANIZATIONS AND THEIR WEB SITES

www.tibet.com
www.savetibet.org
www.amnesty.org
www.healingthedivide.org